"AH, DEATH CHILD, A WORTHY FOE AT LAST!"

Niko knew better than to meet the demon's eyes or listen to its threats, supposed to stun him. He lunged forward, ancient sword in hand and arcing back and, without thought to dodging demon claws, swung it down, right to left, so that even as the demon sought to grapple him, he cut its head from its neck.

Yet those claws screeched on his armor like fingernails on a child's slate, and its body bore him down under its twitching weight, and for a time he struggled there with something that should not be living.

The demon's head, hanging by thick red skin, swung back and forth and jaws clacked near his naked arms . . .

Don't miss these other exciting tales of Sanctuary: the meanest, seediest, most dangerous town in all the worlds of fantasy....

THIEVES' WORLD
(Stories by Asprin, Abbey, Anderson, Bradley, Brunner, DeWees, Haldeman, and Offutt)

TALES FROM THE VULGAR UNICORN
(Stories by Asprin, Abbey, Drake, Farmer, Morris, Offutt, and van Vogt)

SHADOWS OF SANCTUARY
(Stories by Asprin, Abbey, Cherryh, McIntyre, Morris, Offutt, and Paxson)

STORM SEASON
(Stories by Asprin, Abbey, Cherryh, Morris, Offutt, and Paxson)

THE FACE OF CHAOS
(Stories by Asprin, Abbey, Cherryh, Drake, Morris, and Paxson)

WINGS OF OMEN
(Stories by Asprin, Abbey, Bailey, Cherryh, Duane, Chris and Janet Morris, Offutt, and Paxson)

THE DEAD OF WINTER
(Stories by Asprin, Abbey, Bailey, Cherryh, Duane, Morris, Offutt, and Paxson)

SOUL OF THE CITY
(Stories by Abbey, Cherryh, and Morris)

BLOOD TIES
(Stories by Asprin, Abbey, Bailey, Cherryh, Duane, Chris and Janet Morris, Andrew and Jodie Offutt, and Paxson)

BEYOND THE VEIL

JANET MORRIS

ACE FANTASY BOOKS
NEW YORK

This Ace Fantasy Book contains the complete text of the original
hardcover edition. It has been completely reset in a typeface designed
for easy reading, and was printed from new film.

BEYOND THE VEIL

An Ace Fantasy Book/published by arrangement with
the author

PRINTING HISTORY
Baen Books edition published 1985
Ace Fantasy edition/February 1987

Ace Fantasy Books are published by The Berkley Publishing Group,
200 Madison Avenue, New York, New York 10016.
PRINTED IN THE UNITED STATES OF AMERICA

BEYOND THE VEIL

Book One:

DEATH IN TYSE

Two Rankan couriers rode into Tyse three hours apart on the last day of summer. Neither was aware of the other; both carried the same information. The parties in the Imperial Rankan court who had dispatched them to seek out a man known as the Riddler needed to be sure their message would be delivered.

The sun was setting when the first courier, who went by the name of Belize, urged his exhausted horse the last few miles up Broadway and into the souk, Tyse's open-air bazaar. Where the horse traders had their stalls he was supposed to meet the Rankan agent who would lead him to the Riddler.

But no one had warned Belize of the curfew. They had warned him not to go to Embassy Row and check in with his countrymen. They had warned him not to trust the Rankan intelligence chief, Grillo, and thus effectively barred him from making use of his upcountry peers and doing things the easy way. They had warned him not to depend on the mageguild network or on anything but the evidence of his senses. Imperial Ranke was beleaguered

1

and embattled from within and without; every diplomat and cabinet functionary who favored peace over this protracted and expensive war with the Mygdonian Alliance was well aware that summary execution awaited anyone caught conspiring against the Empire—even to bring peace to it.

In the souk's maze, he dismounted and led his blowing, sweat-drenched mount through a stinking, narrow-eyed throng hurrying home with the days' profits, bargains, or spoils. Everywhere, stalls were being shut and locked. Pickpockets lurched and fumbled their way through the thinning crowds.

Belize looked up: an early-rising moon, full and pale, smiled down on him. An armored cavalryman wearing the yellow-lined mantle of the "special" occupation forces didn't: "You don't have one of these, traveler." The soldier, frowning down on him from his saddle, tapped an embroidered armband. "You'd better find a guest house. Curfew's in effect." This last was spoken around a chunk of lamb pulled from its wooden skewer and into the soldier's mouth by teeth bright in the light of torches being lit along the rows of wooden stalls, goat's-hair tents, and brightly colored yurts of the souk.

As the "special" kneed his horse on by, Belize took a chance and asked for the stalls of Palapot the trader—a chance because the special forces in Tyse were Grillo's men. A chance because the armband he'd seen had on it the unit device of the Stepsons—bulls and lightning bolts—which marked the wearer as one of the Riddler's own elite squad of Sacred Band pairs and seasoned mercenaries (just the men whose attention he did *not* want to attract). A chance because the rider's fine-featured face was Syrese, not local, and the sharp eyes in it had sized him up with cold and minute precision.

Belize knew his own kind when he saw one; the mounted officer was no less observant.

The rider turned in his saddle, his helmet swinging by his knee, his bare head, in profile, somehow vaguely familiar. "Sure you don't want the mercenaries' hostel? Or the east barracks?"

Belize had to fill the pause the soldier left empty. "Palapot the horse trader. I'll swap this horse and then find a bed."

"*Swap* it? You ought to put it out of its misery. The only place you'll get anything for that poor beast is in the free zone. And," the soldier looked up at the sky, "you don't have any time to speak of—curfew's upon us." He cast the half-eaten skewer of lamb into the dust, then with his free hand motioned to the rapidly clearing street. "Palapot will still be there tomorrow. As for that horse, you owe it at least one good night's rest. It'll end up in somebody's stew pot if you trade it looking like that. Come on, citizen, I'll ride with you as far as the first guest house."

Belize had to agree, had to show his papers when he got there—which was, he thought, what the special was waiting for, since the tall officer in cavalry-issue leather and mail had insisted on escorting him inside and stayed on, chatting with the innkeeper, after he'd been given a room key and a chit to stable his horse around the back. He looked back once at the short-haired Syrese leaning on the counter and caught the Stepson unabashedly staring after him. "Life to you, Belize," said the other, a professional's farewell.

He didn't answer with a mercenary's response—Belize wished no man life, or glory. The Stepson had guessed wrong, after all. Belize wasn't a member of the mercenaries' guild, nor a professional soldier. He was an assassin.

The guest house the Stepson had escorted him to was at the Tysian city limit, where Commerce Avenue and Peace Falls, the adjoining township which observed no curfew, cut into Tysian discipline and Tysian jurisdiction. He had only to stable his horse, secret his effects in his room, cross a street no wider than an alley, and he would be within a stone's throw of Commerce. The Stepson had done him a favor, showing him to the merchants' quarter which abutted the souk and spilled over into Peace Falls' anarchic bustle.

The inn was called the Dark Horse; he memorized its salient features—back doors, overhanging roofs, rear balconies, and adjoining buildings. As he bargained with the head groom for liniment, sweet feed, and a better stall for his mount, Belize kept an eye on the intersection of Commerce and Souk avenues visible from the stable yard, hoping to see the Stepson on the big bay horse ride away.

He didn't. So he went inside the stable to examine its box stalls while the head groom, biting the Tysian half-crown between his teeth, began trying to make good his promise to "have him road-worthy in the morning, generous sir. Just pick any stall you like and I'll move out the other nag."

Belize had everything he needed: local currency, genuine travel papers issued by the Rankan chancellor's office that afforded him safe conduct empirewide, a free hand in accomplishing his mission. But his gut was telling him he'd missed something, some detail more troublesome than being a day late to meet a man who didn't know he was coming. Damn the mages, every necromancing, oversold soul among them. If the mageguild network had been trust-worthy, things would be much easier. In fact, if the mages weren't suspect, Belize wouldn't be here at all. He was a little bit more than your average courier. But then, some messages require specialized delivery. Whether the Riddler agreed with the proposition he carried or not, the parties Belize served wanted their dictates expedited.

He put the third horse he'd run into the ground to get here into the stall he'd chosen for it when the groom had cleared and cleaned it, then headed for the rear stairs to the inn.

He heard no sound out of the ordinary in the summer night: laughter wafting on a southwest breeze from Peace Falls; horses behind in the stables and before on the street; the snap and hiss of oil-soaked torches. He took the back stairs two at a time despite the deep and dancing shadows: a few minutes in his room and he'd be ready to see what Commerce Avenue had to offer. Just a quick prayer to his god, some security precautions . . . it wouldn't take long.

Halfway up the creaking staircase, he thought he heard a sliding foot, leather scraping on wood. He stopped. He turned full around. He saw the stables, the head groom, horseboys. Nothing more. He wiped his hands on his thighs. Why was he so nervous?

Turning back to vault the last few steps and begin his quest, Belize felt a sharp sting at his throat. He slapped the spot. There was a marsh nearby, but mosquitoes didn't usually. . . . His palm felt the little dart even as he slapped it more deeply into his throat so that its point pierced a nerve. He halted as he pulled the barb loose, thinking about the scuffling footstep he had heard. Then his eyes began to tear and a burning sensation spread out from his throat to reach up into his brain and down toward his heart. As he grabbed onto the railing for support, sensation left his extremities and his tongue felt as if it had swollen to thrice normal size and was suffocating him.

He didn't feel the impact as he fell to his knees on the board stairs. He was a western-trained fighter; the mind-over-body discipline he'd relied upon for years to prevail against his enemies and endure rigors most men could not survive allowed him what he craved most then: a look at his assassin.

What he saw, as his body fell forward like a sack of stones, was an urchin's face, grubby and beardless, with hair like straw and huge eyes that seemed colorless in the torch light. He felt himself being turned, soon enough, but by then the fire in his blood was consuming him entirely and there was a light far up in the night sky which he must follow. He felt the young mugger's fingers searching out his purse and his wallet, and even the belt at his waist in which was secreted . . . something . . . something he'd been at pains to protect. Anger pushed back death's croon for a moment. Then it could not.

The body still lay as it had been found, askew on the Dark Horse's back steps, when Randal the Hazard-class mage arrived on the scene, the iron grip of the Stepson, Straton—who'd come banging on the mageguild gates, disturbing half-cast spells with this unwelcome summons —clamped numbingly upon his arm.

Around the corpse was an efficient cordon of uniformed specials, keeping back the idly curious stablehands and a few patrons. On the staircase itself, crouched over the body

in a pool of torch light, were two of the most shadowy—
and deadly—personages in Tyse: the specials' commander, Grillo, chief of operations in Rankan-occupied
Tyse and the entire northern theatre, a black marketeer of
renown; and Critias, the Stepsons' task force leader and
second in command of that private army of Sacred Band
pairs and mercenaries which the Riddler, called Tempus,
had brought north from Sanctuary to the front a few
months back in search of "honor and glory," as well as
riches and territory, in the ongoing war with the Mygdonian Alliance.

They'd gained some of each. Randal ought to know.
Randal had fought in the war to drive the rival Nisibisi
mages off Wizardwall and make all Nisibisis free. Thus
he'd come to know these men, whom no safety-conscious,
self-respecting mage of the Tysian guild should be seen
consorting with, and become embroiled in their affairs of
war and death. It hadn't been Randal's idea: it had been
fate; the intervention of Aškelon, the lord of dreams; and
the urging of his own venerable First Hazard, which had
made Randal the favorite sorcerer of the armies. The Tysian First Hazard had jumped at the opportunity to make a
pact with the Stepsons' commander, the virtually immortal
and redundantly bloody Riddler, Tempus, who had been an
enemy of the black artists for better than three centuries—
ever since an archmage had laid upon him a far-reaching
and horrendous curse. Randal's mentor, First Hazard of the
Tysian mageguild and nameless, as were all top-echelon
wizards, had "offered" Randal the "honor" in a way Randal
couldn't refuse: Randal had been a *junior* Hazard for two
years longer than was appropriate for further advancement;
it had been his last chance to revitalize his ascent through
the ranks of magic. Perhaps, the ancient archmage had
prognosticated with glittering eyes, Randal would acquire
attributes sufficient to outweigh the debit of his allergies—
Randal was allergic to furry animals, especially when he
became one. And the First Hazard had been proved right;
Randal gained sorcerous spoils in the razing of the Nisibisi
wizards' high keeps. He'd acquired a globe of power. He

was now a fledgling adept, a Hazard of the seventh level, a person of power.

But Randal now had a curse of his own to contend with: the murderous crew of fighters called Stepsons considered him one of their number; the scrofulous Sacred Band pairs counted him as a brother. Whenever their superstitious fear of wizardry was overcome by the reality of need, it was Randal they called upon to banish impotence or make a lame horse sound or grant them luck in gaming. And this was happening more and more frequently, as it became clear to the followers of the Rankan war god that their deity was not answering their prayers. It was said that Vashanka, one of the primary gods of the armies, was planelocked, bound away from his followers by magic—or dead. It was also said that this disappearance or neutralization of the Rankan state-cult's Storm God portended the fall of the Rankan Empire.

As the unyielding hand on his arm steered him through the nearly silent crowd of well-disciplined specials and nervous horseboys toward Critias and Grillo and some poor dead fool who was as likely a victim of mundane greed as of anything more interesting, Critias sighted them, touched Grillo's arm, and left the corpse, heading their way. Grillo's handsome Rankan head came up and, as his gaze fixed on Randal and his escort, Randal tried to shake his arm free. "Enough, Strat! Unless you want to lose every hair on your head, let me go."

"Can't have you disappearing, can we?" Straton's grip didn't ease. Strat was Critias's partner, bound to the task force leader in some infernal degree of relationship the intimacy of which varied. Sacred Band pairs swore to fight together, shoulder to shoulder, to die together (if need be) while defending some elusive overdevelopment of honor only they understood. From a core of ten Sacred Band pairs, Tempus had created the shock troop squadron called Stepsons, augmenting the pairs with distinguished single mercenaries from a score of nations. Within the elite unit, differences existed—one could be a Stepson without being a paired Sacred Bander—but all Stepsons were committed

to carrying on the nearly mythical tradition of peerless fe-
rocity begun by the original Sacred Band under the leadership of Abarsis, the Slaughter Priest, of which many of the
pairs had been members.

And of which, due to circumstances and politics, Randal was now considered a member, though he was celibate
by choice and nonviolent by nature, though his "partner,"
one Nikodemos, had withdrawn from Tyse and the Outbridge barracks/estate and the much-vaunted camaraderie
of the Sacred Band to a western sanctuary far, far away.
Broken pairs, however, were common. Once a Sacred
Bander, always one, went the saying.

"Listen here, Straton. For *appearances'* sake, let me
go!" Randal wished he could do half the magic that the
superstitious Stepson thought he could—disappear out of
the iron grip which held him without taking Straton with
him; make Straton's hand go numb . . . something, anything
short of turning himself into an animal form. But since it
was that or nothing, he forebore a shape change, wishing,
not for the first time, that the globe of power he'd earned
on Wizardwall was small enough to carry around with him
or simple enough to employ that by now he'd have mastered its use. But it wasn't either, so his threats were
empty. And if they hadn't been, Critias's taciturn right-side
partner was no man to curse unless one was cursing to kill.

"Life to you, Randal," Critias said formally as he joined
them. "How are you faring?"

"My arm hurts." Randal stared steadily into the eyes of
Tempus's task force leader and saw them crinkle with
amusement.

Critias had a very cynical smile. "Strat, I think our
friend can stand on his own two feet."

Randal knew that Critias didn't like him or approve of
his induction into the Stepsons. Suddenly, his resentment
faded and he realized that Critias must have had a very
good reason to send for him.

But Straton was already detailing Randal's reluctance,
his voice very low and very angry. ". . . had to wait in that
godless hellhole and state my business; to one mincing
mageling after another. Half of 'em need training bras.

And when this... *Step*son finally deigned to give me a humping *au*dience, *he's* asking *me* why and what for, with the gods know *how* many witchy ears as big as his pressed to the damn walls. By the gods, Crit, he'd not *have* his pink-and-lacy suite in the left wing of that Fun House if not for us, and he's giving me an argument—*or* the balls to tell me he's too *busy*, there's spells need casting, and—"

"All right, Strat. All right."

"Not all right. What do we need him for, Crit? What do we put up with him for?"

Randal didn't like the way the conversation was going, or being spoken of as if he weren't present. And nobody argued with Critias. Even Tempus was very careful to *explain* matters to the task force leader... He thought he'd better try it: "Critias, I'm sorry. You caught me at a bad time."

Straton snorted.

Critias said, "Strat, take a look at this. It's the murder weapon." He held out a little dart in the palm of his hand.

Randal, shorter than the other two, craned his neck to get a better look.

Straton took it, held it up to the light, squinting, then put it to the tip of his tongue.

"Straton!" Randal objected. "It's obviously poisoned."

"Not as dumb as he looks," Strat marveled. "I'll take it around to some of the snake milkers. It's not arsenic or cyanide—tastes too sweet. Want me to go now?"

"If you would. I'll be here until high moon, anyway. Then I'm going over to the farm. If the Riddler's not at Brother Bomba's, he'll be there. I sent somebody over to see if he was with Madame Bomba, but maybe you'll drop by to double check." Though Critias answered Strat quietly, his gaze never left Randal's face.

"Pleasure. Just answer me: What do we need him for?"

Randal felt his neck grow hot, the flush crawl up his cheeks.

"Read the dead. You *can* do that, can't you, Randal? Tell us what his thoughts were? Maybe what he saw, who put him down?"

Strat grunted. Randal temporized; the big officer, about to leave, clapped a bearlike hand on his shoulder. "Do a *good* job, mageling. Prove you're worth the trouble I went through to get you here." And then Strat was gone, more quietly and quickly than Randal would have thought he could move.

"He's not at ease with this," Critias said softly. "Neither am I. But *I* didn't have to go *into* the mageguild, so I'm not angry. Don't pull this sort of thing again, Randal. You're a Stepson; you come when you're called. You don't ask questions unless they're strategic, and then not until you're given leave. Come on."

Randal found himself trotting along beside Critias. "That's what I want to talk to you about. I'm not at all happy with this arrangement—"

"Neither am I. Talk to the Riddler. Or Niko. Later. Now, you're going to read this dead man and tell us who we're looking for."

"Whom."

"What?"

"Looking for *whom.*"

Though Randal, angry himself, had been correcting Critias, the task force leader misunderstood. "I saw his papers before he was robbed. The name on them was Belize. Very comprehensive safe-conducts, issued in the capital. Grillo says he hadn't heard anything about a new agent being sent up here, which is what this man *must* have been. I know one when I see one; the papers just confirmed it. I want to know if Grillo's lying. Can you tell me that?"

"Perhaps." Randal squared his shoulders. They *did* need him. He didn't feel so short, so put-upon, or so resentful. "But reading the dead . . . it's not pleasant."

Crit's grin flashed. "I imagine not."

"So you'll have to bear with me. Ask me again what you want to know when I've got him—made contact with whatever's left, that is. It's just impressions . . . I might act . . . strangely." They were passing by a pair of specials who had a groom with them.

Once they were past, Randal continued. "So bear with me. It's . . . frightening."

"I understand. No one's going to draw any conclusions about you from this. Just don't let on to Grillo that we're wondering how it is that he didn't know about this fellow. I'll buy you a round of whatever strikes your fancy afterward. But my gut's telling me this isn't just a random incident. I came upon this Belize in the souk about curfew and escorted him here *myself*. Checked him out. He didn't know anything about the town, not even enough to get a room before dark."

So that was it: Critias was afraid he might be implicated. The task force leader didn't make friends easily, and he and Grillo were de facto rivals. Of all the private militias in Tyse, the Stepsons and the specials enjoyed the most open contention. When they weren't chasing Mygdonian-backed death squads or Nisibisi refugees in the free zone, they were rousting each other. The army, of which Tyse had a surfeit—four garrisons, one at each compass point —was Rankan, and thus Grillo, should he choose to, could call on garrison aid. None speculated on what arrangement existed between Tempus and Grillo, but everyone knew it was strained, now that they weren't fighting a common enemy. During periods of inactivity, with no declared or obvious foe, mercenaries and career soldiers engaged in urban war gaming to keep sharp their "edge." Part of Grillo's "edge" was caravaning contraband surreptitiously; Critias had recently interdicted a shipment entering Tyse which Grillo couldn't have owned, but in which he surely had invested heavily. The proceeds from the auction of this "unclaimed" salvage were now in the Stepsons' pension fund.

It was, Randal knew, a war within a war, kept under wraps only by Tempus's and Grillo's need to keep up appearances—and to some extent by their shared interest in the continued survival of Free Nisibis and its charismatic leader, Bashir. Technically, Tempus outranked Grillo, being a Rankan general. Long off the active-duty list, however, in order to employ questionable methods and lead the mercenary life with his Sacred Band without being subject to the constraints of Rankan oversight, he'd come to Tyse seeking vengeance upon the Nisibisi mages. Some said the interests in Ranke he served weren't those of the emperor. Randal didn't want to find out the truth of it. Even a seventh-level Hazard was mortal; the Riddler was not.

Critias was talking to him as they mounted the steps, where Grillo could hear every word. ". . . a woman's weapon, or a child's. Just lay your hands on him and give us your impressions, or whatever you do. Then we can close the matter."

"Maybe," Grillo amended. His features were aristocratic, Rankan perfect; he was dressed like a Tysian hill-man, but then he never wore a uniform, and even his hair changed colors. Grillo's eyes, however, were a piercing Rankan blue, and his intellect was not to be underestimated.

Randal would have lied for Critias, but he hoped Critias realized he wouldn't be able to: one read what one read; one saw what one saw. In the deep trance he'd need to summon to see what Belize had seen, such matters as white lies and quotidian advantage would fade from him: he would be Belize. And he would be dying.

He shivered, told both agents to back off a bit. "I need quiet, room to relax."

They did, and he saw Critias's hand slip into his pouch where the Stepson carried his charms and amulets.

Then Randal touched his own amulet, whispered a ward so that his mind could not be snatched or tainted by hostile forces while he gave it up to a dead man, and folded into a squat beside the corpse who'd been called Belize.

His fingers brought incense out of his belt. He lit it with a flint and steel, feeling the tingling of trance begin in his toes, and put the joss stick in the dead man's mouth.

Even before his palms had gone to the temples of the dead man, as he felt the cool lips touch his fingertips, he got an impression: another pair of lips the dead man had seen, lips with a gold coin between them, teeth biting down on a Tysian half-crown to prove it was no gold-washed copper: he saw the face of the head groom.

Then it faded. Randal's heart was pounding, pushing the trance-calm away. He called it back, breathing deeply of the joss, causing his knees to feel as if water ran over them and wondering why the "he" he sought could not remember that Belize was its name. He called that name thrice, got no further impressions, and then realized he was trying too hard.

He didn't want to call *back* the dead, only visit a fading mind. He closed his own eyes and felt the cold flesh, telling the corpse he would avenge its death, if only the murderer could be determined. Then he was in a stable with the smell of marsh hay in his nostrils, then coming out.

Belize was not this man's real name, he realized as he recalled like his own memory the rooftops and escape routes this sharp-eyed operator had detailed before he climbed the steps. Then he lost all sense of "Randal." His palms were sweating and he was wondering if the bad luck he'd had in meeting a Stepson who fastened on him like a leech in the souk was an evil omen as he climbed the stairs. . . .

He'd heard a footfall, he was sure.

Snnk! His throat stung. He slapped a mosquito. Then there was a burning pain and a determination to beat back death and see his assailant. The dart in his palm. Falling. Being turned, paralyzed, helpless. Wanting to hold the mugger off; then hands at his belt, at his wallet. Belize saw the face of his attacker, but it was swimming in pain and death: pale eyes, pale hair, dirt obfuscating what the poison did not. A child; a girlish, beardless face; a youth . . .

"Randal? Randal!"

He knew that voice: Critias. He opened his eyes, knowing he couldn't yet feel his extremities, and then realized he was sprawled on top of the corpse in the exact position as was the body under him.

Legs like wood, his heart pounding loud in his ears, he scrambled off it and sat, arms around his knees, to quell his shaking. "What did I say?"

"Nothing," Grillo replied. "Not a thing."

"He's . . . he was . . . up here to contact someone, deliver a message. He wasn't thinking about that until the girl, or boy, or whatever, robbed him. Then he was just thinking that he'd been at pains to protect the message."

"The face, Randal. Did you see a face?" Crit asked.

"Blond. Pale eyes. Teenager. Girl or boy, can't say. Very dirty face. And he was partially—almost fully—paralyzed by then. But it was a child, an urchin, a street waif —someone from the free zone. Or a Rankan." Randal looked at Grillo: There were many blond Rankans; even Grillo's dark ash-blond head might once have been pale.

"Or a Mygdonian?" Grillo countered.

"Yes, a Mygdonian. There aren't that many Mygdonians in town. Plenty of youngsters in the free zone who'd fit what I saw."

"So you don't think you could recognize him or her again? If you saw a group of children, could you pick out the right one?" Critias, with narrowed eyes, asked clipped questions, no relief evident, but tension spelled out clearly on his Syrese face.

"No. Not unless I were dying of the same poison. It was a chance event, a mugging. Nothing more. Can I go? Oh, one more thing."

"Yes?" Grillo leaned forward.

"The head groom. The man gave him a gold piece for extra service. Maybe he saw something."

Grillo pulled on his nose and unfolded from his squat. Looking down, he said, "I've got to admit I didn't think there was any point to calling in one of you people. I was wrong. Thank you, Randal. And my best to your First Hazard. Crit, I'll have my man interrogate the groom. We don't want Straton's overzealous sort of assistance on this. Or yours. It's a local item, now, something for the garrison police squads. Our regards to the Riddler." He stepped over the body and descended the stairs.

Critias blew out a long breath. "Bless you, Randal, or whatever equivalent thereof is acceptable to your kind. Ready for that round of krrf I owe you?" Critias helped the shaky young mage to his feet.

"That's not necessary. It wasn't even really magic . . . merely a mental trick." But Randal was proud of himself, and he'd developed a taste for krrf, the stimulant which was the fighters' recreational drug of choice. When he'd been working closely with the Stepsons he'd used it frequently; it kept his allergies in check when he was assuming animal forms.

They were walking away from the specials then and Crit

gestured toward the alley which would lead them to Commerce Avenue and Brother Bomba's.

"What about Straton? Aren't you going to wait for him?"

"He'll find me." Crit bent down as if to pick up something from the dusty street, then straightened. Randal saw him peering behind to see that no one was in earshot. Then Crit said, "You'll need the krrf. I'm not through with you. And I have a feeling you've not told me everything."

"Wrong. You're wrong. See here, task force leader, I've paying customers to attend to: a spell to cast for no less than Madame Bomba herself, or one of her girls will get pregnant . . ."

"Randal, did the face you saw remind you of anyone? Anyone at all?"

"No. Yes. I don't know." He could see that face now, wide-eyed and towheaded. But he was telling the truth; it looked like any of a dozen urchins' faces. In the free zone, where refugees from the war lived in a squalor too bleak to be contemplated, he'd seen more faces like that than he'd like to count. He said so.

"Was there anything unusual, then—anything at all?" Crit was like a dog worrying a bone.

"No. But *you* know something, don't you?" Randal ventured.

"Indeed. A number of things."

They came out onto Commerce, where no curfew was observed and ladies of the evening escorted gentlemen into establishments which catered to the siege mentality that prevailed in Tyse: anything, these days, could be had on Commerce for a price.

"Something specific, something you want me to confirm."

"That poison isn't local; it's Mygdonian."

"Oh. Oh, my." The Stepsons had a hostage from the war, a highborn youth who was pale and blond and very valuable: the son of General Adrastus Ajami, the Mygdonian warlord's brother.

But before Randal could object that the boy, Shamshi, was surely well guarded and not running about the streets in rags, Critias posed a question. "That man was too good a skulker to have been surprised by a free-zone delinquent. Magic had to have been involved, or one of these mind tricks you spoke of. Did it seem like that to you?"

"No. Yes, Maybe. Please, Critias, I've got to go back. I don't think it's wise for us to be seen together in public."

"You're not going back for a while. You're going to Bandara."

"Pardon?"

"You heard me. You are to seek out your partner and inform him he's returned to active duty."

"You jest! Do you know how long that will *take?* You don't send an adept of the mageguild to *Bandara*. They won't let me in the gates. And, on top of that, what if he won't come?"

"If he'd been here, I wouldn't have needed you. Niko could have tracked down the assailant before sunrise."

"Well, he won't be able to do it by the time we get back here. He tracks by aura, so he says, and that will be long dissipated; heat trails disperse."

"Randal." Critias stopped still, fists on his sword belt. "Read my lips: You're a Stepson, dispatched to fetch your left-side leader. You've received a direct order. You don't ask questions, unless they're pertinent. Ask me how long you've got to get back here, or what I expect you to do with this money." Critias pulled a pouch from his belt. "Here."

Randal was speechless, hefting the pouch. He thought of all the reasons he couldn't do this. Then he realized he was wondering whether Nikodemos would come back at all.

"Now, let's go snort some krrf, Stepson."

Randal found that he was pacing Critias and heard himself say, "As you wish, Critias. But I do have to know what the money's for and how long I've got to bring him back. He probably won't want to come by cloud-conveyance."

"You're getting better, Randal, much better. The money is for a boat. Buy one in Caronne and sail over to the Bandara Islands. Tell the secular adepts there that it's our gift to them if someone sails back to Caronne with the two of you. While you've got Niko there, have him stop by his uncle's. He's to finalize some business he's doing for Madame Bomba with his family. And you've got," Crit looked up at the sky, where the full moon was clearing the rooftops, "a maximum of ten days."

"*Ten* days? I was *jest*ing when I said cloud-conveyance," Randal sputtered.

"Ten days. You're a Hazard, aren't you? You've got Datan the archmage's mighty globe of power, don't you?"

"Well, yes, I do, but . . ."

"Ah, I forgot." Critias grinned. "You don't have the stand for it, do you? The golden stand with all that funny writing on it, the one it spins on. Well, I forgot to tell you: I took the stand as part of my share of the spoils. And I'll give it to you, Randal, as soon as you bring your partner back."

"*You've* got *that?* Oh, Crit . . . that is, *sir:* it's invaluable. I'll be able to utilize the globe much more effectively. Bring Niko back more easily, more quickly, if you'll just let me have it now. . . ."

But Critias was shaking his head, chewing a piece of marsh hay he'd had behind his ear. He said around it, "Later, mageling, later. Go fetch Niko home."

As a haughty young philosopher, ages ago, before the curse which had made him a tireless wanderer, bereft of sleep and love and what men call peace, Tempus had said that "God is day/night, winter/summer, war/peace, satiety/hunger . . ." Further, he had proclaimed that out of all things can be made a unity, and out of a unity, all things.

The most daunting consequence of the curse which afflicted him was that he must live and learn the truth of those things he'd said when talk was idle and wisdom cheap. He called himself Tempus because time was his, unending: he was the river of it—always changing, always the same. Once he had been called The Obscure by those who knew him; now they called him the Riddler, the sleepless one, and worse behind his back.

For he was death's prophet, a living talisman of war.
Those who loved him died of it; those he loved were bound
to spurn him: this burden an archmage had laid upon him.
He never slept; he could not die. His body regenerated
itself tirelessly, even without the help of the Storm God
whom he had served so long and who finally—like everything else he loved—had deserted him.

He was alone among men, no matter their quality or
their number. Even surrounded by his Stepsons, his curse
kept him solitary: he loved them dearly. They were mortal,
to a soul. Every one of them would die and he would
not. There would be many requiems to be said for them,
many biers to light in the days and years ahead. So he tried
not to care too much for them, the Sacred Banders and the
rest.

And yet, he thought, sitting in Brother Bomba's with
Bomba's wife in her office, looking down and over the
patrons in the ground floor barroom through alchemically
crafted one-way glass, he was not quite so alone or quite so
unhappy as he customarily liked to think he was. The
woman whose hospitality he enjoyed was unabashedly
middle-aged, a former barber-surgeon of the armies,
tough-minded and pragmatic in the face of fate and dissolution. A weathered and wrinkling smile (which would
have sent a lesser woman running to the mageguild to sell a
bit of soul for the illusion of youth and beauty) always
greeted him. Eyes which had looked on fields of casualties
sustained in defeat and victory always met his steadily. She
was what few were to him: a respected, trusted friend.
Once, long ago, they might have had congress; he couldn't
remember. Women in general he found tiresome, even less
likely than men to live up to their potential. But Madame
Bomba had no illusions: she knew death intimately, she
was free from fear and loved life too much to forget what
lay at the end of it. Like her bones, her spirit was yet
strong.

With her, he could speak freely. With him, she always
did. If not for her husband, he continually teased her, their

liberties could be extended. But that was not what they spoke about tonight.

"That woman there, the one in silk and leather like a Rankan fighting lord—you *do* see her, Riddler?—came in asking for you."

"How long ago?" He had come up the back stairs, as was his custom; but not gone down into the drug dens beneath as he usually did. He was avoiding someone—a female someone, a Froth Daughter from the twelfth plane come to earth to spend a year as a mortal. Six months of that year were up, and the rest of it loomed unending before him. Jihan, daughter of the nameless Stormbringer who'd spawned the world's pantheons, was spending her mortal year with him. She was his companion, perhaps his equal, but not his friend. He peered down through the smoke and the crowd. The woman who had laid her Machadi helmet on the bar and wore cavalry boots like a Syrese fighter and a cuirass some smith had had to mold from a plaster cast made live on her physique was not Jihan. This woman was not muscular enough, nor tall enough, nor was her hair burnished like copper. Jihan, though she had many superhuman attributes, could not change the shape she had chosen, the shape in which she had entered the world of men.

"How long ago?" Madame Bomba repeated, shrugging and holding up one hand to indicate with thumb and index finger the span between knots on a Tysian rope which a flame would have burned in that interval. "A Rankan hour, perhaps. She ate and drank; now she waits."

The woman drank between mercenaries at the bar; more, she drank *like* one. The man on her far side had his head bent to hers: a dark head, short-haired. "That's Crit with her?" Tempus ventured. The angled face was hard to make out from his vantage point.

Madame Bomba's hearty laugh rang out. "You're ruining my story. Yes, that's Critias. Thou art popular with thy band. He's the third to come here asking for you this evening."

"Would you know why I'm in such demand tonight?"

"No more than I know where the gods hide their treasure. I'd sooner ask your Stepsons for their favors than their secrets, as you well know. But of course, one hears of doings on the street."

"One does, of course," he prodded.

"One hears that there was a murder at the Dark Horse tonight, and that the victim was a man Crit recommended into the innkeeper's care. One hears that both Crit and Grillo were at the scene soon after, and our own Randal summoned from the mageguild's crypts."

Madame Bomba had appointed herself surrogate mother to the Stepsons; she loved good fighters, Sacred Banders most of all. They were her "boys," and it was to the benefit of everyone, even Tempus, that this was so. But she liked to draw out her tales and had a penchant for innuendo. Tempus didn't try to hurry her or to interrogate her; he wouldn't spoil her fun; her eyes danced with glee over something. He had all the time in the world. He leaned his chair back on two legs and poured some umber krrf carefully into the well of his fist from a silver box, snorted the powder, offered her the box.

She pinched two piles, lay them on the black marble table at which they sat, and inhaled them through a golden straw that hung between her satined breasts on a delicate chain.

She sniffed loudly. "Aah. Good. Very good. When this woman was done eating and beginning to drink—just after Crit came in and he and I were talking at the bar—one of my staff came up to us saying the woman wanted to go upstairs."

Madame Bomba kept girls for whoring, but no boys: it was a personal prejudice of hers. She was, in her way, straight-laced: even her girls must be over twelve. Tempus fingered a smile. "You ought to let her, if she wishes."

"Oh, pish. Don't interrupt me. I was about to, when Crit asked which woman we were talking about. When I pointed her out and mentioned she was looking for you, loyal Critias offered to pretend to be one of my whores long enough to turn the tables on her and find out what she'd thought to learn from one of my bellywarmers. If she's tipped him, we'll share the gratuity."

"They're done, then?"

"So it seems. And very friendly, yet. So what's your pleasure, sleepless one? See the girl? Crit? Both? Neither? I've a nap room behind that curtain—" she pointed behind her with a naughty smirk "—you've not seen yet."

"You've got me curious. Go tell Crit I'm here and follow his lead as to whether or not she should know. And—"

Bomba was already getting up. She paused quizzically.

"—should Jihan come in," he warned, "your answer's still the same: you haven't seen me."

"Seen who?" she teased, tossing back gray-streaked hair once chestnut, now faded. "But a question, dear friend and guest, in case there's no time later or you suddenly are invisible to me as well as to your other ladies."

"Speak it."

"Stealth, called Nikodemos? Any word of him?"

"None." He didn't want to talk about Niko. She sensed it and, though her question had been prompted more by business considerations than idle curiosity, let it pass. Niko had been Tempus's favorite among the Stepsons; he'd left Tyse abruptly. Tempus would not conjecture about or try to alter Niko's decision. Those the Riddler loved were bound to spurn him. In Niko's case, it might be better this way. The young fighter's soul had been coveted by a Nisibisi witch, who for a time possessed him, and his patronage was still sought by no less a power than Aškelon, the entelechy of dreams. Nikodemos had retreated to the western island sanctuaries, where he'd been trained. If ill befell him there, it would not be Tempus's fault.

When he looked up again, the curtain in the doorway was rustling and Madame Bomba's tread could be heard descending the stairs. Niko's immediate family was long dead of war. He had an uncle in Caronne who purveyed the finest and rarest of drugs; it was this that Madame Bomba wanted with Niko. The boy had written a letter of introduction for her and she'd sent it on to the uncle, but so far there'd been no response.

He watched the woman and Crit at the bar, now, as Bomba sidled nimbly through the crowd, then whispered in

Crit's ear. The foreign woman's gear was eclectic. Only in
the Rankan capital, or perhaps Mygdon proper, could such
an assemblage of international craftsmanship be procured
—or in a mercenary hostel near a hotly contested front
where there was much dying and hiring taking place and
camp followers pitched their mercantile, mobile cities.

The two women and Tempus's first officer conferred
briefly. An ancient, dusty jar of wine was produced from
behind the bar, its seal broken, lid sniffed by the madame's
educated nose, a bit poured into three goblets. Then a bar-
maid headed toward the stairs with the jar.

Only Madame Bomba followed, and that a long interval
later. Crit and the foreign woman had by then disappeared
through the bar's far portal, whether to the drug dens beneath or the playrooms above, Tempus couldn't tell.

"Crit says," Bomba announced, her smile dropping
away into a frown as she poured the fine wine for herself
and Tempus, "that he's not done with her. He'll bring her
out to the farm in Hidden Valley when he's through—on
the 'off chance,' he told her, that you might be there. He
wants you to know that she claims to be of the Rankan 3rd
Commando. Is that possible?"

"Why not?" He sipped the elegant wine. "Because she's
a woman? Because she's so far upcountry? Or because
she's looking for me?" Tempus had formed the 3rd Commando a quarter-century before. It had been instrumental
in Ranke's northerly expansion during the so-called long
wars. It had been used badly, in his opinion, for purposes
other than honorable; it had obliterated city-states and con-
tributed to the downfall of a worthy empire. He'd left it to
those who had perverted its purpose; he'd not served as a
Rankan field commander on active duty since that time.
There was not a death squad or even a remnant of the once
ferocious Nisibisi mages (who had a well-earned reputation
for viciousness) that rivaled the 3rd Commando in fielded
cruelty or gratuitous violence. Ranke's fame as barbarians
second to none stemmed directly from the "unending
deaths" the 3rd Commando inflicted on its captives. Taking
to heart the doctrine that an army has failed in its purpose if
it must be fielded, a war already lost once one must be

fought, he had conceived them, hand-picked them, trained them, and spread word of the scourge they had become— to use them as a deterrent. But the emperor had turned them loose on subjugated peoples and rebel city-states and the slaves they had taken and sold off had made of the original members rich landowners, lords, and statesmen.

But nothing could change their true nature: they were assassins, experts at torture, skulkers, and berserkers— true followers of the Rankan gods of war. If this woman was one, she was seeking him for good reason: there was nothing in Tyse worth the time of even one of that unit's members. Years ago they'd conquered the north and deported its peoples, and driven the feared Nisibisi wizard-caste up into the peaks known as Wizardwall.

He was curious, riding toward the Nisibisi border on one of his steel-gray Trôs horses, as to what the 3rd Commando wanted with him.

He was also interested in Crit's reasons for handling the matter as he had.

Preoccupied thus, he forgot all about his determination to avoid Jihan. And so as he crossed the border into Nisibis through a narrow canyon which led directly to Hidden Valley, where he and Niko had recently agreed that the stud farm (which belonged in part to all Stepsons but mostly to Tempus and Niko) would be established, Jihan spurred a second Trôs stallion out from behind a rockfall to intercept him.

"Ha! Riddler! You are found out!" On his horse, she was an arresting sight in her brown/green/gray scale armor of metaphysical manufacture, her proud, classically beautiful head high and bronze hair streaming, her broad shoulders, impossibly tiny waist, and muscular thighs shown to her best advantage as she cantered up beside him astride a horse than which there were only two better in the known world.

As the horse was not hers, neither was she responsible for the beauty of her form or the perfection of her accouterments: she was a Froth Daughter, a supernal sprite, and her eyes glowed with red flecks of anger as she brought her mount alongside his and reached down to grab his horse's reins below its bit. "Where have you been, slaggard? I have searched everywhere for you. You must not leave me alone so long." There was no womanish whining in her voice; rather, there was a warning tone.

She was as strong as he, perhaps stronger; her stamina was unparalleled. She played at womanhood as she played at life. As a bedmate, he found her suitable; as a companion, she wore upon his nerves. Six months on earth was not nearly long enough to have mellowed her.

He squeezed his knees against his mount and muttered, "Hai," to it. It reared up on its hind legs and walked three steps, forelegs flailing, breaking her hold on its reins and causing the second Trôs to back up rapidly.

She pouted and put her hands on her hips. His horse came down on all fours again, and by then, she'd thought better of her behavior. "Let us start anew, surrogate husband. I have missed you. Let us hurry to our quarters and reacquaint our bodies with one another."

He was not through punishing her for having been taken in by the Nisibisi archmage Datan during the summer war for Wizardwall and turning against him; she was not yet through punishing him for the loss of her betrothed husband, Aškelon, lord of dreams, to Tempus's own sister, Cime.

That they both enjoyed the strife they engaged in, neither would admit—out of bed.

But tonight there was something new about Jihan, something he didn't understand—a sense of urgency, a tension in her. "Race me to the barn, Tempus," she called out, and the Trôs she rode lunged homeward.

She still had a half-length lead on him when they thundered into Hidden Valley between the sheer rock walls which curved in narrowly to make an easily defensible choke point. One could climb out of the valley other ways; one could not ride out. Bashir, warrior-priest of Free Nisibis, had given the land to Niko and Tempus in gratitude for their assistance in routing the Nisibisi wizards who had long oppressed his people. They had taken it gladly; Mygdonia and Ranke might war unto the death of both, but

Bashir and his Free Nisibis would endure. Sometimes
Tempus considered throwing in with the warrior-priest permanently: the Stepsons would settle in gleefully among the
free men. As it was, they were half at home here.

Nisibisi free men, braided sidelocks confining their long
hair, lounged around the paddocks and trained desultorily
with his Stepsons, even now as the moon neared its zenith.

Two of each sort of commando ambled over to take
their horses. It was a measure of the easy atmosphere and
mutual respect at the farm that Tempus could leave his
animals to others to tend.

He slipped to the ground and caught Jihan as she slid off
the blowing Trôs, rump to horse in cavalry fashion, lowering her gently to the ground. "Come, now, Jihan," he said,
kissing her brow though he hadn't meant to. "What's the
matter with you? You're not trying. You could have beaten
me by two lengths, perhaps three."

And she melted against him as the horses were led
away, so that he was very much aware that they stood in
public. She said, her words muffled against his leathers: "It
occurred to me today, alone and friendless, that I've only
six months left with you. Then what, sleepless one, will
happen to me?" She raised her head and the red flecks were
muted, saddened.

"Happen to you? Whatever you choose, I'd dare say.
Your father is not one to withhold his blessings."

"What if I told you I want to stay? Be with you permanently?"

"Permanently, with me, is a very long time. You'd become bored, restless. Already you complain that I spend
too little time with you. We would be at each other's
throats, eventually. You don't want that."

"I want to stay."

He disengaged her and walked toward his quarters, an
arm over her shoulders, thinking he knew what she needed.
Jihan's appetites, like her abilities, were greater than a
mortal woman's.

"Then you will stay," he said to defuse a possible argument. "But I doubt that even your father could allow it

without some reduction of your . . . extraordinary gifts."

"But then, if I gave up some . . . things, you would accept me? Marry me?"

"No!" It came out of him unbidden, a pure reaction. He tried to mitigate it. "I don't believe marriage would improve our lot. But you may stay with the band as long as you wish. Of course, there's the dream lord to consider. . . . You might yet take a year with him, when my sister is done."

"Hhmph. Come serve my needs, Riddler. That's all I want for you."

She vented her anger on him, but he was used to it. He rather enjoyed her attempts to make what was consummately enjoyable for them both a pleasure for her only. Jihan was an infant in an adult's body; her tantrums were part of her charm for him, and would be until she realized it.

They had worked up a good sweat on his wide, feather pallot when someone came knocking. "Send him away," she muttered blackly, "or I'll freeze him where he stands." Jihan's flesh was cool to the touch; that she sweated now was an indicator of the degree of her passion. She got up on her knees and slapped his thighs. "Banish him, or I will! Irrevocably!" Cold was her weapon, as was to some extent all water: she was born of the tides of the primordial sea.

"I'm expecting someone. You've had more than your share tonight. Go look in on our hostage. You wanted to keep the boy, to 'discover your motherhood'; you cannot in good conscience neglect him."

Jihan's guilt was stirred by Tempus's inference and she slipped, naked, corselet in hand, out his back door while he was dressing to let Crit (whose knock he knew) in the front.

Crit had the foreign woman with him and she was gracious, comely in a businesslike fashion, lithe, and possessing a handshake as firm as most men's.

"I hear you've enjoyed a joke at my expense, you and Critias," she said without preamble.

"Critias? Me?" Tempus feigned ignorance. "Crit, you look weary. You know where everything is. Refresh yourself." And Crit did look exhausted; his lips were bluish and his eye-whites red.

Crit saluted Tempus and inclined his head. "She's got a message for you. She wouldn't give it to me, no matter the persuasion. I'm going to collapse back there until you decide if she's staying. If she's not, wake me and I'll ride back to town with her. Night, all."

"Pleasant journey, Stepson," she called huskily after him, then unlatched her mantle, putting her helmet, black-crested and visored, on a hook next to his.

Tempus noted the little unit device on her cuirass: a red enameled horse, the workmanship raised, the horse rearing with three lightning bolts clenched in his teeth—3rd Commando.

But there was no rank designation beneath it. "Have you a name, sister?"

"Kama. Of the 3rd, but you'd know that, my lord. Permission to sit?"

He waved his hand. "I'm not your lord, unless you're offering yourself in service. We've a fighting woman or two . . ."

"Something like that." She was reaching up under her armor and into her loinguard. From it she extracted a folded parchment, sealed with red wax. She held it out. "This may explain, my lord." She handed it to him, then sat at the simple board table which dominated his front room, pushing the oil lamp on it toward him.

He slit the seal. He knew the crest stamped in it; it was from a Rankan whose bidding he still occasionally did— for large amounts of money. Tempus had gone south to the empire's nadir, wretched Sanctuary, for this man's faction.

The note was in code, introducing the messenger, Kama, and offering a mission: take the boy Shamshi home to Mygdonia as a special emissary of the Rankan government; negotiate a settlement of Rankan/Mygdonian differences which would ensure that all borders reverted to their former status—that is, return Machad to Rankan control; de-escalate the conflict along the fronts; draw up an agreement of nonbelligerence which would put an end to Mygdonian-funded revolutions and the feud between the

Rankan mageguild and the remnants of the Nisibisi mages who had fought for and fled to Mygdonia. Tempus was authorized to sign any such agreement in the name of the emperor.

"Sorry," he said, handing it back to her, "not for twice the amount they're offering."

The woman had thick eyebrows, a broad, high forehead, and a generous mouth tapering to a pointed chin. One eyebrow raised and she bit her lip. He could almost see her mind work behind wide brown eyes. Then she said, "May I ask why not?"

"It would mean returning Wizardwall to the Nisibisi mages. I like Bashir; I've fought beside him. I won't fight against him or stand aside while someone else tries to take from him what's his by right."

"I can't argue with you, my lord. Certainly not about rights. But I don't think that anyone considered that angle. If you could see your way clear to act in our interest and somehow allow Bashir to retain Wizardwall—after all, he's not a Rankan treaty signatory—we'll be more than content with that."

"How is it that you can speak for them? Is that a royal 'we'?"

"Not exactly. The man whose message you hold is a distant relative of mine. They trust me. I had a chance of getting through. I can offer the 3rd's support, if need be. Or if need arises. Of course, should the Mygdonians refuse our offer, we would have no choice but to redouble our efforts to wipe them off the map." Kama grinned like a gargoyle and then sobered. "Either way, we think it's fitting if you make the initial overture. If we're accepted into Mygdonia and get to Lacan Ajami, anything can happen. We'll see their true strength, that's certain, and gather useful intelligence."

"We?"

"I'd be along as an observer. And to convene my unit, of course, if you decide you want us."

"How much of this did you tell Crit?"

She chuckled, leaning back, one foot up on a chair rung, her legs spread enough that he saw a stain on one leather-covered thigh. "More than I'd thought to tell, I admit. But only that we had a lucrative proposition which might lead to him and me spending more time together."

"Convene your unit? In Mygdon?"

She shrugged. "I'm going to need an answer before we discuss details. Let me assure you that the 3rd can do what we say it can do, and would be honored to work with you again. After all, it's a sort of poetic necessity, having you along: no one wins without you, do they?"

"That's a myth."

"Or coincidence. But having coincidence on our side couldn't be bad. Oh, yes, one thing that we didn't want to write down, although it might already have been solved..."

"Go on."

"A man named Grillo, here, is no longer trustworthy. We feel it's time to retire him without honors."

"You'll have to do that yourself. Stepsons don't do Rankan dirty work. As you say, it's not in the message." He held it out, letting its feathered edge catch fire from the flame of the oil lamp.

"Is that an acceptance of the commission? And me?"

"Twice what we've been offered, and whatever spoils we happen upon during any battles we walk into—but no territory. We're mercenaries, not a country or part of any Rankan expansion cadre. You may stay until we hear from them that my terms have been accepted, on one condition."

"What's that?" Kama's eyes were sharp and clear, and for some reason, he didn't doubt that she could convene the 3rd, be it in hell itself.

"That you don't wear out Crit. He's got a rightside partner and he's my first officer. Find someone else."

She waved her hand, "Condition accepted," then extended it. "Let me say I'm reasonably certain that your terms will be met, and thus I'm personally gratified that we'll be working together. I've been looking forward to this for a long time."

"Why is that?" he asked politely, expecting her to respond that it had to do with cadre integrity and the history of the 3rd Commando.

"Because," Kama responded with just the hint of a smile pulling at the corners of her mouth, "unless my mother was in error, you're my father."

Before the Stepsons had joined forces with Bashir's guerrillas and taken Wizardwall, there had been nothing between Tyse and her northern enemies but the four Rankan garrisons at the town's compass points. Tyse had been —and still was, in Crit's estimation—one of the most fragile buffer states of empire.

As dawn broke and he and Straton rode past the gate guards into the free zone, Crit's eyes strayed to the peaks of Wizardwall, brooding like angry gods over the town.

They were riding toward the altar pits where a score of gods from nearly as many lands were worshiped. They could have avoided the Rankan sentries who officiated at the break in the free-zone wall, reciting their rote disclaimers that law in Tyse stopped at those ruined gates, by slipping inside through the tunnels; Grillo's specials and Bashir's commandos often did. But Crit had established a drop point in the free zone, one of half a dozen he'd put together for his street men and his plainclothes agents. As task force leader, he'd established a network of infiltrators and turncoats and cheaply bought spies: this was a routine part of his job.

It was information he was after this morning, dressed in Tysian homespuns on a nondescript horse, looking for a horse trader named Palapot whom Grillo had been at pains to make sure he and Strat didn't have a chance to interrogate.

"*Seh,* Crit, I don't like it." Straton had mastered enough Nisi to be fluent in its invective, curses, and taboo nouns; this one meant offal. They spoke in the polyglot mercenary argot, gleaned from worldwide campaigning, which if overheard was unlikely to be understood by the refugees who traded rags and family jewels and favors for winter wheat and goat's-hair tents. The refugees thieved from one another, every factional bloodfeud and hatred—brought with them from obliterated homelands now part of Mygdonia—alive and well here so that beyond the altar pits mass graves grew like an infestation of moles, and crematoria had sprung up to handle the overflow.

"What would Palapot be doing in here?" Strat shifted in his saddle; their horses, reins flapping loose, picked their way slowly through the human detritus. "There's no business for him here, not a customer for the kind of horseflesh he sells."

Crit didn't think his street man, who'd sighted Palapot coming out of Grillo's office in the Lanes behind Embassy Row just before sunrise, could have been mistaken. He said so. And he admitted to Straton that he didn't like it either. "Let's quit and go south and hire on as retinue guards in the emperor's palace. Or go back to Sanctuary and chase third-rate criminals. The whores there shake down quicker, and that vampire lady you've got a crush on would just *love* to see you again."

"Bastard." No Stepson, especially Straton, missed Sanctuary, southernmost outpost of empire; they had a stake in matters here: they had the Hidden Valley horse farm and respected allies in Free Nisibis. They had the Riddler, under whose command each was honored to serve; they had one another and the integrity of the Sacred Band to think of. "This isn't to be taken lightly," Strat complained. "While you were off twiddling that twat in man's clothing, *I* was working. That dart's steeped in Mygdonian poison and that fellow who took it in the neck was somebody's very special envoy—hard as nails and with weapons in his kit the likes of which I've not seen since I was in the capital. And you know it."

"Want any of it?" Crit reined his horse left through a break in low black tents where those who vended rice and onions were just building their morning fires. Up the way a knot of children huddled in the packed-dirt street, fighting over scraps or throwing bones to double the take from a night of pilfering. Keeping the waifs inside was the hardest, and saddest, part of free-zone duty: they died in the family feuds or starved if their parents did; they were worked to death by the orphans' gang bosses or sold off, if they were just a bit luckier or sturdier, by slavers who came up out of the tunnels on moonless nights and hustled them away, drugged and senseless, to fill coffles headed west to Azehur or east to Syr.

When Strat responded that assassin's garrots and incendiary kits weren't exactly his style, Crit had forgotten his teasing offer. There was something about *this* knot of children that seemed wrong: it didn't disperse as they rode up; it drew tighter, as if protecting something.

"Let's take a look." He kneed his horse. The filthy, big-eyed urchins should have scattered to all sides by now. Though he and Strat weren't uniformed, they had weapons and horses and were adult strangers, therefore enemies.

"Doesn't feel right," said Straton, urging his sorrel into a slow, crowd-dispersing canter. Still the children held their ground.

"It's *not* right," Crit confirmed, as they bore down, and to either side, veiled women gathered daughters kneading flatbread or sons hauling panniers of water and scuttled with them into tents behind the flimsy stalls.

For some reason, all the night's anomalies ran through Crit's head: the murder at the Dark Horse, Grillo's interest, the woman who'd come seeking the Riddler. Then he had to stop his horse or trample the ring of little belligerents before them. Strat swore softly; Crit saw him slide his crossbow from his saddle and lever a bolt to ready. "Easy," Crit said under his breath, and leaned forward, arms on his pommel, hands obviously empty.

The foremost child was well into his teens, with a bristly young chin defiantly outthrust, and arms folded. His garb was free-zone nondescript, his physiognomy essentially northern—broad face, almond eyes, flat nose: no wizard blood in this one. He might have been Machadi, or of Nisibisi peasant stock, or from a subjugated buffer state of Mygdon; his hair was mousy, full of straw or dirt or dung. Beside him was a girl who might have been his sister or his wife: she was pregnant, perhaps thirteen. On his other side was a snaggletoothed youth with a dying eye; beyond, Crit saw one with a short leg, another disfigured by fire. Not slaver's meat, any of these: the hale one was too old, the others too unlucky. All were doomed to the free zone.

Crit felt like the villain they obviously thought him, but said, "What's the attraction? Clear out of here, pud, and take your classmates with you," in Nisi as he told his horse with his knees to move slowly forward. The children to the rear began to drift away but those in the forefront held their ground. Behind him, Crit heard Strat's unnecessary warning: these desperate youngsters weren't harmless.

He knew that. All their eyes were on their leader, who hadn't answered Crit's question or said a word, just stood with legs widespread and eyes unblinking as if Crit, his big bay, and Straton with crossbow behind were invisible.

Then Crit's mount crowded the youth and the boy either had to move or be moved by the horse. A scabbed hand reached out toward the horse's bridle; the beast flattened its ears, tossed its head, and snapped at the boy in warning.

"Rankan scumsucker!" the youth said then in a loud voice. His gang froze in mid-retreat as their leader glared around at them; he took the hand of the pregnant girl beside him. "This your handiwork, bully-boy?" the youth said. "Maybe he didn't drop his pants fast enough? Or maybe he wouldn't play along with—"

Crit used his horse to break the handhold between boy and girl and knock the boy aside. The youth sprawled on the ground; unfortunately, the pregnant girl fell, too.

He heard Strat's pornographic warning to all concerned to stay very still, then he saw *what* the group had been protecting: one of their number, this one pale-haired, askew in his own vomit, gray upper-class eyes staring blankly at the rising sun.

Dismounting with little thought of the vicious children all around him, Crit knelt beside the corpse. The boy had died on his face; they'd turned him over. The smell of vomit, blood, and defecation was strong, this close, overwhelming the background stench of the free zone. The slain youth had once had a pretty face, arch features, and he wore a better grade of clothing, which his winsome looks had doubtless helped provide. He had bled to death;

he was nearly disemboweled. It was a particularly agonizing way to die, and a slow one.

Crit could see a brownish trail where the boy had pulled himself along the packed clay of the free-zone street for some little distance. Patting him down for evidence, Crit found nothing—not a wallet, a pouch or a coin—then turned to the circle of children around him. "Your friend, let's have what you took from him."

Half of them were gone, he realized. But the boy who'd stood up to him had helped the girl to her feet despite Strat's bow trained on him, and now looked Crit straight in the eye. "If I was you, sirrah, I'd get on my horse and get my professional killer's ass out of here. We don't want *more* truck with your sort. We ain't nobody's—" He blinked and Crit realized that, hard as he was, the sparkle in those brown eyes was not simply from anger; tears welled there.

"More? I don't know what you're talking about, but you're making me want to find out. We don't know you; we don't know him. Maybe you'll come along, sonny, and tell us just whose business you've been doing, to get one of you killed like this—" Crit made a sign with his right hand; Strat moved his horse up.

The youth looked nervously between them, realized he'd said more than he should have, then gave his own handsign. The others scattered, and as they did, he broke for it. Straton collared him with one lunge of horse and held the urchin suspended by his tunic, feet dangling while his arms flailed.

His girl, clutching her belly, sank down next to the dead boy and began to weep, then to beg for mercy for her friend, her hand extended toward Crit. "Here, here! Take it; it's all we's got. He's a good boy, let 'im go, let 'im go. . . . We don't know nothin' 'bout what Tip, here, died for, can't read none of this . . ."

In her hand, Crit realized, she had a crumpled parchment. He took it. "What else? Whose boy was this?"

"Don't say nothin'!" the boy Strat held called out.

Crit didn't look over his shoulder. He toed the dead boy. "Whose?"

"Worked . . . sometimes, now and again, for the spe-cials, is all. Carrying messages . . . and like that." She ran her hand under her nose. "Please, sir, that there's my baby's father. We don't hurt nobody."

"Right. What else was on him?"

Her eyes shifted. There had been money, then.

"Just give me the papers, keep the coins."

From under her dress she pulled a leather security belt, a wallet. From behind, Crit heard the boy's muffled objec-tions, Straton's curse.

"Strat, let him go." And: "That's fine, missy. You be on your way. And take this—" He gave her a copper piece. "Buy your Tip a prayer or two."

With a sour smile at her, the best he could manage, Crit turned away. The operator in him told him he could get more from these children than the wallet belt and papers: he could use them. But he didn't want free zone runners enough to risk them paying the price the slain boy had. Nor was he touched enough by the girl to offer her work out at Hidden Valley: when children like these passed ten, they were more dangerous than useful.

He heard the boy's stream of invective resume as Strat put him down, but by the time he was mounted, both chil-dren had disappeared.

"Somebody's running us in circles," Strat complained. "Grillo's specials, maybe. Convenient, finding Belize's killer so soon, with every bit of incriminating evidence in place."

"At least we know it's not as simple as it seems." Crit fingered the little reed blowgun he'd found and palmed when he patted down the dead boy.

Straton grunted. "Still want to see Palapot?"

"Twice as badly," Crit affirmed, holding his horse steady while the two of them sorted through Belize's papers—those he'd seen at the Dark Horse which identi-fied him and gave him permission to travel freely where he would in empire, and those he hadn't seen: a coded mes-sage with a highborn Rankan family's seal on it, opened by greasy fingers; a collection of receipts and vouchers; a map of Tyse with Palapot's trading stand in the souk and

Grillo's Outbridge estate circled in red—a map so sketchy and imprecise it hadn't been made by anyone who'd ever been here.

Straton, as they threaded their way among the morning crowd of the hopeless and homeless, was persistent. "Somebody lost an agent. Grillo didn't want us talking to Palapot until *he* had. The agent's murderer turns up dead, and he's known to have worked with the specials. If Grillo were behind this, he'd point the finger in some other direction."

"If he could. Maybe Belize wasn't his man. Maybe Grillo was Belize's target. I don't know. We'll hear what Palapot has to say."

"What about the coded letter?"

"Can't read it. Maybe the Riddler can." Passing the Spring of the Prophet, they stopped to let their horses drink, sitting on the ochre mudbrick well's edge while their mounts quenched their thirsts in the adjacent trough. He'd been thinking that the oddest thing of all was that two couriers had arrived in town the same night, when Straton, who had an annoying habit of reading his mind, said, "Didn't that lady you took out to Hidden Valley, the one Madame Bomba put you onto, have a message in code?"

"Kama? She's no lady. Let's get going."

They looked for Palapot for the better part of the day, first in the free zone, then in the souk. His horse-line was there, tended by a nephew, but he wasn't.

At dusk they headed homeward—not to the Stepson's Outbridge barracks or the Hidden Valley farm, but to a safe haven in the Lanes. Crit sent word by messenger to the Riddler that he'd appreciate a meeting and gave his evening's itinerary. He had no intention of leaving town until he'd found Palapot and given him over to Straton, whose forte was interrogation. And he wanted to see Tempus alone. If this coded message had anything to do with Kama of the Rankan 3rd Commando, he and his commander ought to consider the implications privately.

* * *

"Shamshi! Shamshi!" It was Jihan's voice; there was no mistaking her deep, resonant tone.

Shamshi had been hiding in a thicket, shaking, shivering, letting his tears flow and his terror ebb. He was covered with blood from his scuffle in the free zone with the Maggot wretch. Finding a Maggot—a refugee—who looked enough like him had been harder than the disembodied voice of Roxane, the Nisibisi witch, had led him to believe it would be. Since the murders, he had not heard from her.

Now Shamshi was alone, her voice gone, the deed done, weak from the implications of it all. Fear had spurred him on during his mad, predawn dash through the tunnels. He'd found his pony right where he'd left it, in the burned-out barn the Nisibisi free men used to hide their comings and goings; he'd flung himself upon his pony and raced toward the Nisibisi border and safety.

Crossing it, he'd been elated. It was done. He'd turned eleven with the rising sun and become a man during the night; destiny was his.

"Shamshi! Shamshi!" he heard again, an urgent call, not quite a yell. The Froth Daughter would soon find him.

Wiping his tear-swollen eyes, he crawled forward on his belly. He hadn't seen the blood, soaked into his linen tunic, until the sun had risen; he'd almost reached the Hidden Valley choke point by then; he'd panicked; he found he couldn't think at all. He'd done away with the Rankan assassin, sent to ruin everything, with ease; then he'd let the scapegoat Maggot he'd found in the free zone bleed on him. Guilt had splattered him; he was covered with blood he couldn't explain. He'd reined his gold-maned pony hard about, and then it had happened: fate, or the Nisibisi mageblood which elevated him above the mortal cattle among whom he hid, had come to his aid. His pony had stumbled; he'd heard a sickening *snap* as they went down.

He'd sat in the dirt, unhurt, listening to its screams, then moans, of agony, watching it try to understand why it couldn't get its fractured leg under it no matter how it lunged, consumed with tremors of his own.

Then he'd realized what he must do: he took his dirk

and approached the exhausted pony, whose eyes rolled in its head but who calmed as he came close, expecting him somehow to make it well, and he slit its throat.

It took longer to die than the boy he'd murdered in the free zone, and this time Shamshi retched: he'd loved his pony.

It had saved his life. He knew the Stepsons wouldn't be able to tell pony blood from Maggot blood; he'd begun the long hike home in a daze of relief. But then the enormity of it all became too much for him to bear: he'd climbed up the valley wall and circled around behind the barns, filled with grief and guilt and confusion.

What had he done? Was it enough? Was it right? The voice in his head which told him what to do and how to do it—Roxane's voice—had gone away. He'd lain shaking on the ground a long time. Now the sun was warm on his back and Jihan was calling: they'd found his pony long since. He wriggled toward the thicket's edge.

They'd never send him back to Mygdonia; he wouldn't go. He'd lived among the Mydgonians long enough. His mother was a blind fool and his father of record was not his father at all. He'd always known it; they were too stupid to be his parents, it had had to be some awful mistake. For years, Shamshi had waited among the idiotic sheep who walked like men in Mygdon for his *real* father to appear. Eventually, they had found each other. Shamshi of Mygdon was called son of Adrastus, the Unescapable, second warlord of the Alliance. He was in reality the son of the most powerful Nisibisi archmage ever to have ruled from Wizardwall.

He'd had scant weeks with his real father, then Tempus's Stepsons and his accursed sister, Cime the magekiller, had murdered Datan and taken Shamshi hostage.

Tempus would pay for his foul depredations. Shamshi lived among the Riddler's Stepsons and pretended to hark to his teachings. In actuality, Shamshi bided his time. The Froth Daughter loved the boy, and he knew it. She'd help him stave off the Riddler, make Tempus relent and save him from being deported to Mygdon. He wouldn't be traded like a horse, haggled over like a gilded chalice.

Jihan was close now, her long legs in his field of view. He stumbled to his feet and, with a distress he didn't have to feign, crashed pall mall through the thicket and threw himself upon her, sobbing out his grief over the pony he'd had to slay.

Her cool, muscular arms enfolded him. Her sweet-smelling breath was upon his cheek as she kissed his tears away, scolding him tenderly, telling him they'd get him another mount—not a pony, this time, but a mighty charger, a warhorse as fine as any man among the Stepsons had.

"These things happen, little love," she crooned. "You must be brave, my prince. For Tempus is right when he asks 'when is death not in our own selves?'"

He struggled back in her arms, searching her face for a sinister inference, found none. He lay his head against her scale-armored breast once more. Roxane, the finest and most powerful witch of Wizardwall, had introduced him to the joys of congress with women; he had fantasies of expressing his love for Jihan more substantially. In time, he would; in time, he'd marry her and make her his consort. Now, he was too small in stature, too lacking in power: she thought him a child. But he could speak freely of love to her, and that he did then, reminding her that today was his birthday; from now on, she must think of him as a man.

"Well, my young man, then you must stop crying."

He knuckled his eyes and she slapped his bottom. "Up, now. We'll have to hurry back and tell them I've found you. The Riddler was very angry with me; he thought you ran away. You'd never do that, Shamshi, would you?"

"From *you?*" He reached out to take her hand and they strolled toward the fenced north meadow together. "Never. Unless . . ."

"Unless *what*, beastly boy? I've been out for hours looking for you. It's nearly dusk—"

"Unless you cannot save me from the Riddler's plans. I can't go back to Mygdonia. I hate it there. My mother can't protect me any longer, now that she's gone blind. My father is a craven fool. Lacan Ajami longs to see me dead; he won't have his own sons—my cousins—outshone in

valor or intelligence. The time I spent on Wizardwall, I
spent there because they say in Mygdon that I'm possessed
by demons. What worse, now, might they be saying? If
rumors have reached my father's brother that I'm not his
son at all, but a child of magic, they'll execute me!" He
pulled his hand from hers, peered up at her. "Promise me,
Jihan, that you'll not let him send me back."

"I . . . can only promise that I will let no evil befall
you," she said in a deep, troubled voice. "You are as a son
to me, Shamshi. I will protect you as if you issued from
my own belly."

He hugged her; she kissed his hair.

"Now," she said, "let's get you bathed and fed. Then, if
you're up to it, we shall pick out a horse for you, finer than
your wildest dreams."

When the soft night fell, Tempus had ridden into town
with Kama and Gayle, a former special of Grillo's whom
Tempus had made a Stepson for services rendered. Gayle
was half Nisibisi, half Tysian, sensitive to magic or treachery afoot, and knew nothing which would be damaging if
Kama worked her wiles and debriefed him all night long.

He left them on Commerce Avenue, the woman who
claimed to be a daughter of his and the game commando
he'd thrown to her like a haunch of meat. Gayle's seawater
eyes twinkled merrily in his hawk's face. He liked this
duty, wasn't underestimating it, and threw himself into the
part of tour guide with a confidence Tempus wished he
could share.

Still, other matters were pressing, and the man into
whose arms Tempus himself had collapsed in the aftermath
of a battle with sorcery only the two of them had survived
should be able to handle a single woman, even if she was
3rd Commando and spawn of his loins.

She might not be, he told himself. One couldn't recall
every ceremonial rape or wench taken in battle. A full
quarter of the Rankan nobility claimed him as an ancestor
when deep enough in their cups. Kama was looking for a
saga, she'd told Crit, a bit of history to make. She wanted

to restore the 3rd to its former glory and have its finest hour ready for the telling at next winter's Festival of Man. The festival was held once every four years, and at it the best Rankan charioteers, riders, wrestlers, spear chuckers, runners, bowmen, swordsmen, and poets met to compete. Medals were awarded by the emperor himself, and treaty signatories sent teams of contestants. It was a likely story, but he wasn't sure he believed it. Her eyes told him she was after honor and glory of a more immediate sort, as her bearing and her boldness told him she was deadly serious. Moreover, he remarked to Crit in the Lanes safe haven, while from under a closed door came muffled sounds that meant Straton was making progress interrogating Palapot the horse trader, "she might just *be* a child of mine. If so, she bears watching. I didn't marry her mother, or even ask the woman her name. In fact, I can't recall the incident at all."

"You don't like her, do you, commander?"

"Not particularly, no. But it's more accurate to say I'm wary of her. She told you and me two different tales; that in itself confirms much of what she's said. She's from the 3rd, I own, and full of deceit. I don't want you fraternizing with her. I've told her, and I've put Gayle on her. Keep clear of her, Crit, until I decide whether we've any use for her."

"Meaning we can afford to lose Gayle?"

"Meaning we can't afford to lose you. We'll see how she comports herself. She'll be here until we hear back from Ranke whether they've accepted the exorbitant terms I've set for the Stepsons' hire. If she causes no trouble by then, perhaps it will prove me wrong."

Crit was rolling a smoke; he lit it from a candle on the single bluestone table in the spartan Lanes haven. The windows' iron shutters were drawn and they'd pulled up benches. Leaning on his elbows in only a linen undershirt and loinguard, Crit dragged deeply on the broadleaf he'd licked into a cylinder and squinted at Tempus over the blue smoke. "Mind telling me what kind of trouble you're looking for from her? What the mission under consideration is? What the tale she told you was?"

From the other room came a muffled shriek of agony; Crit didn't look away toward the sound. Tempus's voice was gravelly and clipped. "Ranke still thinks that we can trade Shamshi to Lacan Ajami for strategic advantage. We'll be emissaries, there to negotiate. The 3rd will be our backup in case of treachery."

"Sounds reasonable," Crit said cautiously. "I've always wanted to see Mygdonia."

Crit had given Tempus the coded message and watched his commander read it without comment. Tempus had volunteered only that the two messages—the one Kama had brought him and this second which Belize had lost in transit—were the same in every particular. Crit had remarked that someone wanted very badly to make certain Tempus received the information.

But intelligence was Crit's speciality; more had to be said. Because this man was task force leader and his second in command, he needed to know not only what was certain, but also what was probable. Tempus said quietly, "After a day of verbal fencing, I'm still not certain what she's holding back. However, she's very interested in our estimate of how many and which Nisibisi mages still fight for Mygdon. Given that the Rankan mageguild insists that victory for the empire is impossible while their Storm God remains planelocked by hostile magic, my guess is that once we get to Mygdon, we'll find ourselves part of an attempt to exterminate the remaining Nisibisi adepts who fight for Lacan Ajami. Mygdonia has no magic of its own. With the war god freed, Ranke would rally."

Crit was leaning back, nodding slightly, a nasty little smile on his stubble-fringed lips. "Suits me. I have dreams about vengeful witches—especially that Roxane—dancing on my chest. And it makes sense—why else involve the 3rd? We're strong enough without them to protect ourselves on any regular sortie, invited or uninvited. Are we going to do it?"

"Perhaps. I'm not sure I'd welcome the return of my tutelary god at this point in time. I'm doing well enough without him. And we must consider what a Rankan victory will mean to Free Nisibis."

Crit whistled softly, tapped ashes into the pool of hot wax collecting in the candlestick's base, then stared at him.

For a long while, all that could be heard were the soft whines and thuds coming from the next room. Then Crit inclined his head in that direction. "Stepsons have no love for Ranke; every man of us thinks highly of Bashir. What about Grillo's involvement? He won't take kindly to what Strat's doing to that double agent of his."

Tempus and Critias had attended just enough of Palapot's interrogation to determine that the horse trader was a Rankan agent who, unbeknownst to his masters in the capital, had fallen into Grillo's web of power and now served two masters.

"I'll talk to Grillo. But only about the chances of continued autonomy for Free Nisibis." He got up, took his leopardskin mantle from a hook, strode to the door.

Crit said, "That's it, commander? No new orders? Want me to watch Kama from a distance? Dispose of this piece of Rankan rubbish we've got in there?"

"Nothing yet. Just let me know if Strat learns anything more of interest." He didn't want Critias thinking too much about Grillo, or Kama, or a second campaign against Nisibisi magic. "And put a bodyguard on young Shamshi; we don't want him disappearing again. I'll be with Grillo for the balance of the evening, if anything urgent comes up that you can't handle."

"Nothing will," Crit promised. Tempus hoped he was right. This interview with Grillo was going to be very sensitive.

Gayle was sticking as close to Kama as a loinguard, squiring her along Commerce Avenue with the insouciant swagger of an old Tyse hand breaking in a new recruit. Worse, he had ideas in his head, communicated to her by the occasional accidental brushing of their girded hips while entering this fortunetelling establishment or that drug den. Worst, whenever he met a garrison soldier or one of his fellow Stepsons or Grillo's lurking specials, he introduced her. She had to shake him.

Kama knew by the time they'd come out of the third of a seemingly endless array of ale houses that she'd never outdrink him; her head was spinning, her steps chancy. "Gayle, I've had enough to drink. You promised to show me Tyse, not Peace Falls." She'd been issued an armband which made her immune to curfew; all she had to do was rid herself of this accommodating soldier and she could be about her own business.

"Tyse. Well, there's not much to see at night. The Maggots are in their tents and the Tysians locked up tight behind their walls. What about a little krrf? Or pulcis?" He didn't quite leer, but his hawk face inclined to her conspiratorially. She fought the urge to put this sanguine-skinned local in his place. Pulcis was a mildly hallucinogenic, aphrodisiac stimulant—rare, expensive, and illegal everywhere but Caronne; krrf was a berserker's drug—the Rankan army ran on it. Perhaps she could outsmoke him or outsnort him. Otherwise, she was going to have to outsmart him and make an enemy. Gayle wasn't her type, but she wanted them to become separated "by mistake," not cause him to fail in his duty or make it clear she'd purposely disobeyed the Riddler's orders. Kama wanted to leave him snoring somewhere, do what she had to do, and get back to him in short order, so that he wouldn't know she'd been gone.

She let him take her elbow as they descended ill-lit stairs into a smoke-filled cellar subdivided by paper partitions (most of which were already pulled shut), wishing that he were Critias, then growled aloud so that Gayle said, "Excuse me?" and she had to cover the lapse. She'd been solitary too long; she had a habit of growling wordlessly when frustrated and of striking out at innocent walls or furniture with a balled fist to quash errant, troublesome thoughts. She'd have to watch herself. Though Tyse seemed primitive and simple by Rankan standards, these men the Riddler had collected were not.

She let Gayle secure them a private booth and wondered who was paying for this debauch, then answered her own question: her father. Kama preferred not to think of Tempus that way, but it was her kinship which had secured her this

assignment. Meeting him had been something she'd
dreaded. Having him immediately start dictating to her
whom she could see and with whom she could keep company had been unexpected. First she'd felt disbelief, then
cold fury. And the legendary Tempus sitting across from
her had watched her curiously, his high brow smooth, and
a defensive little smile dancing at the corners of his mouth.
Tempus was all that he'd been reputed to be, that was certain. It was hard to remember that he was older than the
city-state of Tyse itself, harder to discount his mystique,
his animal magnetism, his sheer power.

Kama liked power in men, the sort which seethed
under wraps and was sure enough not to need demon-
strating. She liked Critias better than she should; she'd
always taken to his type—quiet, intelligent, manipula-
tive. Her father had probably done them both a favor by
registering his disapproval, but it only fanned her interest. Crit was just what she needed: someone who shared
the Riddler's confidence, who knew what was worth
knowing. Any man who could play whore for a possible
information advantage, and do it so convincingly, was
special. Forbidden fruit. She swore aloud, pushed the
hour they'd spent together upstairs at Brother Bomba's
out of her mind. Crit be damned.

Gayle was here, now. He must know something, be
useful in some manner. She began to open him up with
canny questions and careful flattery. When she learned
he'd been one of Grillo's specials, she redoubled her efforts. *"That's* what I want to see: the specials' barracks,
the east garrison, Embassy Row . . . I need orientation, not
recreation," she said hoarsely over the smoke she'd just
exhaled.

He cocked his head. "Rankan 3rd Commando to the
bone." He tsk'd. "You'll be sorry. Leave's scarce enough
around here. They'll work your butt off, starting tomorrow.
Can't you just relax and have a good time on the Stepsons'
credit?" He toked deeply on the bubbly pipe between them,
then rasped, when she didn't answer or take the pipestem,
"Women. All business. Fine. You don't have to worry
about me. What's first? Mercenaries' hostel? Mageguild?

The Lanes—that's offices and safe havens, drops and such? Want to check in with the Rankan ambassador?"

Then, finally, Kama realized Gayle was a bit smarter than he'd seemed, a bit more than he looked. These grunts of the gods bore watching, especially since they were so concerned with watching her.

So she did take the pipe, and toked again, and while he drew, at her request, a little map of the town with resiny pipewater on the low bronze table between them, she flipped open her ring and emptied the sleeping powder from it into the pipe's bowl. Then she handed him the pipestem.

But he'd had enough. "Not if we're going to do some serious reconnoitering. Is that your job with the 3rd? I like long recon patrol myself . . . out there, you can win, not like standing in a porking line wondering if your field people really have their strategy down. . . ." He was on his feet. She followed, thinking, *All right, Gayle, let's see what you've got.*

What he had was a knowledge of Tyse she began to envy, and a way of letting his questions hang in the air until she had to answer them or appear as what she was—someone who was hiding something.

They'd crossed over into Tyse proper via the mercenaries' hostel ("Pretty quiet, lately. Everybody worth having's already spoken for and deployed out of here"), the mageguild of rose quartz which sat back among giant cedars in a vacant park ("We've got to just ride by quickly. Sometime when my friend Randal's about, we'll get you in for a look if you've got the stomach for it"), and had turned up Embassy Row toward the palace square ("Never did find the poor royal family when the wizard war brought all that granite down on their heads, but Rankan aid's been sent to rebuild the palace. The stone lions are still standing, though. Lions used to be sacred to the kings hereabouts. Nobody else could hunt them . . ."), when she noticed Gayle wasn't treating her like a lady any longer.

They stopped at an intersection. "The Lanes," he said, pointing northeast. "Outbridge begins there on your left."

His hand gestured west. "There's a Nisibisi eatery a couple of blocks down the Lanes. They've local delicacies and an outhouse that's porking-well bearable."

In the Lanes the streets were narrow and torches far apart. The buildings were ancient, many attached to one another—windowless, mudbrick facades which had been there when the free zone was an independent contoured city and the Lanes its posh suburb. In the Nisibisi tavern he ordered in Nisi and toasted her.

The wine was foul and made her stomach lurch. She grimaced. "What *is* this?"

"Goat's blood, garlic to keep it thin, and hill wine. Better drink the whole thing; Nisibisi free men are touchy about their cuisine."

She looked around. Sidelocked Nisibisi were watching her; she was the only woman in the place. And Gayle was telling her that she'd better be as tough as she'd given him to think she was. Without a word, she drained her goblet, meeting his challenge. He gestured to the leather-clad barkeep to refill it. "Hungry?" Gayle asked, deadpan, as a customer eased up to the bar on her right and her escort gave an offhand greeting to someone she couldn't see. She turned.

It was Critias and another Stepson, both in Nisibisi tunics and breeches.

Gayle said, "Critias, this is—"

"We've met."

"That's the commander's—?" asked Crit's companion, heavyset and taut, with swordsman's shoulders and bleak eyes that stripped her without apology.

These two were old friends; Crit didn't need to hear the rest of his companion's question. He slipped familiarly into the other's pause. "Straton, meet Kama, attached to the Rankan 3rd Commando. Kama, this is my right-side partner and better half, Strat."

Sacred Banders, then. Who would have thought it? Her heart sank, unreasonably. She offered her hand to Straton and his grip was cool, firm, and noncommittal.

Then Strat said, "Gayle, I have to talk to you. Alone."

Gayle and Straton excused themselves and threaded their way among scattered tables to take seats against the far wall.

"I see Gayle didn't spare you the obligatory hazing," Crit said, his finger tapping the goat's-blood cocktail before her. "I'm sorry; Nisibisi comestibles take a little getting used to."

"You were looking for me. Let's stop toying with one another." In the bronze mirror behind the bar she could see Straton and Gayle, their heads together, watching them.

"That's right. I have a problem I'm wagering you'll help me with—and not tell Tempus I asked you."

"Which is?"

"A man named Belize was murdered here just before you arrived. Ever hear of him?"

Belize? "An assassin," she said carefully. "A good soldier, though. Special work." She couldn't afford to guess which lie would do, how much or little Critias might already know about the man in question. "But why ask me? The Rankan army's widespread."

Crit shrugged but watched her steadily; his eyes were level, his mouth a straight line. "Two strangers, both from Ranke. Both with safe-conducts issued from the same office. Both with coded messages for the Riddler which he says read exactly alike. . . . Redundant."

"Are you implying something?"

"Not really. Just tying up loose ends. You weren't in competition with Belize to get here first, by any chance?"

"I didn't even know they'd sent him," she said honestly and with real anger. "If he was a decoy to make sure I'd get through, they needn't have bothered. Is that what you think?"

"I'm just doing my job. Asking questions. Trying to make sense of the answers. An assassin, you say. Does that mean you are, too?"

"I've told you what I am." Flustered, she reached out for the pottery goblet of blood wine. His hand closed over hers. "You don't have to drink that, or prove anything to me." This voice was deeper, more intimate; she looked at her hand in his, up at him, then away.

"Your commander told me not to fraternize with you," she said.

"He told me the same thing. Maybe because you two are related . . ."

"You've got a right-side partner. Sacred Band, isn't it?"

"To the death with honor." He grinned. "What's that got to do with anything?"

"Anything . . ." she repeated, telling herself she had to consider her assignment.

"Anything I do on my own time is not Tempus's business; Strat and I are an old working team—no problem."

"Is this a proposition?" She slid her hand out from under his.

"A declaration of intent." He told her where his Lanes drop was. "I've got an office there, sleeping quarters; I run lots of agents. I'd like to consider you one of them. Think it over. Sometimes the Riddler sees things in terms of black and white—good and evil; sorcery and religion; men and women. He'll keep you around and give you busywork. I'll *use* you. We'll both like it. I'm sure you can keep secrets; I can smell it. If you want me, you know where to find me."

Then he collected his partner, waved from the doorway, and headed into the night.

Gayle motioned to her to join him. Before she did, she reached into her beltpouch and pulled out a pair of dice. She threw them three times: eight, nine, nine: power and increase; money. She'd thrown for the outcome of Crit's offer. Nodding, she put the dice away and caught sight of herself in the bronze mirror as she turned to join Gayle across the room.

The spells she'd bought from Rankan magicians in the capital had been worth their price: so far, she'd outmaneuvered her competition, though she hadn't known she had any; she'd met the man she had to meet, the one who'd help her; she'd found her father, for what that was worth.

Grillo could live a while longer. Belize's death changed things; she'd have to be more careful. Perhaps she'd hire a take-out artist from the mercenaries' guild to put an end to

Grillo. Perhaps she'd merely discredit him, make him suspect and thus useless here, ruin his career and force an early retirement. It was her choice. And Gayle, who knew his former master well, was going to help her make it.

Kama had been sent to deal with Grillo, infiltrate the Riddler's confidence, make sure that the Mygdonian child they held here was sent back to Mygdonia where he'd die along with his father and his uncle, Lacan Ajami.

She'd made sacrifices to the gods openly and contracted success spells on the sly because everyone knew that the gods weren't what they used to be: sorcery and hard work were the only ways to get anything done.

She hadn't yet caught sight of the fabled Froth Daughter, or Shamshi of Mygdon. But Crit was going to be a very fruitful contact; her dispatcher had been wrong in assuming that enlisting the Stepsons could be accomplished only through the Riddler himself. Tempus was, as her hired mage had predicted, too bound up in the affairs of Free Nisibis. That, too, she hoped to rectify. Wizardwall had been taken by dint of Rankan effort: Grillo, Tempus, the Stepsons—all were fielded on Rankan gold and sworn to Rankan service. Free Nisibis should not exist; Nisibis should be a Rankan client state. And so it would be.

Kama had an open mandate here, and beyond Wizardwall—one which extended into Mygdonia itself. Sliding into a seat beside Gayle, she began expertly to guide the conversation toward Grillo's extracurricular activities: bribe-taking, smuggling, lending his forces to the Nisibisi guerrillas. Gayle was proud of all that; her credentials, vouched for by Straton, she assumed, while Crit was propositioning her, were no longer in doubt so far as Gayle was concerned.

He began to explain the complex political structure of Tyse, the personal militias, the provisional military government, the insurgent substructure funded by Mygdonia, the difference between "good" and "bad" Nisibisi and how Tempus managed to keep the Stepsons nonaligned.

She listened very closely; Kama's work here for the 3rd Commando had begun. At the end of it might lie a palace coup in Ranke, an end to the mismanagement which had the empire teetering on the very brink of collapse. But first the 3rd must be reunited with its founder and reconsecrated in the fiery sack of Mygdonia. On this, every Rankan mage and seer of the armies agreed. If they were going to get their god back, His avatar must toil in their cause.

"You'd better watch Critias," Grillo warned, his handsome head upon his fists, tapers burning low about them in his office. His bleary eyes narrowed. "By Vashanka's bunioned balls, Riddler, I'm tired. Not everyone can go without sleep as long as you. Where *is* that woman?" He picked up a mallet from his desk and desultorily struck the gong hanging on its red-lacquered stand.

"Any particular reason?" Tempus asked evenly. Grillo detested Crit, and vice versa: they both were expert at the same sort of work and rivalry was too gentle a term for what existed between them, especially now that Crit had interdicted a shipment meant to fatten Grillo's wallet.

"My sources in the mageguild network tell me Randal's gone to Bandara. I'll lay this whole lot of krrf—" he patted the gilt quartz box from which they'd been reviving their wits all evening "—against an equal amount of muck from your stables that you didn't know about it."

"Should I have?" Tempus responded mildly as the widow Maldives, a brown-haired wench he'd have taken home himself if she weren't Grillo's mistress, brought steaming *cha*—an aromatic, bracing tea—in delicate Rankan cups with saucers, smiled at him, switched her hips and left.

Tempus took a cup, sipped. "This would wake the dead." The brown liquid was opaque, so long had it been steeping.

"Good," Grillo grunted. "Then maybe I'll be able to keep up with you. You asked me why you should have known. I'll tell you. Because he went at Critias's behest. There's only one reason for that . . ."

"I'm mystified," Tempus admitted. "What's your point?"

"See! You don't know what your own people are doing."

"Critias has the authority to send for any Stepson. I'm not babysitting Tyse, he is. If he wants Niko back, that's his business."

"Maybe. Maybe it's all of ours. You come to me with some half-assed story about dead Rankan assassins and a daughter of yours you don't like and questions about Bashir's security. Niko and, for all I know, other Stepsons on leave, are being recalled by your first officer without your knowledge—"

"I didn't say that. I only said I didn't know Randal had gone to Bandara. We think it's time to consolidate our forces."

"Even the adepts? You used to stay clear of wizards. Now you're all but a mageguild sponsor."

"Grillo, this isn't getting us anywhere. *Will* you increase your personal security for a while? Go up to Wizardwall and talk to Bashir about stationing more men up there— yours, mine, the garrisons', I don't care whose, but we need to be able to secure Nisibis's northern border."

"*Why?*"

"Standard procedure."

"Yours, not mine. I wish you'd tell me what's bothering you."

Tempus drank deeply of the *cha,* stared into it ruminatively. He couldn't tell Grillo any more than he had—not that Kama had orders to make an end to Grillo; not that the 3rd would descend on Tyse like the wrath of gods; not that an incursion into Mygdonia itself was in the offing; and not—*especially not*—that given the foregoing, an attempt at coup d'etat in Ranke was almost a certainty. All Tempus had was suspicion, instinct, an itch he could not scratch but which, over centuries, he'd learned never to ignore. He sighed rattlingly, his normally smooth brow deeply furrowed. "I don't know what more I can say. I've warned you."

"Of what?" demanded the exasperated operations officer. "Tell me that the god is whispering in your ear! Tell me *something* substantive!"

Tempus sighed once more. "Of the Logos, which is as I describe it, men always prove to be uncomprehending—both before they have heard it and once they have heard it. They fail to notice what they do after they wake up just as they forget what they do when asleep."

"What's that supposed to mean?"

"You see? Consult your gods; I am not one."

So it was that he left Grillo in an ill temper, not certain that he had succeeded in his purpose of protecting his friend from his daughter while still looking after those Stepsons whom he loved. They, as he, craved only sanctified battle with those who threatened not only their way of life, but their gods themselves.

As for these others, the Grillos and Kamas and Bashirs of a world his soul disdained, their Logos—what cosmic reason expressed itself as the source of world order and intelligibility—must sustain them: he could not.

He was girding for a second battle with Unreason in the guise of Mygdonian-sword sorcery, and he was going to have to win it with only his Stepsons to wield—without even the help of friendly gods.

One particular god, whom the Rankans called Vashanka and the south called its Storm God, had been humbled or routed or vanquished—or perhaps even destroyed—by the Nisibisi mages who served godless Mygdonia and labored against even gods for pay.

Too long had his tutelary god's voice been absent from Tempus's ear. And though once the man called the Riddler had considered deific possession to be an affliction, he missed the battle of wits and wills in which the man and his god once were prone to indulge.

Though he did not love the berserker god, Tempus respected Him. Rumor had it that the once-mighty Pillager was plane-locked, a laughingstock among deities. He didn't quite believe it. But if his Storm God needed rescuing, he was bound to see to it.

In search of the once-mighty lord of rape and pillage, Tempus would venture even into godless Mygdonia. A bloodletting was coming; Kama was the sign of it, she who was conceived upon the battlefield while Vashanka was yet in him. Her message was the line and page of the mandate the Logos had sent him. Not only would his Stepsons be able to settle their score with the Nisibisi wizards who'd murdered wantonly among their number, but his own 3rd Commando was being returned to him.

And if none of this were so, he would still have gone forth, eventually, into Mygdon: he was bored, and he was lonely.

And with all the portents teasing him and events goading him, with Jihan plaguing him and the Mygdonian hostage Shamshi worrying him, he chafed to be upon his quest.

He could hardly wait.

Book Two:

MASTERS OF MYSTERY

Leeward of the Bandara chain's main island, nestled like a sleeping child between the crescent of its harbor and the northerly mainland coast, lies Ennina, The Lord's Eye, an islet reserved for returning masters of Bandara's mysteries and initiates in retreat.

Here mornings are misty and seasons tender; even on dog days, the gentle haze reaching up to heaven seldom burns off before late morning. The sea warms Bandara in winter and cools her six islands in summer. The prevailing steering currents from the west coax her pine and willow into wondrous shapes and conspire with easterly trade winds to keep her veiled in clouds impenetrable to curious, unsanctified eyes.

It was to Ennina that Nikodemos had repaired to heal his soul and put his life in order. No one in Bandara called him by his war name. Here he was simply Niko; "Stealth," the Sacred Bander, decorated leftman of the Stepsons, shock trooper without peer, did not exist. It didn't matter to the masters of Bandara that Niko was a blood brother to

Bashir of Free Nisibis or that he'd become landed and wealthy employing the skills he'd learned here as a boy: silent movement; peripheral sensing; Death Touch; meditation's hunches, self-help and stamina; weapons at hand.

It did matter to them that one of their number had come home wan and troubled. Niko had claimed the attribute of *maat*—balance, equilibrium, and the strategic mental arsenal a quiet heart can bring to bear—during his boyhood years here. Few had attained as much. The mysteries of maat were the most elusive and difficult to master; induction into its study in no way ensured success. Many sought maat; the majority failed.

To have an initiate so gifted return hollow-eyed and sick at heart was distressing. To show overmuch concern might make matters worse. Niko had exercised his right to solitude and gone straight to Ennina, where by tradition he must be left alone. He'd said only that he needed more healing than his mental rest-place could provide and sought its equal in the phenomenal world. This was a formal request couched in the requisite language—not a revelation, just a ritual invocation any initiate might use to assert his prerogative.

No one who had tutored him from the time he'd come to the oracles' islands at the age of nine—or who'd trained with him during those four years he'd spent there locked away from "the world," as the Bandarans called the mainland—had dreamed, at first, that this time the words spoken were literally the truth.

They respected his privacy; they could not sympathize with his plight. Every man heals himself, said the sect. Every oracle makes his own truth. A wise one determines his own fate. It is upon each soul to recognize its limit. They let him be.

He'd brought a girl with him, a mute with a baby boy on her hip. This, too, was his right. They took in the homeless girl and prepared to cleanse her and adopt mother and child as their own. It was then that the oracles began boding ill, and nightmarish interludes afflicted the dream masters.

Eventually, a former instructor named Levitas was sent to speak to Niko. A Bandaran adept must not bring the world home with him; Niko should have left his wordly troubles behind.

"Our dreams are full of blood and death; witchfire fouls the sybils' caves; wizardsign has been seen: a red tide came in." The instructor Levitas, well over one hundred, lowered himself to the immaculate boards of Niko's cabin and crossed his bony legs.

The hazel-eyed fighter watched his former teacher, unblinking, unspeaking. An exotic mage-strain whispered in Niko's flaring cheekbones and pointed jaw, in his thick ashen hair and his long clean limbs. This was as Levitas remembered. But the thin-lipped mouth drawn tight had been split in battle; the nose was not so straight as once it had been, but bent from a blow. Nikodemos yet gave the impression of being an athlete or a sporting noble rather than a warrior from Bandara's arcane schools, but that was a bequest from his parents. The venerable instructor could feel the unrest in Niko by its effect on his own heartbeat and the pounding of his pulse.

Though in a pose meant for meditation, Nikodemos was far from calm.

The teacher, having elicited no response beyond an initial nod of greeting when he'd slid back the partition and entered unbidden, tried again. "You bring the world with you, Niko. You must let go." Still no response. Levitas sighed. At least Niko's eyes did not avoid his. He made his voice as intimate, as gentle, as possible. He was about to cut deep with it, begin an excising ritual he'd never once in all his life had to employ. "Have you killed men?"

A response to that question was not a matter of choice; it was a duty.

"Yes, sir. I have." In the boy's gaze was nothing. Niko looked out at his onetime mentor from an unthinkable distance, emotionlessly as if his eyes themselves were still in the world, where the flat emptiness in them served a mercenary better than impregnable armor.

"How many have you killed?"

A spark of anger flashed, then subsided. The old man's heart thumped in his chest.

The boy said, "Men? Close up? Face to face?" His eyes slid away, as if counting memories, then back. "Nine or ten."

"All told?"

"Hard to say. Covertly, from shadows, indirectly in battle . . . I don't know, perhaps thrice that number. But you're wrong, it's not that."

"Then what is it?"

"Demons. Fiends. Witches. Magic." Niko unfolded from his squat abruptly, his hand outstretched to the startled instructor. Taking it, the old man let the youngster help him up. "I've got to show you something," Niko said quietly. "Come this way."

Out behind the little cabin was a gravel "pond," neatly raked but without any artful design. Niko walked barefoot out into its midst. "Please," he said over his shoulder. "See this."

The gravel was a meditation aid; it was nearly sacrilegious for anyone but the cabin's occupant to walk on it. Yet, so bidden, Levitas couldn't refuse. The blankness of the gravel gave him pause and made him worry more.

When the old tutor reached his student, the boy had brushed away enough gravel to reveal what he had buried there: an enameled cuirass of priceless antiquity with snakes and glyphs twining its breastplate; a sword in scabbard and matching dirk with the demons of the elder gods raised on it in a way metal had not been worked for centuries.

"Where did you get these?" Levitas spoke before he thought, and the trembling in his voice reached the boy's ears clearly. Half horrified, half astounded, he knelt down beside Niko on the stones.

"They were inflicted upon me by Aškelon, regent of the seventh sphere, after my left-side leader's death. I tried to offer this," Niko tapped the cuirass, "in sacrifice upon my partner's bier, but it came back to me again. Since I've had it, I've lost a second partner, been possessed by a witch, and shunned by my brothers. The possession, supposedly, is over, but the witch still lives and none of my Sacred Band can believe I'm cleansed of her taint, no matter how they try." Niko sat back on his haunches. "Neither can I. I want to be rid of this accursed gear—" He pulled the sword from its scabbard, held it out by the blade. "Feel it. It's warm. It's from Meridian, the dream lord's realm. He's after me, wants my . . . wants me."

Touching the hilt, it seemed to the old man that it burned him. Instinct made him drop it.

Niko looked at it, nodded, took it with a mixture of tenderness and revulsion, and put it back in its sheath. "Does that explain your bad dreams and evil omens?"

The teacher nodded, speechless, at a loss as to what he might suggest.

The uncanny youth chuckled then and helped him up. "It's not your fault, Levitas. It's not anybody's fault. Don't look so stricken. I feel better now that I've told someone. I'd thought to give it to the sea or to the coffers, but I can't defile either one. So I'll deal with it. I just need time and peace to think things out."

"You have that. Here. Always." Tears in his eyes, Levitas embraced his former pupil. "I'll go down into the vaults and look through the scrolls, and I'll have my students scour the literature. These weapons may have come to you by way of an archmage, but they were forged in the smithies of the gods. It's Enlil and Kubaba's demons who romp on them, not some godless sorcerer's minions. Take heart, Niko. We'll solve it."

"I don't think so. But I've heart enough, as it is. I told you, I need time."

"Time you shall have," the instructor promised, though his temples throbbed as if a demon squeezed them slowly in a vise and he knew that what Niko had, and didn't have, would be a matter in which the secular adepts of Bandara had little say.

Soon after, they sent the mute girl to spy on him, since she could read and write, and her reports declared that Niko was improving daily. Under the circumstances, they could do little else but respect his wishes and retranslate ancient texts, hoping to establish the provenance of the armaments or fit what was happening to one of the prophecies of old.

The square-sailed trireme Randal had purchased once the cloud-conveyance deposited him in Caronne was decked fore and aft; amidships, the slanted benches which accommodated twenty-five rowers per side were empty: Randal had no need of muscle.

The galley's lofty prow, gleaming with the polished wood and bronze of its ram, cut westward through the sea, its gold-painted eyes wide and fearless, its rainbow sail full of a conjured wind so fair and constant that the slim little vessel made thrice the four knots her optimistic seller had claimed she might.

Randal was glad to be away from the cozening shipwright who'd lied and chiseled his way to a fine profit on the little warship during protracted haggling. It had been five soldats extra for this sail, three per pair of oars, twenty for the teak decking. . . . If he'd needed to crew her, the ship would have taken all his funds.

As it was, she was barely seaworthy—triremes seldom were. They were too light, too much the instruments of war they'd been designed to be. And no craft built without the benefit of incantations, with a mage at hand from the day her keel was laid to the moment of launch, was meant to course the seas at the speed the Tysian hazard demanded of this one.

When Bandara's mists came in sight, the shivering, sea-wracked sorcerer spoke an anchoring spell through blue lips and went below the foredeck, where he shut and warded the stout teak door behind him, sank onto a bunk upon which he had not dared to lie once during his three-day journey hither, and fell immediately into a long and dream-studded sleep. He'd never been happier than when he'd left Caronne behind for the open waves; he dreamed he was back there yet, arguing with the seafarers on its busy quayside until his throat was raw. Caronne the seaport was one of four known Caronnes that cartographers had charted. The name itself was unlikely to have originated in any of the six languages of the civilized world. Legend had it that in ancient times a king named Caronne had gone conquering, naming the cities he founded after himself. Another, more arcane tale said that the original Caronne, city of legend, lay beyond a dimensional gate not unlike the one through which gods and demigods and the likes of Tempus and his sorcerer-slaying sister, Cime, gained entry into a world already plagued by a surfeit of gods and their get, a world whose phenomenal base was magic and where gods and wizards unceasingly warred.

Whatever the truth of its origins, this western port of Caronne was the trading center from which drugs and slaves and other contraband issued south and east. No mageguild or civilized government oversaw her mercantile anarchy. Randal had been glad to be quit of Caronne's pernicious carnival; the place had an air of jolly menace about it which made him very conscious that its wicked folk supported neither gods nor archmages. Caronne laughed at heaven and disbelieved in hell; it recognized only the Lord Commerce and the taste of gold between the teeth. Its highest officials kept the Seals of Weights and Measures; before them, priest and mage alike bowed low.

In Randal's dream, a Bursar of the Customs House had discovered the young mage's globe of power and was trying to pry its gemstones loose.

Reality reminded him that he didn't have the globe with him just as he burst out of sleep, bolt upright, in his gently rocking bed. Fumbling with the door jammed by his own forgotten wards of the night before, he stumbled out and up on deck.

Bandara lay ahead, misted and lavender in the pastel morning light. He splashed fresh water on his face from a bucket and set about calming himself. There was no similarity between Caronne and Bandara; the Tysian junior Hazard faced a totally different set of problems here. Mages of the guild, who dealt with demons and took power from the seething magma of the underworld, were anathema to the Bandarans, who aligned themselves with neither gods in their heavens nor sorcerers in their hells, but held man himself to be an expression of universal power. Nascent powers were developed here, true, but only "natural" powers. Randal's sort of alignment with elemental forces was considered by Bandarans a perversion. As he had told Critias, the young mage might be denied admittance if he walked up the steps hewn into the quayside, knocked on the great red door, and announced himself.

Therefore, he wasn't going to knock. He knew they'd know he'd come: the bright-sailed ship—his calling card, his trump—was obvious. Even without it, they'd have sensed him; probably they'd been aware of an "evil" force approaching long before his sail became visible on their horizon. He would let Niko explain to his fellow Bandarans whatever the Stepson thought necessary. They weren't going to like it, but by the time they heard about it, Randal would already have had his say.

And he was curious. This was a potent sect; under less extenuating circumstances, he'd never have had the opportunity—the audacity—to study it close at hand. He'd find out what was fact and what was fiction among the tales told of the veiled isles. He had more than an excuse—he had a duty to deliver to his left-side leader their task force commander's recall order.

Still, it was an insolent and outrageous thing he had in mind to do. An uninvited guest is never welcome. And his heart was not quiet; the mercantile marauders of Caronne had left him angry enough to put a pox on that town or turn all the precious gold in its underground treasuries to salt.

Wishing he'd brought his globe along—with which he could have accomplished the shape change he had in mind regardless of the intensity of his concentration—he took from his girdle a vial of special salts, and on the deck before him, poured it out into the shape of the closed spiral, each arm of seven spinning outward to join the wheel at its edge from a central sphere. This was his most potent glyph. Staring at it, he muttered his favorite spell as he stripped off his clothing, warding the ship against intruders or capricious Nature, demanding success in his encounters, then changing his shape.

Moments later a seahawk beat with mighty wings from the deck. Spiraling upward, it alighted on the stout pine

mast, gave its high-pitched piercing cry, and struck out
west, deviating only once from its shoreward course to
pluck a young sunfish from the bounteous sea.

Niko was raking the gravel of his pond into a pleasing
design when a hawk's shadow fell over his labors.

Wiping his sweating brow with a bare arm, he paused
in his work to watch it soar, master of the air, its wings
hardly beating. The day was hot, autumn's last heat
wave. The haze had burned off early and the sky was a
deep, exhilarating blue against which the hawk was a
graceful curve.

Niko thought to take an omen from it: right to left was
the best of signs, left to right the worst, and he knew every
variation's meaning. But this hawk just circled, as if following the waves and tides Niko's rake made in the gravel
under his feet. He'd discarded his chiton and worked now
in only a linen loinguard; the sun felt good upon his back
and legs and his thoughts were immersed in the pattern he
was making in his gravel.

He'd started at the center, working backward, never
stepping on the furrows his rake was making once he'd
used its toothed side. The flat side he'd long since finished
with; the gravel was nearly smooth, even where he'd had
to walk. All his training was his to command once more;
he could step on nails or crushed glass or wet parchment
and leave neither blood nor footprint. When the design he
saw in his mind was realized, ordered in the myriad stones,
no dissonant irregularity would mar it. He could climb the
hill and meditate upon what he'd wrought to his heart's
content.

Niko wasn't impatient; he was enjoying the process as
much as he would appreciate the result. It was the doing,
here, which was important. An ordered mind was already
his; its expressions were added joys, benefits he knew were
consequences of an accomplished result. With his maat encompassing all that had troubled him and his soul at peace,
he merely wished to return some of the pleasure he felt to
the natural world from which it emanated.

He hoped the hawk liked his pattern. He felt increased by its presence, as if it had purposely come here to float above him while he worked—a harmonic expression that made the pattern of Niko making a pattern, which expressed the pattern he felt within, all the more singular. There was a piece of art in the world now which only the hawk and whatever looked down upon the hawk from even more supernal distances could see: Niko in his gravel pond, behind his cabin on the narrow shelf halfway up Ennina's wildly fertile bluff, making something for the joy of it, something for the gods with which they could do what they willed.

This moment, however, was complete, everlasting, and reasonably perfect. Niko conceived of gods as the spiraling arms connecting the central unity of his mental pattern with the outward, resonant unity of his as-yet-unfinished gravel circle. Gods in the world were angry, jealous, destructive, and mean while being instructive. Niko in the world was no better than the world he was in. Yet when he rejoined it, he would carry back his maat, his unity, and not ask the world to remake itself or meet any elevated expectations. What he brought to life, often enough, was the transformation of death. But he brought also the unity of his perception, the essential calm which allowed him a duality of his own with which to meet Nature's duality. He could endure any amount of hardship, once again, without complaint. He could strive toward perfection without ever being disappointed that he could not attain it. He could excuse the frailty and treachery of his fellows without question or fear. His spirit was once again intact.

Niko knew he was ready, like the hawk wheeling above his head, to venture forth wherever the wind led him, to engage in strife and do battle, as his mystery prepared him to, with the imbalances abroad. He was in no hurry to do so. He was imbued with maat at its purest; he gloried in the restfulness of Ennina and the equilibrium he'd regained here. This was as it should be.

But also he was aware once more of the paradox of the Bandaran schools: what was pure here was sullied beyond, where it was most needed. The test of his mental disciplines lay in how long they were effective against chaotic, hostile forces.

A Bandara-trained fighter must leave the sanctuaries when all elements became equal within him. Here he would waste what he had gained. Should the abstract ever outweigh the world's allure for him, he could enter another mystery, one whose mastery could be claimed in solitude and whose dictates did not send its initiates out to ascend its degrees in the field.

So when the hawk spiraled down and down and came to rest on a cherry tree just beyond the gravel pond's edge, Niko was not surprised.

He'd been drawn to it; he'd even fancied he'd looked down on himself through its eyes.

When it alighted on the ground and disappeared behind the tree's trunk, Niko began to feel a certain suspicion. A bit of his placidity ebbed.

Not even an archmage, he thought to himself, would dare to send someone after him, not *here*. But his inner sight detected a bluish tinge, in retrospect, to the hawk— more than its sea-roving plumage would warrant. Blue was for magic, the kind made in witches' crying bowls and mageguild crypts.

He didn't stop raking immediately, but he was suddenly cold though the sun was at midheaven. He finished the spiral he was working on and stepped carefully back out of the gravel pond to retrieve his chiton.

When he'd slipped it over his head and secured his belt with its utility knife on his hips, Niko was certain he had a visitor. Whether it was friendly remained to be determined. He recalled old Levitas's reports of disturbed oracles and portentous dreams, then his mouth twitched. He let the rake fall and strode toward the thick, ancient tree determinedly. "Whoever you are, show your—*Randal!* I own you gave me a turn." Hands on his hips, Niko regarded Randal critically. The mageling Tempus had forced on Niko as a right-side partner was still slim, long-necked, big-eared, and fey. But Randal's auburn hair had grown over his ears now and the clothing he'd doubtless materialized while out of sight behind the tree consisted of the mottled gauze tunic and tight-ankled trousers Nisibisi guerrillas wore in summer.

"Life to you, left-side leader," Randal said, his freckled nose wrinkling as he grinned and stepped forward, arms outstretched in greeting.

"And everlasting glory, rightman." Niko completed the ritual salutation, endured Randal's comradely hug and, stepping back a pace, squatted down. "Do you approve of my pattern?" He didn't care. He was wondering how long it was going to take for the school to be alerted and send initiates or masters to deal with this travesty; whether he would be blamed if Ennina was judged befouled and in need of purification; whether he could chance secreting Randal in his cabin; or even if he would protect the mageling, should push come to shove, from harm. Niko had taken an oath to do so, but his ties to Bandara were more profound.

"Pattern? You mean the power glyph?" Randal knelt down also, excitement obvious on his peeling, wind-burned face. "I knew we had things in common, Stealth, but I never dreamed you Bandarans and we mages were so closely—"

"Randal, it's a sacrilege, you being here. Don't *say* things like that. You'd better have a good reason for putting me in this position. . . ."

"Position? It's your po*si*tion I'm here about. You are recalled to active duty. Critias sent me to fetch you back. Immediately." Crestfallen at being reproached, Randal was now peevish. "If I get you back to Critias within ten days from when he dispatched me, he'll give me the stand for the globe—the stand I need to wrest from it the finest of its secrets. So come along now. I'm under orders, you see, from Critias, as to just how this is to be handled. I had to stop in Caronne and buy a ship to give the Bandarans—it's anchored offshore—as a gift from the Stepsons. All they have to do is send someone with us as far as Caronne . . . but it took three days to sail it here, and longer than I anticipated to buy it—"

"Just three days? What did you do, hitch it to ocean-going demons?" Disgust and wariness wound around

Niko's words. "No master will set foot on it. An initiate
who's ready, perhaps, might join us, but not if you tell
them your rate of sail. And what's the hurry? Surely we've
a few days left. Can't you get us there with your magic—
by cloud-conveyance, whatever? Snap your fingers and—"

"*Our* task force leader has given specific orders, Stepson. You still *are* one, aren't you?"

That was insupportable insolence. Niko got to his feet.
"Randal, don't try me. What are you hiding?" Though
Niko's right-side partner had saved his life on Wizardwall,
Randal was still a mage: untrustworthy, a trickster.

"We're to take one Bandaran as far as Caronne, where
you are to complete negotiations with your uncle for the
drugs Madame Bomba wants. Now can we gather up one
of your brethren and *leave?*" Randal, rising, brushed off
his seat, then his knees, fastidiously, complaining. "You
should be glad to see me. I admit my feelings are hurt, but
they'll mend if you'll show me around. . . ."

"No chance. If I take you inside my cabin we'll probably have to burn it afterward." Niko, who had been heading toward the rake he'd dropped, stopped still.

"What's wrong?" Randal caught up with him.

"All I have is your word that Crit sent you. Did he give
you a token to prove it? A letter?" Again he moved toward
his rake, then stooped to pick it up.

"Nothing like that. Niko—" Randal, frustrated, wiped
his brow in a habitual swipe. "You really are angry, aren't
you?"

Niko was fondling the smooth, worn wood of the rake's
long handle. He dug its teeth into Ennina's rich earth,
watching the furrows it made, considering matters. "Not
angry. I left Tyse . . . abruptly. Do you know if the Riddler
is aware of this?"

"Of what? You, me, Crit? I'm not supposed to ask questions, remember? If you're not coming back, just say so.
And why wouldn't Tempus know?"

"I'll come. I wonder if he does, though. I wanted to
bring Shamshi, the Mygdonian boy, here. The commander
and I disagreed about it. That's all." It had been worse than
that; he'd desensitized his memories, but he still didn't like

to think about the circumstances that forced him back to
Bandara. He'd left his fine sable stallion and his pregnant
mare with Tempus, a renunciation of all they'd done and
all they'd shared. Most of it he couldn't bring himself to
explain to Randal, who was a newcomer to matters of
honor such as concerned a member of a Sacred Band.

But the six pairs who'd been his closest allies—before
Tempus, when they'd fought for Abarsis the Slaughter
Priest—had *known* that Niko was possessed by a witch and
not told him. Tempus had known. Critias had known.
They'd conspired "for security reasons" to keep from him
their doubts and the nature of a problem Niko had had to
surmount without any understanding of his own. He'd only
pieced it together after the fact, when men who'd been his
most trusted friends were obviously uneasy with him once
it became clear to all that the witch Roxane, who'd possessed him, had lived to escape to Mygdonia.

Niko could forgive many things, overlook failings and
lapses in courage and even changing allegiances. But he
could not forgive the look in those Stepsons' eyes or
Tempus for having lied to him. So he said, sighing, when
Randal only stared at him, "Never mind. Let's go. We've a
long boat ride over to the main island, a longer negotiation
ahead if we're to secure a traveling companion. Don't explain anything. Don't *say* anything unless you have to . . .
I've got to make this as painless as possible for everyone
involved." Letting his rake fall, he had a feeling it would
be a long time before he'd see it, and Ennina, again.

Walking into his pond carefully, Niko brushed the gravel
from the cuirass, dirk, and sword that the dream lord had
given him and, still on his knees, put them on. Then he
tried to reinstate his pattern. But it remained unfinished,
disturbed, randomized by human events when he left it.

It didn't matter—the next occupant of his cabin would
make a different sign, need a different sort of healing.

By the time they'd docked their little tender at Levitas's
private pier, Niko had made Randal realize that they could
be incarcerated for this—at least Niko could be—and that
the mage himself might be in some considerable danger.
Niko was not the only fighter in the isles. Many, he assured

the mageling, were twice as skilled as he.

Levitas's lacquered door opened promptly and the mute girl Niko had brought over from the mainland smiled with her eyes and touched first her lips, then his own, with a finger, ushering them into the cool, slate-flagged home with its tree-trunk pillars and expansive shadows. Niko gave his apologies for disturbing the household but asserted that he must see Levitas as soon as possible.

During what seemed to Niko an interminable interval of waiting, Randal began to sneeze uncontrollably, exclaiming in a choked, congested wail, "Cads! By da Wrid, 'e's god cads! Aah! Ach*oo!*" his t's becoming d's as his allergies flared.

"Cads?" Niko had been paying little attention; he was worried that Levitas might decline to see him. His integrity was on the line because of Randal; he was likely to be expelled forever from the single refuge the world could offer him. . . . "Oh, you mean *cats*. Yes, he breeds them. If the dander bothers you, why not ensorcel it away?"

"Nod funny." *Sneeze*. "'Ave you any krrf?" *Sniffle*. "Or an 'andkerchief? Or I *will* conjure one."

Niko had extracted from Randal on the boat ride hither a promise to refrain from magic while in Levitas's presence. Now, he ripped off a piece of his chiton's hem, wadded it up, and threw it to the mage whose Hazard status had been delayed by these allergic reactions no spell could quell.

Randal, catching the wad, bowed his head and blew his reddening nose, his shoulders hunched in misery and shame.

When Niko looked up, Levitas was standing before a translucent silk screen beyond which the softly rolling harbor could be seen, the master almost as insubstantial as the diaphanous cloth which kept out insects but let in the salt-fragrant breeze. Levitas's bald head nodded on his fragile neck; his parchment skin glowed like a candled egg. He frowned at Randal, then seemed to float across the flags toward Niko, one frail hand outstretched.

Niko met him and took it, brushing it to his lips. "Teacher," he said tautly in a very low voice, "I have brought the world to Bandara. It's time for me to leave."

"So it seems," Levitas said gently, no trace of emotion on his palimpsest face. "How could you allow this ... creature to gain such a hold on you?"

Then Niko had to say it, for on his right and left, silk-stretched partitions slid back and into the room filed six initiates, robed and girded for war, ceremonial masks upon their heads making them so fearsome in their approach that Randal scrambled over to Niko and tugged at his arm. "Levitas, this is Randal, Tysian mage of the Hazard class —Randal, what's your current level?"

"S-s-s-seventh," said Randal, at Niko's right, his gaze fixed on the six night-robed initiates who closed in with slow and measured steps.

"Seventh level," Niko continued conversationally. "Randal is my right-side partner, master; my Sacred Band teammate, here with orders from my task force leader. Randal, this is the master Levitas, my teacher."

The two exponents of opposing philosophies gazed at one another frostily. Neither spoke. The six initiates converged in perfect synchronization on soundless feet; soon they would be so close that Niko would have to step back or be physically accosted. He continued calmly. "The omens the sybils spoke—the red tide, the oracles' dreams —all were forewarnings that my partner had been dispatched to find me, nothing more."

Levitas spoke now. "Nothing *more?* Niko," he shook his head sadly, "not even for you can I excuse this ... obscenity."

"I'm not asking that. I'm merely saying farewell. In a civilized fashion." Niko looked pointedly about at the students gathering to protect their instructor. Then he said even more quietly, "Stop them where they are, or I will. You owe me a hearing, with so much at stake."

Levitas reached out a hand and tapped the cuirass Niko wore. A single blue spark snapped. "You mean you owe me a better explanation for bringing this demon's pawn into my house."

"Now waid a minude!" Randal demanded plaintively. *"I'*m here wid—excuse me . . ." He turned his head aside and blew his nose again. "That's better. I'm here with a gift from the Stepsons, regards from Tempus the Sleepless One. You *do* know who *he* is? And none of this is Stealth's fault.... The least you can do is be polite. You see that armor there? Niko's? It's from the benighted entelechy of dreams, by the Writ. Where do you get *off*—?"

"*Randal!*"

"Well, Stealth, he's not very understanding for a high-minded spiritual type, is he? As I was saying, Lord Levitas, we've brought a trireme for you from the Stepsons. We need a man to sail in it with us as far as Caronne—"

Levitas's hand came up and the six initiates stopped, legs spread, folding their arms. "A *gift?* From Tempus the Obscure? For the school?"

"Not exact—" Niko began to explain.

"Stealth, *you* keep shut. This is my muddle, and I'll make it right," Randal interrupted. Then, to Levitas: "If you're going to hold this fighter of yours responsible for events beyond his control, go ahead. We can't stop you. But be assured that he's in great demand elsewhere—on this plane and beyond—" Randal sneezed again. "Damn cads. Sorry. So anyway, either give us a man to sail with us to Caronne, or reject the gift. We don't care."

Niko saw the skin quiver around Levitas's eyes. Piously, the old teacher bent his head. Then he raised it. "I regret to say that none of that justifies what I see here. But we will send a man to return with the sleepless one's gift. You!" Levitas's pointing finger shot out with a speed which belied his age. "Come here." One of the masked initiates stepped forward. "The rest of you, back to your labors. I appreciate your concern, but it is misplaced. And no word of this beyond these walls! Go!"

The five melted back into the shadows. Niko blew out a long breath as the partitions whispered shut. Under his cuirass, perspiration trickled down his backbone. He'd forgotten he'd had it on until Levitas touched it. Now he wished he'd thrown it into the sea as once he'd intended.

Levitas's eyes were on him, unyielding as stone. His bony finger, pointing Niko's way, drew a sign in the air. It burned Niko's soul as if its passage through the air between them had turned his cuirass molten.

Thus, without a word, was it done: Niko was banned from Bandara henceforth; not Randal's lies or even Tempus's name could mitigate the ritual's finality.

Having lost everything already, Niko felt lightheaded. A rebellious part of him, angry with the Stepsons for sending Randal where no sorcerer should ever have trod, had been toying with the idea of resigning when he reached Tyse, turning about and coming straight back here on the excuse of seeing to Ennina's purification personally. Now he had nothing to come back to. . . .

". . . send my own son," Levitas was saying. "No other could I expose to such peril in good conscience. Sturm, my child, you are ready for the world, you say. You will go with these . . . people . . . into it and return with the Riddler's gift." Levitas's eyes carefully avoided Niko. From now on, for the instructor, the failed student must cease to exist.

By the dawning of their second day at sea, Randal was utterly exhausted from the demands of sailing the ship by spell while casting illusions to make his magic more palatable to the two Bandarans on board.

If he'd had only Nikodemos to deal with, the sorcery required would have been considerably less strenuous, but Sturm, son of Levitas, was a stranger and one of unknown proclivities. Sturm was beefy and sullen and younger than Niko. From the moment it was clear that Levitas was sending his son along, Niko had been at pains to make sure Randal took every precaution.

Waiting in the little tender for Sturm to gather his effects and join them, Randal had ventured: "I'm sorry about . . . all this." He'd waved his hand, encompassing the shoreline of wind-sculpted pines and wave-smoothed rocks and the pastel sea which rocked them. "It's my fault that you lost it."

But Niko's quick, canny smile came and went. "I haven't lost anything I need. I love Bandara, but I love to leave it. I shouldn't have come here. There was no need. I was sulking." He shrugged. Then: "Here comes Sturm.

We've got to minimize apparent magic. He's a big boy. We don't want to frighten him. I don't know what he can do, and a boat's no place to find out."

"Boat?" Randal hadn't thought about how he was going to transport his two companions to the trireme. Now he did. "You mean we're going to *row* out there? Yes, I see you do. All right, *you* row—don't let him—and I'll give us a bit of help by way of friendly currents. Agreed?"

Niko had time only to clap him on the shoulder in assent before he went over the side into knee-deep water to help the burly, horse-faced Bandaran with bound-back hair and a scraggly moustache distribute his three heavy sacks and considerable bulk so that the little dinghy didn't list hopelessly. Low in the water and heavy with the uncomfortable silence of the ill-met, they headed out to sea where, in the low-rolling mist, the trireme's mast was visible on the horizon.

In the prow, facing back the way they'd come, Randal was struck by the contrast between the two initiates—Niko's easy, flowing motion as he rowed; Sturm's quick, wary movements which caused the keel to dip and sway. Having received from Niko assurances that Stealth didn't blame him, it was natural for Randal to compare the two Bandaran adepts and find Sturm wanting in experience, wisdom, physical culture, and style. Three is never a happy number, and Niko was Randal's left-side leader. As always when in Stealth's company, Randal felt taller, more formidable—fierce and brave and worthy. Although at times being both an upwardly mobile wizard and a Stepson was a dangerous combination, and the mystique of his pairbond a daunting responsibility to live up to, it was indubitably worth it.

Randal had come by fortune and study to an estate which as a youth he'd despaired of ever being able to attain. He just wasn't cut from hero's cloth—this had been clear early on. Only as a black artist or a court-bound intellectual, his father had explained gently one gray day, would Randal ever make a name for himself. If only the kind old warrior—who had gone to great lengths not to show his disappointment in a frail and overly bookish

child, who had bought Randal into an apprenticeship at great
personal cost and died still worried that not even magic
would avail his son—could see him now! Not only was he
comporting himself with integrity and risking life and limb
at the behest of his guild, he was doing it in the company of
a lion among Stepsons! Niko was, with the exception of the
Riddler and his old-guard officers, the best of the Stepsons.
Even Critias called Niko "one hell of a boy-soldier" and
judged no expense too great to recall him to duty.

Randal was trying to explain some of this to Sturm,
whose task it was to prepare the morning meal from ship's
stores before Randal went below to sleep. Niko had the
tiller and the watch. Had the strange Bandaran not been
aboard, they could be eating whatever Randal chose to
fetch from any nearby shore; as it was, they were eating
raw fish, cold rice, and dried figs.

The oars were shipped and the galley made good time.
Part of Randal's intention was to keep Sturm from dwelling
on *how* good; he'd asked about the mainland shore due
north of Bandara and drawn the islander into a discussion
of the fertility cults and priestesses that dwelled there. A
man climbed the steps hewn into those sheer basalt cliffs at
his own peril; some boys of the western nomadic tribes had
to make that journey to claim their manhood. All of this,
Randal knew, but when Sturm had sneered that, as Sacred
Banders, neither Niko nor Randal could be very interested
in the flowers of womanhood growing high on those preci-
pitous bluffs, Randal's patience with the sharp-tongued son
of Levitas found its end.

"If they taught you everything but respect for others in
Bandara, they've taught you only how to die in the world,
Sturm," Randal said, his voice quaking with rage, and
stormed out of the cabin, first throwing a strip of red tuna
in the Bandaran's face.

Sturm followed, eager to continue the confrontation
which had been brewing under beetled brows and polite
snubs since they'd set sail. Ignoring him, Randal headed
aft, between the slanted rowing benches and up again.
"Niko, watch this! I've been practicing." Though using
powers for display was frowned upon by wizards of scru-

ple, and he'd promised Niko not to flaunt his magic here, something had to be done to take Sturm down a peg. From Randal's belt, seemingly of their own accord, three throwing stars floated upward. When they were at eye level, Randal sent them speeding, one after another, through the air. They thunked into the mast so close to one another that the grate of metal upon metal could be heard, on their journey whizzing past Sturm's startled face.

"Maggoty queen," Sturm cursed, big hands on hips.

Niko looped rope around the tiller to keep the trireme steady and came toward them without a word. When he reached Randal, he said only that he was hungry. When he'd passed him and come abreast of Sturm, words Randal couldn't hear were exchanged. The Bandaran glowered at the mage a moment longer, then followed Niko's retreating back.

So it was that Randal alone saw the emergence of a thick mist, the size of a large island or small land mass, from the sea, its expanse crowned with arching double rainbows, its position dead ahead. Staring at the spot, which only moments ago had been clear water, he blinked and rubbed his eyes. The mirage persisted. The mist was thick as marble, impenetrable as a burial shroud. They would sail right into it on their present course. Randal's first instinct was to alert Niko. But to what? He sat on the afterdeck, chin propped on his fists, trying to determine what kind of manifestation awaited them. Things didn't normally pop up out of the sea. There was no fog anywhere else, no rain clouds even on the far horizon. The sky, elsewhere, was clear. When he thought he knew what he was looking at, his fingers and toes were numb and his throat dry with excitement; his little display of temper and the lesson he'd thought to teach Sturm were forgotten.

In the afterdeck cabin, they were talking as he entered:

"—take that scrawny little *partner* of yours and break his back across my knee. *Then* we'll see what kind of powers he's got."

"I won't protect you from his wrath, Sturm. You've a lot to learn. It's too bad you're going right back to the islands. You've been too long under Levitas's skirts.

Things don't work the same way in the world . . ."

"Ram's balls! I'm not going right back. Mad as your
necromancing paramour I'd be, should I do so. I'll sell this
ship—it's too tainted, they'll just sink it when they realize
how much sorcery has seeped into its every plank—and
buy another, when I'm ready. No one's given me a time
limit. As for my *fa*ther, he's addled with age. Frightened of
his own shadow—so frightened of your fabled Riddler
he'll do anything to accommodate him. Gods' mung, I'd
have thought you'd realized it, after what he did to you. I
don't like magic, and I don't doubt you're not half what
you're touted to be, but the old ones have forgotten what
it's like to have blood in your veins—" Sturm paused for
breath.

"Excuse me," Randal murmured, coming the rest of the
way in, where Sturm, as well as Niko, could see him. "But
there's something . . . in our way, you might say. We could
try to change course, but—" Randal spread his hands
"—you know these archmagical abodes . . . I don't think it
will help. If you'd like to step on deck, Niko?"

"Archmagical abodes?" Sturm repeated, frowning.

"In our way?" Niko rose up, steadying himself on the
table. "What is it?"

"Meridian," Randal said offhandedly, aping Niko's
habit of delivering the most startling news in the calmest of
demeanors. "The shadow lord's home. Surely you've heard
of it, Sturm, even in Bandara? Aškelon's archipelago? The
land of dreams?"

Entering Meridian's harbor through clouds rainbowed
like its furled sail, the little trireme shipped its oars and
glided by dint of magic smoothly into port.

The waters she plied were calm as glass; the crystal
quays she sought, inviting. Few mortals' craft had made
this harbor in all the days of time. Meridian was not kind to
uninvited guests. The island chain which was part and parcel of Aškelon's mystique partook of more than the dream
lord's legend: it shared his power, knew his thoughts, and
when it manifested as a phenomenal place with latitude and

longitude it had awareness all its own. Treasure-seeking plunderers who thought to fill their holds with the gold pavings of these streets found themselves in sinking ships whose iron nails deserted oak and pine and flew off through the air and whose bronze rams and boarding hooks melted like flaming wax long before their prows parted this harbor's waters.

For Meridian belonged as much as Aškelon to the seventh sphere and that shadow life that men forget while waking. Her populace, her golden streets and homes and barques and palanquins—all became wholly real and fully living, here and now, only when the trireme's hull passed through the rainbow gate, so that the joy of its denizens at this visitation was nearly boundless.

And Aškelon, lord of Meridian, of dream and shadow, entelechy of the seventh sphere, deep below the quayside in his foundry where fires roared high and metal poured like water, readied gifts for these two most welcome guests: Nikodemos, whom Aškelon's heart desired beyond any other earthly adherent, and the promising junior wizard Randal, whom the dream lord had used as a proxy to help young Niko more than once before. The third party with them, Sturm, late of Bandara, was an unexpected guest.

Through every eye and ear and wave and dolphin dancing playfully alongside the trireme, Aškelon kept tabs on the galley's progress. He had too much to accomplish and no time to spare to greet them with mere ceremony: Meridian had arisen from this foreign sea half a world away from where it was accustomed to manifest; even the lord of dreams could hold the archipelago here only so long.

Thus he had sent Cime, his consort for a year, a half-reformed sorcerer-slayer and free agent, to greet his guests. This woman, who squatted now like a soldier on the outermost quay, was Tempus's sister and the one who had come to Aškelon with this scheme to engineer a meeting with the mortal Nikodemos. She had almost killed Aškelon once, nearly destroyed Meridian when it manifested in its accustomed place as it did only when the gods and elementals made their millennial peace and Aškelon took a wife to ease his loneliness. Then Cime had come in the guise of that wife and used her arcane evil and her diamond rods to wound him so that Meridian shriveled into clay and settled back into the sea. Later, he had forgiven her, made a bargain with her, traded with the gods upon her account and left his betrothed, Jihan the Froth Daughter, with Tempus in his hellhole world to seal the pact. But still, he could not trust her.

So he watched, very carefully, as she boarded a barge and, with three nymphs attending her and six dolphins gaily towing her, put out to meet their guests halfway. Cime, who called him "Ash" as her brother dared to do and pronounced him "boring," "dull-witted," and "vain," was still both assassin and whore: the curse which made her thus would not be lifted until her year with him was done. And mages such as Randal were her favorite prey.

In the pot of white-hot metal, nearly ready to be worked, he could see her clearly: her hair black and silver like his, her statuesque beauty like a figurehead tall against the wind in the pleasure-barge's prow, her fine and haughty features the double of his own save for what animated them from within. For Aškelon's face was scored with compassion, with the weight of a race's broken dreams and all its dreams to come. Cime, on the other hand, did battle with all the nightmares of excess; she knew the opposites of virtue thoroughly: she was queen of harpies, mistress of the cutting tongue, priestess of murder and lust.

As such, he thought—smiling to himself as he thrust bare hands into a cauldron of boiling hot metal to draw out ensorceled iron for a special blade he'd create with the hammer of his fist—she was an admonition to those he'd brought here: what Aškelon offered could not be had without cost.

He knew what they dreamed of having, both the mageling and the young warrior; he knew their dreams more intimately than even they, as he knew Cime's nightmares and her brother's dreamless soul. He could offer much, but he could not coerce.

He'd sent young Niko a gift horse as fine as any Tempus had received, and the boy had abandoned it. He had sent Randal intimations and guidance fitted for so noble and mystical a spirit. He had sent Cime to greet them because temptation and danger must accompany them hither. Aškelon, who had traded away much for regency of the seventh sphere and become a contractee to what abided on the far side of heaven, knew better than his visitors how important was tribulation and the element of choice in life. Greatness accretes; one pays as one goes.

He knew this because he was not selfless; he had goals and troubles of his own, gargantuan efforts under way. Success with Niko, his choice among a multitude of possible mortals, would secure Meridian so that never again could a well-meaning but accursed soul like Cime threaten destruction upon it.

For this, he had labored. For this, he would take Randal as his apprentice and even move an archipelago from one side of the world to the other. Already, he could feel the strain of his labors, the possibility of failure like a sad mantle weighing down his shoulders. These were not wise, seasoned souls, but just the children of men. And Aškelon had learned, on the brink of dissolution Cime had brought him to, that inherent value in a cause is no guarantee of success.

And so he had embarked upon this program of honorable risk, with a world to lose and a viper in his bed—this creature Cime who did not understand the value of salvation through dreams or even the meaning of love.

Lovingly, he drew out the white-hot iron in his bare hands, cupping it, speaking over it, enjoining it to serve rightly in his cause. Then, ladling it slowly onto the anvil of his knee, he began creating the recurved *kris*, a short serpent of a sword which would serve his purpose in this world long after he and his archipelago had faded from it.

As the nymphs beside her twittered girlishly, and the dolphins drawing her barge slowed to come alongside the trireme, and Niko, boarding plank in hand, scowled when he recognized her, Cime mused that killing was as much a social function as was mating. Cime had been doing both for hundreds of years. She killed mages, mostly. In her

mating partners she could not be so choosy: an archmage
had cursed her to wander eternally, giving herself for pay
to all comers, yet incapable of love.

If she had been capable of love, she would have bestowed it on one like the Stepson, Nikodemos. Twice before, upon encountering him, she had found herself deeply
in lust. And, after dull aching months on Meridian, where
its surfeit of peace and beauty made her feel as if she'd
gorged on sweets, she'd concocted a plan to coax him
here, playing on the dream lord's weaknesses. It was she
who'd come to Critias in a dream and moved him to send
Randal for Niko. Now she intended to convince Aškelon to
let her leave with them to win her brother's war. She knew
she could: Aškelon had everything he wanted but the allegiance of the young fighter Nikodemos. Ash hadn't been
able to resist a meeting face to face with Niko, who wore
Ash's smithery, but so far—by dint of luck and mental
discipline and Tempus's protective intervention—had not
acknowledged Aškelon as his patron.

Cime rose, fixing her diamond wands in her hair and
smoothing an aspect of youthful, raven-haired beauty over
herself like fine raiment. Though she'd met Niko before,
she'd never succeeded in seducing him; though he knew
who and what she was and thus could not be fooled, he
might yet be vulnerable to the sort of spell she had in mind.
She held out her hand, a signal she was ready to come
aboard.

Niko took her wrist, steadied her as she trod the boarding plank, his mouth tightly drawn with wariness. Randal
the young adept was behind him, oblivious to the nymphs
who should have been distracting the mageling by now.
The nymphs, foolish and full of laughter, hung upon the
virile, hulking stranger who stood by the trireme's tiller.

He was no problem, but Randal, the wizard in training,
might be: she could feel the mage's ties to infernal realms.
Her fingers itched to slay him—it was her curse and her
vocation, together, taking hold. But Randal didn't feed on
souls; if wizards ever were benign, as Aškelon claimed to
be, then this Randal was such a one. She controlled herself, smiled at him, greeting him civilly in Nisi. She might

need him to bend his left-side leader, Niko, to her will.

Niko had not spoken to her, only nodded. As soon as she stood safely aboard, he had let go her hand and retreated toward the bow where he now stood, watching, as if physical distance could protect him from his own desire.

It was Randal who questioned her as to why they had been brought here, and Randal to whom she responded that he must ask Aškelon, who had contrived this meeting. And when Randal, pulling on one ear, insisted that she must know some salient details, she smiled. "I can't say. But I will give you a hint, which you may pass along to your silent, shy friend up there." She indicated Niko with an inclination of her head. "Adherents in the phenomenal world are necessary to 'benign' powers, who get lonely in their semimaterial realms. And who is *this?*" Ignoring any response Randal might have made, she moved sternward.

The young mage scrambled out of her path as if her touch would scald him, saying hastily, "Sturm. Sturm's a Bandaran . . . student. Sturm . . . Cime, her ladyship, mistress of Merid—"

"Mistress of the land of boredom, Sturm," she interrupted, the while thinking that, though she needed Randal, this insolent adept of the Bandaran school qualified for the kind of death she yearned to bestow. "All this beauty, the sparkling piers, the azure harbor, the crowd on the dock . . . look closer, don't be dazzled like the parade of fools before you. Those nymphs you fondle—" The three were hanging on Sturm like nubile courtesans. He had one hand on a pair of breasts, one between two buttocks, a third nymph cuddled between his legs.

"Meridian's out of step with human needs and human blood. Three days among these smiling, dazed denizens and the place will wear upon your nerves," she warned truthfully.

"As it does on yours?" Close behind her, Niko's voice sounded.

She turned and looked up at him, reached out to touch the dirk slung on a belt at his hip. This close, her body could woo his, calm his fears, ease his doubts. She stroked the hilt of his dirk while he tried to ignore the innuendo but

held his ground, protective of his fellows. She answered
softly that Meridian had become a prison, an irritant, that
she was a damsel in distress, in need of rescue, a boon for
which her brother would repay him handsomely.

"Are you sure? If I were Tempus, I'd want you right
where—"

"Give me a token, Niko, and we'll see where you want
me," she said sotto voce, hoping to twine their fates by the
mechanism of her curse. "This dirk will do, or even a Tysian copper." She caught his gaze in hers, then, and held
him fast by it. Her nymphs, as they had been instructed,
did what they could to distract Randal. Dreams told her
this young fighter who could not back away from her ad-
vances had been celibate for months; her fame and her
illusion did the rest.

She'd wanted the dirk, but even half-entranced, Niko
was too cautious for that. He dug in his pouch slowly, like
one moving in a dream, and came up with a coin. It was
gold. She took it, dropping it between her breasts. He
watched it disappear beneath her white tunic and when it
was gone he still stared there, his brows knitted.

"I didn't mean—" he began.

"It's the gods who move us, Nikodemos, you and I.
We'll fight my brother's war together, and win. You know
how he is. Without my help, he'll make a fiasco of it."

"That's why Aškelon did this?" Niko's hand gestured to
the quayside, coming close now. As he did, Sturm roused
himself to prepare to make the galley fast.

Cime smiled at Niko. Beyond, the singing throng thick-
ened; behind, she heard Randal's tread, his admonition to
the nymphs to "Stop hanging on me! I've got to dock this
ship!" She said, "That is why *I* did this." She took her hand
from the dirk's hilt and Niko, as if released, stepped back,
muttering that he'd better help Randal.

Cime didn't realize, then, that taking the coin she'd
craved from Niko had set in motion forces she could not
control.

The sorcerer-slayer Cime, who had killed more mages
than Randal had teeth, leaned close to him as the ivory-

screened wagon in which they were riding stopped and
Niko vaulted out. "So, *you're* twirling Datan's globe these
days?" she whispered sweetly, her thigh brushing Randal's
knee as she moved to follow Niko. Sturm growled in word-
less frustration when she patted his head in passing, saying, "Come, come, my little Bandaran monk, there's
nothing to fear here but a chance meeting with your own
inadequacies."

The mention of Datan, the vanquished Nisibisi mage,
had sent a chill down Randal's spine which did not pass,
but curled now around his tailbone as it often had when as
wolf or dog he'd done covert business for Tempus or the
archmage he'd served but never met—Aškelon, entelechy
of dreams. Randal had never expected to meet the dream
lord. Meridian was a state of mind, a mythos, not a place
to wrestle with one's fate in daylight.

But in daylight they had ridden through halcyon streets
where curious folk without the pinched faces of want or the
rags of despair had smiled at them from doorways or
shaken gaily streamered tambourines in their honor. Randal
was sure beyond doubt that this was no dream or illusion.
He and Niko and Sturm were really here, abroad in Meridian. He should have been elated. But here, where the
benign Aškelon ruled, he felt the tremors of his own
foreboding, even distress.

Following Sturm out of the wagon, and coming abreast
of the Bandaran as Cime's swaying hips led them like a
beacon up a shimmering walk into a cyclopean hall moist
with ancient shadows, Randal admitted to himself that it
was Cime the free agent who troubled him: her presence;
her slightly crooked, ageless, and somewhat sullen smile
which boded well for no mage or man; and especially the
coin she had taken from Niko, who was innocent of the
ways of magic and vulnerable, fresh from Bandara with all
his ideals polished bright.

So as they descended in Cime's wake down ill-lit stairs
up which a tangy metallic smoke wafted hot and stinging,
Randal worked a protective ward over Stealth's ashen head
bobbing before him. Of Sturm he took little notice—the
Bandaran had not been at pains to make a friend of Randal.

If Cime's attention could be turned to the son of Levitas, Niko might have time to come to his senses. So Randal took his warding spell for Niko and turned it into a reflective one; thus, whatever Cime aimed at Stealth would gravitate to Sturm.

More than that, Randal could not do. He had ethics, a moral code to which he must adhere. And in Meridian, more even than on the average day, his behavior must be above reproach.

Down they came onto a torchlit landing opening into a subterranean hall illuminated by fires that threw grotesque shadows against rough-hewn walls and aged pillars.

In the midst of this roseate light stood Aškelon, tall and full of grace, his brooding beauty underlit as if he stood over the infernal pit of hell.

Niko, up ahead, stopped still and said something to Cime, who slipped a hand through his arm so that Randal once again was sure that peril emanated from her fetching, ageless form. She hung on Niko, guiding him toward the fire and the cauldron and the entelechy of dreams who, in the captious light, seemed to hover, insubstantial, far above.

It was Sturm who saw the forge and who pointed it out to Randal. It was Sturm who invoked a timeless ward and warned the Tysian Hazard, "Be careful," as Aškelon raised a hand in greeting.

Then Cime stepped back from Niko's side. Randal shivered when she turned his way, not liking the way the firelight glittered in her eyes. She approached him, taking his arm, saying, "You, too, mageling. The dream lord waits . . . don't fear." And: "Sturm, not you. Stay here; I'll rejoin you presently. *We* are merely witnesses, onlookers, you and I."

The distance Randal had to cross with Cime's arm in his was not great or far, but somehow, it took forever. And while he put one foot before the other, the combination of the seductress next to him and the white-hot forge ahead of him made Randal start to sweat. His mind raced with wards and spells and wizardly protections and, suddenly, like a bolt from heaven, a revelation came to him. He said, just before he and Cime came abreast of Stealth, who stood quite still, as if entranced, "Cime, my lady, I hope you know that this coin you've got isn't his, but mine." And as he spoke, he raised one hand breast-high and made the gold piece Niko had given her arise from its resting place between her breasts and hover in midair above them.

It was true: Niko had come out of Bandara penniless; Randal had given him all the extra gear, goods, traveling cash, and papers a right-side partner should thoughtfully provide.

Cime's perfect features quivered, folded into an aged crone's, reformed again into the beauteous mask she wore. "What's this? It's so—I see it now. Tricked me, have you, Randal?" In one swift movement she snatched the coin from midair. "Though I can't move against you while I'm in your debt, hear me well: you'll pay for this once our contract is fulfilled. And don't think you can hold me off forever—" Her hand flickered out, stroked up his thigh, patted him insolently, and then withdrew. "You'll succumb; it's good as done. And yet, I promise, you'll enjoy it—in spite of all you know."

Smiling sweetly once again, she drifted toward Sturm as Aškelon called Randal's name and drew him close by the sheer power of those eyes like melting ice.

Shoulder to shoulder with Niko, then, Randal stood, while the dream lord welcomed them to Meridian, saying, "Both of you have earned a special place in my heart and thus have special tasks awaiting you in the world of men."

"Such as?" Niko asked him brazenly.

Randal would have touched his partner, hushed him, but the dream lord raised an eyebrow, chuckled like spring's first breeze, and nodded. "Fair enough. I'll answer all your questions later. But as yet you don't know what to ask me, Nikodemos. I wish with all my heart you did." Aškelon raised a hand and the obsidian tailsman known as the Heart of Aškelon glowed dark red with reflected firelight—or the blood of its wearer, if legend was truth and the dream lord's heart was really in this amulet upon his wrist.

"Randal, you must help your partner. More than stealth, more than strength, is needed." As Aškelon spoke, he picked up a short sword, not a forearm's length, whose blade wriggled like a snake frozen in mid-slither. "This *kris,* magician, is for you. You have pacted with a dead man to avenge his murder; a dreaming soul you call 'Belize' has taken you at your word."

"I—" Randal began to demur, to object, to explain.

"What?" Niko demanded, staring at Randal with a mixture of respect and confusion.

"This blade," Aškelon continued, as if neither had spoken, "has certain powers, as all your panoply, Nikodemos, has charms and strength you know not of. Listen closely, Randal, for only once will I—"

"I don't want any magical weapons; neither does my partner. I tried to give these back before. Now I'll leave them here with you—" Niko, as he spoke in anger, began to strip the cuirass from his shoulders.

Aškelon stopped him with an imperative glance and a pointing finger. "Listen. Learn. Profit. Or not even I can save you from the witches and the murderers intent on that boyish soul of yours. Any other would have let his weapons speak to him, so that I'd not have to bring you here in person."

The shadow lord turned to Randal, the *kris* held out. "Take it. Hold it with the hilt toward you. Place your right thumb across the flat of the blade where it meets the hilt, your left next to it, so that it just touches the right. Walk down the blade, thumb over thumb, until the tip is reached."

Randal did so, working his way over the nine undulations until his thumb, at last, met the tip of the blade exactly.

"It fits him perfectly," Niko whispered.

"I made it for him with these hands." Aškelon held them up. "Among mortal smiths, the thumb test proves a *kris* lucky, proper for an owner. Among those of us who can do more than men, its power is assured. Listen closely, Randal: by its power you may dispatch a man merely by stabbing his shadow or his footprints. Hold its point near fire and move the blade, and the flames will follow the

point. From its tip, should you wish it, hornets will issue.
You may draw water from it by squeezing the blade and
making this sign." Aškelon's fingers flickered.

Randal, accustomed to this sort of instruction, let his
own fingers follow suit. He nodded.

"If you are righteous," Aškelon continued, "merely
pointing its tip at an enemy will end his days. If you are
loving, it may on occasion jump from its sheath to fight
your battles. If you are careless and thus endangered, it
will rattle in its sheath to wake or warn you."

Randal stroked the recurved blade. "Thank you," he
whispered, frightened and yet proud.

"I warn you: never use these powers unnecessarily,
never for display. And do not trust your *kris* to ferret out an
enemy or to know good from evil. It knows no more than
you, is neither benign nor malicious. It is your character
and your nature which animate it, nothing more."

Feeling fragile and yet lightheaded with joy, Randal noticed Niko staring at him. Catching his eye, Niko shook his
head.

"And now," Aškelon said softly, "I must show Nikodemos the stables, where the sire of his horse holds court
—and another place which, I wager, will be familiar.
Niko, if you will. . . . Perhaps you'll learn something about
your own weaponry on the way."

Niko didn't move.

"Go on, idiot," Randal whispered, giving Niko a shove.
"We can't offend him."

"Cime will see to your wants, Randal, and to your
friend's, while we are gone," the dream lord decreed,
coming so close that Randal could see opalescent whirl-
pools in those deep-set eyes.

Then all things became confused. Cime was beside him,
saying that so fine a *kris* had not been given a mage in all
the time she'd lived, and Sturm was there too, congratulat-
ing him with downcast, covetous eyes and unmistakable
envy in his voice.

When he looked up from the blade whose nine undulations were so fascinating and so perfect, Nikodemos and

the dream lord were nowhere to be found and Cime was
offering to show them such wonders of Meridian as few
mortals had ever seen.

Sturm had gotten lucky; right-living was its own reward. He'd escaped Bandara with its uncountable rules and
antiquated dicta. He was free at last of Levitas's
handwringing and out in the world with a fine ship and
having adventures, straightaway, the sort all young heroes
dream of.

This Meridian, he thought, was not a dream realm;
his Bandaran perceptions knew it to be real. His youthful
impatience and boundless hubris deduced that Nikodemos
was a burned-out coward and Randal, the junior Hazard,
the true source of Nikodemos's overblown reputation.
Just the fact that Niko had found need to take a partner
proved this, as far as Sturm was concerned. Sturm
needed no man's help.

Women, however, were another matter. Let Niko and
Randal fondle and "support" one another, each womanish
soul finding its mate timorously close at hand.

This Cime was most beautiful. If the truth be known,
she was the first woman Sturm had craved to have. He
wasn't worried about her rejecting him: he had a plan.

There were two things he wanted from Meridian: one
was the magic dirk Aškelon had given Randal—a little
magic never hurt anybody; the purists of the school did
magic all the time, simply called it by another name and
thus created exclusivity where nothing special existed—
and the second was to give up his virginity in some silken
bed with this obviously experienced, indescribably enticing
creature, Cime, sweating under him the while.

He had a ship, he had his mental skills, and he had a
good idea that she'd welcome his proposal, if he could just
get her alone long enough to make it: he'd take her with
him, rescue her from Meridian—it was this she'd said she
wanted.

The rest would be between them, alone on the rolling

sea in the fine little ship Randal and fate had so thought-fully provided.

Walking through a high-hedged maze gardened with statuary and tinkling pools, he finally had a chance to whisper in her ear. The perfume of her skin was heady.

She looked up at him coquettishly, appraisingly, then tapped her lips with her fingers. "Leave? Together? We two? What a twist of fate!" Her fingers moved from her lips to his, traced them, trailed down his neck. Everywhere she touched him his flesh seemed to flame. "Perhaps we will, my dear . . . Sturm, isn't it? . . . a bit later on. You must be sure you can do it; make a good plan." Having whispered this conspiratorially, she added, "As for the *kris*, all I can do is . . . distract . . . Randal. You must secure it on your own." Then she turned on her heel, flouncing off to join the mageling where he sat on a stone bench before a reflecting pool, and began to do such things as nuzzle the junior wizard's big ears so that they flared bright red.

Soon after, with Sturm scuttling along behind them, Cime guided the entranced young sorcerer toward a likely bower.

On the pretext of showing Niko Meridian's stables, Aškelon was attempting to explain his great plan, his hope of restoring to men control of their dreams.

But Nikodemos, accompanying him down the aisle between box stalls from which horses of unparalleled quality whickered greetings, was far from receptive. "So you approve of this magewar in which so many have died? Or are you part of it?" The fighter who was known as Stealth walked at arm's length, regarding the archmage warily.

"I want," Aškelon rejoined, "my name to be known and invoked among men—it is this I ask of you."

"Why?" Niko stopped, crossing his arms and leaning back against a stall whose occupant poked out a blazed, wedge-shaped head to nuzzle him.

"To secure the stability of the seventh sphere through its human connection; to prevent the possibility of someone like Cime again threatening the right of man to salving dreams. You, Niko, will be my avatar, my chosen instrument, and Randal also, whom I have plucked from among warlocks."

"The way Tempus serves as the war god's avatar? No thank you. I've got to make you understand . . . I don't want this. I have my maat; it entitles me to fight for my freedom—spiritually as well as physically. I want no master, in any realm." The youth's expressionless eyes met the dream lord's and held them. "Between a balanced soul and its destiny, no power has a mandate to interpose itself. Not you, father of magic, not an angry god or facile demon. No bribe will lure me from my center: I belong to no one but myself—especially to no magician, of any sphere."

"I'm sorry you feel that way. Let me try to explain."

"There's nothing to explain."

"You fear what you do not understand. Magic is not an end but a tool; its use assures your partner Randal an opportunity to attain true power. You two are wedded. Will you deny him your love and respect—worse, deny him his heritage—because of the ignorance of *your* prejudice?"

Niko pushed away from the mare nuzzling him. "Are you threatening me? With Randal? If his soul's at risk, it got that way long before we met. Taking him as a partner wasn't my idea; we paired in spite of, not because of his wizardly bent."

"Again, your prejudice blinds you." Aškelon sighed. "Nothing is sadder than willful ignorance. I had thought you more open-minded; it is unlikely that in such a matter I was wrong. Your spirit is braver than your waking mind, Nikodemos, and less troubled by the baggage of experience. But I will try one more avenue via which to convince you . . ." The dream lord waved his hand so that a blinding light came to be among the stalls full of fragrant straw and sleepy horses.

When it was gone, Niko and the entelechy stood in another place, a broad meadow of waving grass, ringed by distant mountains, where a sighing wind played gently with Aškelon's silver-starred hair.

Niko's reserve and determination fell away with the rev-

elation that he stood, corporeal and awake, in his treasured
rest-place—not a mental refuge, now, but a physical loca-
tion exact in every detail, the reality for which his soul had
searched so long and which he had never described to anyone. His eyes, so noncommittal previously, filled with
tears. He sank down upon the grass and let his hands rove
in it, seeking by touch alone to determine how real was this
overwhelming revelation. Niko (as all who studied the
mystery known as maat hoped, but never expected to do)
had found his rest-place in the phenomenal world.

"Still, do you fear me? Doubt me? Reject me?" Aškelon
asked quietly, taking to the grass beside the dumbstruck
fighter, who only shook his head.

Aškelon smiled upon his "avatar" and spoke at length,
gently, reminding Niko that Randal had received his *kris* at
Aškelon's behest and that similarly would he, Niko, attain
his fondest dreams—even come back here, eventually, to
end his days where his spirit longed to be. "No gravel pond
or guarded island can ever offer you more than a facsimile
of this; you have lost nothing, losing Bandara, only shed a
too-small skin. This is your place that *your* mind has
claimed, and your body will return here, to our common
ground, when your tasks are done. Right now, you know
that what I say is true. Remember it. Your destiny lies with
Randal's; together you will hasten one another's spiritual
ascent and free your people from the *misuse* of magic and
the fear which creates evil. Evil comes only from the
minds of men. It has no objective reality, no power beyond
what unscrupulous mages and immoral priests and ignorant
fools have given it. As father of magic, lord of all creatures
of nightmare as well as dream, I say to you that only men
can put to rights what men have perverted. Thus I cannot
act directly upon this travesty men have made. But you,
my avatar, can and will act boldly. Drive a stake through
superstition's heart, young fighter, and she will shrivel.
Decapitate ignorance and demons will fade away. Vanquish
the evil of men's creation and no greater principle of evil
will survive it. You need not even believe in me, but only
in yourself." Aškelon, having finished the generation of a
hero, lay back upon the grass.

Pristine clouds wafted across a sapphire sky and under them a man swiped away tears a youth had shed. Niko, overcome in this moment by the truth of these words spoken in his rest-place, could not argue further. He sat where all initiates dreamed to sit: in his private place of power. As much as he hesitated to believe that he could do, or should do, all that Aškelon had decreed, he was determined to win his way back here, his right to be here, to live out his aged days here—to win, in his own terms, all a soul could claim.

So he said, sighing shakily and lying back in unconscious imitation of the dream lord, "All right. Teach me about the panoply. Teach me what you will."

Just before Aškelon began, Niko had time to wonder if it had been this way for Tempus, once long ago, and then gone bad. Had Tempus, a youthful pawn of fate and ferocious forces, given up, given in, willingly signed his soul away to labor in a "higher" cause? He didn't know; he couldn't say. The last thing Niko ever wanted was to be any power's avatar, let alone the willing servant of the entelechy of dreams.

He hoped the dream lord wasn't going to plague him, appear to him, dog him like a shadow as the Rankan Storm God breathed down the Riddler's neck. But then, no true parallel could be drawn: Tempus was immortal, undying, and resoundingly accursed.

Then came a torrent of instructions, some in words he heard and some in words which issued forth in red and flaming characters from Aškelon's mouth to burn among the clouds of Niko's private place forever, so that even though his conscious mind might not remember all that was said and done here, his spirit-self could never forget.

When Randal came running, disheveled and short of breath, into the stables shouting Niko's name, it seemed to him that the dream lord and his left-side leader appeared from nowhere.

"Niko! Thank the . . . *ah—achoo!*" Horses! Horses' hair stopped up his nose and made his eyes water and his throat close up, despite the fact that now was no time for it. Miserable, enraged at himself, Randal skidded to a stop before them. Then, with an effort of will greater than any he'd ever mounted against this internal problem with which he'd lived so long, he blurted out what had happened while tugging on Niko's arm in an attempt to drag his partner bodily from the stables.

Niko's eyes were red and he seemed disoriented. If Randal hadn't been so full of remorse and horror at what had just occurred, he would have marked it.

But he did not. He only tugged and gasped out, "The kris! It *did* it. *It* did it. I didn't. By all the—"

Coming out the stable door, Niko shook off the mage's grip and demanded, "What? What did the kris do?"

Aškelon, his hollow cheeks deep with shadow and his mouth downdrawn and sad, handed Randal an embroidered handkerchief. Somehow, from the long-suffering look on the entelechy's face, Randal knew that this news, no matter how terrible, was not going to be entirely unexpected.

He blew his nose, a furious honk. He breathed deeply. He said, "The kris rattled in its scabbard, just as you warned." He faced the lord of dream and shadow wondering if, after all, what had happened was somehow his own fault. "I—I wasn't wearing it. You see, the free agent . . . she took a coin she thought was Niko's, but it was mine. So she was bound to . . . to—" He couldn't bear to tell the entelechy that his consort had seduced a lowly Tysian Hazard. It was going to sound bad. Yet, what had happened after that should not have occurred here, not in the land of dreams. On his way here, Randal had passed weeping, white-faced residents who knew, somehow, the travesty in which he'd had a part.

"Spit it out, man. Get hold of yourself. *What* happened?" Niko demanded, suddenly coming close and taking hold of his partner's shoulders. "Are you all right?"

Randal took a deep, shuddering breath, closed his eyes, and told all. "Cime, she tried to make love to me, to discharge a coin's worth of debt. I took off the kris; it was lying on the grass in its scabbard. It rattled. I didn't pay attention. She's dangerous, might have killed me after-

wards—still might—and I knew it but I *couldn't* fend her
off. She was . . . *do*ing things to me . . . when the kris—it
flew out of its scabbard and through the air right at this
bush. . . . I thought it was a bush. It *was,* I mean, but Sturm
was behind it. Then he screamed and fell out, with the kris
sticking out of him. . . . And she laughed. She *laughed!*"
He'd vomited, right then, and fled. He didn't tell them
that. "She's after me, maybe."

"Sturm!" Niko snapped. "Is he dead?"

"Oh, yes. Dead."

"And your kris, Randal?" Aškelon said evenly, as if he
weren't surprised, as if Randal were a very junior prestidi-
gitator who'd made a rabbit disappear and couldn't bring it
back again. "Did you leave it there?"

"I— She— Yes, yes." His anger flared. "I don't know
if I want it. Look what it did! It killed someone! I mean—
Do you think *I* did? Am I to blame? You said, my lord, that
it was a mirror of my—"

Aškelon snapped his fingers, and in his hand the bloody
kris appeared, gore smeared on its scabbard. "You had an
enemy who wished your death. You knew it; he knew it;
the kris knew it. Were she not so powerful, Cime herself
would have been skewered. It is said of the kris that one's
enemy's body is its only rightful sheath. And you, Randal,
who use meekness as a shield and pretend to weakness,
must come to terms with what else lies within yourself. It
is unfortunate that Cime has brought violent death to Meridian, but she *is* its manifestation." Holding out the kris,
the dream lord, seeming all of a sudden much taller and
much harsher in his wine-dark robes, took a step toward
Randal, then another. "Take it. It is yours. What it does,
you rightly feel, is your responsibility. Succumbing to
temptresses of Cime's sort never leads to a good result.
Take it."

Randal's hand, of its own accord, followed the dream
lord's order. The kris's sheath and grip were sticky and
cold in his palm. With Niko watching, his imperturbable
mask again in place, Randal knew he could not refuse the
lord of shadow's gift.

"And Sturm?" Niko said, looking away toward Aškelon, once Randal had girded on the kris. "What of him?"

"What of him? We all hold our own fate. I will send his body back to Bandara. A ship the double of your own will take it. A self-inflicted death is not your concern, nor is this violence in my realm. Go down to the dock and board your vessel now, quickly. Neither I nor Meridian will be here much longer. Get you to the harbor and head due east, out to sea."

"Out to sea?" Triremes were seldom sailed beyond sight of land; one hugged the coast, sailing in so unseaworthy a craft. Randal, having questioned the dream lord's orders, met that gaze like hell frozen over and thought again. "Right. Out to sea. Immediately. Come, Niko." He began to back away. But Niko was still staring at Aškelon, unmoving, his mouth drawn tight.

"Niko!" Randal said more loudly, exasperation coming to fill the void where terror so recently had been. Aškelon wasn't holding him responsible for Sturm's death; he wasn't to be punished, or even damned, for what had happened. He wanted to quit Meridian before Aškelon changed his mind. Or before the treacherous, murderous Cime found him and made good her promise. *"Niko, let's go."*

"I won't thank you, Aškelon, but then you know that." Niko took a step back.

"Just go." The entelechy flickered; his aura flared into visibility, as if the moon came before the sun. Then he disappeared.

Aškelon, facing Cime in his study, drummed long fingernails upon his table. He was wan and weary-looking; death always made him tired.

She was wild of eye, defiant. He'd snatched her from Randal's rainbow-sailed trireme just in time; she'd been hiding below decks. He'd whisked her hither effortlessly, his power here so great she could not even attempt to forestall him.

"You! How dare you!" From her hair Cime took down wands of diamond, arcane weapons which once before she'd used on him and nearly wiped Meridian and all it stood for from the planes. Their tips she touched together and a baleful blue light began to shine.

But she had made a bargain with him, lived with him, and benefited from him: the time she'd spent here plus the ill she'd done today gave him power over her she hadn't known he had. Now she would: he raised his own hand and the blue light faded from her diamond rods. They glowed now red-hot and still she held them, so that he smelled her skin searing.

Yet she did not speak or lower her wands or look away, but held her ground.

This tableau of a woman consumed with hate and full of scorn for even her own pain then touched him: he felt pity for her as strongly as he had the day he plucked her out of misery with a promise of salvation should she but spend a year with him.

And thus he waved his hand again, and all light drained from her rods of diamond. She turned them, dim and harmless now, in her fingers.

He said, "Free agent, murder doesn't suit you. In this, of all abodes, hell's fury is out of place. Let your temper fade away; we've so much more to live for. If I can overlook a death here, you can surmount your disappointment."

"You promised me," Cime spoke at last, "that I'd find peace here. Peace?" She laughed, flipped around her deadly wands in one sure motion, and fixed them in her hair again. "I've found just deadly boredom, servitude, despair."

"Give yourself a better chance. All you've done today is weaken your own power; this land itself now looks at you askance." And as they spoke, the islands of Meridian were fading from their place in space and time; a mist grew thick and closely cloaked the isles and all upon them, then closed in upon itself, lifting harborside and city street and every quay and denizen away. There was a crack like thunder where they'd been but none on the archipelago of dreams could hear it: all were safe and sound upon another plane, returned now to the seventh sphere, which nestles in between the heavens and the hells and the ball of earth from which everything man knows has sprung.

Even as it happened, Cime sensed it. Her shoulders slumped, she felt behind her for a chair. Sinking down upon it, she said to him, "You've done it, have you not? My exile is complete again. It isn't fair. I brought you your prey, let you twist and taint the purest soul I've seen in thrice a hundred years. And what is my reward? Further bondage? A greater sort of debt to you? Our bargain not-withstanding, I put it to you, soul to soul: I want your leave to fight this war of magics by my brother's side."

"You should have asked me outright. This murder on Meridian needs expunging; you've penance to do which you, not I, decreed. Do it, and you have my leave to so-journ—but not an instant before the soul you've freed here is at rest, placated, back where it belongs among the heavens known to men."

Her chin raised; her eyes met his. "Your word, Aškelon, this time, and no trick about it?"

"My word, dear Cime, is good until eternity itself wears out."

Niko and Randal had been amidships in the trireme when a peal like thunder sounded and a blinding fog came down about them. A giant shudder tossed the trireme so that, though they couldn't see their hands before their faces, their stomachs and their inner ears told them how completely and abruptly the very sea around them heaved.

Niko had been teaching Randal the basic etiquette of weapons, how to clean and oil and care for this kris a dream lord had bestowed. While the weather raged and decks below them bucked, he held the junior Hazard close as if Randal were his lover. Should the budding adept fall overboard, or let go the kris, then what was lost would never be regained.

Soon enough, the deck and sea beneath it calmed and the fog dispersed and blew away, leaving them becalmed on a sea which ended, perhaps an hour's sail away, in a fine and busy harbor.

By then Niko had loosed his grip on Randal's bony

shoulders. Embarrassed, he'd turned away, and thus was the first to spy the port before them. "Look! Randal! What's that? Where are we?"

And Randal, who'd recently visited Caronne, recognized the ramshackle dockside district, the chock-a-block warehouses and sprawling mudbrick inns that lined the shore and, up the rolling hills agleam with whitewashed houses, the cedar courts and crowning walled and domed estates of the mercantile rulers of Caronne. "We're here!" he sputtered, quivering with excitement, soaked with salt spray, and chilled with cold. "Oh, Niko, the dream lord surely loves us: we've made Caronne this very day! There's still a chance I'll get you back to Crit in time and thus lay claim to my prize! My globe's stand! I'd despaired of it, but now I may yet win it!"

"Caronne? But how?" Niko saw Randal's quizzical look, then continued, "Never mind. Don't answer that. Let's get some rules straight before we make landfall."

As he spoke, Niko headed toward the mast to hoist the sail again, which he'd been at pains to furl when the eerie fog had enshrouded them.

"Rules?" Randal followed after.

"Rules. Tell no one where we've been—they won't understand it. I know I don't. If not for that kris at your hip I'd disbelieve the lot. And the kris—you've got to keep your wits about you. We can't have it flying off at will; they'll hang us here for murder without a care for what ensorceled weapon did the deed. Understand me? Mages are not well liked here; you've no powerful guild to help you. We're just a pair of mercenaries back from adventures we'd as soon not discuss. *My* guild has better standing here. We'll check in, see my uncle as Critias ordered, sell the ship, and be off overland by dawn."

Then he rattled off a dozen orders which sent Randal scurrying to find the title to the ship and make it ready for inspection, scouring it for signs of magical "infestation"—any implements or protective amulets or whatever Randal might have brought on board.

When Randal came up again on deck, he had the handkerchief Aškelon had given him on Meridian clutched in a trembling hand. "I've still got it, Niko, I've still got it!"

"That's nice," the fighter said, his thoughts with the slain Bandaran, Sturm, not understanding or caring to understand what special value a handkerchief from Aškelon might have. "Remember, we aren't talking about *him* or anything else. If you must, you can say that we were in Bandara, but no one should ask you even that much."

Randal, wiping his nose fastidiously and secreting the handkerchief in his belt, came close.

Niko noticed a new determination in the mageling's eyes and, without taking his own gaze from the portside or his hand from the tiller, said, "Yes? Out with it."

"I—We'll never make it in time overland, Niko. It's too chancy."

"You know a better way?" Niko frowned. He'd been hoping not to argue this; he'd prefer to make it back to Tyse without the aid of magic.

"You know I do. We'll sell the ship, see your relative, and be at the Hidden Valley farm by dawn. Please. I need that stand. The globe's not all it could be—nor am I— without it."

"You're what you are, with or without it. Don't depend on artifacts or even special weapons." Niko eyed the kris. "What's given can be taken back. What's found can be lost."

"You'll let me do it, though? Bring us home to Tyse however I may?"

"We'll see what happens onshore."

Six hours later, they reclined in Niko's uncle's dining hall, soft pillows under their elbows and sweetmeats before them on gilded trays.

The uncle was glad to see his nephew, so glad he threw a formal feast with the official town beggar in attendance to bring their reunion luck.

The drugs Crit wanted Niko to secure for Madame Bomba were promised—not just a single shipment, but a steady stream by caravan, the first load leaving late that night.

Niko's portly uncle, misty-eyed and long of tooth, waxed voluble, full of drink and stories of Niko's father's heroism in days gone by. But when the old merchant leaned an oiled head so close that scented curls brushed Niko's nose, and offered him a place in the family's trading empire, Niko once again refused.

And Randal, watching carefully, detected the discomfort in his friend at all the largesse shown and confidences given. Old wounds were here, ones not even a right-side partner should try to tend.

So when they'd bid their host farewell and sought the fresh air of the streets, Randal said only, "Ready now, left-side leader, to quit this town for home?"

Niko, uncomfortable with too much hospitality, had given the trireme to his uncle as collateral for the first transshipment of Caronne krrf and mountain pulcis. "I suppose. There's nothing holding us here, is there?"

Randal, fingers resting gently on his kris to make it fast, agreed and suggested that they seek a quiet clearing where a cloud-conveyance descending from the heavens would not alarm the natives.

Near the docks, where a cliff rose too high and steeply for commerce, they found themselves alone. "Ready?" asked Randal, raising his arms to heaven.

"Ready," Niko said with a touch of resignation, and let his partner spirit him home.

Book Three:

WITCH'S WORK

On the west bank of Peace River, directly across from the ruins of the Peace Falls house Tempus's men had burned down about her head during the summer war, Roxane the Nisibisi witch put her scrying bowl aside. This swampy haunt she'd made her home was called Frog's Marsh because no greater creature used it. It stunk of putrefaction and the sinking death it offered to deer or dog or wayward child who wandered lost among its quagmires and its moss-hung, gnarly trees.

A perpetual dusk reigned here, relieved only at night by the glowing marsh-gas rising, which smelled like belch or fart and bubbled, gurgling, from mulch and mud to cast its eerie light. A fine place, this, to meet the local revolutionaries; the perfect base from which to whip Tyse's burgeoning insurgency into shape.

Roxane's bower, itself, was clean and dry and hung with claret velvet. She quit it now to meet her pawns, who waited under an overhung swamp-giant two thickets and a lily pond away. They'd never see her spell-spun home. She had no need to make the rebels comfortable; she wanted them atremble with superstition and frayed about the nerves. She climbed her conjured stairs, then closed a mossy door behind her, casting a holding spell, which made her subterranean abode all but disappear. It was impregnable now, almost nonexistent; it would not really *be* again until she returned to stoop beneath the arching roots which hid its portal from the world.

Roxane stifled a curse which, these days, was more than rhetoric: curses from her lips were potent weapons. She'd risen in rank among the warlocks of Nisibis; though she was female, she was strongest of them all. None among the remnants of the once-proud Nisibisi mageguild—those who'd fled Tempus and his Stepsons to far Mygdonia after the war for Wizardwall, or even those who'd been at Lacan Ajami's side casting spells and curses upon the enemies of Mygdon when their routed fellows arrived with tales of deific intervention and pleas for asylum on their lips— dared challenge Roxane's suzerainty.

She had now what she'd always wanted—control of all Nisibisi magic. She answered to no one. It was Roxane who ruled magic's precious roost.

Of course, she was sworn to aid the warrior-lord of Mygdon; her clan labored in his cause. Threading her way through swamp cypresses whose treetops made a nearer, darker heaven, she reflected on her task. Spying for Lacan Ajami upon his Rankan enemy meant spying on the thrice-cursed Riddler. The 3rd Commando—should she fail in stopping Tempus as she had failed in stopping Imperial Ranke's second, covert messenger from reaching him— might soon be pillaging at Mygdon's Lion Gates.

Roxane didn't blame the wizard-spawn, young Shamshi. An agent could do no better than he was bid. Some Rankan witch or treacherous enemy adept had cast a protective ward over this hell-child, Kama—a pall of invisibility, a cloak of insignificance—so that her real mission and her message were submerged beneath a guise: she'd been seeking out her father. None among the seers and portent-readers had even marked her. Now she was marked— marked for death. Roxane would not assign this task to her hand-picked rebels, nurtured long ago and straining at their leashes. The news Roxane brought and the plans she'd implement would be fresh meat to these Mygdonian sympathizers: far too long they'd had to content themselves with baying at the moon.

Now Lacan Ajami, affronted beyond measure by the Riddler, who kept a son of Mygdonia hostage, sallied forth, the total destruction of Tyse uppermost in his mind.

These minions of hers would clear the path for his army of conquest and retribution. By the time Mygdonia's fierce hordes arrived, screaming "Lacan is great!", Tyse's forces would be in disarray, divided, her people terrorized from within and thus easy prey to Mygdonia and her allies when they attacked from without.

And then Roxane would be free to leave this foul and vaporous swamp for more suitable surroundings: the newly rebuilt palace in Tyse would do for starters, though she wanted, most of all, to raise her arms to heaven atop Wizardwall once more, to regain for all her kin their lost ancestral home where now Bashir of Free Nisibis held obscene services in the names of odious gods. Wizardwall must once again shimmer blue at midnight with the light of working wizardry: this she had sworn, as she had sworn to find out whether Tempus was truly an immortal and whether a Froth Daughter might be turned to drizzle upon the air.

Coming abreast of a patch of red-dotted mushrooms as large as human heads and so poisonous that even Roxane took care not to step on one, lest a bit of powder from a crushed one make its way onto her lips or into mouth or nose, she reflected that hatred and destruction were all well and good, but not the only thing she had on her mind. Nothing she'd seen in Tyse or on Wizardwall or in far Mygdonia troubled or angered the finest Nisibisi witch as did what she'd seen in her scrying bowl just tonight.

This unsought vision bedeviled her. Unbidden, it had come and turned the clear water of her scrying bowl viscous and putrid. Water had never defied her before. But it was not the audacious fluid which worried her, but the vision it insisted on showing her—one of the mortal Niko-

demos being compromised by Aškelon, meddler in human
affairs, bleeding heart among plane lords, the overpowered
and obscenely greedy entelechy of dreams.

If Niko was to belong to any black artist, it was she,
Roxane, who would have him. Niko's soul was hers, even
loved her. She had, quite plainly, a prior claim. But con-
testing with the lord of dream and shadow outright was
tricky business—bold and canny as she was, Roxane well
knew she just might be outclassed. She'd thought, when
the vision formed in her water bowl, and blinking or even
stirring the water's surface with a finger would not change
or mend it, that she ought to move her headquarters, find
some sunny place where shadows did not lurk, where their
lord could not make use of them to observe her.

Now she dismissed the impulse to flee. Darkness was
hers as well as his; shadows have no allegiance. Like
souls, they can be persuaded to an unjust cause.

Waiting for her, in a clearing ringed by tall swamp reeds
with bushy tips like the tails of frightened cats, were five
men and a pair of women, each holding close a torch and
talking loudly to one another, proving by their raucous
laughter and coarse diction how fearless they were.

She cast a little ball she'd taken from her pocket into
their midst. It exploded with a blue and fiery light, then
settled down to burn steadily and clean. She had brought a
gross of these incendiary pellets. Her laughter followed,
then her piquant form dressed in spotless satin raiment.
The proper entrance made, she coaxed the awed and trembling rebels from their cover behind logs and arching roots,
even those who were face-down among the reeds, soaking
in the mud.

Only one was dry of muck and sweat and had his torch
and knife in hand. This was Oman, the rebel leader,
swarthy and built like a bull, with a strangler's hands and
squinty eyes. His expression, looking around at his
comrades, all so recently buttocks up in the mire, was un-
forgiving. When he turned his gaze to Roxane, it hardly
changed.

Their eyes locked in a silence an owl saw fit to break.
"Whoo! Whoo!" came from the trees behind Oman.

"Who, indeed?" Roxane took control. "Who among you is ready to do battle with our enemies? Who is anxious to slit a Rankan throat or two? The moment is at hand." She still stared at the insurgents' leader, who was smarter than he looked, but vain.

"At hand, is it? What have we been doing for the last year or so? Knitting sweaters for our Rankan overlords?" Oman spat by his booted foot. "And you, Cybele—" For this was what they called her, an alias she'd used and a disguise she'd worn here in days gone by "—where have *you* been? Cuddling up to demons to sway them to our cause? We've seen what sorcery can do against the Rankans and their gods! I hope you've something better, this time, to offer us. Better plans, better aid, better information, better—"

She stopped him then, reaching once more into her pocket and bringing out a palmful of the little incendiary globes. "These little balls, as you have seen, will temporarily blind and sore affright your mortal enemies. Just drop or cast one—" She started to let them fall groundward; Oman lunged forward to catch them . . . and succeeded— just. The others, behind him, tittered. He scowled around at them, straightening up.

Roxane continued: "Cast them in the midst of your enemy, then strike while the terror lasts. Come, come close, all, and get your share." She gave out the gross of pellets, making sure that Oman got the lion's share.

This mollified the rebel leader somewhat and he began telling her what progress his group had made. She interrupted, saying that she knew what he and his had done and it was not enough, but just a start. "The merchant class must be disrupted, totally. Food shipments, drug caravans, wine and water poisoned or cut off entirely. Lacan Ajami sorties south even now with a mighty army to join with us, but—"

"Ajami!" One of the women squealed with delight. The other hushed her.

"Before he arrives, our part in this must be done. Now, I wish to meet with Grillo, either by his leave or without it."

"Grillo? But he's a Rankan—" Oman interrupted.

"I *know* who he is; it is you who have been fooled. He is a profiteer who must be swung to our side or discredited and destroyed as having been, if he cannot be."

The rebels muttered among themselves. She let it go on a while, then added: "Bring him here to me, willing or no. It will go ill for all if I have to come to him."

Cries of consternation rose from the group, now huddled together, except their leader, who stood nearer Roxane, fists resting on his hips. Grillo was their enemy, sworn; he'd put prices on every head assembled here. Oman, who by day was a minor noble whose estate north of Tyse had been commandeered by the Rankan army and who now, to support himself, had a smithery near the souk that specialized in fine weaponry fit more for show than duty, spoke the mind of his group, saying that their necks might stretch on this one and asking how soon it would be before the Mygdonian force was close enough to be sighted by Rankan outposts or reconnaissance patrols.

"A month, no more. Perhaps less. There's no time to delay. Of course, if you've come to love your Rankan masters like the Maggots in the free zone love their begging in the streets, I'll find a bolder crew, men and women who remember what freedom was like. . . ."

She was interrupted, this time, by a flash of blue light: Oman had thrown one of the incendiary pellets at her feet.

Almost, she controlled her temper. But not quite: a purer flash of blue poured forth from Roxane's pointing finger, whipped round Oman like a lasso, then like a net of power, and when the brightness faded so that mortal eyes could look, a giant frog squatted, man-sized, where the rebel leader had just been.

Screams and pandemonium broke out among her minions. The women threw themselves on their bellies at her feet and wept for mercy. Their tears falling on her toes and the terror in the wide-set eyes of the hoarsely croaking frog (too new at the amphibian life to realize either that it had a weapon in its long and sticky tongue or that it was far too heavy to live long, out of water: death lurked in its very size) convinced Roxane that her point had been well made.

"Close your eyes, fools!" When they did, she waved a

hand and recalled the spell, at which point Oman, the proud, fell over backward to sit, knees up and hands covering his face, in the mud.

Roxane left him, then, with orders as to when and where and how she expected them to report; with targets to terrorize and businesses to destroy. One of these was the establishment known as Brother Bomba's, thrown in for good measure, to make the Riddler mad.

As for herself, Roxane had a child named Shamshi to tend, a Froth Daughter to harry, a Rankan or two to compromise, and a legend named Tempus to defame. This, she told herself, was plenty even for the finest Nisibisi witch to do. But the matter of Nikodemos still vexed her and thus, instead of heading in appropriate guise into Tyse to put certain plans in motion, she retired once more to her underground bower to meditate upon Niko's soul, its jeopardy, and some suitable method of countering the machinations of Aškelon, shadow lord, lord of dreams.

Wizardwall had once glittered with blue wards of magical power; now it glowed faintly pink with the blessing of the god Enlil, lending Tyse, nestled at its foot, an aura of sanctity that Tempus's knowledge of the town belied.

Riding downward from Bashir's high peaks stronghold, over tricky ground at a speed only one of his Trôs horses or this Aškelonian mount would have dared, Tempus reflected that though all the laws of men are nourished by one divine law, in Tyse that law was in the habit of fragmenting itself, even destroying itself. Those who lived in Tyse and those of Free Nisibis fancied themselves at cross-purposes and no one, not even the Stepsons he loved or Bashir's Successors whom he respected, had any tolerance for another's viewpoint or considered it at all odd that prejudice had replaced community and every mother's son suffered from a curse of selfishness and self-importance only Tempus seemed to recognize.

A whole town accursed? A whole race of mountain-dwelling people frowned upon by the very gods they sought to serve? Even to Tempus, who knew Disorder like a mother and fancied that Strife marched ever on his right, these were daunting questions, chilling suppositions to entertain.

But Bashir was taking his priestly role too seriously, and frowned upon any who didn't have the god's ear. Jihan was threatening to marry Tempus and have a child by him, even give up immortality for him. Death squads and dead squads roamed Tyse's byways and even ventured into Peace Falls to torch grain magazines and fuller's stalls and, if what Crit's message said was true, were bold enough to swagger into Brother Bomba's, white eyes gleaming, and demand blood pudding and tripe and worse to eat, then vandalize the premises when they couldn't get it. And no one, not Grillo's specials or the Rankan garrison or Critias's task force, could ever be alerted in time to roust or intercept even one member of this rebel force of shades and gypsies.

In fact, talk was that certain elements of the various private armies and estate militias doubled as terrorists when off duty. Even his Stepsons had been implicated, a matter of a lightning-embossed silver concha being found in the rubble of what was once Brother Bomba's pride and joy—his public dining room.

This last had occurred while Tempus was with Bashir on Wizardwall trying to make some accommodation between the Free Nisibisi and the Tysians below. If the war Tempus smelled on every breeze—which made his pulse pound fast and his instincts cry out that he'd better be off to Mygdonia with the hostage Shamshi before he couldn't go at all—was really blowing hither, then the populace of peak and plain must make a pact that would hold despite the exigencies of war to come.

He'd spent six days in the acrid smoke of the gods, stirring sacrifices with a golden poker and mumbling prayers he'd had a hand in writing before Bashir was born, trying to convince the warrior-priest to consider the townies as part and parcel of his flock.

But Bashir belonged to one god, and Tysians venerated nearly threescore; because of this, Tempus had made no progress with Bashir—he had no proof to which he could point, beyond the recent increase of Mygdonian-sponsored agitation in Tyse's narrow streets, that war blew down on them like the thunderheads now massing above him, driven by an unseasonable wind from the northeast.

The horse, Niko's sable Aškelonian stud which Tempus had inherited when the boy gave up all he owned to sojourn west, snorted disapprovingly at the clouds which suddenly masked the autumn sky, but kept picking his way southward. Any horse of strong and noble breeding could partake of Tempus's own speed and stamina, twice that of a mortal man, but this beast didn't need his help. He'd taken it to Bashir to bribe the Nisibisi leader with the gift of breeding privilege. It hadn't worked, as nothing else had availed, to change Bashir's isolationist mind. If nearly fifty Stepsons couldn't quell the town's unrest, Bashir had pointed out, then it was fate. "Come up, sleepless one, and join with my Successors. Sanctify our cause and we shall hold this mountain firm against all of magic's demon armies and even jealous, foreign gods."

This wasn't like Bashir. Tempus had given up then, thinking that Crit had sent for Niko and perchance Niko could do better with Enlil's priest, his boyhood friend. Then Crit's message had arrived, wrapped around the leg of a homing hawk—no polite suggestion, or timely missive, as might have been expected, but a summons: all the men and gods and laws of nature Tempus had dared to trust were acting far too strangely for less than magical intervention to be at the root of it.

Thus he rode homeward, summoned by Critias to the Outbridge station like a truant groom to his muck-filled stable. If only Kama's Rankan masters would send the money he'd requested, he'd be out of town with all his Stepsons. He'd neither tarry nor delay, just leave.

And he'd leave Jihan in Mygdonia when he got there. It had occurred to him that either the Froth Daughter or her Mygdonian charge were the fount of all this ominous display.

The clouds above kept massing as he rode, so that the ground beneath with its furrows and chasms and rocky slopes became difficult to see and the Aškelonian stud stopped, its flanks aquiver, craning its neck around at him with a snort and a reproachful look as if to inquire which of them, man or horse, was the more foolhardy. It was nearly dark as night by now, madness to go on.

Yet he slapped its rump and kicked it hard: he had an idea what this daylight-devouring cloud might be.

Looming above them, it stretched north back toward Wizardwall so that no gleam of pink or mighty peak was visible; ahead, the cloud seemed to rise up from the ground so that no Tyse, indeed nothing whatsoever, could be seen.

Nevertheless, the horse, not one to defer a challenge or refuse a dare, started resolutely forward, each foot held long above the ground, then pawing tentatively before trusting its next step.

This continued until thunder roared and the Aškelonian halted once more, raising its muzzle high to let out a scream of challenge to the very sky. There was no lightning with this thunder, no lessening of the cloaking dark about them, so that the proud stallion, who had never in his life known fear, broke out in frothy sweat where he stood on trembling legs and hid his head between his forelegs, partly from terror, partly from shame.

Tempus, touched by the horse's plight, slid down and took it by the bridle, tying a kerchief from his neck about the sable stallion's white-rimmed eyes. This done, he led the blindfolded beast slowly forward, trusting his own sense of direction to guide them safely over ground he thought he knew, until, directly in his path and on a level with his own eyes, two burning orbs of red appeared, like the eyes of some mountain cat piercing inky gloom.

"Stand!" He stopped the horse and held it still, not going for his weapons: he'd fought an apparition quite like this once in Sanctuary, most venal southern port of empire. He'd fought it to a draw for a god. He couldn't win against it then. And now, he knew, he'd fare no better.

Its name could not be spoken by a human tongue. The thunderous sound they'd heard had not been lightning, but its growling as it came to be on this unaccustomed plane. The sound from that cloud-throat he'd heard before, much louder. He'd hoped never again to hear Jihan's father's voice ringing in his ears.

He spoke to it, calling it by its manifestation. "Storm-bringer, what is it you want here? Your daughter, Jihan, is not with me. She's back at the barracks station, playing mother to a human child."

Thunder roared. The sheer volume of that sound buf-feted man and horse, and the blindfold was blown from the stallion's eyes. The steed emitted a high-pitched squeal and reared. For an instant, Tempus's feet left the ground and he dangled from its headstall. Then he brought it down.

"Scare my horse, will You, inhuman lord of turbulence? I've cast off godly love for affronts to my mounts before. Begone, if You've no purpose here. I've no time to—"

"Silence! Mortal toad, spawn of dirt and blood! Have you not said that the soul is water and from water comes the soul? You know your danger!"

"So You think to cow me? Am I not plagued with Your daughter? Is it not enough to torture me, that You must threaten me into the bargain? I've called it quits with gods and Their untimely aid and comfort. Get Thee back to Thine unearthly home!"

Thunder without words roared so that the horse dragged Tempus back a dozen steps and the very ground beneath them shook. "And, too," Tempus added, anger rising in him, not just at this inarticulate, incomprehensible father of weather gods, but at all the gods who throughout the ages had used him, plagued him, made sport of him, and af-flicted mortals through him, "you've quoted me wrongly: I said that for souls it is death to become water, for water it is death to become earth; out of earth water comes to be, and out of water, soul! So if it is death You've come to offer, Ineloquent One, give it here! I'll take it! Otherwise, Weathermonger, piss off!"

The ground beneath his feet began to split then, so loud was Stormbringer's thunderous response, bereft of words but full of emotion. The red orbs grew and grew and seemed to come much closer. A fetid wind like breath from the earth's bowels blew in his face. *"My daughter, mortal-lover, is with you. More, she craves to stay with you, at*

*any cost. Her power and her heritage she petitions to for-
feit, to be a wife to you and spread her legs for you and
bear a child to you when, but for you, she would be the
honored consort of the entelechy of dreams! I hold you
responsible for this! Dissuade her, afflicted demigod."* The
roaring which carried Stormbringer's words had become
softer, a rumble viscious and full of threat, *"Or the suffer-
ings of your wasted youth will be nothing to the torture of
your endless old age! Be warned!"*

And with a last, gusting breath which nearly made
Tempus retch, and from which the sable stallion turned his
head away, the red orbs, so close and hot, dissolved. The
thunder ceased, and the black clouds scudded and dispersed, the last inky wisps of them blowing away on a
crisp autumn breeze.

When the sky above was clear, Tempus raised his fist to
heaven. "Crap!" he shouted. "I'm not afraid of you, Wind-
bag!" And he wasn't.

Roxane held court in Frog's Marsh when the moon was
high. She had a brace of minions, human, ex-human, and
inhuman. She had conjured a throne of red granite and a
pavilion of summer sky to illumine her where she sat above
the throng. She fingered a small golden effigy of a man (or
of a god, none could say, so old was this talisman of
power) as Grillo was brought forth through the crowd with
a red demon on his right and a gray fiend on his left and
Oman's death squad—which included seven white-eyed
undeads—trailing along behind.

Some humans in the crowd gasped and murmured, as
humans will. The fear in them—in their voices, their
sweat, and their minds—pleased Roxane. She fed upon it.
It was not a meal to her, but a sumptuous snack, a delight,
an appetizer fit for the feast she hoped would come.

This Grillo she would not sup upon in one single evening; gluttony was not Roxane's way. A nibble now, a nibble later; the meal she'd have would be a sacrifice from
this crowd, one they'd choose of their own number, if

they'd failed in their endeavors and come without a suitable victim for her enjoyment.

For this was a god's night. On such a night, a witch works hard. Many sacrifices were going up to heaven; many prayers must be countered; many priestly efforts circumvented and earnest prayers blasphemed.

Roxane was a defiler by nature and a spoiler for sport. Sacrilege during the harvest festival could ensure famine and evil throughout the coming year. To that end, she had brought out her finest weapons—those of the spirit, those of the flesh, and even those of material nature. Beside her, on its golden stand, was her own precious globe of power, inset with colored stones; in her palm was the tiny golden man.

When Grillo was brought by Oman to the foot of her dais, still dazed and under a spell of compliance so simple even Oman or an undead could recite it without error, Roxane reached out and spun the globe so that it caught the light of her conjured canopy of daybright sky.

Then she held up the little golden figure. It was bathed in the reflected light of each diamond, sapphire, ruby, and emerald in her globe as it spun.

Grillo teetered, swayed on widespread feet. Roxane waved Oman back and he, along with her throng of adherents, went down on bended knee at her signal.

Where the globe of high peaks clay stood, the very air began to shimmer and coalesce. Stroking the golden talisman, she bent the powers which loved her to the task of summoning one more guest: the Mygdonian-raised Shamshi, son of Datan, the deceased Nisibisi archmage.

Around the globe, the air now shone unbearably. People below shielded their eyes. Undeads chuckled. Demons chortled. Fiends cackled.

At the proper moment, Roxane reached out and stopped the globe's spinning with the flat of her hand.

An "Aah" of wonder escaped the bravest of the humans in the crowd who gazed upon a miracle through narrowed eyes: the materialized witchchild stood still for an instant, startled to be snatched from bed and sleep, then rubbed his eyes with his fists, lowered them, blurted: "Roxane!" and threw himself onto her lap.

For all to see, she caressed him. Stroking his flaxen hair with his head against her breast, the talisman in her other hand, she bade Grillo come forward.

"You," she whispered to the child whom she had afforded his first experience of a woman's body and so many other, more arcane matters, "follow my lead, beloved Shamshi, and soon we will be united forever."

"Anything," Shamshi replied thickly, and she realized that his voice was beginning to deepen with age as Grillo mounted the top stair of her dais and with an effort visible on his face began to try to make sense of what he was seeing.

"What? Who are you? Where am I? There's nothing like this place around—" His hand indicated the throne, the dais, the canopy of sky splitting the darkness. "—Tyse. What do you want with me?"

"Shamshi," Roxane murmured sweetly, as if she had not heard, "fetch me my water bowl." The boy scrambled off her lap to find it.

"Grillo," she said then, "surely you know who and what I am. Or is *this* my more familiar aspect?" With a wave of hand before face she became Cybele, the fair-haired girl whom Niko had loved during the summer war. Another wave, and she was the dark-tressed, magnificently torrid Roxane again. "You may call me Roxane, since we are to be cohorts."

"Cohorts? Witch-bitch, you've got the *wrong*—"

"Gently," she warned. "I'm your only chance for salvation. Do not offend me. These are my . . . troops of revolution, those who have previously been your enemies. Join with us now and survive what is to come." As she spoke, she probed his soul, finding the weaknesses of greed and fear and ambition that she knew were there. "Before you declare your loyalty to the Rankan empire and suggest that I kill you, if I must, but you'll never join me, know that I speak for Lacan Ajami."

Grillo crossed his arms and widened his stance still more. His mental acuity, she knew, was fully returned now.

She wanted him to know exactly what he was doing. It was much more satisfying when a soul turned upon itself in full understanding that it was choosing evil over good. He said, "Fine. Speak," and she knew this to be only a ploy. He thought to trick her, gain information from her, escape with his life and soul intact. This, though he did not yet realize it, he could never do.

She nodded to the closest demon, red and snaggle-toothed, and to the nearby fiend whose eyes looked in every direction at once, and they came up the stairs and took Grillo by the arms. At the same time, Shamshi brought her scrying bowl. "Good. Go stand there." The boy went to stand beside her globe.

"Take your hands off me!" Grillo ordered the non-humans.

"Come look in my scrying bowl of your own free will, Grillo. Come, see the riches awaiting you. See Lacan Ajami and make your pact with him. What difference is it to you whose banner flies over Tyse, so long as you prosper?"

And he came forward to look into her bowl and see what she would have him see. He couldn't know that he pacted with a dark father, not Ajami, or that his soul would be the interest charged on every gold coin he gained and moment of pleasure he enjoyed. He need just look, and he was hers.

When he did, a hiss of ecstasy escaped her as she tasted the bit of him she then acquired.

He looked up, but then looked again into the bowl, where he saw not only Lacan Ajami, but the caravan of drugs and precious wares headed overland from Niko's uncle in Caronne to Madame Bomba's Outbridge warehouse.

Again Grillo raised his head, his eyes somewhat glazed, for Lacan Ajami had just, as far as he knew, taken an oath of allegiance from him in far Mygdonia.

This one was not afraid of witchery; she'd known she could work with him, own him, and savor him. "Our gift to you, this caravan of contraband. Surely you'll confiscate it all and remember our generosity."

Grillo nodded, stiff and cold, not knowing that he was minus a fraction of his soul and that at every future meeting he would lose still more, so that someday he would be too weak to crawl from her presence and she would have him, in entirety, to feed her needs. No, now he was still suspicious, able to fight the euphoria she was offering him. But soon he would not be.

"What do I have to do? And who's that kid? He looks familiar . . ."

"Kid? There are no goats here." The boy, Shamshi, saw her signal and hid his face. The demon clacked its jaws, hoping Grillo would refuse her offer and all would dine on rare fare this evening. "Ah," she said, putting the golden talisman down before her slippered feet, "this, you mean." She nudged it with a toe and it seemed about to topple. Then its tiny golden legs spread and it took a step, then two, toward Grillo.

"That's right," Roxane purred, "take him. Pick him up. He's our contact. Our go-between. This little one will summon me whenever you need me. Just tell him to fetch me. Or even to fetch help. Or to carry a message."

Grillo's hand reached out, touched the diminutive golden statuette, clutched it. "Ouch! It scratched me!"

The closest demon smirked; beside him, the fiend giggled out loud and the demon elbowed him.

"Nothing but a rough edge. His gold was smelted long ago." There was no turning back for this soul now, fight though it might. Grillo was hers. He had yet to discover this, but that delight she could wait to savor. Roxane had many things to attend to, and the wizardspawn of Datan was not the least of these. "Shamshi," she said softly, so that Grillo could not hear, "come spin the globe and deliver this new ally of ours back to his office." Then, to Grillo, in a normal voice: "Since you will be among us, go you down and study the faces of those who are your friends and cohorts. Study well, and work well. Prosperity is thine, and success whilst all of Tyse fails. Rejoice, Grillo, thou art saved."

Before the fiend and demon could assist him, Grillo backed of his own accord down the stairs.

Probably, she admitted to herself, the operations officer would still fool himself into thinking he could spy among her people and walk away, tell all he'd seen to his Rankan allies, double-cross, even triple-cross her if he had to. Soon he would know better.

As he walked among the undeads, the insurgents, the peasants to whom it was an affront that others suffered less than they, these greeted him. Only her finest spell kept Grillo calm among the white-eyes, whose cold hands he had to shake, the demons, who fondled him wistfully, and the fiends, who kissed him, lapping the salt sweat from his skin with rough and hungry tongues. But she was up to her tasks: she was Roxane.

When she nodded and the boy, Shamshi, utilized a power globe to alter a human's fate for the first time, Grillo disappeared from among those hideous and pathetic celebrants she'd picked to counter the harvest fetes in town.

Then she sent the boy down into the crowd to choose the sacrifices from among the living. He'd touched a fifteen-year-old girl and two strapping youths before she called him back. Tonight, Shamshi would sup on tortured souls, an indescribable and addicting experience the likes of which did not exist among all the addictions and perversions of mankind.

But first, they would have some sport with them, so that the souls would be filled with concupiscence. It was this giving of pleasure and of pain that made a soul tender. It must not want to give up its life, but find that the very thing it lusted after would kill it.

When Shamshi came up from the midst of the revelers, Roxane gave the signal that the pleasuring begin. Succulent pigs on platters and whole roasted lambs appeared, and cushions and amphorae of wine and gurgling pipes wafting sweet blue smoke. She called the boy close.

It was Roxane's teat, she knew, he wanted to suckle; her legs were those he longed to part. Since he couldn't stay for the entire feast—he might be missed—and because she was kind, she allowed Shamshi a few moments with her.

And so, in as fine a fashion as had ever been done, the witch Roxane and the wizardspawn Shamshi began the debauch that would counteract, desecrate, and defile the harvest prayers which even then rose to a score of gods in Tyse's behalf.

Above the Outbridge barracks station, the moon was high and full and seemed to smoke, so misty was the night. Some of the Stepsons hustling about with ribbons and streamers and gilded wooden weapons for their harvest festival float peered up at the sky occasionally, muttering to one another about "wizard weather" and mumbling favorite wards.

Wizard weather come upon the town during harvest festival would be the worst of omens, all agreed. Second worst would be the failure of the Sacred Band's float to join the processional up Embassy Row. In it, effigies of the Storm God and his consort, nine feet tall and painted gold, must ride in honor and glory to the Spring of the Prophet where, if all went well, the squadron's entry would win the governor's prize.

As it was, their float might be the last to join Tyse's favorite parade, for which the provisional government had even lifted curfew—for the entire harvest month, martial law had been suspended. It was because of this that Critias was in a blacker mood than the oxen being hitched between the wagon's traces, who kicked and bellowed and generally behaved like the foul-mouthed mercenaries who struggled against time and superstition and the bad luck which had put the first pair of oxen that the band had purchased down with colic.

At times like these, Crit longed for bygone days, regular army postings, simpler men, and simpler wars than those he managed now. Belize's death still bothered him, although officially it was solved and because of it the resilient trader Palapot was an agent of his task force. But since that night when he'd sent Randal off for Niko and Kama had come into his life, everything smelled of fate and wizardry. He often wondered, now, if he had any free will left—if, by taking up with Tempus's daughter on the sly, he hadn't inherited some part of the family curse.

Straton thought he had. Strat didn't like Kama one bit. And now Strat was sick, and Madame Bomba, the only barber-surgeon any of the Stepsons trusted in this faction-ridden hellhole of a town, had to be persuaded to tend him—no easy task, since Brother Bomba's dining hall had been razed by hostiles pretending to be Stepsons, who'd left "evidence" around to prove they were.

Gayle came up, panting, stripped down to his tunic. "The porking porker's porking-well porked, pork it."

By this Crit deduced that the wagon's front axle wasn't salvageable—it would have to be replaced. "God's breath, man, then find another! Wait!"

Gayle had turned to go. He swung about, lines deep on his brow in the moonlight. "If you ask me, what we need is a priest to lift the curse off this whole job."

Crit jumped at his chance. "Fine. You find one. As a matter of fact, I'm putting you in charge of this mess." He waved his hand to encompass the oxen being unhitched once more from their traces, the obscenity-spouting work crew, the menials hanging about pretending to be useful but in reality gloating that so simple an undertaking had gone so undeniably and comprehensively awry. "As I remember, it was you who were telling me just last week how much good will we'd earn by joining in the local rites."

"But—"

"Stepson, that's an order. I've got better ways to waste my time." Kama was in Crit's quarters, waiting. Strat might need help at Bomba's. "If Tempus comes in, tell him I'll be at Bomba's or the Lanes station. And *get* that float rolling before dawn, or we won't be able to hold our heads up in the town."

And Crit set off at a brisk pace, ignoring Gayle's sardonic, "Yes, sir, commander."

Discipline, Crit well knew, was breaking down in the face of Tempus's absence, death squads with incendiary pellets, dead squads with all-white eyes—and the prospect of the band quartering in Tyse for the winter. If they didn't get another assignment soon, and quit this town, the snows would come down over Wizardwall and none would fight in the north until spring.

This depressing thought weighed on everyone's mind and made personality clashes inevitable, Crit told himself, though the senior Sacred Banders had come to him, all six expressionless and icy-eyed, and blamed this deterioration of the esprit de corps on the return of Niko, with his "witch taint," and on Randal, whom no one among the Stepsons was anxious to call a brother. Crit had told Tempus that he'd see that the band accepted Randal. He'd given his word and he'd see it through, though Critias had never dreamed that the Riddler meant to keep a magician—worse, a Hazard-class adept—as a permanent member.

So consumed with his private problems was Critias that he paid no mind when a horse came galloping full-tilt through the double gates—everyone was in a hurry, these days.

The task force leader had almost reached his quarters in the smaller officer's wing of the rambling estate when the rider, now on foot, reached him, panting. "Crit, Critias! We've trouble."

"Don't tell me . . . the goddess can't keep her skirts down, even for one night: the god's having her on the float."

"What? No, sir." It was Ari, one of the few locals the unit had absorbed, who'd been one of Grillo's specials and, like Gayle, was an expert on the town. "It's Grillo, sir, he's disappeared. Right out of his office during a briefing. Three specials were there, told me themselves, after a couple ales to ease the telling. There's no formal alert; only those who saw what happened know he's been snatched . . . or gone missing, or been witched away. But they'd like our help, seeing as Tempus was talking up the need for better security around him. . . ."

"I'll be damned and accursed. Disappeared, you say? Tsk, tsk." Crit and Grillo had too much in dispute to settle. "Luck's not all bad tonight, is it? All right, I'll take care of it."

Ari, falling in alongside when Crit moved away, wouldn't let it go at that. "I'd like to pick a search party, lead them myself. It'll look better—look like we *tried,* at least."

"Don't tell me you think I won't try to find our favorite Rankan? I'll put Niko and Randal on it. You can't compete with their kind of expertise, not without slogging knee-deep in magical attributes and Bandaran tricks of tracking. If you insist, you can accompany them—"

"No, no!" Hands up, Ari backed away. He was a friend of Niko's, but none of the Stepsons wanted to be seen with Randal—they sneaked off to consult him when they needed help, but took pains that no one else would know.

Crit had just entered his quarters, tiptoeing through the front room to his tiny bedroom where Kama lay, a wet rag over her eyes and a candle guttering on the bedside table, when he heard a knock at his front door. He ignored it.

"Critias? Is that you?" Kama had been on the street doing task force work one night when the insurgents struck. She'd see again, most probably, but no one knew how long she'd have the headaches or whether the fever which racked her now was related to the swordcuts she'd taken and the claw-mark scabs that scored her upper arms. It wasn't going to be easy to explain to her father how he'd let her get into this kind of shape.

"It's me, all right. Grillo's missing. Your father hasn't come in. The float's in trouble. I've got to go into town to see Straton." As he spoke he rummaged in his trunk, the room's other piece of furniture, and came up with a blanket-wrapped bundle—the stand to Randal's globe, part of the spoils from the summer war. Crit couldn't put off the junior Hazard much longer. And Randal was right—whatever rendered the single mage committed to the Stepsons more effective served them all.

The knock he'd heard forgotten, he bent low over Kama, touched her face. It was hot. He put his lips to her forehead. "I'd like Randal to have a look at you, in case there's more than simple fever here—a curse, some evil eye or poison in those wounds. You should see it out there —it's mages' mist and—" Having told her she should see what she could not, he bit his lip.

Her fingers found his wrist, brought his hand to her

mouth. She buried her dry, cracked lips in his palm. "Come back soon," she said in a childlike voice.

"I will." He really hoped she was going to live.

Closing the bedroom door behind him, the blanket-wrapped stand under his arm, he realized that the knocker had entered. It wasn't good protocol and he was looking for an unfortunate upon whom he could vent his wrath—Critias wasn't used to problems he couldn't solve. A scathing rebuke on his lips, he looked up and saw not a Stepson or a hired townie, but Jihan, Tempus's Froth Daughter, glowing with health and eerie beauty.

First he noticed that she was frowning, then that she had on her scale-armor, gray/green/brown and impossibly supple. "Jihan, what's the occasion?" This inhuman creature made him nervous; her eyes held the fire of unnamed, primeval gods.

"Shamshi has disappeared. I missed him less than an hour ago. From his bed, he disappeared."

Crit put the blanket-wrapped parcel down on the table; he had never seen Jihan distressed: her eyes glowed.

She crossed the room and took his shoulders in a crushing grip—Jihan was as tall as he, and twice as strong. "My sweet child . . . Tempus will never forgive us. You must help me, Critias. My father, who abides in the primeval sea, will show his gratitude. Now and forever, you will be blessed. But we must find him before the sleepless one returns, or my life will be ruined! The Riddler will spurn me! Do you understand?"

Crit understood that she was crushing the very joint upon which his sword-arm depended. He said, "Right. Got it. Don't worry, we'll turn him up," and was rewarded by a lessening of pressure on his shoulder. But then she slapped him in a display of good fellowship and he almost staggered. What could even Tempus want with such a woman? He couldn't fathom it. But, all things considered, any blessings from any god would be welcome right now—he'd take what he could get.

It was shaping up to be one hell of a night.

* * *

Madame Bomba stood over Straton, a prizing tool a foot long in her hand. The big Stepson, mouth firmly closed, was shaking his head, arms crossed, his eyes watering with pain.

They were upstairs in Brother Bomba's, in the Madame's private quarters where the smoke and water damage had left no mark. "Strat," Madame Bomba said, "you've got to let me pull that tooth. It's not going to hurt any more than it hurts right now."

Niko and Randal had come by to pay their respects and to convince the Madame, as Crit was sure only Randal and Niko—or Tempus himself—could, that no Stepson had had a hand in the destruction of Peace Falls's—indeed, all of Tyse's—finest inn and victualer, and had walked in upon Straton, hand holding his jaw and his temper raw, and the Madame arguing.

Randal glibly confirmed her diagnosis. "A tooth. Yes, I see it now. It's a tooth and no magic can heal it: it's dying and if you delay it may just take you with it."

Straton declared in language which made even Madame Bomba blush that Randal was addled—it wasn't his tooth that hurt, but his ear which ached, his head which throbbed, his neck which had been strained and now was too sore to turn.

"You see?" Randal said to Niko with exaggerated sorrow. "It *is* his tooth. The tooth demon has visited him. It lives inside his tooth and it means to kill him by way of it. But first, it eats up his reason with its pain. Too bad, Straton. We'd thought, Niko and I, that you were the bravest, the strongest, of all the Stepsons. Even Tempus, we were saying just the other day, seems unable to excel you in feats of valor and stamina. But tooth demons bring the strongest men to their knees. We will remember you," Randal winked at Niko, urging him to agree, "the way you were before—a man of bravery unparalleled and a paragon of common sense and soldierly pragmatism—"

Strat eyed Randal with a look so promissory that Randal's kris rattled in its scabbard.

"He means," Niko cut in, realizing that Randal's choice of words was not making matters clear to Straton, whose face was white with pain and who shuddered every now and again and even closed his eyes once in agony, "that you'll die a coward's death, when you don't have to, if you won't let the Madame pull that tooth. Then what place will you have in heaven? You'll meet the Storm God and he'll say, 'What enemy hath slain thee?' and you'll have to reply, 'A tooth I wouldn't let my friends pull out.' After a life of honor and glory, you'll lose your place in heaven after all. What heroics you can claim will never stand against a fool's death. You'll go down," Niko pointed repeatedly, dramatically, to the floor, "and wander eternally in the dark and rocky caverns of—"

"Cease! Desist! It hurts my head to listen to you both. My lady Bomba, do it, then. But be quick about it, before I change my mind." Straton eyed the iron, long-handled prizing tool of the sort a vet might use to pull a horse's tooth, and shuddered.

Niko couldn't blame him. He and Randal excused themselves to go downstairs to fetch Strat a drink "—with your leave, my lady, the strongest draught you've got; he'll need it."

Brother Bomba's wine cellar was extensive, a maze of casks. A steward at its entrance bade them wait and disappeared within to fill their order. Niko, waiting and counting what casks he could see, estimated that even his uncle in Caronne had no larger or finer cache. From his vantage he could see amphorae bearing crests and devices of a dozen nations, some so old that the countries of their origin no longer existed. Niko hadn't realized the Bombas were so wealthy or so cultured.

Critias caught up with them as they were climbing the stairs with a jar of anaesthetic wine in hand meant for Straton and told them he'd take it up. "Grillo's disappeared— right out of his office," Critias said. "Some kind of magic, no doubt. Find him."

Randal, hand firmly on his kris, bristled. "When you give me my globe's stand. If there's witchery about, we'll need all the help we can—"

"Randal." Niko shook his head. "Let's go."

"Go? *No!* Where's my stand, Critias? What's your new

excuse? You come here without so much as a thank-you when without us your grumpy rightman would never have consented to—"

"*Randal!*" Niko could sense the excitation in Crit's aura, the heat coming from his task force leader, and didn't understand why Randal would force the issue now, when Crit obviously had other things on his mind.

"Tonight, at Outbridge, when you've brought Grillo back. I meant to bring it with me. I just forgot. Niko—"

"There's something else?"

"Jihan's outside. She's misplaced Shamshi again—the boy's an inveterate runaway. If you should come across him, Stealth, make sure he gets back to Hidden Valley safe and sound—under guard. Questions?"

Niko didn't have any and Randal withheld his, following his left-side leader's example, until they had slipped out the back door where their horses were tethered.

Once they were mounted and safely away, sneaking like thieves through the back alleys to avoid an encounter with Jihan, Randal began complaining about Critias. "Besides being a welsher and an unprincipled scoundrel who's holding back the stand he promised me despite the fact that I brought you home in plenty of time, he is an ungrateful lout. Madame Bomba's faith in the Stepsons is restored, thanks only to you."

"No thanks to me," Niko said absently, guiding the bay he'd taken from the Hidden Valley stables toward the Lanes, where he hoped to pick up Grillo's trail. "And the Madame never believed that rot about Stepsons gutting their favorite watering hole—it was her husband who had to be convinced. She's too much a woman of the armies not to have realized that if *we'd* sacked her place, we'd have burned it to the ground."

As he spoke, Niko was casting about for some trace of Grillo in the astral, some indication he might notice of a disturbance, an abduction, a struggle. His maat could help him only so much; he wished Randal would be quiet, let him think. He wished his mare was fit to ride, not fat with foal in her stall, or that Tempus hadn't taken the sable stud up to Wizardwall. But he'd given the Aškelonian horse up, along with any part in the profits of breeding farm or invested spoils from the summer war. If now he twinged with regret and wanted back everything he'd spurned, it was only a sign that he'd come to terms with his problems and was comfortable again in the world he'd fled.

Tempus, Niko knew, would return the horse to him if he asked or even allowed it; as for the rest, he'd not decided what he'd do. If he had to swear allegiance, become an adherent of some personage, man, immortal, mage, or god, it was and had always been Tempus he longed to serve. Aškelon's demands lay heavily on his shoulders now, here where his commander's spoor was strong.

Somehow, Niko was not surprised when, as they crossed Broadway to head up Embassy Row and from there enter the convoluted alleys of the Lanes, young Shamshi called their names and came running up to them. Even in the misty dark, the youth's towhead gleamed in reflected torchlight from the sconces high above Tyse's best-kept secret.

They stopped their mounts, and while Randal scolded the errant child for sneaking out of bed, and the boy answered in a defensive tone with just the slightest whine that he was only looking at the floats and the preparations for the sunrise parade, Niko wondered, peering up at the overhanging three- and four-story embassies which lined the wide and sidewalked avenue, if it was out of one of these the boy had come.

And thus he saw, on a balcony above, half-hidden by a curtain, a girl staring down at him, an oil lamp in her hand. And the look upon that young face was so wistful and so comely that he could not look away. Their glances met. She smiled. Niko waved.

"Who was that?" Randal demanded, sliding back to accommodate the young prince of Mygdon before him on his horse. And: "Come on, boy, use that statue there to climb up on. That's it." Then again to Niko, with an odd grimace: "I'll take Shamshi out to Hidden Valley right away, if you'll be all right on your own, Stealth."

Knowing Randal as he did, Niko understood that the mageling was discomfitted by the proximity of the Mygdonian boy and trying to hide it. Why, he wasn't sure, but he too had heard Randal's kris rattle like a diamondback and seen Randal's jaw clench tight.

"Good. And thanks. We'll meet at Outbridge. I want to be there to see that Crit makes good his promise. Task force leaders, Stepson, always keep their word."

"Hrrmph. We'll see that you're right, I hope. If not, this is the last night I spend as one. By the Writ that serves me—"

The Mygdonian boy broke out in a fit of coughing then and Randal turned solicitous. "Poor thing. Come along then; both you and I are better off far away from horses." The junior Hazard snuffled meaningfully and brought out his most precious prize—the handkerchief Aškelon had given him, which eased his allergies enough, with an occasional swipe or whiff, that he could ride a horse without tearing eyes or congested nose—and put it over the boy's nose and mouth. "Breathe deeply, thrice. That's it. Good boy." Randal put the linen carefully away and kicked the fat old gelding into a lethargic lope.

Niko wondered if Randal had noticed how the boy had stiffened, frozen still, when Randal put the linen to his nose, but then dismissed it: the girl he'd seen had come downstairs. The building's thick oak door opened and there she stood, smiling. She waved again.

It was the Machadi embassy's threshold which she lit with an elegant presence, he realized. Machad had been taken by Mygdonia in the summer war; refugees of high estate from Machad often asked for and received asylum here. The free zone was not for girls like this, accustomed to damask gowns and delicate lace and tiny sandals with heels. The girl's heels tapped as she came a few steps farther toward the street.

"Greetings, soldier," the young girl said, her cultured voice full of wicked pleasure at speaking first and coming out unescorted.

"My lady." Niko's horse danced forward in response to the pressure of his knees. "What service can I do a guest of the Machadi embassy?"

"I was just wondering, young sir," she replied, coming

yet another step forward so that he could see the wide brown eyes and sun-gilded hair in gentle curls about her throat, "where the best vantage might be for tomorrow's parade. We're so far from the reviewing stand that I can't even see the Spring of the Prophet from my window."

Almost, he dismounted. He wanted to get a closer look. But he was under orders to find Grillo, and so he said, "If my lady wishes, I'll come by an hour before sunrise and take you to the reviewing stand myself—every Stepson is entitled to one guest."

"A Stepson? Oh, I didn't know." She backed a pace. "I've been forward. I can't accept. I don't even know your name. And my uncle . . . might not approve."

"I'm Nikodemos," he said softly, toying with the helmet at his knee.

"And I am Aisha," she replied, "niece of the Machadi ambassador."

"I'll be by to collect you. If your uncle disallows my invitation, I'll understand, Aisha, but I hope he'll let you come. Where are your parents?"

"My parents," she blinked back tears, "are prisoners of the foul Mygdonians in Machad. My uncle, the ambassador, takes care of me."

"Tomorrow, then." Niko had met the Machadi ambassador. His heart lightened; a well-bred girl with earthly problems was just the thing to soothe him. "I've got to go."

"Bide well, then, soldier—Nikodemos," said Aisha, raising her skirts to turn and go inside.

An hour later he'd ridden every byway in the Lanes and found no heat-track, reddish trail, or even wisp of Grillo fresher than a half-day old. He was giving up. This job needed a magician, not a western-trained fighter with a bit of maat.

He dismounted and tied his horse before the door of Grillo's Lanes office, climbed the steps, and knocked. Within, he could sense the men in agitated discussion— some passion there, hot argument, even Grillo's peculiar aura: red and pink and tinged with bluish lines which shouldn't be there. Blue, in Niko's private mental code, was for mages, the ensorceled, the bewitched, the witches, and the damned.

When the door opened, to his consternation, Grillo's aide slipped out and shut it, then leaned back against it. "Ssh! Stepson, *never mind!* We sent out a dozen messages, trying to call off the search. Grillo's here—guess he never left. Or anyway, that's what he says. Some kind of witchy prank of harassment from the mageguild. He swears he never left the room, but couldn't see us the way we couldn't see him. He'll be mad enough to break us all to stable duty if he hears we let news of this slip out. Now go, go on! Get back and tell your Critias what I've said—we'll owe you one if you Stepsons keep our secret. Otherwise," the pasty-faced aide shrugged and looked away, "it's nastiness as usual, your side and ours. A deal?"

"As far as I'm concerned. Good luck with this deception." Niko turned and left, angry at this whole affair—his wasted time, crossed lines of communication—and certain that this explanation was not going to satisfy Critias.

As a matter of fact, it didn't suit Niko either, but he had no choice. He headed his mount toward the Outbridge station to give Crit his report, and as he was about to round the corner, heard a horse behind him and turned to look. A local type, a man named Oman who made ceremonial swords and rich-man's armor, was just riding up to Grillo's door. Stranger agents than Oman might be used by Grillo, but Niko had never seen one. He filed that bit of news away for further study without halting his horse or giving any sign he'd seen or recognized the man.

He had more pressing concerns: Randal would have his globe's stand this night, or Niko was going to have from Critias the reason why not. And in the morning, he would escort a lady named Aisha to the harvest festival's most wondrous event.

When Oman, self-confessed leader of one of the rebel groups which had been making Grillo's life miserable for the last few months, left his office, Grillo seriously considered siccing his specials on the fool, consequences be damned.

But it was Grillo himself who was damned. And Oman knew it: the cocky, puffy-eyed Tysian, whom Grillo had met in Frog's Marsh, coolly proclaimed just how and where Grillo's specials would interdict a shipment of Caronne krrf and mountain pulcis meant for the Stepsons' den mother, Madame Bomba.

Grillo knew he should have thrown the revolutionary out on his ear, at the very least—better, he should have arrested him. But he just *could not.*

Sitting at his desk, alone in his office, he nudged the little golden statue a witch had given him. It was proof that what he remembered was no nightmare.

Beside his oil lamp, it gleamed dully, no bigger than his middle finger. He touched it again and its slightly conical head turned; its golden legs quivered, separated; it moved a step, then two, toward his finger, then rubbed against his knuckle like a lonely cat.

He drew his finger back slowly and it followed, just as slowly, but moving more steadily with every step.

All his hackles raised, he sat back in his chair. He knew he was in deep trouble. He couldn't forget the witch's face as she'd passed her hand before it and her countenance changed from raven-haired, sultry Nisibisi to pale and fair young girl. In the midst of its transition, he had seen a crone, ancient lips pulled tight over a jutting chin. He imagined rheumy eyes staring at him even now.

What could he do? Report the witch? To whom? Plead for help from the mageguild? Rankan magic had fared poorly against the Nisibisi wizard-caste in the summer war. And what the witch had said was right—he really didn't care which faction held Tyse, although he did care deeply about Bashir and the mountain-dwelling folk of Free Nisibis. As long as she didn't ask him to betray Bashir, Grillo told himself, he'd go along with her.

The homunculus, or whatever it was in front of him, had reached the edge of his desk. One more step and it would tumble into an abyss of air and crash upon the floor.

Perhaps if it could be destroyed by fall or fire or a stamping foot then he could shake this feeling that he was helpless —that the witch was watching him, that his soul was in danger of forfeiture.

Grillo prided himself on disbelieving equally in gods and magics, in luck and fate. And yet, no logical disclaimer had availed when the witch had spirited him from his quarters into the midst of her followers. Something inside him knew that she'd been controlling him ever since.

It wasn't like him to give up without a fight. Even now, knowing it to be futile, he thought to free himself from Roxane's gossamer web.

He nudged the little golden figure, cold as metal but indubitably animated, toward the desk's edge.

It teetered but, arms flailing, righted itself.

Again Grillo extended his finger toward it, his knees well out of the way so as not to break its fall. Sympathetic magic, symbolic action, call it what one willed, he had a hunch that if he could free himself of this evil little trinket, he could break Roxane's hold.

It reached out its tiny arms toward the finger inexorably approaching and, as Grillo jabbed at it to force it over the brink, it grabbed his finger with both arms, its metal hands digging into his flesh, its grip tight as a vise.

Grillo sucked in a breath; there was pain, surprise, anger. Then, even as panic set in and he started shaking his whole hand violently to throw it off, the room began getting hazy.

Desperately, Grillo grabbed its feet with his other hand and pulled as hard as he might. But strength was leaving him. With it went purpose; even the fear he had been experiencing was gone. In its stead came a fatalistic calm, a feeling he could only term foolishness. He didn't recall why he had been hostile to the tiny golden statuette—it was his future, his good luck charm.

He cradled it in his palm now. Only tiny, dry punctures showed where its claw-sharp fingers had gone deep into his flesh. He didn't notice the imprint of minuscule teeth, either, or understand that he was drugged by its venom, rendered tractable and pliable by magical means.

He held it up to his face in the lamplight, kissed it, put it to his ear.

It began speaking to him in a chirping voice, giving instructions to which he could only nod his assent: now he understood that the golden figurine that Roxane, Death's Queen, had given him was the best friend and protector he would have in this world or the next.

Tempus, cloak and helmet covered with trail dirt, on the great Aškelonian steed whose flanks were caked with dust and sweat, slipped unremarked through Tyse's back streets under a fey sky shot with colored light.

There was mist everywhere, steaming up as if from the cobbles themselves. This combination of mist and preternatural light in these last few hours before the sunrise parade to the Spring of the Prophet sent veterans of the summer's wizard wars hustling off to temples and open-air altars to pray, or to soothsayers and card-readers to buy prognostications, or to magicians in their lair on Mageway for protective amulets and all manner of prophylactic spells.

No one doubted, even before the paving stones on Embassy Row cracked wide apart and then smacked back together, catching men and oxen and wagon wheels in bear-trap jaws, that magic was abroad. Those seasoned in the field or long of memory worried most: if there were a worse sign than wizardry against the populace during the harvest moon, nobody could think of one.

More than a flock of birds lost their lives that predawn, pinioned to fortunetelling boards, copper nails through their wings. More than fifty livers of sheep and goat and pig were lifted quivering out of still-warm bellies to see how the bile was flowing. Virgins were hypnotized and sent walking, blindfolded, through the mageguild's garden maze, but not even this produced unequivocal results.

Tempus's return, however, when at last he had urged his filthy sable steed through the Outbridge station's gate, lightened the mood of the Stepsons quartered there.

The fact that their commander had already reconnoitered the town and knew in more detail than they just what sort of sorcerer's mischief they were up against made the senior Sacred Banders smile covertly and nod their heads when he'd passed by: they had orders from the Riddler now, orders none would hesitate to obey. It wasn't that any of them distrusted Crit or found him wanting as a tactical officer; it was simply that holding Tyse was more a task for gods than men—everyone knew that Tempus, now and always, had the Storm God whispering in his ear and the favor of the higher heavens.

Men who had been sullenly chewing straws on doorsteps set off trotting to their tasks. Swords were whetted, bucklers checked for rivets or straps worn thin; horses came out of their stalls and amulets out of their pouches— if the Riddler said a disruption of the parade was in the offing, then they'd be ready to keep the peace at any cost. Those who'd ridden through gouts of molten rock spewed from restless mountains with the Slaughter Priest would ride through worse for Tempus—he'd led them to victory on Wizardwall against the massed defenses of the archmage Datan and all his Nisibisi warlocks.

So as Tempus left his stables and the sable in the care of a grinning, zealous groom who mumbled shyly, "Glad to have you back, sir," he heard Stepsons whistling battle airs and Sacred Band pairs harmonizing hymns of war.

But before he'd reached his quarters, where he'd thought to shed his mud-heavy mantle and quench his thirst before seeking out Critias, the sight of Randal the Tysian Hazard on a *horse* made him halt, his fists upon his hips.

"Randal!" Tempus's gravelly voice rang out so that men paused in their tasks even on the battlements and looked on in silence. "I'd like to see you for a moment."

Randall dismounted, slapped his gelding's rump, and the old nag ambled toward its stall alone. The mageling, hitching up his swordbelt, approached Tempus with an uncertain but relieved smile upon his freckled face.

Swordbelt? Tempus looked again. By the time Randal was greeting him as befit a Stepson his commander, Tempus had determined that it was indeed a swordbelt

Randal wore and that a kris, of all weapons, depended from it.

Ignoring protocol or even politeness, Tempus demanded: "Where did you get that kris? What are *you* doing with a weapon like that?"

The startled mageling blinked twice, his feelings hurt; even in the oddly colored light of this enchanted dawn, his flush was obvious. "Doing with it? Nothing much, as yet. Aškelon gave it to me. Isn't it wonder—?"

"*Aškelon!*" Tempus thundered, one fist pounding an open palm. "*What* have you done?" He cursed himself silently. No mage was beneficent. No sorcerer was trustworthy. Not even this harmless-seeming youngster had a single moral or ethical fiber in his entire body.

"Done?" Randal almost shouted back, his voice quavering with temper. "*Done? I* brought Niko back, as I was ordered—as a Stepson, I've so often been told, always does obey his orders. *Without question!* No one said to me, 'Bring him back but keep shut of Meridian, if it should appear in your path in the middle of an empty sea!' I brought him back by way of Meridian and I assure you, commander, the choice of port was hardly mine! And I'm supposed to be paid for it with the stand to my globe, which Critias promised—"

"I'll *pay* you for it, if you've let Aškelon get his claws into—" Before he could speak Niko's name aloud, where so many ears were pricked, or before he said the next thing on his mind and expelled the mageling Randal from the Stepsons with an appended prohibition from associating with any man of his henceforth, Tempus marshaled his anger. If things were getting witchy, as they seemed, he needed Randal, his one sworn mage, right now. So he continued, in a quiet tone, "I'm assuming that both you and your partner suffered no ill effects from this visit—correct me if I'm wrong."

Randal, his bony arms crossed, inclined his head, his face suffused with blood from rage or embarrassment—Tempus hadn't time to determine which.

"Good. Then go in my behalf to your archmage and ask him for an opinion on the meaning of this weather and whether he will join with us in attempting to ensure an uneventful and pleasantly routine harvest festival. Then—"

"I'm not going anywhere until I get my globe's stand . . . sir!"

Tempus had to chuckle. "Who's got it—Crit, is it? Yes? Well, come along. We'll see you in possession of your trinket and you can tell me your opinion of how Niko fared with Ash."

"Ash? Oh, the dream lord. I can't tell tales, not even to you. You know the Stepsons' oath—you wrote it. As for that 'trinket'—give it here, and we won't *need* my archmage . . . or any help from anywhere but *here!*" Randal tapped his shallow chest, puffed out to its fullest.

"Indeed? Then let us hurry."

So it was that Randal, on the way to Critias's quarters, told Tempus about the evening's dual disappearances—those of Grillo and of Shamshi—and explained that he'd just returned from Hidden Valley, where he'd left the Mygdonian prince in Jihan's "capable hands."

"Good. Thank you, Randal." On Crit's office steps, Tempus paused and gave his orders gently. "Find Niko, will you, and bring him here. I'll have your reward for you as soon as you return."

"Niko? All right." Randal seemed disappointed, then he brightened. "We'll soon clear up this foul weather, once I've got it."

Tempus nodded absently and the mageling hurried off, a slight figure in the cobalt-shadowed dawn.

Crit, when Tempus found him pacing back and forth in his bedroom where Kama lay bandaged and a local healer was applying leeches to her wounds, was more troubled than Tempus had ever seen him. Even Crit's sardonic smile sat askew on his stubbled face as he suggested softly that the tiny room was too crowded and they'd best talk out front.

"I told you to stay away from her," Tempus said without preamble.

"I thought we'd burn that bridge after we'd crossed it. I couldn't leave her alone . . . not like this. She's virtually a stranger here—the locals don't care for fighting women,

Jihan avoids her, she makes the pairs nervous. . . . This
state she's in . . . it's my fault. I sent her out with a task
force patrol and they ran into a death squad with incen-
diaries as well as superhuman members . . . demons, white-
eyes, the lot."

This speech, Tempus realized, was one Critias had long
been preparing. He gazed at his second in command steadily.

Crit, crossing to his front room's table on which lay a
blanket-wrapped bundle, an oil lamp, a half-eaten meal,
and a copper humidor, motioned to one of the two chairs.
"Have a seat, commander. I've got some flat beer and
this . . ." As he spoke, Crit rolled a smoke, then another,
and held one out to Tempus. "Say some damn thing . . .
relieve me of my command or whatever you're going to
do."

"Is that what you want?" Tempus took the broadleaf Crit
held out and lit it from the oil lamp, sinking down into the
chair opposite his first officer with a deep, rattling sigh.
Since the god had left him, though his regenerative abilities
remained and his stamina and sleeplessness also, physical
fatigue was no longer strange to him: his muscles ached
from riding.

Crit didn't answer until Tempus had blown out a long
stream of blue smoke. "Want? I don't know what I'm supposed to want. I'd like Kama to recover, but the leech in
there says it's no simple poison—it's some witch's brew.
Of course, that's the kind of excuse you'd expect from one
of them, but . . ." He spread his hands. "Strat's in town
with Madame Bomba—he's sick too, and Strat's as strong
as one of the god's bulls. Tonight, so far, we've lost and
found both Grillo and Sham—"

"I know."

"Then you tell me whether we've got another sorcerous
infestation on our hands or I'm just trying to excuse a total
botch of things. I'm sure *I* don't know. But the pairs think
it's Niko—as soon as he got back, this weather boiled up
and everything I've tried to do turned to dung." Crit's
smile, this time, was its normal, cynical self. "Stealth says,
by the way, that he saw Oman the once-noble coming out

of Grillo's Lanes hidey-hole tonight. He also says that—"

A voice interrupted Crit's dour monologue from the door which Tempus had left ajar: "—that it's more likely my fate than Crit's, causing all this trouble."

Tempus turned his head and saw Niko, wet hair slicked back from a recent bath, leaning in the doorway, Randal's head visible just behind. The young fighter wore no armor, only hillman's shirt and trousers, and his feet were bare.

Tempus wondered where the charmed panoply the boy had gotten from Aškelon was now—buried, most likely, in some forsaken spot; or on the bottom of the sea. Tempus remembered his own struggle against supernatural forces who craved a mortal representative. He thought he saw in Niko the loneliness of a man who fought a private war he knew he couldn't win. It was there for any knowing eye in the subtle changes this young fighter called Stealth had undergone: Niko's eyes, once merely shielded and blank to a casual observer, had retreated into his head. His movements, as he eased inside, made room for Randal, then closed the door and slid its bolt, were fluid, economical: no earthly threat weighed on Niko now. The boy had learned that death was not the worst that might await even him.

"Life to you, commander," Niko said with a commiserating smile, "and everlasting glory. I've come to see that Critias makes good his word and gives Randal, here, the stand for his warlock's globe. We need the use of it, from what I saw in town tonight," Niko reached behind and urged Randal to come forward, saying more softly, "Claim your prize, rightman. Then take it to the mageguild and see what you can do for us—for *her*." His gaze flickered to the other room, then returned to Tempus, where it stayed. "Randal thinks Kama's in receipt of some witchery meant for me or you from our old friend, Roxane. He needs a leave of absence."

"Done. Give it to him, Crit." Tempus took another drag upon the broadleaf and stubbed it out among the bones of quail on Critias's dinner plate.

Crit reached out without rising and hefted the blanket-wrapped bundle, then tossed it through the air toward Randal, who lunged forward fast enough to catch it.

Crit's lips twitched in disgust and he muttered, "Maybe it's fine and dandy now we've got our own resident Hazard-class adept, but I'm glad it's you, Riddler, not me, who gave the order and dispensed the weapon."

Randal, wrestling with the wrappings on the gilded stand, hadn't heard, but Niko did and gave his task force leader a withering look, saying, "I told you, Randal, that Crit would keep his word. Among Stepsons, it's necessity, not choice," and turned to open the door, adding: "I've got to see my partner to the mageguild gates. I'll be right back—"

"I'll go with you." Tempus rose, chuckled as he looked down at Crit, and clapped his first officer on the shoulder. "Don't blame yourself, or worry. Neither does a bit of good. What fools and gods and witches make, each party freely shares. As for the rest of us—those in between the victims and the manipulators—we simply do our best to help the innocents and save our own lives."

Crit stood up then. "Fine. Good. Then go say something to your daughter, who may not last the night, who only wanted to help—to earn her sire's respect, to take part in a saga worth retelling. You should hear her poetry. If she lives, she'll surely win first prize at the Festival of Man. Or rather, would have done: if her life's in Randal's hands, we'd best start felling timber for her pyre."

"Wait outside, Randal, Niko," Tempus ordered, putting himself between his task force leader and Niko's eloquently reproving look until the pair had gone.

Then: "Crit, you're not in love with that woman? She's 3rd Commando," Tempus reminded him. "She's not capable of love, only of using you."

"What's she using me for? To find herself an early death? I've done my best at that. I'd rather light her bier than have her live because of magical intervention. She won't like it if she owes her life to Witchy-Ears, out there."

"I want you at the reviewing stand in my place this morning. Get Straton and put your task force out among the populace. Keep off the actual parade route, in case the ground is hungry yet, though." The only cure Tempus knew for what ailed Crit was work and lots of it. "And watch this Oman; Niko's hunches are worth heeding. When the parade's done, send every Stepson not on crucial duty over to Bomba's to help rebuild her place. Put two senior band pairs out at Hidden Valley; I want the Mygdonian boy under surveillance, around the dial. I'll be keeping Jihan with me. From what I understand, her father may be looking in on us, by and by."

Crit raked a hand through feathery hair. "Anything else, commander? Raise the dead? Move Tyse lock, stock, and barrel out of harm's way?"

"Yes, now that you mention it: stay away from Kama. I don't want to have to tell you again. You've got a task force to love and nurture. She's not a member of it. Once we hear yea or nay from her superiors on the proposed sortie north, she'll be on her way. I don't want her taking you with her."

"You're sure she'll live that long?"

"I'm sure. When it comes to women plaguing us, this unit doesn't get that lucky."

But when Tempus was alone with Kama, he found himself moved by her plight, even distressed. Touching each leech in turn with wooden swabs lit from the candle by her bed, he caused them to loose their hold, then slowly and methodically he crushed each one beneath his heel.

"Healer?" Kama's voice was weak, uncertain. "Crit? Critias, is that you?" Her hand reached up toward the wet cloth over her eyes; his met it there and grasped her fingers.

"It's Tempus. I told you to stay clear of Crit. When you're well enough, I'll spank you until your bottom's blue."

She smiled faintly. "I can't wait. I'm . . . sorry."

"I see you are. Any word from your friends in the capital?"

"Not yet." Her face was shiny with sweat and he could see her frame twitch as the poison did its work. Her grasp was weak in his; she shuddered and he wished he'd known her better. Then she seemed to forget that he was there; her grip grew limp and her mouth moved as she whispered

words he leaned close to hear. But these words she spoke
were not for him: she recited poetic works in which he
figured in some heroic part.

He shook his head and, as quietly as he could, left her.
So foolish, to think that words in songs or stories were
worth this kind of risk. Words of power belonged to the
archmages and the politicians, to the generals in the field.
And they had no time for art or hidden meanings. She
sought what? Some ephemeral glory for herself through
making a folk hero out of him? Some propinquity of the
spirit she had not had, indeed *could* not have, in flesh?

If Kama died of this foolishness, Tempus decided—
leaving Crit behind with just a wave answered by a smart
salute—it was no worse a death than that a killer wolf
might earn by exposing himself to crossbow quarrels atop a
mountain where he must bay at the moon. But it was no
better, either. A woman who craved heroics was like a dog
who longed to talk or a horse who ached to fly: what could
not be had was imbued with a value beyond what was
natural, or attainable, or real.

But then, she was *his* daughter, after all.

In the mageguild, Randal sat alone in his little tower
room. He'd said goodbye to Niko and to Tempus behind
the Outbridge stables. It was no more difficult for him to
remove himself to his quarters by means of magic than to
endure another trek by horse. Aškelon's handkerchief
might not last forever; he didn't want to waste its power.
And he didn't want Tempus to interrogate him or Niko to
watch over him with that fondly distant look.

Here Randal was secure, alone, an upwardly mobile
Hazard, not a fumbling semi-Stepson.

The floor of his room was flagged with marble. He took
the precious golden stand with its arcane runes and ball-
and-claw feet and set it in the middle of his spiral power
glyph.

Why couldn't Stealth be content to be chosen by Aškelon, more humane and more powerful than many a bloody
god who demanded never-ending sacrifice and laughed

with garlicky breath in its desperate penitents' faces? If Aškelon had chosen Randal for such an honor as the one Niko deemed a curse, the seventh-level Hazard would have risen to the occasion with all his might.

But the fighters were inscrutable; they loved their war and death and picking through the bones of time to sort out right from wrong, good from bad, evil from holy, honor from dishonor.

Even Tempus, who knew better, played this silly game and justified it by the end results, whatever they turned out to be.

So, as Aškelon's single *willing* adherent and Tempus's single magical ally, Randal could not fail to prove himself worthy.

With hands atremble in anticipation, he got his globe from its warded chest, almost forgetting the power-lock he'd spoken over it so that he had to say the reversion spell twice.

With the globe poised over the stand, Randal cleared his mind and ordered his tasks: in these he must not, would not, fail. He'd foil the curse which wrapped Kama tight, which any adept could clearly see and even Niko had noticed. He'd give Niko the courage to accept his fate and the strength to meet his challenges. He'd help the Riddler win his peace—for that, he knew, was what Tempus wanted most of all—and protect Bashir on high Wizardwall, even if it *was* Roxane whom Randal had to oppose.

And his gut told him it was in truth Death's Queen, she who coveted Niko once and perhaps lay in wait for Randal's partner still. Randal had previously found within himself the bravery to fight against Nisibisi wizardry, against Roxane herself, for those he loved. And though he was a mage, committed, he neither felt nor was evil. He supped on no souls. The energy he needed, he took from the resonance around him as planes rubbed upon planes; he worked in harmony with nature, not against it.

But this was a Nisibisi globe he sought to use, to tame and turn to his purpose, the very globe the Nisibisi archmage, Datan, had used to bring coherent evil upon this and other towns.

So Randal was very careful as he set the globe upon its stand. It could be that in order to save those he loved and prove himself the whitest of mages, he must expose his very soul to all the evil he'd these long years been content to do without. He might become a soul-sucker, a contractee of powerful demons, or worse. But he would do it for the best of reasons, without a thought to personal gain.

And thus he finally let go the jeweled and prodigious globe so that it rested in its stand. And then he knelt before it and, with his palms outstretched to set it spinning, began the incantations which could put his eternal soul's survival in direst jeopardy, but which would lift the curse from Kama, deflect all evil directed at the Riddler back unto its source, and, if love could heal, might even set poor Niko free.

Roxane sat bolt upright in her bed, hands clapped to her skull in agony. The pain that lanced there tore a howl from her throat and made the human boy beside her scramble up, a sheet around him, and dash for safety to the corner of the room.

This disturbed her new house snakes, which hissed and rose up on their coils to threaten the child with darting tongues.

"Have him!" She freed the snakes to feed upon the twelve-year-old she'd chosen from the free zone.

Before his wails had ceased she was out of there, seeking her own globe of power in her Frog's Marsh summoning room.

Only one power tool in the known world was stronger than her globe. And that, a greater globe than this one she now spun with fervid invocations while sweat beaded on her upper lip, had belonged to Datan, the vanquished archmage whom Roxane had served so long.

Who had it now? Who dared to turn it on her, spin it contrary to her wishes—use it on Death's Queen as if she had no recourse?

Her water bowl beside her on the table, she watched the light her globe spilled out and held her breath against the pain that beat upon her flesh and bones like hostile wings from unknown hells.

When she had spun the pain away, Roxane was nearly exhausted. To refresh herself, she conjured up a fire in the stone hearth and called the snakes that ate the boy and ate the snakes, first one and then the other, roasting them in turn upon the hearth. Too bad—she'd thought to keep this pair. But snakes were expendable right now.

Her strength replenished, she gazed into her water bowl while across the walls colors spun from globe-light danced. In the water there formed an image of the mageguild, Tyse's home for hubristic prestidigitators.

She tried to see inside it. She waved the water with her palm and spoke words so ancient she had needed them but once in all the summer wizard war—that once, when she'd escaped the wrath of Tempus and his summoned gods unscathed, had been the first time in her life she had had to use them.

She used them now, for whomever or whatever had that globe within Tyse's mageguild was turning Roxane's own spells back upon her—the wasting death and anguished agues and lingering ill-fortune she'd cast upon the Riddler's spawn called Kama and on Straton, Critias's 'friend,' and on all the other Stepsons...that bad luck which hung over the entire Sacred Band, a dedicated pall, had been thrown back at Roxane from a canny hand within those high stone walls.

She couldn't see her enemy's face, but just a hand, busy at its spelling and its spinning.

The results of this meddling fool's endeavor, though, lay clear upon her water bowl's bright surface: Kama sat up smiling; Straton swaggered down Brother Bomba's stairs with Madame tucked against him; the Stepsons' float rolled bravely down the middle of Embassy Row toward the reviewing stand in the midst of a parade unspoiled.

Roxane howled with fury once she'd gobbled the last bit of tasty snake and the last spell had been tried and failed to change the tableaux that her scrying bowl reflected. The worst, her bowl had left for last: young Niko, in his precious armor, with Tempus by his side and grinning; and

Grillo, not out with Oman on the way to seize the caravan as he should be, but attending to law and order in the town.

Then did Roxane bend her head to magic as she'd never done before: she wrenched and molded time and space and even rent reality as she rent her own black garments before she cast off clothes and human form and, quenching her own fire, went soaring up her chimney in a falcon's form to wreak havoc upon the town and her enemies among men.

Her shadow, where it fell that sunrise morning, blighted ground and crops and sickened animals and men it touched while passing over.

When it fell upon the mageguild, stones groaned, foundations trembled, roofs began to quake. When it darkened Brother Bomba's doorway, the buttressed bottom floor gave way and fell in to crush the magazines and wine cellars and what luckless individuals were caught inside.

As she soared over the parade route, the governor's own float was beginning, with great fanfare, the trek up Embassy Row; beneath its wheels cobbles turned to muck and paving stones opened wide to reveal sharp teeth and gaping maws so that in moments the entire float, its oxen, attendant outriders and revelers by the tens, were swallowed up or sucked on down and crowds surged backward, fleeing.

Roxane screamed a challenge from her falcon's throat; this bird, the fastest winged warrior nature ever made, dodged with ease the crossbow bolts Tempus and some Stepsons launched at her. She veered; she dived; she dared to defecate upon the Riddler's very head and wing away, toward the eastern pass between mountain peaks where Oman's insurgents waited for Grillo's specials, and for a certain caravan from far Caronne to come.

Meanwhile, on her orders, certain death squads and three dead squads made up of subjugated souls and led by demons marched on through the rent she'd made in Frog's Marsh. These met and joined forces at Peace River and by the demons' aegis went raiding in the town, headed toward the reviewing stand.

And as they did, in the blighted free zone, the holy Spring of the Prophet which fed the town turned red and ran with blood and bile, and overhead, a rain of toads began to fall.

Grillo, despite himself, had ended up deploying specials and Oman's grisly crew of "troops" at the eastern trade route's pass, called the "general's route" for some reason lost to antiquity.

He didn't remember riding out here. The little golden figurine he'd found somewhere was fastened to his collar; it was bringing him good luck.

Ahead, the caravan's dust could be seen in the first true light of dawn.

His specials silently assumed positions high above the pass where boulders had been rolled into place and fulcrums, wedges, and pushing-poles of freshly trimmed pine were waiting to box the contraband carriers in Grillo's trap. His men were uncharacteristically reserved this morning, either spooked from rubbing elbows with the death squads, whom everyone was sure had devils' help, or just overworked.

Grillo couldn't worry about them—control, command, communications: these were his main concerns. Morale in times like these was always dicey. The same could be said of his allies—death squad members, revolutionaries who kept their hoods well down over their faces.

Watching a segmented, tiny procession far below, Grillo gave a whistled command. From fore and aft, boulders should have tumbled.

But pine saplings snapped and cracked, and boulders tottered, not to fall, as planned, upon the caravan below, but to roll backward, like living things with wills of their own, over the men who tried to move them—and over some who were not men, who lost their robes to rolling rocks and then, naked, unfurled fishbelly-wings and turned batlike heads about, and whirred and leaped into the air.

Thereupon, as only pebbles fell below and rocks chased men and crushed them flat in weird pursuit, the attackers broke in rout and fled, the humans stumbling as they ran, the others taking to the air or disappearing in a burst of sparks.

Men were turning now upon untrustworthy allies— Grillo's specials drew their blades and hacked at nearby revolutionaries. Javelins flew and crossbows spat forth quarrels and everywhere pandemonium raged, so that below, Grillo saw as he too began to scramble for higher ground where a boulder couldn't roll him flat, the caravan was warned and picked up speed to make it safely through the pass.

Scrambling on scree which wouldn't hold his weight or afford him purchase, Grillo found that his mouth was dry and darkness edged his vision. Among the screams of wounded men and fleeing fighters run down in their tracks by hostile boulders, or pushed over precipices, or skewered by recent allies, he heard a fiercer, piercing cry and looked up in time to see a falcon circling high above, wings motionless upon the air.

He was just cranking his own crossbow, bead drawn upon Oman, the traitor who had set this trap to kill every special worth his salt, when a dark shadow from those wings above passed over him and Grillo knew no more. He never guessed that it was Roxane who wheeled above him in falcon's form, furious that her own spells had been turned upon her minions and powerless to stop the unknown mage who spun Datan's globe against her, spoiling everything.

There was madness in the streets which sought to swallow every Tysian and refugee and celebrant alive. Niko, riding his sable stallion at Tempus's behest, thought he might be the only one in town who could tell from the color of the ground ahead where it was and was not safe to tread.

He'd gotten out his panoply at Tempus's suggestion. At the time, he'd resented his commander's order to dress for the occasion, knowing Tempus meant him to don his Aškelonian weaponry; now he was glad he had it.

Niko had no sooner picked up Aisha at the Machadi Embassy and headed with her toward the reviewing stand when havoc broke out along the parade route.

Chaos about him, his first thought was for Aisha, astride a white pony right beside him. One hand on her mount's red bridle, he'd thought to see her home. But he'd lost her in the crowd somehow. He didn't understand it: a white horse was hard to miss.

So he was seeking her among the terror-stricken throng, restoring order where he could, using his steed to stop the desperate who'd take any risk to loot, when he saw the white pony, running, bolting out of control, southwest toward Peace River.

Giving the sable a kick, Niko set out after the white rump he now could see, now could not. And thus he galloped right into a pitched battle at an intersection which was cracked and heaving: Stepsons fighting death squads. He had to lend a hand.

He fought his way into the thick of it, the sword Aškelon had given him warm with recognition of magic close at hand. And when it sliced a human-seeming throat, its owner burst apart in flames. A blue wing whickered by his ear. He'd seen it coming, but not in time to duck away. It seemed to Niko that the flying wing had veered off as if his armor had deflected it.

A crossbow bolt which struck him between the shoulders shattered on his cuirass; another, coming low, went deep into his thigh, but he was infused with excitement and the lust of battle. He kept after a particularly enticing foe, one whose cowl never slipped away and who had taken swordcuts and even been pierced through by a peltast's spear and not been fazed.

Niko's stud, teeth clacking, did its share and once (as it snapped about it, not knowing friends' mounts from foes' and certainly not caring), it bit a Stepson's horse and Gayle shouted, "Stealth! Pork-all! Keep that porking nag of yours away from our horses or you'll be fighting by yourself."

As if Gayle were prescient, soon enough Niko was alone: his horse and quarry had led him to Peace River. They forded it in a froth of water, this indestructible foe who did not seem to bleed still well in sight.

His sword sheathed now, Niko cranked and sighted
through his crossbow, but every bolt aimed true seemed to
go astray.

Frog's Marsh was on the far side of Peace River here.
Approaching it, his horse slowed, snorting, head tossing,
showering Niko with foamy spit from gaping jaws. "Come
on, horse, we've gone this far . . . a little undergrowth
won't hurt us." His quarry's trail was clear ahead, bilious
blue-green and supernatural; so was the pinkish trail of the
girl he'd promised a safe-conduct to the festival. If the
wizard, or demon, or what-have-you, was chasing the
girl's white pony, then Niko couldn't let it go.

The sable danced in place despite Niko's urging knees.
Had Tempus made a coward of this horse? Or exhausted it?
No, the Aškelonian was neither fool nor weak: Niko knew
this beast and respected it more than many men he'd met.

Stealth dismounted, rubbed its muzzle, held it by the
headstall and looked it straight in the eye. "Either we go
together, horse, or I go in alone. I left a pitched battle back
in town to run this murderous creature down; I can't fail to
do it. And I've my word to an innocent to make good.
Come or stay behind, horse, it's up to you."

He realized then that he'd never named it. He should
have, perhaps, to make a stronger bond between them. But
he'd given it to Tempus and really had just borrowed it
tonight.

It cocked its head at him and then, deliberately and
slowly, pawed the ground three times, its tiny ears pricked
forward.

"I hope that's 'yes,' horse. I haven't got time to argue."
He swung up on its back and this time it moved ahead with
little urging, testing each step as if it trod on eggs before it
put a hoof firmly down.

At this pace, they'd never catch someone fleeing fast,
but the horse was right: this ground was tricky. In it were
deep hoofprints; as long as daylight lasted, he'd have no
trouble with this trail.

He had a moment then to realize he was almost glad the
town had erupted in confusion; Tempus had been slowly

and methodically drawing from Niko everything that Aškelon had said. Niko didn't want to explain about his rest-place, or that through it Aškelon had a hold on him that the western-trained fighter was powerless to break. Another time, perhaps, he'd tell the Riddler. As it was, he'd been saved from a discussion more perilous than a hundred-to-one encounter with assorted demons: he couldn't talk about Meridian yet.

And so, after what seemed an hour of reflection, he came upon his quarry: both the cowled figure and the Machadi girl.

She was backed against a cypress, her festival skirts heavy with soaked-up mud, a little sticker in her hand. Her white pony lay on its side, blood running from its mouth red as its trappings.

The cowled insurgent, if such the figure was, had its back to Niko and was closing in on the girl, who was telling it, "Stay away! I warn you, stay away! I'll kill myself before you'll touch me, you warty salamander!" And she called on a Machadi patron goddess, so that all around the trees began to shake their limbs.

Niko dismounted silently and crouched behind an ancient bole big enough to hide him and his horse, squinting through his peep sight: a crossbow bolt could go right through the foe and impale the girl from this angle. And if the bolt went wide, as bolts had done before when launched against this perhaps unhuman target, it might do her more harm than good. His throwing stars were likewise suspect.

He judged the distance, put the crossbow by, and slid his dirk from its sheath. He'd not used it since the summer war. It was yielding in his hand, warm and eager, proving magic lurked here, if Niko needed proof.

He thought an instant more and then, decided, cast the charmed dirk and followed right behind it, drawing his enchanted sword as he leapt toward the girl and her tormentor.

The cast he'd made, though even Niko doubted it would serve over so much distance, went true, and before him, as he closed upon his enemy, a back shivered. Then it seemed to swell and, from the wound around the dirk, in flesh up to its hilt, green and steaming ichor spurted.

An arm raised to fend off the acid blood, Niko met his enemy as it staggered full around and with clawed hands raised came toward him, jaws open wide, its disguise—if ever it had had one—gone away and a red and awful demon face there in its place.

It spoke. "Ah, death child, a worthy foe at last!" It hissed. "Well and good to meet you: I'll be an angel of high estate once these teeth have torn out your throat."

Niko knew better than to meet its eyes or listen to its threats, supposed to stun him. He lunged forward, ancient sword in hand and arcing back and, without thought to dodging demon claws, swung it down, right to left, so that even as the demon sought to grapple him, he cut its head from its neck.

Yet those claws screeched on his armor like fingernails on a child's slate, and its body bore him down under its twitching weight, and for a time he struggled there with something that should not be living, while the head, hanging by thick red skin, swung back and forth and jaws clacked near his naked arms.

Niko heard the girl's screaming coming closer, but didn't realize what that meant until her face appeared, mud-smeared and contorted, over the severed neck spouting acid blood, and she joined the fray, plunging her little lady's dagger into the demon's back and tugging at the weakening corpse, trying to get it off him.

Niko yelled to her to get away, to watch the claws, to avoid at any cost the stinging demon-blood and especially its spittle, but in the end it was the girl, Aisha, who pulled away the corpse, now foul and steaming, heating up as it started decomposing while it hugged him.

Freed from its deathly embrace, he rolled over on his stomach, wiping his face in the moist grass and dirt, seeking to clear away the stinging, viscous stuff that covered his face and made his eyes tear.

He heard a tearing sound and hands were on him. He felt something touch his face and wipe his eyes. It was her bodice, soaked in water, he realized when he could focus

his eyes again. He saw her fair young breast as she sought
to tend him, heard her soft, sweet voice assuring him that
he'd been marvelous. "You are my savior, bold Nikodemos, and the finest hero that's ever lived since ancient
times. There now, just be still." She leaned close, first
wiping his eyes with her wet cloth, then kissing them with
gentle lips. "You'll soon be all right. And my uncle will
show his gratitude when I tell him how you saved me.
You're a lucky one, too. Except for that—" she pointed to
the crossbow bolt embedded in his thigh "—you're not
badly hurt at all . . . a few burns and scratches mostly."

She sat back and smiled at him. "Say something."

But he could only take deep breaths and fend off pain
and watch her, this noble wench so soft and fair, who perhaps had just saved his life.

If not for the timely arrival of forty mounted strangers,
who joined right in without awaiting orders and moved the
panicked crowd back from the heaving streets, roped the
floats to drag them to safety by dint of horse and muscle,
and generally took up the slack left by Grillo's absent specials, Tempus knew they would have lost the day and perhaps the town to sorcery.

At one point, when he had turned a corner near the
reviewing stand and seen Jihan, on his other Trôs, working
at crowd-control like a veteran, Tempus had found himself
next to one of the nondescript riders who'd chosen to lend
a hand.

The Trôs that Tempus rode was greeting its brother with
a belly-shaking squeal just at that moment. The dark-clad
rider whom Tempus didn't know turned in his saddle and
saluted, "Hail to thee, founder."

Then Tempus saw the 3rd Commando device high on a
leather breast plate and grinned his wolfish grin. "And to
thee, soldier. Glad to have you with us." And he was.
"There!" He pointed with his sword and charged toward a
small group of insurgents, fleeing counter to the press of
the crowd.

The 3rd Commando member kept pace, using his horse

skillfully to part the crowd. "We didn't think you'd mind. We're tired of waiting for the seers to tell the omens," he called to Tempus as their horses leaped in tandem. "We're here without portfolio—or money—but we thought you'd have us anyway."

"How many are you?" Tempus grunted, leaning low to avoid a flying missile passing close. And so, as they fought their way toward victory, he learned that his terms had not been met in the capital and that, because of this, the 3rd had detached itself from the empire's army. Unless a coup or natural death made a change in emperors, these fighters were his for as long as he would have them. That they could keep their unit separate and distinct from the Stepsons was all they asked.

As the two of them backed six insurgents against a mud-brick wall, and the commando on his right put bolts enough into spread-eagled forms to hold the prisoners by the fleshy parts of arms and thighs until they could be collected for interrogation, Tempus allowed that the 3rd could stay, although silently he added that the rivalry between these fighters and his Stepsons might be more difficult to handle than even the three undeads among this captured cadre right before him, who calmly tore their flesh from the crossbow bolts pinioning them, leaving muscle, and in one case, a whole arm behind, and with a final, white-eyed gaze of taunt and silent fury, dashed away in three directions.

They chased no more rebels after that; they had the floats to tend and magic on their minds.

Over the reviewing stand the sky had darkened and Tempus pointed there: he had a suspicion blacker than those roiling thunderheads as to just what he might see when he got close.

To do so, he jumped his Trôs across the yet-heaving street where paving stones were restless and cracks had claimed extremities of man and beast.

When he looked back from the other side, the 3rd Commando fighter was crouched low and forward on his horse's withers, leaping it after his. Judging horse and rider, form and fettle, brains and courage, Tempus had to admit he was impressed.

The true test of this commando came, however, when they rode up to the reviewing stand and found the spectators who had huddled there, afraid to leave, with hands over their heads, and Jihan and her father, his red eyes piercing heaven and his growls making people hide their faces, arguing with lightning bolts and thunder claps over whether or not she would remain.

"Jihan," he shouted, "Stay or go, the choice is yours. I'll miss you," Tempus could not resist adding, "if you should leave. But ask your father's help with this—banish the curse from our parade."

"For you, my darling, anything!" Jihan's eyes were as red as her sire's and it seemed that sparks flew from her hair. She raised her hand and, in a way he still could not understand, she "spoke" to her father, Stormbringer, progenitor of all the weather gods, and things began to fall from heaven.

Falcons, eagles, condors, and winged things Tempus had never seen before came crashing to the bleachers so that the crowd there broke and ran.

The ground ceased its complaining and the paving stones of the street undulated like a troubled sea and came to rest in perfect order.

The mist that clung yet to byway and alley sparked bright and blew away.

At Brother Bomba's, lumber raised itself, casks reformed and filled themselves with wine, and all was as it had been before.

In the free zone, the Spring of the Prophet no longer ran as red as blood, but was clear and bubbling, pure. The toads that had fallen from the sky became stationary, turned to diamond, ruby, and emerald effigies which the starving free-zone Maggots trampled one another in their haste to grab.

The mageguild roof snapped tight again; no mortar fell or timber groaned.

And on a Trôs horse before the bleachers, Jihan, whose

hands had been raised to heaven, lowered them until they were extended straight out to Tempus. "Your word is my command, lord of my heart. My father, too, accepts your gratitude. Look!"

Above her head, the clouds dispersed; a sunny morning blazed down upon her glowing form. "Now kiss me, prodigious human lover, for I have earned it!"

Tempus cursed himself for allowing her to construe his words as a deal he'd made with her and, worse, her father. But Stormbringer was gone, the sky was clear, and there was nothing right there and then that he could do but make the best of it.

Book Four:

IN THE SHADOW OF THE WALL

A fortnight after the harvest festival parade, the Machadi ambassador gave a dinner party in honor of the "valorous souls, men and women, whose bravery, above and beyond the call of duty, saved Tyse from peril and destruction during that night of horror . . ." etc., etc.

"What he's really grateful about," said Straton to Critias sourly as, on the pretext of checking their horses, stabled with the other guests' in the Machadi embassy's rear court, they marked with jeweler's files the horseshoes of mounts and dray beasts whose destinations later this evening might prove to be of interest, "is Niko having saved that niece of his from some Frog's Marsh demon. The rest of us are just here to make it look good."

Straton didn't like this sort of party, where a man had to dress like a fop and act like a politician, where the portions of food were small and the drinks smaller, where he had to laugh at bad jokes and be polite to the seldom-seen Tysian nobility, commanders of the local garrisons, and functionaries of the Rankan government.

Strat especially didn't like the feeling he got when Cri-

tias set eyes on Grillo: Tempus had taken Strat aside and
told him that no matter how obvious it was to Crit that
Grillo had been out to interdict the caravan bringing drugs
from Caronne to Bomba's (and not, as Grillo maintained,
to escort and, as it "turned out," *save* the shipment from
insurgents), there was no proof of Grillo's treachery and
thus Tempus was counting on Straton to keep Crit from
going on record with his suspicions.

"Good?" Crit grunted, putting down the hoof of the 3rd
Commando leader's roan and straightening up. "There's no
way to make this collection of power brokers, rogues, and
well-placed back-stabbers look civilized, let alone 'good.'
Five Stepsons certainly won't do it, not when one's Niko,
one's a Froth Daughter, and one's a damned Hazard."

Crit, palm sliding along the roan belonging to Sync, the
3rd's commanding officer, spat over his shoulder in disgust
when Straton didn't rise to his bait, and added with a theat-
rical sigh, "That's the lot. Let's gird for the forthcoming
war of words and go back in there." From his pocket he
fished a broadleaf sprinkled with pulcis, lit it with a flint
from his beltpouch, then passed it to Straton.

Taking it, Strat tried not to notice how tired his partner
and left-side leader looked. In the light of the flaring leaf,
the dark circles under Crit's eyes seemed to dominate his
face, the lines around his mouth were deeper, his forehead
was crisscrossed with furrows. Strat had been careful not to
argue with Crit lately; though he might survive it, it wasn't
going to do any good.

Handing the smoke back to his leader, Strat inclined his
head toward the party in progress, its laughter and music
spilling out into the courtyard through open doors. "Let's
go, Crit. Maybe Tempus needs us in there."

"Maybe the sapphire toads that bought passage out of
the free zone for some of the worst criminals in town will
turn back to warty flesh and hop away," Crit said cynically,
but came along with no further urging.

Critias's problems in Tyse stemmed as much from a
flaw in his character as from the town itself: Crit didn't
know how to fail, never gave up on an operation in progress, couldn't turn away from a job—even an impossible

one. Worse, he couldn't say no to Tempus. And Tempus was asking Crit to sort out the bad apples in a barrel which increasingly seemed to contain nothing but.

Not only had Tempus decreed that Crit must officiate as his first officer of record and liaison with the garrisons, but also work with Sync and his 3rd Commando, although the forty fighters billeted at the northern garrison were here as much to prove their superiority to Stepsons as to assist their founder in his endeavors.

Perhaps Crit could have done it if Kama hadn't been in the picture, but the woman was 3rd Commando first and woman second. When the 3rd came into town, she'd picked up and moved in with her unit, leaving Crit with all the problems she'd caused him and nothing to make it worthwhile.

So Crit had thrown himself into an operational tizzy, trying to turn up the culprits responsible for the destruction of the governor's float and prove that Grillo had been up above the pass when the Caronne caravan came through it *not* to preserve order or capture insurgents, but to give the Stepsons tit for tat in repayment for a shipment of Grillo's that Crit had interdicted earlier in the season.

The only cure for Crit's troubles, Straton was sure, would be a month or two out of town on long reconnaissance. When Strat had mentioned this to Tempus, the Stepsons' commander had said slyly, "I'm working on it."

Strat had chosen to take Tempus at his word, let the veiled promise buoy him as he'd sortied into the mageguild earlier this evening to collect Randal, who'd been sequestered there since parade eve and who, Crit had insisted, probably wouldn't come with anyone *but* Strat.

Now, as he and Crit reentered the embassy ballroom, Strat felt as if he were walking into a snake pit.

Everyone was there who shouldn't be: Niko, his leg healed and his witchy partner beside him in mageguild velvet and lace, was seated at the head table with the Machadi ambassador and Aisha, who might well be as guilty as her uncle of intrigue in Mygdon's behalf.

Strat, as chief interrogator, had produced from three different subjects the information that had led Crit to the

conclusion that the fat Machadi ambassador was a pawn of
Mygdonia: the girl's parents, the ambassador's sister and
her husband, hadn't escaped when the Mygdonian Alliance
conquered Machad. If the girl was personally involved,
Niko wasn't going to take it well. Right now he bent his
head to hers and smiled through a close-trimmed beard at
some private joke. Only Niko was fool enough to pretend
that any relationship could proceed normally in the middle
of this muddled, treacherous war.

Beside Niko's girl was Sync, the 3rd Commando leader,
dark and rangy in his formal panoply. Next to him sat Madame Bomba and her husband, a scarred veteran as tall and
stoutly made as Tempus. Then came Kama, with Grillo on
her left, and those two were getting on like old friends. On
Grillo's left was the Rankan lieutenant-governor, fair and
supercilious and vain; then Tempus and Jihan.

Crit had gone to Tempus earlier in the week and suggested that if Tempus was serious about quelling unrest in
the town, four assassinations would do the trick: Grillo, the
Machadi ambassador, Palapot the information-monger
from the souk, and Oman.

Tempus had replied, "Find another way." However, Crit
had not been willing to let the matter drop: he tried to tell
Tempus what Niko had learned from the Caronne caravan
master and while watching Oman's weapons shop. Tempus
had dismissed Critias abruptly, the first time Strat could
remember him ever having done so, and come later to
Straton wondering how deeply, in Strat's estimation, Crit
was involved with Kama and to what degree his association
with her might be coloring Crit's perceptions.

The whole situation made Straton very uneasy. Crit's
tenacity when on a trail was legend; eventually, the four
were going to end up dead, and most likely Crit would
deserve the credit.

So Strat was trying, as best he could, to keep four enemies alive while at the same time amassing incriminating
evidence against them all as he'd been bid.

Just as Strat and Crit reached their table, parallel to
Kama's, and Crit slid his chair back until it bumped the
wall, the Machadi ambassador rose, tapping his electrum

goblet with a two-pronged fork so that metal rang on metal and all fell silent, then joined him in a toast to "Tempus and his worthy fighters, every one."

Then, as luck would have it, Tempus proposed an end to "internal strife and the formation of a united front against our enemies, the foul Mygdonians and the Nisibisi adepts," and Straton noticed those who dared not drink to that one: Oman, present because of some accident of birth, Grillo, and their Machadi host himself—all had empty glasses or mouths to wipe or dropped cutlery to retrieve.

Neither Strat nor Critias noticed that Kama had leaned over to Madame Bomba and both had left the table to seek the ladies' lounge until, when music commenced and folk began to circulate, the two women approached Crit and Straton's table to take seats a local merchant and his wife had just vacated.

Crit had been watching another girl across the room who looked, to him, entirely too much like the witch Cybele, a/k/a Roxane, to be coincidence, and asked Straton what he thought: "Would she *dare*, Ace, come *here*, brazen as a free-zone whore? Or am I—?" He broke off in mid-sentence as Madame Bomba in red satin, her mighty breasts powdered and perfumed, sat down beside him and Kama, in gray silk loose enough to have accommodated any manner of weaponry or armor underneath, slid into a vacant seat opposite him.

Crit greeted Madame Bomba profusely, ignoring Kama.

So it was Strat who noted the red-rimmed eyes and fresh-scrubbed face of the 3rd Commando's unit historian, Strat who saw Kama flush, then blanch, then pick nervously at the table's soiled cloth, and Strat who had to bid her welcome and wish her well. But his training told him something was *not* well with this one; he'd never seen Kama flustered. He'd never noticed anything girlish about her before. Even enthralled and cursed and bleeding, blinded upon what might have been her deathbed, this woman had behaved like a fighter; Strat had always thought of her as one.

Yet the voice which returned his greeting was tremulous. Her eyes were too bright. Kama had been crying, he realized, and when she'd said, "A pleasant evening to you, Straton. It's good to see you both so well..." and trailed off into silence, he found himself wanting to pat her hand or ask her what the trouble was.

Instead he turned away, to join the other conversation in progress.

Madame Bomba was saying softly, "...better sort this out, Crit, right here and now, before we have a situation no boy of mine would want to have a hand in causing. Straton, would you leave us for a bit? My husband, there, has got a packet of goodies we brought along to lighten up the evening. Tell him—"

"Anything you've got to say, you can say in front of Straton," Crit said flatly, still ignoring Kama, who pushed back her chair, rising, and said, "This isn't going to do anyone a whit of good, Madame. I'm going. Forget I said—"

"Sit down, Commando, if you are one!" Madame Bomba's hand flashed out and Kama, her arm in a grip the strength of which Straton well recalled, sat back down in her chair.

Strat's tongue probed at the hole where a tooth had once been. "Whatever this is, I want no part of—"

"Strat, you move and you can find yourself another partner," Crit said through gritted teeth, his eyes more pleading than angry.

Strat didn't blame him: alone with these two women was something he wouldn't want to be.

"We're all settled in now?" Madame Bomba teased in a dry, unfriendly voice. "Good. You are a little less than brave, the lot of you. I'm disappointed. You're lucky, Critias, that I didn't go over your head with this. The sleepless one might not be so patient as I with rampant childishness among your ranks. Now Crit, give Kama a civil greeting. And you, Kama, say hello to Crit—you know him well enough."

The two ex-lovers mumbled polite phrases neither meant.

"That, I suppose, will have to do. Straton, I'm sorry you're here for this, but perhaps it'll be a help—perhaps you can talk some sense into your leftman's addled head."

"What? He's sensible enough, now he's quit of *her,"* Straton couldn't help but say.

"Marvelous." The Madame tsk'd and shook her head. "I *should* leave this to the Riddler, it'd serve you all right if I did."

Kama buried her face in her hands, elbows splayed upon the table.

The Madame indicated her. "Look at what you've done to her—a noble fighter, once, she was. Now she'll murder an innocent unborn on your account and carry a stain no valor can erase, all the way to heaven."

"Oh, no. That can't be . . ."

"You deny it's yours, Critias?" The Madame's mouth turned down in disgust. "There's ways to figure out . . ."

"Wait up," Strat interjected. "I don't understand . . . oh, yes I do. By Enlil's most holy privates, *is* she—?"

Kama seemed to shrink smaller. Her hands slipped down to expose her reddened eyes, then her nose, then her puffy lips. She said, "All I want is to be rid of it. Madame Bomba seems to think *you,"* she glared at Crit, "have some say in what I do with my own body. I told her you wouldn't give a damn. And she's told me that she can't help me abort—"

Critias put an elbow of his own upon the table and rested his forehead against his thumb and index finger. "Hold on now. Let me get this straight. *She's* pregnant; *you* think it's some business of yours or mine. Is that it, Madame?"

"Good boy, Critias," Madame Bomba nodded with a humorless grimace. "Now, let's do the decent thing and make the Riddler a grandfather, nice and legal. We can't have unwed parents of—"

"There'll *be* no baby, if I have to fall on my sword and kill us both." Kama choked, cleared her throat. "Can you see me at my post, or on my horse, big with child? Do you know how long and hard I've worked to earn the 3rd's respect and pay my unit dues? Crit, *tell* her you want no part of it . . . or me. Then it's done and I can go."

"Tell me it's mine, in there." Crit, raising his head, let

his glance flicker toward her belly.

Whack! The slap Kama gave Crit rang across the room and turned his head with its force, and other heads with the sound it made.

He rubbed his jaw and nodded. "All right. I get the point. Kama, I . . ." Crit blew out a long, slow breath. "I'd like to be consulted, help you with what*ever* you decide." His hands came up before she got a word out of her mouth. "Now, don't yell at me. The damage is done, if damage it is. It's my responsibility but it's your body, I know. Just let's go off and talk about it by ourselves. Can we do that? This is no place for the sort of things I'd like to say."

Kama's mouth closed, her fists unclenched. She nodded wordlessly and Critias, moving quickly, was around the table pulling back her chair before she could get up. "Strat, I'm sorry about the timing. What we started in the stableyard . . . you'll see it through? Use Niko and Witchy-Ears, over there, and some of our 'friends' from the 3rd Commando. Tell Sync I'll need his help."

"No problem," Strat said to Crit's retreating back, then turned away to Madame Bomba, who sighed and remarked, "That's how I like to see those two—arm in arm. Romance, Straton, my boy, is an area I've heard you Sacred Band pairs know as well as any woman." She winked to take the sting from her innuendo. "I'll be moving on now. Accompany me to my table and we'll have a little krrf to celebrate."

Straton went, not asking what it was that they were celebrating: Crit was in worse trouble, having gotten the Riddler's daughter pregnant, than Strat had thought him capable of engendering. And what was trouble for one, was trouble for both.

He'd had less qualms walking straight into the mage-guild to bring out Randal. And when he'd been escorted up deeply shadowed stairs to a tiny room by overly polite junior magelings, into a sulfurous mist and out again and face-to-face with Randal, Straton had only recognized the mage by his freckles and his prodigious ears.

Now, at the head table, Randal tugged on Straton's sleeve. Bending down, Strat said, "What is it, Stepson?"

loudly enough that all would know *he* was not intimidated by this fast-rising Hazard.

"Did you see that woman over there, Straton? Does she look to you," Randal lowered his voice, "like Cybele? Or am I the only one who sees it?"

"Yep. No. Crit saw it, too."

"Can we watch her, where she goes? Keep her away from Stealth?"

Taking orders from *Randal?* Straton bristled, then told himself that he had too many responsibilities this evening to let personal feelings intrude. *"You've* got legs, Randal. And eyes. And you're better qualified than any other to watch that one. Report to me when you've satisfied yourself. Crit's left me in command."

Randal nodded, his gaze weary, yet game. "I can't stay out here, in the open, away from my . . . work . . . too long, you realize. I'm vulnerable in ways you don't understand. I'll give it until morning. Then you'll have to come to *me.* You'll find me where you found me this evening, task force leader."

And that was that; the mage turned away.

Madame Bomba had her krrf out, which drew Tempus down to their end of the table, away from Sync and someone else who'd just slipped in, covered with trail dust. The stranger whispered to the Riddler and left again so fast that Strat was sure only he and the 3rd Commando leader marked it.

And when Tempus bent his head to snort the Madame's krrf through a golden straw, he said to Straton, "Bashir wants to see me—and Niko. We're leaving now for the high peaks. Where's Crit?"

Straton said casually, "Out in the garden with Kama."

Tempus nodded. "Bashir sent a homing hawk to Hidden Valley. He says it's urgent. You and Crit take care of things in Tyse while we're away. We won't be long. We'll take the Aškelonians and send back a message as to what the trouble is . . . two, three days."

"Fine with me, commander. Just let him—" Straton indicated Sync, who was regaling Niko's friend, Aisha, with some exploit or other while Niko, eyes half-lidded, looked

bored to a casual observer but actually studied Strat and
Tempus where they made their plans "—know that the
3rd's under our command for the duration . . . *if* we need
them. Otherwise, we'll be stepping on each other's toes
without you here to say who's doing what."

"I've done that already. But *you* deal with Sync; he and
Crit have Kama in dispute, and other problems. I'd talk to
Crit myself, but we've got to be off."

Straton agreed as if explaining this to Critias would be
easy. It wouldn't.

"Good man." Tempus clapped him on the shoulder with
one hand while he tugged on his own tunic with his other.
At that signal, Niko got up and threaded his way through
the crowd—going to get the horses, no doubt. "If for some
reason," Tempus said, "you haven't heard from us within
the alloted time, make use of Randal. *You* seem to be able
to come and go as you please at the mageguild."

Yet again Tempus had left Jihan in the lurch, alone
among his Stepsons and a clutch of mortals who neither
loved nor understood her.

She left the ambassador's party early and wandered,
distraught, among the jumbled streets. They were full of
filth and crowded. Why the humans here huddled together,
defiling one another and their environment, when just
beyond the city's limits land stretched green and beckon-
ing, Jihan could not understand.

Perhaps they were afraid to be alone.

She was not. After Tempus had left the party, Sync of
the 3rd Commando had propositioned her, either not
knowing who and what she was or hoping to show his
fearlessness in the face of it. She didn't know. Humans
were a puzzlement, though for Tempus's love she would
gladly become one. If that happened, then she would understand them.

Now she merely mingled with them, a bemused specta-
tor, taking note, but taking nothing she saw to heart.

At the party, Sync's proposal that they "get together for
a bit of fag-bashing, now that the Stepdaughters' den-

mother, Tempus, is gone," made no more sense to her than his vow to lay "the right hands of a hundred Rag-heads at your feet to prove my love."

Subsequently Randal had explained to Jihan that Sync was drunk, that "Rag-heads" was what the 3rd Commando called the Mygdonians who wore turbans rather than helmets into battle. But Randal had no time then for her wealth of other questions. "Meet me at the mageguild gates an hour before dawn," the slight Hazard had proposed. "Perhaps we can help each other, since our partners have left us both to our own devices."

Jihan fancied she'd heard in Randal's voice a touch of the resentment and loneliness she felt. Thus, she agreed. Then Randal had bustled off to other business and once again Jihan was alone, embedded in the human crowd like a fly in amber.

She'd drifted out onto the patio, seeking composure from the stars above, which never changed or turned away or played favorites, but gave their light equally to all, and thus she'd heard Kama and Critias, first arguing, then declaring love, fidelity, and passion in thickening voices. Kama was, Jihan learned, pregnant with Crit's child.

Weeping was foreign to Jihan; it still surprised her when water flowed from her eyes and her body gave up her mind to emotion's pain. But when the couple she could hear beyond the bushes began to sigh and murmur and then to gasp in pleasure, Jihan wept and wandered off into the deserted evening streets, letting her tears flow in the Lanes where none might see or ask her why.

It was she who should be pregnant, cooking up a child for Tempus within her human belly. What else was this equipment she'd been given for, and this life on earth she'd chosen, but to live most fully, to love and reproduce and bind the Riddler to her for eternity?

But Tempus would not accommodate her; her father had forbidden her (and, knowing Him, most likely Tempus, too) from earthly parenthood. The Mygdonian child she mothered was no substitute for a suckling babe. She'd not have Shamshi long, in any case. If Tempus had his way, the boy would be given back to his rightful parents; if not, time itself would take Shamshi from her. In the child's own eyes, he was fast becoming a man and even now treating her as if he were one.

Resentment rose within her, the fury of the undervalued. She strode the streets and kicked at garbage, piles of refuse from which rats ran. She'd even offered to give up her super-human attributes for Tempus, to make him love her more. He wouldn't have it; her finest gift he had refused.

She froze a rabid dog who leaped from shadows, mouth dripping foam as it sought to bite her. Its blood now solid ice, it shattered as it hit the ground.

Jihan strolled on, turning left onto Mageway, and as she did she heard a sound, spun around in time to see Grillo and some others from the party headed south by southwest, toward the old amphitheater on the outskirts of Tyse.

When she reached the mageguild, Randal was waiting under a torch set in the gate. His face was flushed and his words came fast. "Froth Daughter, if you'll join me, lend a hand, we'll sneak up on the witch—I think it's Roxane . . . I'm almost certain—and identify, maybe foil, her allies. Think of it! You and I, doing what the Stepsons couldn't! Tempus and Niko will take us more seriously, after this. What do you say, Jihan?"

She noticed then that Randal's right hand rested on a kris slung at his hip, that his pale young face was pinched and his eyes sparkling.

"You can't do it without me, is that it?"

"Yes. No, I can't. Wouldn't dare to try. I've got to be back here to meet with Straton by sunrise. My globe . . . it's given me hints, but it takes its toll. If I leave it and some other power should snatch it from its place while I am absent, then they've got me. I'm attached to it, you see— Never mind." The mageling shook his head. "If you don't want to show the Riddler what you're made of, we'll leave the honor and the glory to Straton and his crew."

"Straton! Never! Honor and glory, you say, Adept? Lead on. When next I meet the sleepless one, I'll speak to him in language even he can understand."

* * *

In the ancient amphitheater, old when even Roxane had been young, she'd met her human allies: Grillo, here against his better judgment; Oman, who had none to go against; the Machadi ambassador, who fretted and paced to and fro and looked at her accusingly, that she would risk him, flaunt him openly where all could see; nearly thirty other rebels, some here because they fought for freedom, some—like the Machadi and the Rankan, Grillo—because they had no choice.

Then there came her unnatural allies—her friends and contract demons, her undeads, two full score.

The Riddler was gone upcountry, taking Niko with him. Now was the time to strike terror into Tysian hearts, take the Stepsons down a peg, send the 3rd Commando running, tails between their legs. For Lacan Ajami's army was closing; soon enough, despite the cloaking spells of her fellow sorcerers headed south, they'd be sighted. By then, the town must be ripe for conquest, inclined toward capitulation.

All this she told her gathered flunkies while, above, two young Nisibisi mages who'd flown in early with messages from Lacan glided, circling upon the predawn's gentle air currents, their hawks' eyes fixed on the surrounds to give her early warning should any uninvited folk intrude.

Tonight, much earlier, she'd dared to join the embassy festivities, brashly donning her Cybele form to see what Niko's response might be.

But the dream lord had his hooks in Nikodemos deeply, so much so that he'd either not remembered her, or been able to ignore his formerly obsessive attraction to Roxane's Cybele persona.

She fumed, reviewing her troops and giving orders. This coming evening, they would burn the northern barracks, where the 3rd billeted, to the ground. And Hidden Valley, too, would flame and smoke, horses roasting—for there Shamshi languished under guard. This second task she assigned to Oman, who was fearless, the one among these human pawns who knew he'd nothing left to lose.

The Machadi ambassador, whose niece sucked up to Niko, would suffer for the girl's audacity. Aisha, like all Machadi slime, fervently believed in an ancient mother goddess, and aspired to be a priestess—not just of Niko's heart, but of the Order of the Earth. As such, Roxane speculated, she'd been a perfect foil for Aškelon to interpose between the witch and her beloved Nikodemos, who boasted Aškelon's protection though the fighter neither knew or wanted it.

She was just about to materialize a plethora of incendiary pellets, fireballs-to-be, and conjured wagons with drays of awful aspect for her minions to drive rampaging through the town when, above, a hawk cried, then another, and both came plummeting to earth to burst apart with a sound like shattering crystal as they landed at her feet.

Before Roxane could pretend that nothing untoward was happening, a demon shouted, "Attack! Take cover, mortals! The rest of you, fan out and find our foes!"

Thereupon others, fire demons from the earth's bowels, took wing, their breath already steaming and their jaws agape to incinerate the murderers when they found them.

Human women screamed as, from a blue-and-purple sky, a roiling cloud descended, black and lit intermittently with bolts of lightning forking down to land right in their midst.

Fiends cackled as the first humans flamed, forgetting their own peril to crouch over fresh-roasted flesh and lick their chops and eat.

A mortal's throwing star, the sort of weapon Niko used, came flashing by her ear; she lost a lock of hair to it and this, at last, convinced her that her person was in danger. Until then she'd thought to calm the crowd and form a cogent plan.

The lightning struck again, snaking around her feet in a full and vicious circle. In its light she saw the Machadi ambassador, robe lifted high, fleeing for his life.

Then the first fire-breathing demon, and his brothers, swooped, and the entire amphitheater blazed as antique wood caught fire.

Running from the deadly conflagration, Roxane caught sight of Oman, his back afire, rolling hysterically in the dirt.

Then above her head the clouds opened up in an attempt by her unseen enemy to douse the demons' flames with a downpour so fierce it beat the fire demons from the sky.

Howling humans and hissing undeads stumbled through the fire and smoke. Roxane saw, as she changed into her eagle-form and took wing above the carnage, that the demons had tried to trap in a fiery circle the adversaries who had brought the lightning and cast the throwing stars and deluged everything with rain.

But only two figures were in the circle of flame: one was slight and robed like a magician; one was feminine but sturdy, overlarge and glowing. And as Roxane watched from high above, all her minions, soaked with rain, began to slow, then stop, then freeze in place as frost and ice encased them and they tumbled over, toppling to the ground to lie there stiff and cold.

Then, when she attempted to spiral down, to dive and pull the encircling net of flame in and over her two audacious enemies, the mage got out a paltry, wriggly sword. And just before the flames would have met above the heads of these two accursed enemies, he spoke a power word and waved the sword. The flames parted, obedient to the sword's command, so that those two walked calmly out of danger on a charred but no longer fiery path.

Roxane screamed her eagle's scream and in her fury dived straight down at the adept who dared defy her, though it might singe her wings to claw out the offending rival's sorcerous eyes or snatch the charmed and hostile weapon from his hand.

But she hadn't counted on the woman-form, whom her eagle eyes now recognized. Jihan, the hateful spawn of Stormbringer, raised her pointing finger Roxane's way and all the blood coursing through her eagle-body turned to ice, so that she plummeted, out of control, into the raging flames with one final, defiant scream of fury which could not form itself into a curse when issuing from a mere eagle's mouth.

Frozen, she fell. Falling, she burned. Burning, she hated. Hating, she hit the ground.

Crit had brought Kama, at Straton's urging, with them to the mageguild gates at dawn.

Strat had suggested that Randal could help with Crit and Kama's joint dilemma. Not sure that he wanted any help, Crit still had to try it: if it were *he* who had a child growing inside him at so inopportune a time, he'd want what Kama wanted. He couldn't take it lightly that she wouldn't bear his child, but he couldn't blame her. She was 3rd Commando first. He'd always understood this.

Morose and full of conflicts of morality and honor, he shifted from foot to foot, leaning against the mageguild's marble-columned gate, leaving it to Strat to fill an awkward silence with small talk and help Kama pass the time.

He wished she'd reconsider; maybe she would, yet. If Crit could face the Riddler's disapproval—perhaps his wrath—then Kama could survive the snickers of her unit. Crit didn't see why she couldn't have their child and raise it with him, bravely, honorably. If the 3rd cast her out instead of giving her a few months' leave, he'd put her in his own contingent.

But because of Straton, who meant well but wasn't helping, they hadn't had a chance to talk about it when Randal, his robes askew and his face black as a chimney sweep and sweating, came hurrying up from somewhere with Jihan, her eyes aglow and her laughter hearty, on his right.

"Task force leader!" Randal chortled. "Straton! What a stroke, you've brought Critias along. We've won! We did it! Jihan and I, we've finally done it. Got her! Congratulate us!"

"Won what? Did what? Got whom?" Crit demanded before Straton or Kama, back to the wall and face in shadow so no one could see her puffy eyes, could say a word.

"The witch! Roxane . . . you know . . . *Cybele!* You saw her at the party, Crit!" Randal rubbed his hands together. "Jihan was marvelous! Freezing rain and thunder claps and lightning from the heavens! What a team we made! If *only* Stealth was there to see it."

"If only Tempus was," Jihan added huskily, and Crit saw that her chest was heaving under scale-armor smudged with smoke.

"Let me get this straight: you routed Roxane . . . Cybele, if they're really one and the same. Where? How? And why, without my orders?"

"Why?" Randal, his feelings hurt, nearly howled. *"Why?* We've a trifling bit of trouble with hostile magic, if you'll recall, task force *leader*. Or are you too caught up with . . . problems . . . of your own creation to remember that?"

Then Straton hastily explained, rubbing his neck as he spoke and with a rueful expression on his face. "I ordered Randal to follow the witch—or whatever it is: Cybele, the one we saw at the party. Tempus, when he left, said he'd told you that for the interim I was to take command. . . ." Strat's face screwed up; he shook his head.

". . . of our joint ventures with the 3rd, that's all. You've overstepped. You know it, Strat, from the look of you.

"Randal," Crit turned upon the Hazard, "since when do you take orders from my right—"

"Critias! Straton!" Jihan intervened. "We have seen the witch, in eagle's form, fall into a cleansing flame. We have seen the end of Oman, the revolutionary, seen him die afire, caught him in the act of plotting evil with a bunch of demons, fiends, white-eyes, and human traitors. We have seen that the Machadi ambassador, and our old friend Grillo, were present among our enemies, though those two got away. A compliment or two would be in order. Praise for our valor, a *medal*, or some such token of esteem that I can show the sleepless one when he returns." Jihan's fists, upon her hips, uncurled and her fingers tapped. "Individual initiative, when the results are good, surely won't be penalized by *you*." She stared at Crit and he felt his flesh begin to cool.

He raised a hand to fend off her freezing glance. "I didn't mean that, Froth Daughter. You did very well, just fine. We'll have a ceremony, some sort of honors assembly, so that everyone will know. Now, let's hear the whole tale, slowly, and in full detail. We'll see where we can go from here. The Machadi ambassador was there, you say? And escaped?"

Kama cleared her throat then.

Crit had nearly forgotten her. He said, "Ah . . . Randal, I've got to talk to you alone."

"Good." The Hazard eyed the sky, where purple was giving way to pink and gold as the sun began to rise over the mountains. "I've got to be indoors and with my globe quite soon. I can't go with you anywhere, not now, and all of you can't come inside—I don't own or run this mage-guild, only work here."

Taking Randal aside, Crit said quickly, "It's Kama. She's pregnant and doesn't want to be. Just a little; it's not too late to do something. If you could help us . . . I'd be grateful."

"A little? Piff. Critias—*sir:* that's not my line."

"But surely you could—"

"Murder, by any other name. . . . Not right now, not me. But I'll send someone around to see her who hasn't got a globe and stand. . . . And, Critias," Randal added as Crit, with a grunt that meant he should have known better, turned away to hide his relief. "Are you *sure* you want to do this?"

"Me? No. But she is." He turned back. "Now, let's get down to business. Give me your expert, wizardly opinion of how best, in Tempus's absence, we might proceed."

Roxane had been thawed by the flames, protected to some extent from immolation by the ice within her veins. But more than her pride was singed. She'd had just enough of her wits about her to avoid capture or death at the hands of Tempus's unnatural whore, Jihan, and her warlock partner, Randal.

Roxane hadn't been able to remove herself from the battlefield, only to make her eagle's body invisible. And she'd had to lie there on the blackened ground until they'd gone away.

Then there was a grisly interval, before she had strength enough to change out of her wounded, broken eagle-form, during which she hopped about, eating the wounded and the newly dead—hearts and souls, where she could find them.

The sun was high above the peaks before she had the energy to transform herself—this time into a lowly sparrowhawk. She'd heard men and horses coming. Though this form was weak, she managed to take wing.

Out of harm's way on a laurel branch, she watched the soldiers root among the wounded and the dead.

When these were gone, she alighted on the ground and shifted shape again—a bleeding human arm dangling useless at her side was less troublesome than a torn and dislocated wing—and trekked in woman's form, still weak with pain from burns and loss of blood, to the first human habitation she could find.

This was a farm or small estate and the folk there took her in, believing her tale of attack by sorcerous insurgents, for they'd heard the thunder and the screams and seen the lightning and the smoke. By nightfall she would have strength enough, thanks to the tender care given her by the farm manager's plump and solicitous wife, to suck the souls from the human fools who tended her.

In the meantime she rested, just a wounded, luckless girl from Tyse, planning her revenge.

Straton and Sync had spent all day following up last evening's leads: they'd investigated the carnage out at the ancient amphitheater, a place which gave Strat chills. There they'd found the hoofprints of Grillo's horse and others Crit and Straton had marked.

Sync's horse, too, had a glyph filed into its iron shoe. When Sync realized it, Strat had had to tell the 3rd Commando leader how it got there. To his relief, Sync had only shrugged and said, "Well, that's one less we've got to track."

Six of Sync's 3rd Commando rangers had been drafted to aid what Crit referred to as the "cleanup." Whatever

Randal had said to the task force leader when they went off alone hadn't eased Strat's partner's mind. Years with Crit made it easy for Straton to tell that his partner was preoccupied. Crit wasn't going to be much good to anyone but Kama until this personal problem was satisfactorily resolved.

So Strat stepped in without a word to fill the gap; he'd done it often enough before.

With Sync, he passed the time relating tales of wizard wars he'd known, in Sanctuary and other places. The Stepsons' tour in Sanctuary had made them experts on sorcery and undisputed masters of endurance. The 3rd had pulled no duty which could compare in terms of hardship with sorting out the foulest town in empire. Sanctuary veterans lorded it over other mercenaries that they'd survived there. Strat had hated the town when he'd had to live there, but now that he'd left, he found it was the sort of place it was handy to be able to say that one had been.

At the end of one particularly grisly story, Sync remarked that, these days in Sanctuary, there was nothing to revere in those who bore the unit designation "Stepson."

Not wanting to fall into any trap of Sync's, Straton let this pass. They'd traced Grillo's horse's prints as far as the double-dealer's home in Outbridge. Short of going in there to arrest him, there was nothing more that they could do.

Oman's horse, however, its owner dead, had bolted on its own and made its way into the souk. They lost its track whenever it crossed a cobbled street like Embassy Row or Broadway, then picked it up again in the dirt and clay of the alleyways.

The souk was a hard place to track any animal; its clay was a palimpsest of wheel- and hoof- and footprints. But one of Sync's cadre was lounging on his horse near Palapot the horse trader's stalls and Strat found out the man had been on duty since last night. "Come to relieve me, sirs? After that fracas at the amphitheater, I don't think I'll sleep for weeks. I'd just as soon stay here—common folk making common mischief's more my style than demons and lightning bolts and what-have-you."

So it turned out that they had an eyewitness to what

went on in the amphitheater. Strat proposed outright that they take the ranger to Crit without delay.

"Don't you want this Palapot?" The ranger had said that he'd followed Oman's wall-eyed chestnut here and that the horse was presently inside Palapot's grooming tent, "probably having his blaze dyed brown and his mane dyed black."

"Wait here." Straton dismounted and went inside.

Palapot remembered Straton only too well. The horse-trader tugged on his greasy pigtail and his face turned white.

"Want to come talk to me in the Lanes, Slime? Or can we do it here, without theatrics?"

Palapot fairly stuttered, falling over himself in his eagerness to please. Grooms were sent packing and tent flaps tied.

Strat took a stylus from his beltpouch: this confession would be one he'd want to have in writing. If it were good enough, and implicated folk enough, maybe it would shake Crit out of his funk.

Aisha's uncle had come to her, his eyes wild and his long gray hair disheveled so that it no longer covered his balding pate, but hung in strings about his face, saying, "My dear, I have to talk to you. In here."

And when they were in the ambassador's study, musty and warm and cluttered with folios, he said, "That young man of yours, Nikodemos—how well do you know him? How far would he go to help a relative of yours?"

"Uncle, I don't understand."

Sinking into the chair behind his desk, her uncle poured himself Machadi brandy from a stoppered jug, for the first time in Aisha's memory offering her strong drink. "Have some. You'll need it. And never mind why, child—just answer me."

"Nikodemos . . . left the party last night abruptly." She sipped the brandy. "He didn't even say goodbye. I might have offended him, paying so much attention to Sync. I . . . don't know. But I'm sure, if it's important, he'll help as best he can. He's a man of honor, one of impeccable—"

"But can he keep his mouth shut, respect a confidence, listen to a proposal and keep it to himself if he can't help or doesn't think it workable?"

Aisha shifted. She was fascinated by Niko. He'd come to her in a dream and taken her by the hand and together they'd approached, by boat, a glowing city on a pacific island from which wondrous music came. He'd been in his best armor, and it had been glowing. She'd been dressed in a wedding gown. A tall and dignified man with silver-starred hair in regal robes had greeted them at quayside. They'd been so happy . . . And *then*, she'd met Nikodemos. The very next night, her uncle sent her down to make sure the Stepson and his partner weren't out to harm the Mygdonian prince who'd been visiting at the embassy. Her uncle's actions, she knew, were dangerous; but what action was not, these days? Her parents languished in a Mygdonian prison camp. Whatever had to be done to keep them alive, both she and her uncle would gladly do.

She said, "This won't get Niko into trouble? Or hurt him? He'll never go against his commander's wishes—Tempus is like a father to him."

"Girl, just answer me: can you arrange a private meeting—him and me. Yes or no?"

"Yes . . . I think so. Yes, I'll try."

Blinking back tears for whatever might have been between them, thinking she'd never be Niko's bride on her honeymoon in the golden city now and that this war was ruining her life, no doubt about it, Aisha got up to go, to change, to set out brazenly to compromise the one she loved for reasons she was not supposed to understand.

When the Machadi girl came riding into Outbridge on a flashy sorrel horse, Crit was up to his ears in trouble. Randal had rushed in not an hour earlier, saying, "Crit! Did you find Roxane's corpse? Or any trace of her?"

"Randal, can't you remember even an occasional 'sir'? In front of my men, at least?" Crit had been with several Stepsons and two 3rd Commando rangers in the courtyard when Randal interrupted. Thinking Randal had come about

Kama's plight, he'd left them in mid-conversation. "Did you find someone?" he demanded of Randal. "Or have you changed your mind and decided to do it yourself?"

"Find someone? Mind? Oh, Kama. By the Writ, *sir*, that doesn't matter *now*. I took a nap, just a doze actually, and when I awoke, this message was scrawled in blood on my power-glyph, this high—" Randal held one hand over his other, a foot apart "—on the mosaic foor." The Hazard closed his eyes and repeated verbatim: "'Thy doom, foul magician, is sealed. One by one your friends will suffer until you beg me for your well-earned punishment." And it was signed, 'Roxane.' Now, answer my question: *did* you find her corpse, some trace of her?"

"No. Strat went out himself and took a look. But what is the big surprise? You got yourself into this, you and Jihan. You solve it. If my problems aren't important to you, what do you expect from me, Hazard?"

Randal looked peeved. "You still don't understand. She got *into* the *mage*guild, somehow. She was *there!* Cut through all our wards like cheese. It's a wonder I've still got my globe."

Crit smiled knowingly. "I didn't want you to have that globe in the first place. I knew it would come to no good. And if she was there, why didn't she take your precious globe? You're imagining things—or she's content with scaring you to death."

"You're not going to do anything? It's your responsibility, taking care of Stepsons and the town while Tempus is away."

"Tell me what to do. Against a witch. When *you* can't handle it. If your knees stop knocking, maybe you can conjure your way out of this mess you witched yourself into. It's not my problem, as long as Kama's not yours. Now get out of here. I've got urgent matters to attend to. And don't come back until you've a magic potion or some damn spell to help the Riddler's daughter. Failing that, you and I are quits."

Later, Crit was sorry he'd been so hard on Randal, but he didn't have time to think about it just then. Strat wanted to arrest Grillo on the strength of Palapot's confession,

though for Straton, Palapot would have confessed to being
the archmage Datan himself, risen from the dead. The saf-
est thing to do would be, Crit thought, to bring in the
widow Maldives, Grillo's bedmate, and see how Grillo
reacted. Personally, Crit wanted to leave Grillo where he
was, untouched, until Tempus returned. The two were old
friends; it wasn't Crit's place to lock up or put into Straton's eager hands someone Tempus was still trying to protect.

Crit was explaining this to Sync without letting too
much slip or allowing the commando to think the Stepsons
were protecting Grillo when Aisha galloped through the
gates on her sorrel, ignoring orders from the gatewatch to
halt for identification and almost getting herself speared.

"Stay here, Sync."

Crit approached her alone, reaching up to take her
heaving horse's bridle. "Aisha, isn't it? To what do we owe
the honor?"

"Niko . . . that is, I've come to see Niko. It's urgent."

"I imagine it is." Arms out to help her down, he continued: "But Niko's not here. Will I do?"

She shrank from his touch. "Not here? Oh, no. What
will I do? When will he be back?"

"Don't know. Can't say. If it's really as urgent as all
that, why don't you let me help you? I'm Niko's commanding officer, after all. Anything you could have said to
him, you can say to me—unless it's intimate, of course."

"It's not. It's. . . ." Then, suddenly, she slipped off her
horse, almost into his arms. As if she'd stumbled, she
leaned against him, whispering, "My uncle wants to talk to
someone in authority. I have a message, but it's meant for
Nikodemos. If I give it to you, you must promise to tell no
one, keep it confidential. . . . Oh, Goddess! What if I'm
doing the wrong thing?"

"You're not. Let's see it." With a gentle demeanor Crit
reserved for horses and street men given impossible as-
signments in the field, he rushed her: if she had time to
think, she'd get back on her horse and ride away. It had to
have something to do with last night's escapade at the old
amphitheater.

The message she carried, when he'd broken the Machadi embassy seal, said, "I want to discuss sensitive matters regarding the Mygdonian forces here and abroad. Come alone. Be prepared to offer assurances of safety for myself and my family." And it was signed in the ambassador's own hand.

"Stay right here. I'll just get my horse." As he spoke, Crit took a flint from his pouch and ostentatiously burned the parchment, turning it in his fingers. "Don't worry, Aisha. Niko, if he truly wanted to help you, would have turned this over to me in any case."

"Really? Oh, good." She let him boost her up on her horse and waited while he extemporized a likely explanation to Sync and his own mount was brought. The ambassador was right: nobody should know about this but the principals involved.

It took only a few minutes to reach the embassy at speed, but when Crit and the girl got there, servants were running hither and yon and three garrison soldiers were at the embassy door talking to guards who looked very unhappy.

Only Critias's rank got them in the door at all, and then one of the garrison soldiers accompanied them, saying, "Now, don't touch anything. Nothing whatsoever, sir."

"I know the drill," Crit snapped.

The soldier, unfazed, continued, "It's pretty bloody in there—nothing for a lady's eyes."

"I want to see him," Aisha said dully, her fingers digging into Crit's arm.

She was tough enough, he saw when they entered the room and viewed her uncle's disemboweled corpse. She didn't retch or cry or faint, just stood there; but Crit could feel her trembling and had to disengage her. "Stay here, Aisha. You've proved your love. He wouldn't want you to see him like this."

The smells of death and the apparent pleasure someone or something had taken in killing this man mixed to make even Critias, a field veteran, woozy in this close and shuttered space. The word "Traitor!" was scrawled on one wall in Machadi; other, nastier epithets in Nisi were appended.

Crit hoped Aisha couldn't read them.

So much for an informer in the witch's confidence. More than anything else, Crit was disappointed. The ambassador's offer was the luckiest break he'd had all season.

He took the girl with him, bought her lunch in a cafe on Embassy Row to see if she might prove useful, but she knew no more than the "whys" of her uncle's entanglement with the insurgents and the Nisibisi witch.

Nevertheless, he took Aisha back to Outbridge with him. Though one more skirt was the last thing he needed to worry about, this one was Niko's, by her own admission. It occurred to him she could be another Nisibisi witch or some phantasm of Roxane's making; but if that were so, Randal would soon discover it—and one way or the other, he'd want to keep Aisha under surveillance for a while.

By dusk, in his mageguild tower room, Randal had finished scrubbing the defilement from his power-glyph and reinstating and rebuilding protective wards and consecrating spells.

He hadn't eaten, he hadn't slept since the one fateful nap he'd taken. He sat on his glyph in rumpled robes and nearly wept with distress: he should really tell the archmage what had happened, that the mageguild had been breached. But he just couldn't. The whole, horrible mess was his fault.

He'd repaired the damage, he hoped. If not, until he'd regained enough composure to consult his globe and meditate upon how to proceed, what he'd done would have to do.

His kris lay on the tiles nearby and suddenly it began to rattle. He reached out and picked it up, stroking it and crooning to it as a man would soothe a child or a jumpy pet.

But his kris wouldn't be calmed; it rattled more. At last, he put it on.

Maybe Niko was right; maybe the sojourn to Meridian was the worst, and not the best thing that had ever happened to them both. But he didn't believe it, couldn't believe it. Anything worth having exacts a price. Stealth knew that. Randal had learned it long ago.

He wished his partner hadn't gone off with Tempus, then chided himself: he was beginning to think like a Sacred Bander, and *that* was something he dared not let himself become. It was bad enough that everyone thought he and the fighter known as Stealth had a much more intimate relationship than in fact they did.

Randal was a mage sworn to his calling, the more so now that true Hazard status was his. He'd never guessed that his relationship with Nikodemos would bring such a conflict of interest, or such a peril, or, if the truth be known, such great opportunities. But Tempus had. Tempus had arranged the pairing—ordered it.

Tempus, though inscrutable at times, was seldom wrong.

A soft knock upon his door interrupted the mage's reverie, and when he opened it, the First Hazard of Tyse stood there, his wizened form drawn up tall and straight as a flagpole.

The nameless adept fixed Randal with a dark and piercing stare. "We trust that all's well with thee, young Randal?"

It was a question, no doubt of that. "Oh, fine. Very well, thank you, master Hazard. And yourself?"

The old adept's sharp nose had sniffed something— probably Randal's fearful, acrid sweat. "Curious, Randal," said the First Hazard, "curious as to how you've been faring and all the unexplained comings and goings of late." The First Hazard craned his scrawny neck and peered over Randal's shoulder, within, where the globe of high peaks clay winked softly in a single candle's light. "Have you unlocked its secrets yet? Or is it unlocking yours?"

"Half and half, my lord. Would you like to come in?" There was nothing for it but to invite the mageguild's highest official inside; it was obviously what the First Hazard wanted. But it was the last thing Randal wanted.

The old man sighed deeply. "Another time, I'm afraid.

You have a guest. Downstairs. A guest of the sort we'd prefer not to have within these walls, but one, you'll agree, we'd best accommodate this time. Randal, if you intend to keep company with the secular and the damned, do it elsewhere from now on. You're disturbing wizards' work and most likely jeopardizing your own advancement here."

"May I ask, my lord, this guest's name?"

"Shamshi, the Mygdonian, and he's blue as a sorcerer, if one uses one's eyes. I'd like to suggest that you not bring him up here—rather, take him somewhere more . . . neutral . . . for this meeting. Furthermore, though I hate to do this, it's come down to it: us or them. Either you terminate your association with these soldiers to whom you've sworn spurious oaths of brotherhood, or take your word seriously and move out of this mageguild."

"My lord!"

"You do understand, then. Your career, promising as it may be, is on the line. We can't have these sorts of disruptions. Them or us, make your choice. Today. I'll be waiting in my office. Other wizards could use this room to good advantage, and without putting the rest of us in danger."

"So you know what's been happening. I was afraid of that."

"Not afraid enough to come to me and honestly explain yourself. Conflict of interest in an adept doesn't last long —he dies of it. For your own good, Randal, quit the Stepsons. Cleanse yourself for a month or so; I'll help you. You've nothing more owed to those god-loving murderers; they *will* destroy you, if you let them." The bald head on its scrawny neck seemed to retreat into the shoulders below like a snapping turtle's into its shell. "Oh, and by the way: we don't do abortions here. Permission denied. If your friends can't own up to the results of their lust, then send them to Peace Falls; there are abortionists on Commerce Avenue, I've been told."

Speechless, Randal watched as his First Hazard glided away, fading as he retreated so that he never turned the far corner, but dematerialized before he reached the head of the tower stairs.

Shamshi? Here? It must be, Randal thought, that Jihan was in trouble.

And when he found the boy, sitting on the mageguild's outer steps with a wan face and dirty nails, this was exactly what Shamshi told him: that Jihan had gone into Frog's Marsh and not come out, so Randal would have to help Shamshi find her.

"I can't. I'm sorry, but I can't. She'll be all right. She can't die, you know. Don't worry. And don't go there yourself. Whatever you think your budding powers have shown you might just be a witch's trick." Randal patted the boy on the head and for a moment, as he caught those pale and guileless eyes, hatred and bloody hunger seemed to lurk in them.

Randal's kris, under his hand, quivered like a living thing and tried to jump out of its scabbard. He held it firmly.

"Come now," the boy said, imperious, insistent.

"No, I've told you, I can't." Randal wasn't going to try to explain to Shamshi that the child had put him in a very difficult position by coming here. He sent Shamshi off with a swat upon his buttocks and climbed the stairs, not for a moment realizing that by doing so he'd saved his own life and foiled Roxane once again.

Riding up to Bashir's high peaks keep with Tempus, Niko felt like a boy again, following his left-side leader without question, free from doubt and confident of the man in front of him as he hadn't been since his original leftman had died and he'd found himself leading pair after doomed pair into magical battles he wasn't qualified to win.

How easily he'd slipped back into his accustomed right-man's slot; maybe he never should have rejected Tempus's offer, back in Sanctuary after his first partner had died, to ride on the Riddler's right. But then he thought of Janni, who'd trusted him and died of it. To denigrate his own performance as Janni's left-side leader was to belittle Janni's valor. This, Niko was not capable of doing; he still honored the memories of both his perished partners.

Following the Stepsons' commander up Wizardwall along trails Niko had known since his youth evoked conflicting emotions.

He'd been bound here in servitude to the Nisibisi archmage Datan, a year of horror so unrelenting he recalled little of it in detail. He'd become one of Bashir's father's Successors after that, and with Bashir had found true honor for the first time.

The guerrilla fighters of Free Nisibis had been high peaks bandits then. Bashir still thought of him as a brother, though time and Bashir's tutelary god, Enlil, had come between them. After the summer's war for Wizardwall, they had parted filled with melancholy, both men wishing the other was still the boy he used to love.

This time, it must be different. Tempus wanted Niko to talk some sense into Bashir. This wasn't always easy. The mountain bandit Niko'd known had grown into a warrior-priest who had the world's oldest and most bloodthirsty deity whispering in his ear.

Lord Storm—Father Enlil—was Niko's patron god once, too: but now there was Aškelon to be considered, and the panoply that Niko wore, the horse he rode, the dreams he had all signified that Niko served a different master these days.

Gods were jealous as a class, Enlil the worst of all. If the god gainsaid the bargain Tempus wanted Niko to make with Bashir, the warrior-priest would never go against Him.

But Niko couldn't fail the Riddler. Even if he must swear allegiance to a war god he'd outgrown and break his pact with Aškelon to assure Enlil's sanction, he'd do it. And if he did that, Niko knew, he might lose his rest-place and perhaps his soul forever. Easy come, easy go, he told himself. What lay ahead was fixed by the demands of honor, of solemn oaths given to the sleepless one who rode before him, calm, untiring.

What would he lose? A panoply which vexed him, which caused more trouble than it cured? Would it dissolve, or turn to normal stuff? Let it, then. And these two horses, who never stopped to rest, who never faltered, but loped peakward ceaselessly as if their hooves needn't touch the ground—would they turn into humble beasts who couldn't climb scree like mountain goats or soar across chasms like condors? If so, Niko was prepared to lose his sable mount. He'd already lost so much to Aškelon—his freedom, access to his rest-place where the shadow lord lurked in his every dream so that Niko wished he didn't have to sleep—he was prepared to lose the rest.

For Tempus—who knew Niko'd gotten entangled with Aškelon, yet during the long journey up to Wizardwall hadn't once rebuked or questioned him—Niko would do the impossible, or die trying, gladly.

When Bashir's forward sentries sighted them, Niko mentioned it: the wolf-calls announcing their arrival came from human throats. "Shall I give the countersign, say we're friends?" he asked, reining his mount abreast of Tempus's where the ledge widened and two horses could safely stand.

At Tempus's command he uttered a long and lonely wolf's howl which made the Aškelonian under him look around at him askance.

Above and straight ahead, the high peaks keep gleamed pinkish in the dusk, as much from Father Enlil's blessing as from the sun that set to their left. It wouldn't be long now; the way was clear and easier than it had been when they fought to take these marble towers. Bashir had built three bridges over rifts adepts had flown or spelled their way across. Checkpoints loomed above the spans, one of which was supported in the middle by a stone spire rising a hundred feet or more from a narrow canyon's floor.

A yipping, feral pup's response meant "Come ahead." He told his commander that and on they rode, across the Successor-crafted spans and up to the gates of the citadel.

The place still gave Niko gooseflesh: he had too many bad memories to believe that every demon here had been banished, all the evil exorcised.

As the thick pine gate winched down and the Aškelonians flattened their ears at the screeching sound,

Tempus asked, "Is there anything you want to tell me? Now's the time, if you've questions or confidences. There'll be none later."

"Commander? We've got to convince Bashir to join forces with us and the Rankan garrisons in Tyse, I know. Is there something else?"

Tempus sighed. "Not until you say so, Niko. Not, that is, beyond whatever it was that made Bashir so nervous that he'd send for me." Then the drawbridge spanning the last crevasse thumped into place and Tempus spurred his horse onto it.

The Aškelonians minced across the piney bridge with snorts of disapproval. Once on the other side of it, Successors crowded around to greet them both with hugs and whoops. Many remembered Tempus with fondness—he'd commanded the joint forces of Successors, Stepsons, and specials which had secured this place last summer. Others knew Niko from before; still others wished they'd been part of the elite squadrons Bashir had sent into that battle and looked with hungry eyes upon the Aškelonians and the heroes riding them.

It wasn't long until, their horses led away, they were ushered upstairs through halls whose elaborate ornamentation had been defaced: wherever demon lords or evil adepts had strode in bas relief, those heads and names had been chiseled away in hopes that the evil they represented would likewise be erased.

Niko smelled incense and bay leaves and myrrh and knew that the cleansing of this black marble palace was still going on. But Tempus, up ahead with one of Bashir's lieutenants, speaking low and climbing steadily, either didn't notice or didn't care.

Most Successors still slept outside in low black tents, Niko saw when they passed a tower window; many of the open chambers to his right and left still showed signs of the fire of this summer's sack. It seemed to Niko that blue phantom-flames still licked at the corners of these slick, cool walls that wouldn't burn. He could feel and almost see with his maat's eye the ghosts that lingered here, unresting, hostile—ghosts that never were quite human and now, in

death, resented the mortals who had banished them. To his
inner ear came sounds of anguish, wails of hopelessness,
and sobs of spirits in the throes of well-earned retribution.

He'd pulled back into himself, shutting down his senses
to an unaugmented mortal five, by the time they were
ushered into the presence of Bashir.

So Niko was unprepared for the worry scoring Bashir's
flat, dark, Nisibisi face when his friend, in humble hillman's trousers and a wrinkled tunic, straightened up from
the altar he'd been tending in a room where once Datan
summoned devils.

"Riddler! Stealth!" Bashir strode to them, embracing
first one and then the other. When it was Niko's turn, Bashir's arms lingered, tight about him, and the ritual touch
of cheek to cheek was full of something more than greeting—relief, perhaps, or compassion.

Disengaging, the Successors' leader said politely that it
was good of Tempus to come so quickly, then: "Shrivel
me, Stealth, you look tired. Even if our stalwart friend here
isn't, you're obviously in need of food and drink—and
rest."

So Bashir sent a hillman for refreshments and they went
out onto a rampart to enjoy the sunset.

While they were waiting, the guerrilla-priest said, "I
have a problem that concerns you. We'll ask Father Enlil's
help, then get down to business." Without waiting for
Tempus to agree and looking straight at Niko, Bashir
blessed them both with a smoking censer, sprinkled them
with "holy dust," and proffered goblets of the god filled
with pure spring water.

Ritual was ritual. *Priests will be priests,* Tempus's
glance said when Niko chanced to meet it. Gingerly,
Stealth took the goblet and sipped from it, half expecting
Aškelon to appear in a burst of light or the goblet to shatter
in his hand. But nothing untoward occurred, unless it was
that Bashir, with one more low-voiced adjuration, sat down
on the rampart's flags and crossed his arms, saying, "Now,
I know you're wondering, Tempus, why I asked you here.
Your sister came to visit me. When she appeared, I sent
word right away. I—"

"What?" Tempus thundered. "That's all I need. She's not *still* here, I hope?"

Niko settled down into a squat beside Bashir. The Successor replied, in Nisi, "I'm afraid she is," and Niko thought uncomfortably that he should have had the wit to warn Tempus that the Riddler's sister was intent on joining in the fight against Mygdonia. He felt small, incompetent, and foolish for having let his personal chagrin at being recruited by Aškelon interfere with his attention to duty.

"What's the matter, Niko?" Tempus had seen something on the Stepson's face. "We won't let Cime get her hooks in you."

Bashir, too, was looking at Niko. Stealth said dully, "I should have told you, commander, that she'd try to do this. I knew. I saw her on Meridian. If it's not too late, I could tell you what happened. . . ."

Out of the corner of his eye, Niko saw Bashir start at the mention of Meridian, and then he loosed his maat and felt it fan out wide. Despite the ghostly horrors hereabouts, Niko needed every bit of warning his expanded perceptions might provide.

"With Ash?" Tempus called the dream lord by a nickname only the Riddler and his sister dared employ. And Bashir looked from one guest to the other with a mixture of distress and distaste upon his face. "It's too late," Tempus declared. "I'll hear it all from her, no doubt."

"I'm sorry," Niko whispered.

"Don't blame yourself," Tempus said brusquely. "You didn't know. You've got troubles of your own. I had them, too, in younger days. It's not your fault, but mine, for involving you with a greedy entelechy and then assuming you could protect yourself. We'll solve—"

"Hold it, both of you. Have I got this right? Is Nikodemus yet and still possessed, in thrall to the regent of the seventh sphere? A slave of the hideous shadow lord?" Bashir's voice was lowering; it became a deep and almost godly growl. "If this is so, why did you wait so long to bring him to me? My friend," he turned to Niko, tears sparkling unshed in his eyes, "have faith. Enlil will fight a war for even your poor, tortured soul that will shake accursed Meridian to its very foundations, if you but reaffirm your oath to Him and—"

"Wait a moment," Niko said, an edge to his slow, deliberate words, "*I* made my choice. *I'll* live with it. Tempus has survived his godbond and his curse. You've flourished, Bashir, with a bloody Lord looking over your shoulder. I don't want to talk about it. And if the truth be known, commander," he turned to Tempus, "not only is it too late for you to step in and solve my problems, but I don't want you to mix in this. My rest-place hangs in the balance, and it's worth too much to me to lose just to make you or Bashir feel better. That's why I didn't say anything before."

Both the priest and Tempus were silent thereafter until the food came. By then Niko wasn't hungry. He'd had his fill of knowing looks and knitted brows and two men no better off than he—both contractees of supernal forces—trying to save him from a fate they'd both embraced.

He excused himself when the food was served, saying he was too tired to eat and sleep was what he needed, worried that this unfortunate row at the beginning of so sensitive a visit was going to make it impossible for him to help Tempus with Bashir—or anything at all.

Once Bashir had told Tempus that Cime was on Wizardwall, all things became clear to the Riddler. There was slaughter in the offing, wizards to slay, hell to pay, and hazards undreamed of ahead. Whenever she appeared to plague him, Cime brought all of these along with her as if they were her personal retinue.

And once Niko had retired, Tempus could be candid with Bashir. "My sister notwithstanding, I'd have made this trip in any case. You and I must make common cause: survival. Not just for ourselves, but for Free Nisibis, Tyse and her people, as well as your fighters and mine. Our first priority must be this: Free Nisibis and Tyse must continue to exist, no matter what."

"This is news? You keep Tyse safe, I'll see to Free Nisibis. I've told you before, I'll have no Rankans under my roof or my protection."

"You don't mean that. It's a different war now than the one they won against your father."

"You mean *you're* not fighting against me, so I can't lose. I don't believe things are quite that simple. Did you bring Stealth here to convince me to send my people out to die in behalf of the Tysians who wouldn't lift a finger to help us when—"

"You hate Rankans, you say, but Grillo's a friend of yours. True?"

Bashir nodded and Tempus could see his pulse beat in a neck thick with muscle. "We've helped each other," the warrior-priest admitted.

"He needs your help now. He'll lose the town. I'm pulling my forces out and we'll be leaving—"

"You," interrupted a voice from the doorway, feminine and sultry, "brother, are right, for once. It must be a coincidence, it can't be luck—you've long ago used up all of yours, and the god you serve is too craven and too weak to be telling you secrets, these days."

"Hello, Cime," Tempus said dryly, not looking away from Bashir. "To what ill fortune do we owe this visit?" But as he spoke he could feel her gaze boring into his flesh and her body calling to his. The old excitement he always felt in her presence rose up in him and he thought that, since the god of rape and pillage who once inhabited him was absent these days, perhaps he'd rape her and find out if the Storm God of the South was truly gone. If Vashanka wasn't imprisoned or incapacitated, the rape of Cime would bring Him back, full force. Thinking this, he bared his teeth.

She hadn't answered. She came around where he could see her. She was just as beautiful and arrogant as ever. He had to remind himself that she was, by pact and consent of everyone but him, the consort of Aškelon, the dream lord. And then he thought that if he dared, he could use this albatross in woman-form for good, this once: he could take her from Ash and make Ash release Niko to get her back.

So he rose up and, for the first time in years, of his own accord and with all the prodigious passion of his person, took his sister in his arms and kissed her. When he let her go, Bashir's eyes were downcast.

Chest heaving, Cime folded gracefully down into a cross-legged posture beside Bashir, where Niko so recently had been, and poured herself some Nisibisi blood wine with shaking hands.

Tempus sat, too, then, watching her, for once sure that he'd gotten the best of her, if only evanescently. Seeing Cime nonplussed was something he'd long dreamed of—as he'd wondered, off and on throughout the centuries, how it would have been for them if, in their youth, his father hadn't insisted that, despite all evidence, she was his blood relation, and given her over to an archmage to wed. From that unfortunate decision, born of passions between Tempus's father and his stepmother only those two understood, had come the curse on both the children, his involvement with the gods and hers with antisorcerous magic, a contradiction, he had often thought, in terms, but one which made her deadly to the adepts she stalked through all the years of time.

She was contrite now, and friendly; she'd gone into her seductress's act. This time, like as not, he'd let her have what she so dearly wanted. . . . *No!* He shook his head, realizing that she'd almost got to him, and said to her, "By the way, does this visitation mean the dream lord's on his way to fetch you? Have you escaped from him?"

Bashir muttered blackly, a petition to his god.

"Still afraid of Ash, my sweet brother? Don't be. He's on our side. He let me come. I'm here with his blessing to make sure you win *this* war *this* time. No one wants a botch of it. You never *finish* anything, your engagements just drag on and—"

"What war?" Bashir broke in, trying to follow a conversation which wasn't held in Nisi, or any one tongue, but a polyglot of dead and living languages brother and sister both knew all too well.

"What war? Oh, Bashir," Cime licked her lips, pretending concern, and ran a finger down his face from his flar-

ing cheekbone to his mouth. Then she patted his cheek
thrice saying, "Poor man. You've been so busy you haven't
had the time to look out your turret window, is that it? Or is
your god, Father Enlil, playing another one of his fearsome
games? Can it be that neither one of you has read the writing on the wall? That magic has conquered heaven one
more time? That you don't know?"

As Bashir demanded that she explain herself, Cime waved
a hand and on the far wall words in Nisi appeared, chiseled
by enchantment deep into the stone: *The Mygdonian army,
two divisions strong, approaches from the northeast.*

As one man, Bashir and Tempus jumped up and dashed
over to the crenelations, Cime's laugher echoing in their
wake. "You two should see how comical you look. . . ."

"There's nothing there!" Bashir glared back at her.

"Tsk, tsk, of *course* there is. You are just too blind to
see it, both of you."

She joined them, diamond rods taken down from her
hair and aglow in her hands, and pointed. "There, in the
far distance. Surely you can see them now, among yonder
hills where the trail is dark."

And they could, though without her ensorceled wands
no human eye could ever have discerned the Mygdonian
army so far away.

By the second night Niko wasn't sleeping well in Bashir's fortress. He was trying not to sleep at all: standing up
on one foot, then the other, in Bandaran exercise postures
that should have refreshed him in lieu of sleep, but weren't
working here. He'd catch himself when he began to fall,
prop his body against a wall, and start the whole procedure
over again. Stand on the right leg, left foot tucked up
against his groin; struggle for balance; gain it; let his head
fall back; lose consciousness; fall forward; catch himself
on his hands; straighten up and begin again.

The blue flames he'd seen licking at these walls and the
moans from hell he'd heard weren't visible or audible to
Tempus. Not even Bashir seemed to understand what Niko
was hinting at, and Nikodemos wasn't about to explain it

outright: he didn't want the Riddler or Bashir to think he'd lost his nerve or that his mind had snapped from too many brushes with witchcraft.

He found himself wishing that Randal were here, worrying that his partner might not come. Despite the Riddler's summons—sent by homing hawk to Tyse to marshal all their forces—one never knew with Hazards, though Niko's heart said that Randal wouldn't desert him.

Meditation soon became the only refuge left to Niko. His rest-place offered refreshment without the loss of consciousness; he could regain his strength in his green and fertile valley without surrendering his volition or losing touch with his conscious mind. But Aškelon was there, sometimes, compassionate and understanding, true—but *there*.

Niko didn't want a consultation; by his own reckoning, he hadn't even begun to fulfill his obligation, honor his word to the dream lord. He hadn't done a single thing to spread the enthelechy's name or glorify him.

Once, when he was too weary to care and ready for whatever lecture or chastisement Aškelon would give him, he lay down in his rest-place on grass he could feel, its every blade distinct and dewy, though he knew he was yet propped against the black marble wall. Clouds drifted overhead, diaphanous, then fluffy. The feeling of relief that overcame him was unmatched by anything he'd known in the world or even in Bandara.

But then a shadow fell and the dream lord's gray and loving eyes transfixed him. "Tell Tempus that Shamshi must be brought to me."

"I argued with him once about the boy—I wanted to take Shamshi to Bandara. It's not my place to tell the Riddler what to do." The ground seemed cold now, unyielding.

"Then *you* bring him to me. Otherwise, my son, young Randal will have a child's blood upon his hands to satisfy Belize's shade."

"Shade? Blood? Wait! I don't understand . . ."

But Aškelon and Niko's rest-place were fading; he could see the furnishings of his chamber like an apparition taking shape. "Wait!"

Aškelon, translucent, turned and came toward him.

"What shall I do?"

Aškelon inclined his head. "The best you can. Heed your dreams. Guard your soul. Follow your heart. That will be enough." Aškelon's hand reached out and Niko knew he was supposed to take it, but as he tried to, the dream lord and his rest-place disappeared and Niko lost his balance once again, this time falling forward to land, breathing hard and sweating, upon the cold stone floor of Wizardwall's second-highest tower.

A woman was there, a Nisibisi girl, with a platter of food and drink and a bowl of water into which she dipped a rag and then came forward with it dripping in her hand.

"Who are you?" he asked. "How long have you been there?" He felt foolish, embarrassed. She'd seen him fall, probably heard him talking—seemingly to himself, as if delirious.

"I've come to ease your troubled night. Lie back. Let me put this on your brow. That's good. That's fine," she crooned as he rolled over.

The cloth was cool and her hands were soothing and he never realized she reminded him of his lost girl-witch Cybele as her touch drove everything but fleshly comfort from his mind and he pulled her down on him.

In the morning, when he tried to apologize to Bashir for taking advantage of a Nisibisi maiden, Bashir denied having sent anyone to see him while Tempus caught his sister's eye and Niko saw the worried look they shared.

An hour later, after obvious contrivance, he and his commander were alone. "I had a dream about Aškelon," Niko said. "There was a message for you in it. Do you put any store in messages that come from dreams, commander?"

"It depends on the dream and the dreamer. Tell me yours."

Niko did, finishing with: "I wish I knew you'd not blame me for bearing bad tidings."

"Blame you? It's Ash I blame, for making you a pawn in this."

"Will you give up the boy?"

"Absolutely—to his lawful father in Mygdonia when the time is right."

Niko grunted. "I thought that was what you'd say. I shouldn't have told you anything . . . it's probably just a dream of mine. I haven't been sleeping well."

"So I assumed. Tell me about the girl who came to you. Describe her."

As Niko did, he started to sneeze and his head began to ache. Ignoring this, he continued, daring to tell Tempus about the phantasms he'd sensed lurking in the halls and poking their heads out of solid walls and the blue flames that licked at the corners of his vision.

"What do you propose we do about it?"

Niko spread his hands. "Sleep outside with the troops? I don't know. I know *I* can't sleep another night in here."

Tempus's eyes narrowed as if Nikodemos had said something important. "Good point. Are you well enough, sniffles or no, to trek on out tonight? Beyond Wizardwall, just you and I, on long reconnaissance to cause what harm we may among the Mygdonians?"

"Blessed be Aŝk—" Almost having praised the dream lord like a god, Niko stopped himself and said hastily, "Yes, sir, commander. I was hoping you would say that."

"Good. Get ready, requisition what we need from Bashir's stores. We leave at dusk, just you and—"

"Leave?" came a silky voice from behind Tempus. "Without *me?* Surely, brother, you can't mean that."

"Niko, please excuse us. I've instructions to leave for those who'll come after us."

He was glad enough to go: the Riddler's sister was the only woman Niko'd ever known who made him thoroughly nervous. He prayed that the Riddler would leave her far behind, that she wouldn't be riding with them.

And in the soft dusk, with the Aŝkelonians snorting their joy to be away from the Nisibisi stronghold and a chill wind in their faces as they headed north, it seemed that Niko's prayer was answered.

Just the two of them, the Riddler and the young fighter, Nikodemos, set out to war among the Mygdonians.

This pleased Niko greatly, and it must have pleased the

gods as well, for as they rode the chill wind died and the whispering pines enfolded them and Nikodemos, safe upon his great war horse at the Riddler's side, dozed in his saddle without a single evil dream or manifestation of the shadow lord appearing to bedevil him.

Book Five:

———

BEYOND WIZARDWALL

An epidemic ripped through Tyse like Lord Storm's lightning, sending the strong to their beds and the weak to their graves. Only strangers and the refugees in the free-zone blamed the gods for their misfortune—veterans of previous wizard wars had suffered through worse in Tyse; they knew sorcery was to blame.

This explanation the Stepsons gave to the 3rd Commando and the priests to their congregations, so that crowds with rotten eggs and moldly vegetables and wine-skins full of lamb's blood began to gather before the mage-guild.

Crit and Sync had to deploy men along Mageway to help the garrison troops control the mobs. As soon as one chanting throng was out of eggs or beaten back, another would form. The only result of this milling and shouting before the mageguild was that the disease spread faster.

The Hazards of Tyse barricaded themselves within ensorceled walls and withheld the only aid that might have helped.

Nor were the 3rd Commando rangers, quartered in

Tyse's northern garrison, immune to this sickness which began with a red rash on the neck and escalated rapidly to sneezing and congestion, then a fever followed by coma and, in most cases, death. Garlic was hung on doorposts; incense burned by every sickbed. Rankan gods were petitioned for mercy but still commandos sickened.

When three of his rangers had died, Sync came to Crit, demanding to know what secret defense the Stepsons had: not one of them had even caught a chill, though they'd been among the demonstrators as much as any man of Sync's.

"The god loves us," Crit had said, deadpan. "We've got divine protection."

"Which one, man, which *one?*" Sync demanded, taking Crit seriously.

They were in the Outbridge station, alone in Crit's front room, poring over reports strewn on his table—including orders brought by homing hawk from Wizardwall to muster their forces and proceed north posthaste: one to Crit, one to Sync, one meant for Grillo and his specials, and one to Randal that Crit had had no luck delivering.

"Which *god?*" Crit repeated, not believing at first that Sync was asking his advice—he'd never seen the 3rd Commando's leader flustered. But the dark, cleft-chinned ranger was deeply shaken by the loss of three of his top men to an enemy he wasn't qualified to fight.

Sync just stared at him.

Crit said, "Look, Sync, why don't you move your unit over here? Those we can't accommodate here we'll send out to Hidden Valley for a day or two—we've got to be on our way north day after tomorrow, at the latest. It's just a matter of who we'll leave behind." He tapped the strewn table top in front of him. He wasn't going to try to explain to Sync about the Slaughter Priest's ghost, who'd appeared to Critias and half a dozen others in a dream the night townsfolks started dropping with the plague. The ghost of Abarsis had given Crit a draught to drink, a recipe for making more, and a litany to recite to ward off "witch's work."

It had been bad enough to have to tell Kama about

Abarsis, the Stepsons' founder who was in heaven, so that she'd take Crit seriously and drink the foul potion made from lichen and mold and toadstools and fertile eggs; he wasn't going to give Sync a chance to scoff.

So they got down to specifics: whom they'd take north and which fighters would have to stay behind in town. Crit was bringing Grillo, as Tempus had requested, which meant he'd have to release the widow Maldives from custody and be polite to the double-dealer both he and Sync detested above all others.

Just then the door burst open and Straton, who'd long ago forgotten how to knock or observe the courtesies of rank where Critias was concerned, stomped in, his face bitten red from the cold outside.

"God's dung, Crit, you've let the fire go out!" The chill coming from Strat's clothing was palpable as he strode past them both and knelt before a hearth gone nearly as cold as the first frost freezing the ground outside. "Greetings, Sync," came from Strat's bowed head. "Come to seek asylum from the witch?"

"Strat," Crit's tone was cautionary; he didn't need more trouble than he had. "Any luck getting into the mageguild?"

"Maybe. We'll see. I got a message as far as the bottom floor. Whether Randal will receive it, or deign to answer, is a matter for the seers, not me." With a poker, he fussed among the banked coals, coaxing them to life. "That's better," he sighed, and turned, still hunkered down. "Let's just go; we've a job to do. One baby wizard isn't going to make or break this mission." Ignoring Sync's presence, Strat spoke confidentially to Crit. "We'd better go while we still can: that girl, Aisha, Niko's friend—she's not feeling well. Neither is the cook. I'd rather die fighting shoulder to shoulder with Bashir than here, if it comes to that. We'll end up killing horses if we wait much longer and you expect to make that rendezvous with the Riddler."

The fire caught behind his back, crackled and blazed, backlighting Straton as if a god had touched him. If Straton, most cautious and pragmatic of men, was hot to leave, it was surely time to go. But Crit was enmeshed in a web

of administrative details so binding that if he didn't know
better, he'd have thought the witch Roxane, herself, had
spun it.

Crit still hadn't figured out a way to keep Kama here, a
safer place, plague or no, than fighting Mygdonians and
Nisibisi wizards in a guerrilla war beyond Wizardwall. His
orders bade him lead his men through Successor-held
passes north to harry and divide an army outnumbering
them ten to one. He had a job to do and so did Kama—he
shouldn't dwell on what grew within her belly so that it
distracted him from work and even caused him to think of
Kama in ways a fighter, regardless of sex, would have
reason to resent.

So he said to Strat, "What about Jihan? The boy?"

With a gusting sigh, Strat levered himself to his feet and
came to join them, his guarded eyes saying he'd give Crit a
moment to reconsider just how much of Tempus's strategy
the 3rd Commando ought to know.

But when Crit still waited for an answer, and Strat, with
a scrape of wooden chair on wooden floor, had slid into a
seat and poured himself some flat Rankan ale, which had
kept its chill because the room was cold, Strat said, "All
set. She's taking him up to Bashir's on the Trôs horses."

Just then Sync, reaching for the earthen pitcher that held
the beer, sneezed, spraying Crit's wrist and Straton's face
with moisture.

"Great!" Strat said.

"Feeling under the weather?" Crit asked, wiping his arm
on his breeches.

"Sorry. Just a chill—the cold air you let in, Straton."

"Let's hope." Crit suddenly wanted Sync well out of
there. He began wrapping up the meeting, creating a time-
table for troop movement and leavetaking. He was nearly
done when the door to his sleeping chamber opened.

There'd been no one in there; Crit's back was to its
threshold. Straton's widening eyes warned him and he
snapped upright, pushing back his chair with his knees: he
couldn't draw his sword or get any momentum behind a
knife-throw sitting down.

As he whirled to face whatever enemy had sneaked up

on them and Straton reached behind him (from the wall taking a crossbow and fitting a bolt, levering it to firing position), a laugh—throaty and distinctly feminine—filled the room.

"Don't shoot, O mighty warriors! Stepsons, I surrender! Skewer me not, or my brother will have both your skulls made into lamps!" Then the figure stepped through the door and into the hearthlight.

Crit already knew by then who it was. That voice, neither he nor Straton would soon forget: Cime, Tempus's fey sister, had healed Straton's failing eyesight and Critias's battle wounds during the Wizardwall campaign.

She'd done more than that for Crit—bestowed her charms upon him and, for all he knew, on Straton, too. This had caused some little friction between the task force leader and Tempus, and because of that, Crit had found it expedient to cut her loose. Or so he chose to remember what had passed between them.

Whatever Straton thought was not mirrored in his eyes, but Sync—who'd never seen Cime, or anything, Crit was willing to bet, as arresting as the Riddler's sister in her Aškelonian blood-brown armor and her fearsome helmet with three bobbling plumes—looked as though someone had just clouted him on the head.

Straton said, "Oh, god's balls, now we're in for it. Lock up your family heirlooms, boys; try to get some sleep during the day."

"Excuse me?" Sync had no idea what Cime's presence meant—an escalation of all conflict, a surfeit of extracurricular problem-solving, division among allies, all the trouble this woman signified.

"Cime," Crit said. "Lovely to see you. Are we that late, that he's sent you down to hurry us along?"

She came toward them, her hips swinging as she moved in a rustle of armor and leather. Her gleaming boots punctuated her words as her heels cracked on the planked floor. "Critias, well met. And Straton, nice to see you. I trust you see me as well, Strat. And no, *he* didn't send me. I thought I'd come down here, though, and facilitate the mobilization of our forces—we wouldn't want the troops worn out from trekking just when we need them for such a tasty little war..." As she spoke, she snapped up her visor and then took off her helmet. Black hair cascaded down around her face, shining locks freed by the removal of diamond rods to whose power Critias could personally attest.

She took Crit's seat, opposite Sync, and smiled. "Who is this? Will neither of you two Stepsons introduce me?"

"We'd as soon not," Straton said. "We need him just like he is."

Crit looked down at Cime. He wished she'd disappear back into the dream lord's realm; he hoped she wasn't the jealous type, and that he could keep from falling under her spell again—for his own sake as well as Kama's and the Riddler's. He said, "This is Sync, captain of the ex-Rankan 3rd Commando, now reunited with your brother. Sync, meet Cime, sorcerer-slayer of renown. As you may know, Cime is Tempus's sister and thus off-limits to all of us—"

"Oh, yes?" Cime's neck craned and, peering up at him, her eyebrow raised, she reached for him and brought Crit's head down to hers. He couldn't do anything but let her kiss him.

He didn't like this at all.

One thing was certain: with Cime here, he'd double-time his preparations; get his people out of town as soon as possible.

When he could disengage her, he wiped his lips with the back of his hand and said, "Can you move nearly a hundred fighters? Or is that too big a job for you?"

"Too *what?* Foolish boy. Sit down." She patted the table where she obviously expected him to perch while she wrested his command from him and started in straight away: "Tell me about this problem you're having with the mageguild—that junior Hazard, Randal, is it? I couldn't help but overhear."

Sync was watching her with the sort of fascination a cornered mouse has with a hungry snake.

Straton finally put his crossbow by and sat, then, saying before Crit could find a nicer way: "Randal's a Stepson, a valued asset. You keep your hands off him. *Our* mage, a good one. Do you understand?"

"I understand, Ace," she called Strat by his war name, "though I'm not convinced that you do. If you really need to talk to Randal, I might be of help. But then, of course, it's up to you." She looked between Strat and Crit. "As for moving the troops by other than natural means, we'll talk about it this evening, Critias, just you and I. Meanwhile—"

She turned the full force of her smokey gaze upon Sync and said, "Can it be that you're not feeling well, soldier? A touch of influenza, perhaps? You wouldn't want to catch that witchy plague going around hereabouts, would you?"

"Is that a threat?" Sync misunderstood.

Crit stiffened, but Cime only chuckled, saying that if Sync would repair with her to yonder bedroom and cross her palm with silver or with gold to satisfy "the ritual" then she'd make him well in no time, and immune to the plague thereafter.

Everyone prepares for battle in his own way.

Tempus, on the night he and Niko came within sight of the Mygdonian camp, got out his leopardskin mantle and his helmet set with boar's teeth and sat quietly before his tethered Aškelonian, oiling his leathers and whetting his sharkskin-hilted sword and wrapping with cheesecloth every buckle, D-ring, and clasp among his panoply and tack that might clink. His horse, like Niko's, had been cooled, fed, groomed, and had its forelegs sheathed in oxhide wraps and its hooves silenced with leather boots. Now it stood above him, head high and nostrils distended to learn all it could from the breeze which brought the scent of Mygdonian horselines, cookfires, and enemies to it through the mixed grove of pine, ash, and maple in which they camped. Its oblong pupils glowed as it stared upwind through the rustling leaves.

Niko's stud was with its master, some distance off among the trees. A while ago, Tempus had heard the susurrus of horses' hooves disturbing fallen leaves, but now no sound came from the direction in which Stealth had disappeared. The boy sought his maat, no doubt, through meditation, or had piled up rocks and now sat waiting for Father Enlil's blessing before an improvised Storm God's shrine.

Tempus sought no divine sanction, no blessings from on

high or even promptings from within. He blacked his face and limbs with soot, donned his fearsome helm, and smoked a broadleaf laced with krrf, his hands cupped around the coal to hide its light. Then, feeling as much the avatar of destruction as he looked, he set out to find his right-side partner. Though he respected the youth's need for privacy and ritual, it was time for them to go.

He found Niko standing in a clearing, his face pressed to his mount's neck, one arm over the beast's withers, and wondered transiently whether Stealth, a boy-soldier of unparalleled reputation with over a decade's experience in the field, was actually afraid. Then Tempus chided himself: in spite of the charmed panoply he wore and Aškelon's "best" intentions, Nikodemos was resoundingly mortal. If the youth knew fear, he had every right to entertain it: circumstances had conspired to put Niko on Tempus's right hand, alone, against a Mygdonian contingent two divisions strong.

In times like these, men went exclusively by war names. The habit was so ingrained in him that Tempus, whose true name was safely buried in his past, thought of himself now as men described him: the Riddler. And when he called to his rightman, he said, "Stealth. Time's up. Let's go."

His words were Mygdonian; they'd been speaking the language since coming down off Wizardwall to brush up on the tongue and thus on the mindset of their enemy. It was lucky Niko had spent time among Mygdonians; no other Stepson had.

As Stealth raised his hand and turned to lead his horse in Tempus's direction, Tempus decided he'd best not fool himself: there was no luck abroad tonight, or any night he and Stealth did battle. As it had been for Tempus long ago, so it was now for the youngster coming toward him—with one glaring exception: Niko was no sleepless one.

Otherwise, they were a true pair, prompted by forces neither venerated into actions neither condoned. The worst thing about tutelary gods and supernal patrons' habits of "helping" chosen warriors was that deific or magical aid took all the honor out of war, the meaning out of sacrifice, and the joy out of winning.

By the time he'd mounted and reined his horse toward the

Mygdonian encampment, Tempus was missing Vashanka, his old companion, Rankan berserker god and pillager extraordinaire: when Vashanka had habitually possessed him, at least in battle his own melancholia was eased and surmounting an enemy made some sort of sense.

If ever he came through this without losing his Stepsons— or especially without losing the particular Stepson slouched on the horse to his right—he'd cut loose the boy and his whole beloved cadre and go alone to seek his missing god in whatever hell or sorcerous prison He now dwelt.

It was as close to a prayer as he could manage.

But then, it had been centuries since Tempus had put any stock in the power of prayer.

He had that in common with the Mygdonians whom he and Niko then set out to spook: Mygdonians were godless to the man. They died without mumbling prayers or even making warding signs.

The first pair of sentries he and Stealth sneaked up on found their throats slit where they sat dozing and couldn't make a sound with their vocal cords cut. Though they had plenty of time before they bled to death to consign their souls to the gods with handsigns, they didn't—they just scuttled toward their camp, stumbling as they ran.

It didn't matter if the sentries made it back to camp, though that would be fine with Tempus: he wanted every casualty of their evening's work investigated, examined, accounted for.

But he couldn't wait around. They vaulted to their horses and split up: Stealth to use his throwing stars and poisoned blossoms along the western edge of the encampment, the Riddler to set tripwires across the southward trail.

When they met again, the youth had used nearly all his stars and Tempus's trap was well and duly set.

"The horses, now?" Stealth whispered, shoulder to shoulder with him and barely out of breath though in the camp alarms were sounding, men running to form search teams and groping for their weapons in the dark, trying to make sense of what was happening and shake off drunken sleep.

"Now," Tempus confirmed, knowing that war upon the horse-lines was distasteful to the youth: the flash of cold eye he met under Stealth's raised visor confirmed that, as of this moment, young Niko loved him less.

Feeling cheered, the Riddler took the wineskin full of naphtha that Stealth held out wordlessly and continued what the boy had started: laying an inflammable circle of the oil-based incendiary around the perimeter of the entire Mygdonian camp.

The poisoning of hay and water and the running off of mounts in which Stealth now engaged would save some beasts from fiery death, which horses fear the most of all.

Only for a moment did Tempus pause to watch the youngster slip through the undergrowth without a sound; one blink, and even the Riddler couldn't see him. Stealth had covered his panoply as well as his skin with soot: it was up to Tempus to affright them, Niko'd said; for his part, he'd content himself with killing them.

Then, as now, Nikodemos had reminded Tempus by his grim attitude more than his words that it was in behalf of Mygdonia that the witch, Roxane, had first tortured, then possessed, this Stepson. Revenge for Niko's ravaged spirit, his partner Janni's horrid death, had been what lured Tempus and his Stepsons north from Sanctuary. To avenge the harm the witch had done while inhabiting the boy and after, to his self-esteem and his reputation among his fellows, from whom Stealth still felt estranged, would take some doing: more Mygdonians than those camped before them would have to die before they got the witch.

Whether even Roxane's head upon his pike would reinstate the love and trust Nikodemos had once enjoyed as a core member of the Sacred Band, Tempus was not certain.

As Stealth slipped off to lime the water, taint the hay, and foul the wine and food on which the Mygdonian army depended, the Riddler circled west and north, the goatskin bag of naphtha ever lighter in his hands.

Twice he encountered sentries and twice he killed where he could not maim.

The object here, as previously, was to let some luckless fools run hysterically into camp with tales of a leopard-skinned apparition, a giant with no face in a boar's-tooth helm who was in a dozen places or more at once: let Rox-

ane explain to the Mygdonians, if she could, what he was
and from whence he'd come.

To make sure it was on him the soldiers concentrated,
after him they searched, and upon his terrible aspect they
meditated, he showed himself at times, riding into jittery,
noisy groups of four and five who combed the woods on
foot, letting his foul-tempered Aškelonian wreak havoc
with its teeth and hooves while he cleaved about him with
his god-given sword in his right hand and an old, beloved
war ax in his left.

He took two crossbow bolts in one encounter, though
he'd judged the quarters too close for archers, and bellowed loudly that they'd better get their warlocks and their
witches to protect them as he pulled out the bolts with
more contempt than he really felt and snapped them both in
twain, casting them back into the midst of Mygdonians
quaking in their turbans as his steed, squealing, galloped
away.

When he reached their due-north rendezvous, Stealth
was not yet there. The Riddler poured the last of the
naphtha sparingly until he found the spot where Niko'd
begun pouring his; then he sat at the joining of a naphtha
circle which would soon be a ring of fire.

All this, without the aid of gods or the appearance of
magical defenders? He could not quite believe his luck—
nary a demon nor a fiend nor a white-eyed undead had
come out to engage him. His horse had suffered only three
superficial wounds on its rump. His own wounds hurt but
they were bleeding less now; the profusion of blood making his right side sticky boded well for healing. Pain was
something he'd learned long ago that one must endure.

Squatting on the ground, he bound his wounds and
walked his blowing horse in circles while, just south of
him, in the Mygdonian camp, chaos raged. By now they'd
be shooting at each other. The point of this sort of harassment was to induce confusion; more casualties would result
from the hapless in the way of their own crossbow fire and

men too frightened to identify themselves before they
started swinging than from what Tempus and Niko, striking
as quickly as they could from all directions, had done so
far.

Time was passing and the sky was getting bluish; they
were losing the darkness. Where could Niko be?

The Riddler *had* to set the fire while the night was still
upon their enemy. Though Mydgonians were godless, they
were not free from superstition. They had no magic of their
own because they feared it more than death. Their con-
tract-mages, Nisibisi black artists, might hold them firm by
threat in the face of mortal enemies, but if Tempus could
convince them that they faced a vengeful god, they'd break
and run.

When, after what seemed an interminable interval,
Stealth had still not appeared, he considered alternatives:
he could set the fire and return to his own base camp,
trusting that the youth would join him when and if he
could; he could try calling upon Stormbringer, or Aškelon,
for aid; he could sortie into the camp himself to find the
boy.

One remark that Nikodemos had made kept coming
back to Tempus as he hesitated: "We ought to have Randal
with us, commander. Much as I hate to admit it, we could
use the Hazard's help."

The Riddler had said nothing at the time. Now he
wished he'd heeded Stealth, back in Bashir's high keep,
and ordered Randal to join them in the field rather than
come up later with Crit's cadre. But like Cime's, Randal's
help was tainted, could turn out for ill as well as good.

And Niko was Tempus's responsibility, if a fighter of his
quality could be said to be anyone else's but his own.

So the Riddler got out his flint and steel and lit the
naphtha, standing well back from it: if a diversion would
be helpful and timely, the racing circle of flame, licking
skyward, would do the job.

Niko had been passing among the horse-lines, his palm
trailing off rump after rump, his work there all but done,

when some ill-tempered beast had kicked him.

Some horse's hind feet had struck him so hard in the chest that the force of it had lifted him off the ground. But for his cuirass, forged by ancient hands and tempered with magic, his ribcage would have been caved in, his breast-bone crushed.

As it was, he woke flat on his back, trying to catch his breath, the sky above, bereft of stars, turning gray and brown, with the screams of men and horses in his ears.

Gray? Brown? That wasn't right. By some piece of ser-endipity he'd landed under a short pine tree with broad and thickly needled branches. As he struggled to his elbows, he caught the breath he'd needed. Then he understood the gray/brown sky: fire. The Riddler had lit the naphtha.

Although he knew what he would see, Niko pawed at the branches hiding him from the Mygdonians, half their turbans unwound to cover mouths and noses now, to see the ranks struggling with balky, fire-shy horses who'd al-ready eaten and drunk enough of what Stealth had added to their hay and grain and water that many were already swelling with colic.

Some steeds had gone to their knees, heedless of the fire and the men who held their heads and tails to try to keep them on their feet. Others snapped at soldiers who tried to blindfold them or remove the tainted food.

From their concern with their mounts, he realized they did not yet know that the fire encircled them; when they did, it might be too late for most of these.

Gasping from the pain of cracked ribs as he struggled to his knees, Stealth sought a likely exit.

But none was immediately apparent: the smoke bil-lowed inward and the Mygdonians ran hither and thither, and from the center of the camp where the brightly colored tents of royalty were pitched, women and robed figures which might be Nisibisi warlocks streamed to seek in vain the water Stealth had limed.

From his waterbag he poured mineral water onto a strip of linen he'd torn from his undershirt and bound the strip over mouth and nose. He tried not to dwell on the fact that Tempus had closed the trap with him inside: he told himself it was a compliment, that it proved his commander thought that Stealth could fend for himself.

He'd better be able to, or else he'd fry.

Standing was too painful; he scuttled on his hands and knees toward the northern perimeter of the camp, where the fire would have started and where, with luck, he'd find a spot where it had burned up all its fuel, or burned thin, or burned low.

He'd left his horse beyond, among the trees to the west. He wished he had it now as his ribs grated upon one another. His breath came hard and stars danced in his vision. He needed both hands to make headway in this thick brush he must keep to, or risk discovery in the midst of his enemy, but reflexively, his arm pressed against his side to try to keep his bones from grating.

He'd made a bit of distance and calmed enough to realize that his cuirass was not even dented when a whinnying horse with tail ablaze galloped by, a rider on it; then another; then three more riders, yelling to each other in Mygdonian that it was time to save themselves.

Niko couldn't have agreed more, but the fire was faster than he was and he couldn't seem to muster courage or equilibrium enough to stand and run or even stand and fight. He must have hit his head as well, he thought, and turned to look behind him just as three Mygdonians came crashing through the underbrush the other way, javelins in hand, faces grimy so that their eye-whites seemed as bright as the all-white orbs of the undead.

But they weren't undead yet—they'd seen him and knew he wasn't one of theirs from his helmet and his gear.

At least they hadn't had the wit to call for reinforcements, though whether they'd have been heard amid the din was anybody's guess.

"There's one! Get him!" their leader called.

"One what?" another replied, but cast his javelin so that Stealth's reflexes threw him to the dirt and he saw pinwheeling stars when he hit.

He had three blossoms yet; one axiom he followed was to always hold something in reserve, a last defense.

"Did you hit him?" Niko heard the leader's voice and

thanked the gods for the smoke obscuring everything.

"I don't think so. Let's look."

Yet lying prone, Niko slipped his dirk from his scabbard and the three blossoms between the fingers of his left hand. He'd try that first: it was his right side that really hurt him; the movement needed to slip his charmed dirk free had made his breath catch in his throat. And that dirk in his hand was warm, telling him sorcery lurked close by.

One thing at a time, he told himself, and when he could see booted feet clearly through the smoke he gritted his teeth and rolled to his knees, casting the blossoms—*one, two, three*—steeling himself for the effort it was going to take to stand, if he missed any of them.

He knew that with his right side in this condition, in hand-to-hand he wouldn't last long against a Maggot from the free zone, let alone well-trained soldiers. But he'd give it all he had.

Before he could gain his feet, one man yelled, another cursed, and Niko heard the unmistakable thump as human deadweight hit the ground.

The third, however, launched himself at Niko from above, telling him, "All right, devil bastard, man or shade, you've killed your last!"

The force of the impact bore Niko, in heavy panoply, over backward; cheek to jowl with the sweating Mygdonian whose turban was flopping, half-unwound, between them, making it hard for either man to see, they wrestled on the ground.

He felt something sticky on the other's back, recognized it as blood, and realized that the poison on his blossom would help him if he could just hold out—he'd grazed this enemy, so some poison had to be in the other's bloodstream.

Meanwhile, there was a short, curved sword to keep from his vitals and a grasping hand to keep from clawing out his eyes.

His dirk was better than his opponent's sword in such close quarters, but it slid along the armor of the man on top of him; he hadn't the strength in that arm to pierce hardened leather, let alone bronze plates.

The Mygdonian's fingers were pressing painfully upon his eyeballs when, as Stealth got a leg around the other's thigh and raised his dirk to bring it down into his attacker's bladder by way of unprotected buttocks, the man went limp upon him: the poison at last had done its deadly work.

He lay under his assailant, breathing hard, listening to the running feet and hooves around him and the fire crackling as it closed in.

If only Randal had come along, he'd have been out of harm's way and back with the Riddler before Tempus torched the naphtha. As it was, he couldn't see a better move right now than playing dead under the still-warm corpse until he could regain his strength.

Suddenly he thought of Aškelon and the dream-bred horse he had. He really should have named it. Aškelon had said that it was special. He wished it would come and fetch him home; he envisioned himself upon its back and the two of them leaping over flames to safety.

All this time he still held the charmed dirk in a sweaty grip. And it was warmer by the second. He wondered if a warlock or a witch was coming close and, if so, whether his pretense of death would fool a black artist.

He knew he should get up, get out of here, die a clean death in the flames if he had to die. If the Nisibisi wizards caught him, he'd wish he'd died that way.

Decided, he prepared to roll the corpse off and make away, and then he heard the chanting, coming near. One voice among that soulless choir petitioning what did not live in heaven froze him: a woman's alto voice it was, so familiar that he didn't have to see her to know that Roxane was among the procession passing by.

And then from high above a squeal of unearthly rage rent the smoke, and the pall was buffeted away by the beat of giant wings.

He had to see: he raised his head and squinted through one eye, not enough that an adept might see him, he hoped, and there before him was a group of six warlocks with the magnificent Roxane at their head. Beside her walked a man in Mygdonian dress armor, embroidered surcoat, curled-toed boots and all. And these walked calmly, as if in a country garden.

Or at least they had been walking so, until the great wings beat down and talons raked their group and a wizard threw himself out of the way, landing crosswise, half atop Niko and the dead fighter sprawled on top of him, so that Niko could feel the man trembling and every beat of a racing heart.

And while the warlock on top of him intoned invocations through gritted teeth, the processional—all but Roxane and the Mygdonian commander—also dove for cover.

The witch had the general by the arm and was pointing, it seemed, straight at the warlock who lay across Niko and the corpse, and was cursing "the damned Roc and all the lesser mages who change shape but cannot change their nature."

At this, the beating wings above, silhouetted now against a gray/brown/red sunrise sky, seemed to shimmer and, as if struck by a weapon, the giant bird whose wingspan was thrice a man's height came crashing to the ground.

A miasma exploded around it as it landed; Roxane pulled the Mygdonian warrior back and Niko saw her raise her hands as from behind the sound of hoofbeats racing grew loud and the trumpet of a war horse in furious assault made Niko's ears ring.

He still had the dirk, almost burning him now with its eagerness to strike the warlock who lay upon him as if he were a cozy couch.

He took the chance: he'd just kill what enemies he might and go with grace to whatever heaven had in store for him. Escape was impossible now, a pointless exercise in cowardice. He hoped the Riddler would say words for him, commend him to heaven in Abarsis's company—that he'd done a decent job here and that the Stepsons would in death forgive him for taking up with witches and magicians.

Then he stabbed the warlock in the loins and ripped on up; used all his strength to push both corpses, old and new, off him, and stood up just in time to see what kind of bird had descended from the heavens and to be knocked sideways by the war horse whose hooves he'd heard.

As the miasma settled, Randal, changed back by a hostile spell to his own form, flickered naked for an instant, then was clothed and armed. Drawing his kris, Randal leaped toward Roxane and the Mygdonian warlord, throwing stars and poisoned blossoms that Niko had given him rising from his belt and speeding on their way toward the warlocks scattered round about—behind dead horses, bushes, or whatever cover they could find.

The sun was rising now, and shadows were long in a bloody dawn. From somewhere a mighty wind came and seemed to spin above the fighting so that all the smoke was blown outward and away.

Niko, knocked once more off his feet, scrambled up, his side in agony, and only then realized that the war horse was his own and in the thick of the battle, trampling wizards, biting witches where it could.

And these could not seem to believe that their pointing fingers would not dispatch this horse, who only was angered more when a hostile spell was cast its way.

Limping as fast as he could, his sword drawn, picking his own blossoms out of his kills along the way, Niko tried to reach his partner.

But Randal wasn't hurt, and though he seemed no more formidable than ever in his hillman's outfit, he was giving back spell for spell and hell for hell among these Nisibisi mages. Hurrying, his kris outstretched (or being dragged forward by it, for all Niko knew), he seemed to skip across the ground, stabbing certain footprints as he went.

Whenever the kris penetrated a footprint, a wizard wailed and flared, or crumbled into dust.

Between the crazed, froth-mouthed horse and Randal—who stabbed, as Niko watched, a standing warlock's shadow so that the mighty mage begged for mercy as he fell to his knees, his body seeming to melt into a multicolored puddle—the wizard-caste was having second thoughts.

Only Roxane held her ground, her hand on the Myg-

donian commander's brocaded sleeve, and pointed, not at
Randal, but at Stealth.

And Niko heard her through that melee and all the pandemonium as if she were whispering in his ear. "Come,
Niko! Come to me, my dear. Right now, I do command
thee!"

"Nikodemos!" Randal's long and mournful call came to
him as if from a great distance. "Don't let her do it! Not
again. Fight her! *Fight!* I'll help you!"

But Stealth couldn't seem to understand Randal's Nisi;
Roxane's summons was spoken in the language of his soul.
His ribs hurt, his breath was short, her arms were out to
welcome him. What was the use of all this fighting, anyway?

He walked toward her. Then his horse knocked him
once more from his feet and the pain of the concussion as
he hit the earth took his breath away.

When next he knew anything, the Aškelonian's wet
muzzle was whuffing against his cheek, the horse kneeling
down with its forelegs outstretched beside him as if waiting
for a dowager or child to mount it.

Randal's words rang in his ears. "Fight her, Stealth. For
all our sakes! She can't *force* you, don't let her take you!
What will the Riddler say?"

That did it. With those galling words echoing in his
head, he dragged himself toward his kneeling horse's saddle: the Aškelonian, its head bowed between its bent forelegs, was watching him with soft, wise eyes that seemed
sorrowful; even his horse didn't have faith in him.

He grabbed the saddle's pommel, levering himself
aboard awkwardly: he'd show the Hazard and the witch
that neither one of them controlled him. He couldn't have
Randal strutting around, boasting that he'd saved his
partner's life. He couldn't go back among the Sacred Band
with the witch's taint renewed. He had to show Roxane,
too, that he was under no sorcerous compulsion or any
witch's command.

Then his horse lurched to its feet and he heard Roxane's
voice again, telling Randal that everyone the mageling
loved would suffer for his hubris.

Behind her, the fire was closing in, its flames licking skyward and its heat rolling over him in waves that made Niko grip his saddle hard and pray he wouldn't faint; it backlit the witch and the Mygdonian general and blazed so brightly behind them that he had to squint.

And Randal was retreating from Roxane's pointing finger, while around her the surviving warlocks gathered, dark, ominous shadows which might yet sum defeat.

Still Stealth couldn't take his eyes from her, and as he watched, he saw Cybele, the girl-witch he'd come to love, and then the Nisibisi maiden who'd healed his fever up at Bashir's, and then their glances met. "Cybele . . . Roxane . . . no," he said to eyes which promised him eternity and an end to strife and pain if he would but get off that horse and walk those few paces to her. . . .

As he said it, Randal's retreat brought the Hazard to the horse's side. A sweaty face turned up to Stealth's; a mageling's mouth formed words: "Good. Ready? I'll just take hold of this bridle and we'll be out of—"

The junior Hazard's hand closed on Niko's horse's reins and everything—the fiery circle; the witch Roxane/Cybele; the Mygdonian general; the tall, robed sorcerers and flickering shadow-forms behind them; the dead men and beasts and, in the distance, turbaned Mygdonians running toward the royal tents now catching fire—disappeared.

". . . here." Randal finished his sentence in a copse of trees free from flames and firelight so that at first everything around them seemed pitch black to Niko, then granular, undifferentiated green, then subsided into daylight.

Roxane, with Lacan Ajami close behind her, had watched helplessly as the accursed Aškelonian steed and Randal, a puny, Hazard-class Tysian mage, stole Nikodemos from under her very nose.

She had to cover her distress before Ajami then, save the man and the body of his troops, regroup her warlocks and set them to snuffing out the ring of fire—which they could only do when well away from all its hellish heat and smoke.

Fire was their nemesis, a cleansing weapon brought down on them by Tempus and his gods.

And Niko...she'd wanted him so much that she'd risked singeing her own hair and losing wizards to acquire him. Beloved Niko, who'd finally realized what the patronage of Aškelon, the panoply he wore, the horse he rode, could mean: he'd said no to her unspoken declaration of love and power and safekeeping. It was well that no wizard had overheard her offer him eternal life, or heard his heart's response.

They'd been too busy, that was something. They'd seen only what Ajami saw, heard only "Cybele...Roxane, no." Oh, they knew Niko had worked free of her control, but that was nothing—the blame for it easily and truly lay with Aškelon.

What Roxane knew that no one else would understand was that Nikodemos, for the first time, had used the power of his maat and of his patron to disavow love in favor of his honor.

He'd spurned her, discounted her, despite everything— their excruciating trysts when she was Cybele, the night she'd come to him at terrible risk on Wizardwall and eased him. In spite of being enemies, on different sides, she'd loved him and looked after him, taken care of him all this time.

Yet love counted for nothing before Aškelon's protection; services done meant nothing to Nikodemos. She'd been playing for time, never turned her full powers of destruction upon him, no matter what the provocation, hoping love would win out over prejudice.

For Nikodemos truly loved Cybele, and Cybele was Roxane as much as Roxane was Cybele.

But this was a final parting, and she summoned hatred from the depths of the underworld to punish him, though it seemed she sat in council with her Mygdonian allies, explaining away failure and saying how the wizard-caste could yet assist Mygdonia in putting the Riddler's men to rout. "We've saved the bulk of your motley crew, Ajami; what you lost, you lost through negligence, superstition, incompetence of the Mygdonian sort. Now here's *my* plan,

since yours has gone awry—and remember as you hear it
that once we're south of Wizardwall, the town, in the
throes of plague and revolution, will fail as one man
whimpering at your feet and beg you to lift its yoke of ill
fortune and Rankan servitude . . ."

All the time she spoke, she was marshaling her anger.
She reached with immaterial hands and struck dead the girl
in the Machadi embassy whom she'd designated a plague
victim but allowed to live this long: Aisha. That would hurt
Niko, make him know what awaited a mortal man who
scorned Death's Queen.

This she did instead of what she'd meant to do: a
splinter of one of Niko's broken ribs could easily be coaxed
to pierce a vital organ. She would have healed him if he'd
come to her; she could kill him just as easily, right now.

But she did not.

She'd laid a curse on Randal and the mage must feel it:
Niko's suffering would teach the hubristic mageling *whom*
he dared to thwart.

And there was Grillo, riding hither with all speed
among a "secretly" advancing contingent of enticingly
human foes, his little golden homunculus—his master, for
that was what the figurine had become—in his pocket.

She told herself that she wanted Nikodemos to be the
last to die, and made herself believe it.

If, among the remaining Nisibisi adepts, any realized
that Roxane was a prisoner herself—a slave to love and a
servant of her own emotions so that her judgment was af-
fected and her decisions not the best—then these kept silent: she was still Death's Queen, still Roxane. If she'd
come out second best against a Tysian Hazard, this was a
combination of two elements: her infatuation with a mortal
and the fact that Randal had possession of a globe of power
mightier than her own, the very one which Datan had once
used to teach the witch her place and keep her in it.

But among themselves, the Nisibisi adepts muttered,
late at night when Roxane was asleep. If only they'd succeeded in capturing Nikodemos, they could have traded
him to Randal for the globe of high peaks clay; without it,
victory was not assured.

Who had the globe, had power others dreamed not of.

In the morning, their consensus taken, the Nisibisi wizards came to Roxane, proposing an all-out offensive: they must retrieve their globe.

Of this there was no question; on this point, no disagreement. But on how to penetrate a brace of warding spells spun by that very globe, many held diverse opinions.

Some Mygdonians would have to be sacrificed, of course. Mygdon's lord and Tempus would have to engage each other. Though not one Nisibisi adept present had ever taken seriously the possibility of Shamshi, Datan's son, heir apparent to the throne of wizardry, being handed back to his Mygdonian mother and her husband, the ploy would do to get them within snatching distance of the coveted power globe.

Then, if Roxane had not demonstrated competence, leadership, and dedication enough, or called upon dark lords powerful enough, they'd deal with her: no one held the highest post among the Nisibisi's black artists without passing certain tests of fire.

"It's all my fault," Randal wrung his hands and paced to and fro before the Riddler, who was bent over Niko's semiconscious, sweating form.

Tempus had pulled the youth from his snorting Aškelonian. He'd had to pry Niko's fingers from mane and pommel. The Stepson was holding onto his mount for dear life and to consciousness by a thread. With Randal's help, he'd gotten off the breastplate and laid the youth down on a bed of pine needles in the clearing which was their base camp. Conjured bandages appeared when Tempus asked for them, but binding those ribs in place by feel alone when Niko's whole chest and side were bruised and swollen wasn't easy.

There was no way to tell if the job Tempus had done would be good enough, or if the ribs would heal improperly and Niko be left with a crippled right side. And Stealth was right-handed.

"Stop whining, mageling. *You* can't heal this; I've done

my best." Tempus sat back on his heels and shook his head. "I hate to say this, but we need my sister. Cime would put this right in no time, or at least make sure I've done it properly. What say you? Can you call my sister, let her know we need her now, not later? Bring her up here?"

"Me? Her? *Here?*" Randal stopped in his tracks and stared at Tempus with real horror.

Cime was, after all, a mage-killer, a sorcerer-slayer who'd put better adepts than Randal in their uneasy graves.

"You. Her. Here," Tempus confirmed. *"Now."*

"Sir . . . my lord . . . commander, you don't under-stand—"

"What's to understand? Your partner's hurt. We've got to help him." Tempus straightened up and walked around the youth he'd drugged with pulcis to keep the pain at bay. When he reached the firepit he'd built inside a low black tent, he called to Randal. "Come here, Stepson, and an-swer me."

When Randal stooped to come inside, Tempus patted the dirt beside him. "Sit down, Randal."

As the Hazard did, his kris jittered in its scabbard.

Tempus raised an eyebrow.

Randal pulled on one ear and explained earnestly: "It's worried for my safety. Because *I* am. What I meant . . . what you don't understand . . . what I'm trying to tell you is that in my room back at the mageguild, when I was last there, the witch Roxane had left a message: those who are my friends and loved ones will suffer until I offer myself up to her for punishment. That's not an exact quote, but that's the gist of it—that's why Niko's . . ." Randal bit his lip, palmed his eyes, then dragged his hands down across his face. "So you see, it *is* my fault. And not just that: there's the plague in Tyse. That's what she meant. If I give myself up to her, all this will stop."

"Don't believe it. You give yourself up to her and she'll have you for lunch and then burp you in our faces. As for the 'curse' she laid on you, I've lived longer than your mageguild's stood, with a curse worse than that one on my head."

Randal's bony shoulders slumped. He bowed his head.

"Then . . . you don't think it's all my fault?"

"I'd like to, but I can't. Anything else I don't understand? Anything that's keeping you from summoning Cime?"

"She might not like it, being summoned, being brought here. Couldn't *you* ask Aškelon to send her?"

"I don't sleep, remember? How am I supposed to contact him? Besides, I'm not asking you for counterproposals, I'm asking if there's any real reason you can't carry out a simple order. You took an oath, Randal, to do just that—no questions."

"I took an oath to protect my partner's life with my own."

"We've been over that. Unless you're telling me you'd rather give yourself up to Roxane than trust me to protect you from my sister, do whatever you have to do to get her here, *right now.* Crit and the rest won't be at our rendezvous until midnight, and I can't move Niko in his condition, nor should her healing skills be denied him that long."

Having finished, Tempus held out his hands and rubbed them before the little fire; though the day was unseasonably warm and the base camp sheltered, Tempus was chilled from within. Earlier, looking back whence they'd come, he'd seen lowering storm clouds, a gray and leaden sky which might mean that the snows had begun among the high peaks. If so, there was no retreating to Tyse.

This boded well for Tyse but ill for the men he'd led here. If Roxane and her warlocks should spirit the Mygdonians south by magic, he'd need Randal and the globe the mage now fondled wordlessly, which had appeared as if from thin air while Tempus watched out of the corner of his eye. It looked as if Randal had opened a box top where nothing but empty space existed; then he'd lifted out the globe nestled in its stand and placed it gently on the ground.

"My lord, if your sister kills me, you ought to know that this globe will hire you any mage of any power you desire. Oaths of fealty taken on it can't be broken; it's the highest power piece an adept can own. So guard it well, if I cannot."

Tempus made a noncommittal noise. He knew what he was looking at. He'd rather smash it on the rocks; in younger days, he would have. But lately right and wrong were not so clear as once they'd been.

From outside, he heard the Aškelonians snorting, then a whinny and a menacing squeal cut the air. "That sounds like Niko's horse."

"Could be," Randal said distractedly, still playing with his ball of high peaks clay and precious stones.

Tempus had left the stallion loose to guard its master.

When he scrambled out of the low black tent to see what was afoot, he saw that the horse was doing just that: protecting Niko's recumbent form from Cime, who had her shield out before her and was backing, step by step, toward the trees, with the horse, on its hind legs, tail flagged, ears back, coming after.

Tempus whistled. The horse came down on all fours and looked around, ears still flattened, teeth bared.

"Some greeting, this, brother," Cime said, both her diamond rods in her right hand, glowing slightly. "What right have you to use your foul witchcraft-monger to pluck me off my horse without so much as a by-your-leave?"

"Niko's hurt." He indicated the youth under a blanket behind him.

"So? Why tell me? He'd not want me to tend him. He doesn't like me." Her smirk was hard, contentious, a showing of teeth which, if he'd been familiar with his own defensive little kill-smile, he might have recognized.

"Tend him."

She let her shield clatter to the ground. "Yes, my lord, right away, my lord," she said scathingly. "You're turning into an old woman, do you know that? Any little scratch your favorite, here, takes, is a major crisis." As she spoke, she stalked over to the fallen Stepson and pulled off the blanket. "Oh. I see. Yes."

That was as close to an apology as Tempus was going to get from her.

He turned away; he didn't want to interfere or even watch her at work. The last thing he saw was the pair of diamond rods, pointed together and glowing in her fingers, poised over Niko's chest, before he ducked back into his tent to steel himself for the forthcoming encounter with his personal nemesis, to think of some way to enjoin her from harming Randal, and in general to gather his composure: she still made him feel like a wayward boy.

When Cime and the Riddler came swaggering into the rendezvous base camp, Grillo felt the world's weight being lifted from his shoulders.

Although Grillo's specials formed one quarter of the joint force fielded against the Mygdonians, Critias was in charge of their deployment. Of the more than one hundred and twenty fighters, only a select dozen were present to meet with Tempus: Grillo himself, Crit and Straton, Sync, Kama, a pair of Sacred Banders, one Nisibisi free man (a scout Bashir had loaned them), and four 3rd Commando rangers, alike as peas in a pod with their deep suntans, short hair, and alert quietude.

Grillo knew that two of these last had been assigned to watch him. It wasn't that he was under arrest—nothing that obvious. But none of his specials, not even ex-specials like Gayle or Ari from whom Grillo might still have expected loyalty, were among the rendezvous party. The two rangers dogged him like bodyguards; even when he sought a tree upon which to relieve himself, one of them would offer to come along or happen to be micturating nearby.

This was making Grillo very cautious. In his pocket was the golden figurine which was no more damning than the bits of abalone shell and eagle's claw and lead statuettes that Crit carried in a pouch with one die and an old field decoration to bring him luck. On its own, it meant nothing. But it spoke to Grillo at night and now it wanted him to deliver a message scrawled on parchment that he'd found wrapped around it when he woke this morning. He didn't want one of the 3rd to discover what the little golden man could do or what the message meant for Tempus was.

With the Riddler here, things would change. Tempus and he were old friends, veterans of other wars who shared a bond of trust.

But when Grillo approached the sleepless one, Crit had gotten there before him and was whispering in Tempus's ear, Straton just behind, and the task force leader's partner was watching Grillo and his two "bodyguards" with obvious disdain.

So Grillo said only: "Well met, Riddler. When you can free yourself from underlings, I need to talk to you alone." In his pocket, Grillo could feel the golden statuette stirring; he put his hand in there to still its movement. All he needed was for Tempus to notice, or for the damned thing to crawl out. He felt a prick, a sharp pain in his index finger. Then he felt better than he had in days.

Tempus, his face gray with remnants of camouflaging soot, toyed with the boar's-tooth helmet he held and nodded, "Right away."

Grillo knew that when the Riddler put away his favorite shabby duty gear in favor of leopardskin and ivories that what amounted to ritual slaughter was at hand.

But the part of his mind which compiled detail and reached conclusions wasn't working as it should. Grillo had a message to deliver; it was the most important thing he'd ever do.

As Tempus bent his head to Crit to hear some last remark, behind him Grillo saw Sync and Kama, so close together that their girded hips were brushing as they walked, coming toward the little group.

Crit turned to stare in Kama's direction as Tempus disengaged.

Grillo, free at last from the pair of rangers who shadowed him, found time to be grateful for the tension in this camp: between Sync and Critias, no love was lost. And the Riddler's sister, looking to see what Crit was staring at, put her hands on her hips when she caught sight of Kama.

Then Tempus led the way into a stand of pine, and Grillo and the Riddler were finally alone.

"What's the trouble, Grillo?" Tempus asked in his rumbly voice. "Why is it that you and Critias cannot get along?"

"He's telling tales of me, I expect. That's just poisonous

politics, not what I want to talk to you about."

"I'm glad of that. Crit's my first officer; this mission is his responsibility and, after a fashion, so are you. And he's worried. You're telling me he has no cause to be?"

"People talk." Almost, Grillo was tempted to tell Tempus about the witch, about his blackouts, about the little figurine now growing hot in his pocket. Instead he reached under his sword's scabbard where the statuette and message were to pull out the parchment. "Crit's a simple man, fine for simple problems. I can't explain to him—or to you—the reasons for my actions, nor should you ask me to. We've worked together too many—"

The little homunculus wouldn't let go of Grillo's finger. He didn't understand why or how it happened, but as he brought out his hand with the message in it, the tiny golden man leaped from there onto the Riddler's face.

Then Tempus was staggering backward, clawing at his cheek. There issued from Tempus's throat a howl of pain and fury the like of which Grillo had never heard a mortal utter.

Crash! Armored man went down, falling over backward.

Stunned, Grillo watched the Riddler thrashing on the ground, rolling to and fro, clutching his face.

In the distance Grillo heard shouts and then running feet, crackling leaves, and cracking branches.

Somehow, Grillo couldn't move; he was logy, lethargic. And he had to *see:* something was compelling him to watch and hoping very hard he'd see Tempus kick and convulse and stiffen in the throes of death. Though the Riddler's life was unnaturally prolonged, an unnatural assault like this could end it.

Grillo hovered, fascinated. Tempus's harsh breathing and grunts and the sounds he made, struggling with the homunculus burrowing into his face, blotted out all other noises, so that when the rangers tackled Grillo from behind and wrestled him to his knees it came as a surprise to him.

He didn't resist. He watched, ignoring the shouting and Crit's attempt to launch himself into the weird battle, so

that now two men and a figurine thrashed on the ground
while around them a ring of onlookers grew: Straton was
there, bellowing orders; then Sync appeared with Kama
and forcibly turned her head away, dragging her backward
to make room for Cime, who strode into the chaos cursing
like a mercenary.

Her hair cascading around her heart-shaped face, gray
eyes flashing, her diamond rods bright blue in both her
hands, she yelled, "Crit, get away from him. Get *back!* Let
me handle this."

When that didn't work, she motioned to the Sacred
Band pair, who dashed in and dragged Critias ignomin-
iously from the fray.

Grillo saw Cime kneel beside her brother, on his belly
now and howling like a wolf, lift his head up by the hair,
and force her diamond rods between his hands and his
face.

Then the whole clearing seemed to explode in a burst of
light, and when he could blink the after-image away and
see again, Grillo saw Tempus sitting crosslegged, one arm
out to support himself, and Cime crouched beside him, her
hands upon his face. From under her palms blood
streamed, and she was crooning to him that he would "be
all right, just let me help you, my brother. That's it, be
still, let me draw out the poison."

And at her feet he saw a little blackened figurine, its
tiny head severed, its miniature fingers spread like claws.
Crit was stamping on it with one booted foot and Straton,
by his side, had out his warding charms.

Soon enough, Grillo was dragged away among muttered
epithets, the parchment message he'd thought to deliver
still crumpled in his hand.

There was no way to make them understand, no use in
telling underlings that he hadn't planned it, or known what
would happen when the homunculus got within range of
Tempus.

Now Grillo *was* under arrest, bound hand-to-foot and
lying on his belly, his face to the earth. There was an interval during which men came to kick and spit upon him and

promise him a slow and unpleasant death. This he
shrugged off until Straton came and hunkered down beside
his head and told him just *how* Strat had it in mind to
punish him for what he'd done to Tempus.

Only then did Grillo think he'd better act in his own
defense, though if Tempus wasn't conscious, or was dying,
nothing in the world would save Grillo from Straton. He
said, "Ace, in my hand. There's a message there, a parchment meant for Tempus. The Mygdonians sent it to me,
somehow, wrapped around the damned idol. How was I to
know the thing would come to life? Please, Strat, you must
believe me."

A boot kicked him in the teeth. He spat blood and chips
of incisor, but continued. "A parchment, crumpled up. It
might be our only chance to negotiate a settlement with
Mygdonia. No matter how you feel about me, you'd better
have a look."

The ploy worked, at least temporarily: Straton's bulk
disappeared behind him; strong fingers took the parchment,
balled up in his fist. Then Straton's footsteps faded.

Alone, Grillo wept. Tempus was a man he'd cared for,
long respected. How had he gotten into this? The witch!
The damnable witch! He cursed her and swore that if
mercy was bestowed upon him and he lived to make things
right, he'd find a way to pay her back for what she'd done
to him.

Some time later, Grillo became aware that he was once
more not alone.

The other knelt and he prepared himself for death or
torture. But neither came: a woman's voice, gentle yet
firm, told him that if he did just what she said, there was a
possibility that together they could save his life.

And since it was the Riddler's sister, Cime, he had no
choice but to agree.

The message Grillo had carried was from Lacan Ajami.
It proposed a meeting and said that if Shamshi was alive
and well and brought along to prove it, perhaps further

bloodshed could be averted.

The last thing Tempus wanted just then was to avert further bloodshed; his face hurt and his pride hurt and he wanted to kick Rag-head butt from one end of Mygdonia to the other.

With his sorcerer-slaying sister's help, he'd be ready for whatever Lacan Ajami had in mind. He had to make it clear to her that Randal, who'd just brought Niko into camp, was off-limits, before he sent her to fetch Jihan and Shamshi. So he called Cime to the tent in which he was recuperating, where none could see the speed of his healing, and gave her a lecture.

When he was done, Cime remarked that there was "something odd about Kama. More than even her heritage warrants, I mean."

He'd been thinking, as he talked to her, that this plague of women upon his head was worse than the letter of his curse: it was one thing to wander eternally, being spurned by whomsoever he loved and bringing death to those who loved him; it was quite another to have this clutch of bitches and witches and antiwitches and superwomen to contend with. He wondered if Datan, the vanquished Nisibisi archmage, had laid a parting curse on him. That would account for it. But he said only, "She's after Crit. I've forbidden it." It hurt to talk. He shook his head. "Bring me Jihan. Forget Kama. Concentrate on the Nisibisi witch if you must war on other women."

Cime stuck out her tongue at him. "Foolish man. You never see what's right before your eyes. Keep Kama out of whatever's brewing, I'm warning you."

He struggled up on his elbows, incensed, all the meddling of these women in his affairs suddenly too much to bear. *"How?"* he thundered. "As I have kept *you* at arm's length? *Jihan* in her place? The *witch-bitch* away from my fighters? If I could banish the lot to any purgatory—Sanctuary, Bandara, a handy underworld, or worse, be assured I'd have done it *long* ago!"

"Ah, Tempus, Tempus. You still don't understand, poor thing." She reached out to touch his cheek and he struck her hand away. "You *need* me, brother, to fight your battles for you. Or will you be content to lose this one, too?"

And she stormed out, hopefully to get Jihan and Shamshi. If not, Critias and he had a backup plan they'd as soon put into effect: descend on Ajami's party and chop the lot into pieces small enough to be sent throughout Mygdonia in presentation boxes. That's what Crit was doing now—positioning one hundred fighters in hidden but strategic emplacements around the demilitarized meeting place, ready to strike on signal.

It was a comforting thought; he yawned, lay back, and stared at the tentpole with its quivering luffing. At times like these, he really wished that he could sleep, avoid the most disagreeable stages of his body's healing. The area in question burned and ached and pulsed at every cut and mending wound and, as he lay there, it began to itch.

He mustn't scratch it. He sat up and yelled for the Sacred Banders who had appointed themselves his sentries. When they came, he said, "Get me Critias and Randal."

But Crit was nowhere to be found. Straton came instead, outspoken and blunt as usual. "What's this about pardoning Grillo? Your sis—the lady Cime—says to let him go, that he's turned informer and now he's worth his weight in gold."

"You don't think he is?"

"Not to me. Not to Crit. We've known about him since before we left Tyse—we brought his bedwarmer in and we'd have sweated him ourselves except for his friendship with you."

"Sometimes Cime's right, you know. We'll give Grillo another chance—he's not going anywhere but with us, not for the winter season, anyway."

"To Mygdonia? You still think we will, no matter how this negotiation works out?" Strat's eagerness was obvious: he flexed his big hands as he spoke.

"We will. Trust me. And, since we're speaking of friendship—where's Crit?"

Straton looked uncomfortable. "Lots of details to attend to, commander . . . this and that."

"Which this? Which that?"

Strat grimaced. "Kama's which 'this and that,' sir."

"Is Crit disobeying my orders?"

"Don't make me tell tales about my left-side leader, commander."

"I count on you, Ace, to keep me informed, in confidence, of what I need to know. I haven't time to confront Crit with minor infractions or the inclination to interrogate him. If whatever's on his mind is affecting his performance, it's your duty to let me know."

"I really don't see that it is, commander. He's got a lot of details to take care of, that's all."

"If the situation changes, you'll let me know?"

Strat took that as a dismissal. He stood up and backed away, stooped over, toward the tent's flaps. "Yes, commander, I surely will."

When Straton was gone, Tempus had a few moments to consider Sacred Bands and loyalty beyond question and to wonder whether it wasn't time for him to show himself, wounds or no, to the men who were about to risk their lives for him—Stepsons, 3rd Commando, Grillo's specials, Bashir's free men.

He'd just gotten to his feet and endured a spell of dizziness and pain when Randal, who didn't have to duck to enter the low black tent, came inside and saw him.

"Here," Randal offered, "let me help."

With an arm around Randal's bony shoulders, Tempus made his way outside where he could supervise the preparations, and where his men could see him—his presence itself was a galvanizing force among these fighters.

"How's Niko, Randal?" Tempus asked the Hazard as he took his arm away and stood unsupported to return salutes and greetings from the men busy breaking camp.

Above Randal's head the day was cloudless but for a roiling gray mass coming toward them against the prevailing wind from the high peaks to the south. "Not as fit as he'd like to be; he wants to accompany us to the meeting with Ajami. He thinks he's paid in advance for the 'honor' and that he's got a vested interest . . . some Sacred Bander's right he can invoke—"

"Go with *us?*" Tempus was watching the cloud behind Randal's head.

"Well," Randal wheedled, drawing himself up tall. "You can't go without *me!* What if the witch attacks again? You'll need me."

"Cime will be there," Tempus reminded the mageling.

"She doesn't scare me now that I've got my globe—except . . ."

"Yes, Randal?"

"Well, you see . . . on Meridian she happened to get hold of a gold coin of mine and . . . ah . . . she *is* your sister and she doesn't care for mages, as you know. I've got to get it back from her somehow."

Tempus's lips twitched. "In other than the customary fashion, you mean? I'll see what I can do."

"*Would* you? Oh, thank you! I really would feel better. I'm, ah, untried in her area of expertise, if you understand me. And I'd prefer to stay that way—makes for more power in an adept if he's celibate by choice."

"Surely you're not saying that you've never—Yes, I see you are. And is that so? Most sorcerers I've run into seem to fornicate with more abandon than—"

"Not *all.*" Randal raised one hand as if giving a tutorial. "Not all *adepts,* that is. Power can come from demonic aides and devils under contract; another sort is had by becoming a pure black artist of the twelfth degree . . . untainted by passion or—"

Randal continued explaining, but Tempus wasn't listening. The cloud coming toward them was arcing low. "Excuse me, Randal. Go see if you can use your adept's gift to help Niko get ready to ride. If he wants to come *and* he's able, then he's welcome." Patting the mage on the shoulder, Tempus walked away from a fountain of protective objections and suggestions aimed at keeping Niko out of harm's way.

Tempus hoped Randal would learn without an object lesson that no pairbound partner has the right to stand in front of the other: not even to protect his life would Niko accept that sort of help.

Then the cloud touched down and in it a vortex spun,

opening like a maw. Through it could be seen three horses
—one sable, two grays—and behind them Bashir's high
peaks ramparts.

Tempus's Aškelonian trumpeted its joy to see him and to
step once more on solid ground. Behind Cime, on the Aškelonian, Jihan waved from the back of one Trôs horse,
who rumbled a softer greeting; ponied to its saddlehorn
was its brother, with little Shamshi riding tall and bringing
up the rear.

Once the cloud had irised in then *popped* out of exis-
tence, Tempus had his hands full: Cime had to be convinced to give up Randal's coin; Jihan had to be greeted
with decorum. He must assuage Jihan's wrath at the damage done him and the slight he'd delivered unto her by
leaving her "babysitting on Wizardwall" while "Cime and
your favorite Stepsons had all the fun!"

"There's more fun to be had, I assure you," he told the
Froth Daughter, and was rewarded: the red, feral flecks
faded from her eyes.

If it was going to be difficult to wrest the mageling's
coin from his sister, it might be impossible to convince
Jihan that for all their sakes she must give up Shamshi, her
all-but-adopted child.

"But he's a wizard's son," she objected, once they were
alone and the murmur of her scale armor as it slithered
over her glowing musculature made him wish he felt a little
better, and then tell himself he might just feel well enough.

"They'll kill him," Jihan continued, "poor little wraith,
when they find out he's not Adrastus Ajami's—and kill his
mother, too. She was blinded by the witch Roxane. Is that
not punishment enough? Besides," Jihan pouted, kneading
his sore muscles where they'd found privacy among the
pines, "he's made me promise not to give him back to the
Mygdonians. He loves me. He wants to stay with me."

"What say we escort him to Mygdon so he can tell his
father that? He's officially a man, by age at least, and in
private, confidentially, we can probably convince Adrastus
to give the boy leave to serve with me—under your protection, of course."

Tempus was grasping at straws, he knew; but Jihan, her

breath coming faster as she ran her fingers over him, was by no means an expert at the machinations of strategy or diversionary tactics.

"And if I say yes to you, sleepless one, and lose the boy in spite of all you say, will you give me a child of my own to love and care for?" she demanded as she straddled him, her lips puffed with passion and her voice thick with longing.

"You know I can't do that," he said, his hands on her waist as he guided her into a position so compromised that he was sure that at least for the nonce she would do just what he told her. "Your father's forbidden it. Talk to him, not me. But short of that, I promise, you'll have nothing to regret."

That was one promise he could make good and one tactic at which he had no peer.

At dawn on the meeting day the sky was clear and a flock of geese passing overhead, right to left, was taken by both the overt negotiating party and the hidden commando units as an omen of success.

Down on the flat of the valley Lacan Ajami had specified, brightly colored tents were pitched and around them a dozen figures darted, setting out two gilded chairs and a laden victuals table under a red-and-black-striped awning.

A string of horses, groomed and black of hoof, stamped their feet off to one side. None of these were saddled; like the hard-steel weapons on display upon a propped-up board and the bubbly-pipes of gold and silver scattered around on little legged trays, they were there to sweeten the pot, to be traded or given up for this or that advantage, or to show good faith, or seal a bargain.

This made Crit think that the negotiation might be a real one, and not a wizard-sponsored trap, as Cime maintained that it was. There had been a row last evening between the Riddler and his sister, something about a coin which had once belonged to Randal. Because of it, Cime had come to Crit and he'd had no choice but to accommodate her: she was one woman he didn't want for an enemy.

Because Crit felt so strongly about Kama, he'd all but ignored her ever since Cime had shown up. Thus Kama was in the peace mission's traveling party; to have forbidden her, Crit would have had to tell the Riddler she was pregnant, or make up some reason which wouldn't ring false to his commander, or to Cime, or to Sync. Crit hadn't been able to think of one.

Niko, too, was there . . . sort of: mounted on his Aškelonian, helmet on, visor down, gloved and armored with his mantle flapping behind, he hadn't said a word to anyone.

Nor had Randal, on a sorrel from Crit's string, sneezed even once, though the horse's thick winter coat was coming in and Crit hadn't had time to curry the fat, battle-seasoned gelding, only to saddle it and leave it before the private tent Niko's injuries had gotten the pair. He'd called out but no one had answered; he'd ground-tied the horse and left.

This silent, almost eerie pair rode right behind Strat and Crit, who headed up the delegation. Behind them were Sync and Kama, both in 3rd Commando dress-blacks and flashing "ceremonial" weaponry that no one was sure wouldn't see real, unceremonious use this day.

Then came Gayle and Ari, experts, if such existed, on Nisibisi trickery. Crit could hear Gayle's profane carping: the ex-special was telling Ari to "pork 'em if we porking-well see those porkers make one porking *move* that don't look right. Otherwise, we're porked," and enjoining Ari to keep his crossbow on his hip in euphemistic language that made even Kama turn her head and stare. Gayle had never talked that way in her presence when he'd thought of her as a woman; these days, with her unit around her, the Stepsons treated Kama just like any other fighter.

Crit wished he could do the same.

In the middle of the procession were Tempus, Jihan, Shamshi, and Cime; close together, side by side, even. Crit couldn't imagine what Tempus was thinking of, offering such a tempting target to the Nisibisi wizard-caste: if *he* were leading the opposition, Crit would gladly have sacri-

ficed the boy to take out the other three. Without Tempus,
Jihan, and the sorcerer-slayer who'd done away with the
archmage of black Nisibis, Mygdonia could camp here
until spring and then march through Wizardwall's passes
with no fear of significant resistance.

No commando worth the title could resist that coup.

So Crit's neck was getting sore from twisting in his saddle and craning his head around at the piney slopes and
wondering whether the hundred fighters he'd deployed plus
the twenty in their party could stand against a mixed offensive of ten times their number when some were warlocks.
If it was just Mygdonians, ten to one were odds Crit was
comfortable with, given that his men were all Stepsons,
3rd Commando veterans, Nisibisi free men who hated sorcery more than they loved their own lives, and specials . . .
well, perhaps, if truth be known, he didn't rate the specials
as highly as the rest. But there were none of them in this
party: just Gayle and Ari, who were now Stepsons, and
proud of it.

Crit heard something rattling like a diamondback and
shifted, one hand on his horse's rump, to detect its source.

Randal's kris, it must have been. The mage's gloved
hand was tight upon its hilt. Like Niko, the Hazard was
accoutered so that no square inch of skin or strand of hair
could be seen. As for the kris, Crit had heard stories of
what the charmed blades could do and of where Randal had
acquired this one.

Crit faced front again. Someone had to look Ajami in
the face and smile and get things off to a good start. That's
what he was doing up front: Tempus wanted things to proceed to whatever conclusion without any provocation from
their side. If Ajami was serious about negotiating, Tempus
had instructed Crit, then negotiate they would. It was the
honorable thing to do.

Straton, privately, had asked Crit if he believed the
Riddler would actually give up the boy and revenge upon
the Nisibisi black artists who had sicced the homunculus on
him, tortured and murdered Stepsons, possessed Niko and
most recently Grillo, just for an uneasy peace which could
extend no farther than the northern border of Free Nisibis

and the southern reaches of Tyse: Tempus had no mandate
from Ranke to make a treaty more far-reaching. "And *I*
don't think," Strat had said, "that the Nisibisi warlocks and
that yumyum, Roxane, are going to *let* Ajami give up until
they've got back their ancestral haunt—or they're all dead
and comfy in their witchy graves."

As usual, Straton seemed to be reading Crit's mind. In
allaying Strat's doubts, Crit had circumlocuted his own,
but failed to convince either one of them. They had too
much combined experience to expect a final resolution, a
fair settlement, or anything but treachery and deception
which, Crit well knew, only led to one thing: war.

But it was the kind of war he liked, not streetfighting or
police actions against civilian populations. Crit had put it
to Strat this way: "Wouldn't you rather fight in Mygdon,
where the pillage is easy?"

"And the women sultry?" Strat had added. They were
curious about the north; only Niko had spent any time
there. Not even the Riddler had sojourned among the peoples of the Mygdonian Alliance. When Tempus was warring this far north, there hadn't been any Mygdonian
Alliance; in fact, there'd been no Mygdonia whatsoever,
just tribal troops and farmers with regional councils and
vigilante groups—no league of city-states.

When they reached the valley floor, and brightly clad
Mygdonians in their best brocade surcoats and pantaloons
came out to take their horses by the bridles, Crit gave all
his worries to the gods: he was going to have to dismount
and pretend he believed in all this pomp and ceremony,
take seriously what was likely going to be a bad and possi-
bly expensive joke. It was his job to make sure that this
joke, when it came to light, was not on him and his, but on
Lacan Ajami's army of turbaned fighters and Nisibisi dark
lords.

He was just noticing that not a witch was to be seen
among the Mygdonian negotiating team and absently cal-
culating the visible odds—five to one in favor of the Mygdonian Alliance—when the sky above turned a seamless,
dirty yellow and the air became very still.

Then everything—the Mygdonian coming toward Crit

to take his horse by the bridle, the tentflaps opening to reveal Lacan Ajami with a witch on his arm whose hand was extended in the direction of Crit's party, even a hawk wheeling high overhead in the motionless air—seemed to stop.

Cime had been expecting something like this—some underhanded trick from the Nisibisi witch-bitch. Cime was prepared and all her allies were at her beck and call.

But no one else of Tempus's party was ready for fielded sorcery, except perhaps Randal, the Tysian Hazard, and the boy-wizard, Shamshi.

Tempus was still moving, if slowly—a testament to his strength of character, his inveterate stubbornness, nothing more. The Froth Daughter was frozen as still as a statue, but for roving eyes, which made her better off than the soldiers of their party, asleep between blinks, arrested in midmovement, all twenty fighters and their horses as inanimate as garden statuary.

Cime kept still: she wanted Roxane to come closer.

But even with so great an advantage, the Nisibisi Death Queen was cautious: she held back, only her laughter coming toward the spellbound group of victims, as she pointed out to Ajami Tempus's languid, slow-motion struggle to dismount. Lacan Ajami didn't look as happy as the witch beside him: he was an honorable man in his own eyes. Wanton slaughter of helpless victims was not his style.

Yet, at Roxane's urging, Ajami gave the order and his Mygdonians rushed into "battle" against a helpless enemy.

Still Cime held her own forces in abeyance, until the witch herself stepped forward, out of the shadow of her magical tent.

Until three Mygdonians had almost reached her brother, who was drawing his sword slowly and from whose mouth issued a war cry distorted beyond recognition into a low, meaningless growl.

Then Cime took her diamond rods in hand, raised one up to heaven and pointed the other straight ahead, calling in a bold, commanding voice upon her consort and upon the powers concerned to render aid unto their constituents: *"Now!"*

And as she did, the boy-wizard Shamshi slipped from his horse, crying, "Roxane, Roxane!" and Randal's armored form vaulted from its horse, kris drawn, with throwing stars and poisoned blossoms streaming from the mage's person like a swarm of bees, downing the ten closest Mygdonians in an instant.

Meanwhile, Niko's armor gleamed and then glowed with antimagical heat and the Aškelonian stallion who bore that weight suddenly blared a challenge, rearing up. Walking on its hind feet, it interposed itself between young Shamshi and the Nisibisi witch across the battlefield who called to the boy while the troops of Mygdonia attacked the sleeping cadre in a multitude, pouring from the pitched tents which could never have held a fraction of their number.

As yet, only Randal's armored form, Niko's—on the ground, dismounted, grabbing up the boy—and the Riddler, in slow motion, moved among the defenders.

Where *was* the help she'd summoned?

Cime, then, decided not to wait, but dismounted, running as soon as her feet touched the ground first to her brother, to tap him on the shoulder and return to him his twice-human fighting speed, then toward the Nisibisi witch to whom young Shamshi was calling out "Roxane! Roxane! No!" as he struggled, held by the waist like a floursack, his fists pounding in vain upon Niko's glowing armor.

Tempus dashed at speed, now, toward the armored figure who held the writhing boy with one hand. Six Mygdonians, howling "Lacan is great," were closing fast upon them with only Niko's sword to worry about.

But even Tempus was not fast enough: the six closed in and with war axes swinging, hacked away the arm that held the child and, from behind, severed Niko's helmet, cleaving it in twain.

The Aškelonian screamed in rage and, riderless, stalked upon its hind feet among the enemy, cracking skulls and pummeling flesh.

All was chaos, by then. Cime glimpsed Tempus fighting
a horde and Randal's crested helm barely visible amid
taller adversaries.

Cime hadn't time to do more than wonder what was
delaying Aškelon, whom she'd called upon for aid, and
Jihan's father, who'd surely come to save his daughter
from humiliation at the hands of the seven Mygdonians
who, with one warlock directing them, were now pulling
her from her horse to "have her now!"

Cime only looked back long enough to see young
Shamshi run, not to Roxane, but to Jihan's side, before she
turned away again to use her rods to clear a path toward her
immortal enemy, Roxane, when from the sky above a rum-
bling, whistling, then whining sound began and escalated,
and she looked up.

A tornado was forming above the combatants. The
sound of it was deafening. Horses and men broke and ran
or threw themselves to the dirt. The tents from which
Mygdonians still came were gone in an instant. The tornado, Cime saw as she sprinted full speed toward Roxane,
who must not get away, was moving slowly through the
press as if it searched for someone: its little tail had not yet
touched the ground.

In the distance, galloping horses could be heard approaching: Tempus's main contingent. They'd never get
here in time, but Cime wasn't counting on the havoc mere
men could wreak.

She'd called upon her consort and now, just before she
would have her way and confront the Nisibisi witch, Aškelon appeared, pallid in the yellow light: Aškelon, shadow
lord, lord of dreams, in black, with an ethereal nimbus
about him, so that even the Mygdonians gave ground.

Walking calmly forward as if in Meridian, not on a battlefield where bolts whizzed by and horses neighed their
pain and fury, he waved his hand and every spellbound
fighter of the negotiating party woke and looked about,
drawing weapons—swords and crossbows, javelins and
flying wings—and launched themselves at the Mygdonians.

Still Aškelon came toward Cime, his arms outstretched

to her, his eyes shadowed with all the death lurking here, so that even the whirlwind picking up fighters, lifting them high and throwing them to earth, seemed remote.

Only Aškelon's voice and Aškelon's presence existed for her.

"Come, my dear," he said to her. "You've done your part. Murder is denied you. You must return with me or forfeit all the time you've spent already."

"Murder is denied me? What about the witch? Shall *she* go free? This war's not over—it's just begun."

"Come, before Jihan sees me and you have a co-wife to share our bed in sweet Meridian." And those compassionate eyes hypnotized her.

Cime's strength left her. Her resolve dissolved.

"Ash," she promised him, "when this is over and I'm free from my vow to spend a year with you, you'll regret this day."

But even as she spoke, the battlefield bled away and Meridian, with all its pacific beauty and its happy, dreamlike folk, appeared around her. She hadn't even had a chance to bid her brother farewell or slay a single wizard.

There would be, she promised herself, another day. She still had Randal's coin.

The whirlwind, dark and moist with the breath of Stormbringer from whose anger it was sprung, chose its targets carefully among the warring press of men.

And when it reached the Mygdonian boy whom Jihan loved, it sought to lift him up. Jihan saw what her father had in mind and dove for Shamshi, catching the youth by both his legs.

The child was wailing, "Help me help me, Roxane! Jihan! Someone! *Please!*" And thus Tempus, dispatching three mortal enemies with one swing of his sword, caught sight of the boy, his body being sucked toward heaven and Jihan's whole weight trying to anchor him to earth, as the Froth Daughter too was lifted, her feet dangling clear of the ground.

Tempus rushed toward Jihan, calling out her name. By

the time he'd closed the distance between them, he had to leap to catch hold of her ankles. Then, like a human rope, all three swayed, suspended in midair.

Higher and higher the three were drawn until Tempus called, "Let go, Jihan! Save yourself, as I must!" and dropped down through the roiling air twice his own height to land heavily upon the ground.

When he'd regained his feet, he saw Jihan, holding Shamshi, disappearing into the funnel in the air. He caught a glimpse of Randal's armor, chasing a witchy woman-form, his kris outstretched before him.

Tempus's Aškelonian mare, sighting him, trumpeted a greeting and galloped toward him.

He saw Roxane, Death's Queen, the Nisibisi witch, one last time before his horse obscured his view: Randal's kris had wretched itself from its owner's grip and was flying through the air toward Roxane's unprotected back, weaving and dodging as did she, homing in on her.

At that moment his reinforcements, mortal troops, arrived, and though they were nonplussed to see such things as Niko's armor—headless, minus an arm—fighting Mygdonians on its own and Randal's, too, doing battle, cleft down the middle, they joined right in.

So much for negotiating with Mygdonia, Tempus had time to think as he caught sight of Lacan Ajami, trying to rally and direct his army while the whirlwind chased them and from its midst, red-glowing eyes glowered down, un-forgiving.

Vaulting up on his Aškelonian's back to force through the thick of battle and engage his enemy in person, Tempus saw many of his most beloved fighters: Crit, unhorsed and standing over Kama, who was on her hands and knees with her elbows pressed to her belly as if she'd taken a mortal wound; Straton, not far away, slashing about him with ber-serk abandon, bloody sword in one hand and a Mygdonian war ax in the other; Gayle, profanity streaming from his open mouth as he and Ari, back to back, held off ten Myg-donians and one wounded Nisibisi warlock whose flesh was beginning to steam and char, a sure sign that death was near.

Tempus took a moment to stroke his steed's sweating, blood-flecked neck. "Ready, horse? That's our man there," he told it, pointing out Lacan Ajami, who was trying to reach a group of wizards standing away from the fight as if they were preparing to call up their tiresome, stupid fiends and a platoon of demons. He reined his horse around and unsheathed his sharkskin-hilted sword. "Let's get him."

The Aškelonian leaped forward, snorting.

Lacan Ajami, as if a warlock had warned him, looked straight at Tempus and shook his fist. Then all the wizards joined hands around the Mygdonian warlord and the whole circle of enemies disappeared.

Kama hardly felt it when some soldiers dragged her from the field. By then she didn't care whose troops they were; she'd lost her child, miscarried on the battlefield. She was in pain she couldn't justify, out of action for a reason she hoped none of these would guess.

Crit had been there, she remembered, protecting her. Now that it didn't matter, she was sure he loved her, and that she loved him.

She'd seen Niko's armor strewn about and Randal's cracked helmet lying on the ground.

She wept in the dark in a low black tent filled with other wounded, none of them silent in their pain. That *her* wounds were not exactly the sort of battle scars she'd like to sing about at the Festival of Man was all her own fault, and nobody else's.

Eventually, she slept.

When she woke, she began to wonder if she'd die of her wounds. Even on her deathbed, she would never tell and shame both Critias and herself.

A light appeared, small and far away in the dark.

She watched it coming closer, thinking it might be her patron deity come to take her to heaven (if she still deserved it) or to hell (if lying and cheating and playing at war and womanhood without committing to either was a sin).

But it was not a shade or even Death that came. It was

her father, an oil lamp in his hand.

He'd never gone out of his way before on her account; when she'd been doing well, he hadn't noticed. If not for her lust for Crit, the forbidden officer, she'd have won this engagement on her own terms: she had put Grillo out of action, sowing suspicions in Critias's mind; she'd brought the 3rd together with their founder and seen to it that all moved north of Wizardwall to carry the battle to Ajami.

None of it mattered, with her belly ravaged and her thighs sticky from her own blood.

At least she hadn't thought it would until Tempus was standing over her, looking frightful with his scabbed and stubbled face underlit by the lamp's flame.

"Life to you, Kama. May I sit with you?" Tempus said.

She tried to see in his face whether he'd penetrated the deception, whether he was here to disavow her formally. The loss of Niko and of Randal would surely have touched him; Tempus's love for his fighters was legend, and Niko was as close to an inheritor of the Riddler's mantle as any offspring of his own loins might have been.

In Tempus's face was only a map of the war ongoing, nothing more. His hooded eyes stared calmly down at her, awaiting her response.

She said, "And to you, Riddler—" she still dared not call him Father; "life and everlasting glory. Sit, if it's your pleasure."

"Hardly that." He sighed and hunkered down beside her bed, placing the lamp on a barrel strewn with bloody cloths. "Why didn't you or Crit tell me you were with child?"

"*I* tell you? And miss the battle? Be confirmed a worthless woman in your eyes—you, who think of women just for raping or bedwarming or as an excuse to pick a fight? As for Crit," she tried to shrug, then winced at the pain racing up from her belly, then continued: "What he does is up to him."

"Stupid."

It seemed that this indictment hung for hours in the air between them.

"Yes," she agreed at last. "You're right." She was weak.

His face swam in granular, colored light that made her queasy. "Am I going to die?"

"You? I don't think so—neither of us will be quit of the other so easily as that. Randal has agreed to see to you—"

"Randal? But he's dead . . . I saw his armor, his helmet —empty pieces strewn upon the ground."

Tempus chuckled. "Randal and Niko sent their clothes into battle with us. Expecting treachery, a last attempt on Roxane's part to gain control of the contested globe, if nothing more, they stayed with the hidden contingent as field commanders."

"They? Then *Niko* isn't dead?" Kama felt better, suddenly: she'd thought for certain that the blame for losing them would fall on her.

"Niko? No, not dead. Cranky and still weak, despite all magic and even Cime's healing—he pushed too hard this afternoon. Randal was supposed to keep Stealth out of the thick of things, but he can't be kept from his calling, any more than you or me."

You? He meant *her.* For the first time she took a deep breath and thought that perhaps her father didn't hate her, or devalue her because she was a woman. She tried to sit up.

Tempus put a horny hand in the middle of her chest and pushed her back onto her cot. "Rest. We're riding tomorrow. Randal will be along to see you—with your permission. We'll have a wagonload of wounded anyway—one more won't crowd it. But I have a feeling that you'd rather ride than be carted behind the troops. One would want to sortie into Mygdon on one's own."

Into Mygdon? "One would. One does."

"Then you'll agree to let our Hazard treat you, with magic if need be? The sortie party will be chasing what's left of Ajami's army. If that's too much for you, you can ride with the main contingent."

"Where will the 3rd be? Sync? Cri—Critias?" She hadn't meant to stutter. But she had to know.

"Where they'll do the most good." Tempus rose then, picking up the oil lamp. "I'm pleased you're with us. Now

that we've lost Jihan to her father and Cime to the entelechy of dreams, we need a representative of the fair sex to
help us guess what Roxane's next move might be. Think
on it. You have the advantage of being similar in bent of
mind."

Advantage? She would have asked him to expand on
that, but her father was gone, just a light bobbing as it
disappeared in the distance and the dark.

From the creator of the bestselling *Silistra*
series, a temptuous odyssey to the farthest
reaches of the human imagination...

Janet Morris's
THE KERRION EMPIRE

*"Not since **Dune** have we witnessed a power
struggle of such awesome intensity...
A literary feast!"* — Eric Van Lustbader

__ **BOOK I: DREAM DANCER**   07688-1/$2.95
__ **BOOK II: CRUISER DREAMS**   07983-X/$2.95
__ **BOOK III: EARTH DREAMS**   07985-6/$2.95

Available at your local bookstore or return this form to:

THE BERKLEY PUBLISHING GROUP
Berkley • Jove • Charter • Ace
THE BERKLEY PUBLISHING GROUP, Dept. B
390 Murray Hill Parkway, East Rutherford, NJ 07073

Please send me the titles checked above. I enclose _____. Include $1.00 for postage
and handling if one book is ordered; add 25¢ per book for two or more not to exceed
$1.75. CA, IL, NJ, NY, PA, and TN residents please add sales tax. Prices subject to change
without notice and may be higher in Canada. Do not send cash.

NAME_____

ADDRESS_____

CITY_____STATE/ZIP_____

(Allow six weeks for delivery.)

137

BESTSELLING
Science Fiction
and
Fantasy

MURDER, MAYHEM, SKULDUGGERY...
AND A CAST OF CHARACTERS YOU'LL NEVER FORGET!

THIEVES' WORLD™

EDITED BY
ROBERT LYNN ASPRIN and **LYNN ABBEY**

· ·

FANTASTICAL ADVENTURES

One Thumb, the crooked bartender at the Vulgar Unicorn...
Enas Yorl, magician and shape changer...*Jubal,* ex-gladiator and
crime lord...*Lythande the Star-browed,* master swordsman
and would-be wizard...these are just a few of the players you will
meet in a mystical place called Sanctuary™. This is *Thieves' World.*
Enter with care.

___ 80595-7	THIEVES' WORLD	$2.95
___ 80590-6	TALES FROM THE VULGAR UNICORN	$3.50
___ 80586-8	SHADOWS OF SANCTUARY	$2.95
___ 78713-4	STORM SEASON	$2.95
___ 80587-6	THE FACE OF CHAOS	$2.95
___ 80588-4	WINGS OF OMEN	$2.95
___ 14089-0	THE DEAD OF WINTER	$2.95
___ 77581-0	SOUL OF THE CITY	$2.95
___ 80595-7	BLOOD TIES	$2.95

Stories
✠ of ✠
Swords and Sorcery

⚜⚜⚜⚜⚜⚜⚜⚜⚜⚜⚜⚜⚜⚜⚜⚜⚜⚜